For my dad.

PRAISE FOR
HARRIET HATES LEMONADE

"Hooray for second chances! A by-the-book widow's world unravels when she helps a neighbor in need and inadvertently confronts the buried truths of her own past."
–Cam Torrens, award-winning author of the *Tyler Zahn mystery/suspense series*

"*Harriet Hates Lemonade* is a deeply important and captivating story that will have you questioning your own preconceived notions of unhealthy relationships. The theme of abuse is explored like never before with both overt and subtle plot lines weaving together to facilitate emotion, compassion and understanding. McCollum's voice is steady and impactful, hooking the reader into Harriet's regimented and quirky life. At first, Harriet presents with neurodivergent tendencies, her opinions and actions questionable and insensitive, but as the novel progresses, a deep understanding and compassion for her character forms, shifting your perspective. I laughed, I cried, and I learned. Although exploring difficult themes, the story is refreshing, realistic, and heartwarming. "
–Megan Jamieson, author of *The Ties That Bind Us*

"Kim McCollum tackles the difficult subject of domestic abuse with sensitivity and unflinching honesty in *Harriet Hates Lemonade.* I rooted for quirky Harriet as she summons the strength to confront the past she's kept so carefully buried, and learns to find joy in the messiness of life. A beautiful story set in breathtaking Montana with flesh and blood characters that kept me turning the page to the very end."
–Linda Avellar, author of *Cassie Linden Finds Her Sweet Spot*

"*Harriet Hates Lemonade* emphasizes love over hate, as characters face heart-wrenching challenges and build new beginnings from difficult pasts."
–Lucille Guarino, award-winning author of *Elizabeth's Mountain*

"I enjoyed every page of this wonderful novel. Harriet may not be the easiest neighbor to have, but she sure does step up to the plate when necessary. I'd give this book ten stars if I could!"
–Diane Hawley Nagatomo, author of *Finding Naomi* and *The Butterfly Café*

"Harriet Hates Lemonade" is both devastating and uplifting. A beautiful, entertaining story that is honestly hard to put down."
–Diane Dickinson, author of *Final Transaction*

HARRIET HATES LEMONADE

KIM McCOLLUM

Black Rose Writing | Texas

ISBN: 978-1-68513-705-2
LIBRARY OF CONGRESS CONTROL NUMBER: 2025944826
PUBLISHED BY BLACK ROSE WRITING
www.blackrosewriting.com

Printed in the United States of America
Suggested Retail Price (SRP) $20.95

Harriet Hates Lemonade is printed in Bentium Book Basic

*As a planet-friendly publisher, Black Rose Writing does its best to eliminate unnecessary waste to reduce paper usage and energy costs, while never compromising the reading experience. As a result, the final word count vs. page count may not meet common expectations.

"Author McCollum serves up a flavorful brew of tension, humor, uncertainty, and high emotion. Keep a box of issues handy! You'll need it for this engaging and ultimately heartwarming story."
–Ruth F. Stevens, award-winning author of *My Year of Casual Acquaintances*

"In the tradition of *A Man Called Ove* and *Olive Kitteridge, Harriet Hates Lemonade* brings us another cantankerous but loveable character whose isolation is shattered when a new family moves in across the street. Harriet's self centered view of the world widens and she finds herself first helped by, and then helping, a mother and daughter stuck in an abusive relationship. Kim McCollum's newest novel shines a light on the dangers of love bombing while simultaneously giving us a heartwarming story of how women come together to help each other."
–JB Harris, author of *The Immigrant's Wife*

"In her second novel, *Harriet Hates Lemonade,* Kim McCollum addresses the heartbreaking issue of abuse with sensitivity and an empowering focus on what supporting one another through tragedy can teach us. She gives us a memorable and unlikely heroine in Harriet, a middle-aged widow with a strong penchant for following the rules, who is both exasperating and lovable at the same time. Through Harriet's journey of realization about her past, foisted upon her by the needs of her new friend, Robyn, and the messiness of her neighbor's lives, McCollum showcases the blessings and beauty of human connection, the rewards of helping others, and the redeeming power of being resilient and open to change at any age. And she even makes us laugh while doing it!"
–Liz Wanic, author of *Under Cover of Chaos*

HARRIET HATES LEMONADE

CHAPTER 1

HARRIET COULDN'T BELIEVE she was the one in the hospital bed, the open-backed gown robbing her of her dignity. After all she'd endured with Les, she thought she knew what to expect. Turned out, when you were the one in the bed, calm, rational thought scurried out the door like a cockroach when the light flipped on. For the first time, she wondered how Les had managed it. He must've been stronger than she'd given him credit for.

"Well, Harriet! Nice to see you awake and alert!" Her nurse was quite handsome, a fact that made Harriet terribly uncomfortable, with her rear hanging out of the back of her gown and all. She was at least twenty years his senior, so her bottom wouldn't be pert like the girls his age. He probably wouldn't look. But if he did, he was sure to be disappointed. Yes, she walked Bibbo twice daily and ate her five to six servings of fruits and vegetables. Even so, at fifty-two, some things couldn't compensate for gravity.

"I'm awake, but I'm definitely not alert," Harriet said, her tongue thick and cottony.

Her nurse chuckled, the sound echoing in the sterile room. "So, is someone coming to pick you up? You'll be discharged in about an hour, I'd guess."

Harriet's heart plummeted. The simple question felt like a pop quiz she wasn't prepared for. "Y-Yes, of course."

"Great. Have them pull around to the side entrance, and I'll wheel you out when it's time."

"Oh." Harriet's finger went to her chapped bottom lip, and she picked at a loose flake of skin. "That won't be necessary. I can manage. I'll see myself out."

He chuckled again. "I'm sure you can, broken ankle and all, but for liability's sake, I have to see you to the car."

"Of course." Harriet glanced at the clock. He said she had an hour, right? She could figure something out.

After he left, she plucked her phone from the tray next to her bed and scrolled through her contacts. Who was Donna? And Albert? She'd have to clean out this haphazard mess when she got home. And make better notes about who people were before she added them all willy-nilly.

She scrolled back up and tapped the Bozeman Public Library contact. She racked her brain to remember the name of her favorite librarian. The one who didn't judge her occasional romance novel snuck in between her literary and non-fiction. Lucy? Lillian? Lori? Shoot. It was something with an L.

"Bozeman Public Library, Susan speaking. How can I help?" The voice on the other end was bright, but edged with impatience. Harriet bristled. Librarians needed to be patient. It was practically in the job description.

"Is this Lucy? Or Lillian?"

"No. This is Susan. Can I help you with something?" Annoyed this time. And condescending. She'd have to have a chat with Lucy. Or Lucille. Whatever her name was.

"Well, I'm looking for the librarian with the long straight hair nearly to her bum. Could use a haircut and a touch of color."

"Uh-um," Susan nearly choked. "I'm sorry. I'm not sure who you mean."

"Her name starts with an L. Her glasses are so strong that her eyeballs bug out like she's staring at you from behind a magnifying glass."

"I believe that might be Lucille. She's busy helping a customer. Can I help you?" Completely irritated this time. Geez. It was so hard to get good help these days. Les would've gone ballistic over this kind of insubordination.

"No," Harriet said. "I'll wait."

A long pause. "You'll wait? Are you a friend of hers?"

"No."

"Then why can't I help you?"

"Because I don't know you. Or at least I don't recognize you, and this is personal. I need to speak with Lucille. Only Lucille," Harriet said. She was almost yelling. She'd had enough trying to be nice to this woman.

"Okay," Susan said. "I'll put you on hold and tell her you're on the line. Who can I say is calling?"

"It's Harriet Henderson." There was a long pause. "I'm the skinny one with the dangly beaded earrings she always likes," she offered.

"Oh," Susan said. "I remember you. You're the one who checks out Austen and Brontë with a dash of E.L. James thrown in."

Harriet cringed. She'd have to remember to check books out only with Lucille.

"She's finished with her customer. I'll put her on. Nice chatting with you, Harriet!"

Lucille came on the line. "Hello?"

"Yes. This is Harriet. I'm hoping you might do me a favor."

"Um." Lucille paused. "I'm sorry, but I don't recall a Harriet. Could you remind me how I know you?"

Harriet's heart sank. This was a mistake. She felt the desperate urge to disappear. She'd tell her nurse she'd sign a waiver or whatever.

"Never mind," Harriet said, moving the phone from her cheek, her finger hovering over the red hang-up button.

"Wait," Lucille said. "You're the one with the earrings and Jane Austen, right?"

Relief flooded Harriet's body. "That's me. So, would you consider doing me a favor?"

•　　•　　•　　•　　•

Just over an hour later, a dented and rusty Toyota Corolla pulled up to where Harriet was waiting in a wheelchair. Her nurse opened the passenger door as Lucille threw clothing, papers, and McDonald's wrappers into the back seat.

"You must be busy," Harriet said, peering into the car.

"Hi, Harriet," Lucille said, a tight smile cracking her face below her glasses. She looked a bit like Mr. Magoo. "I am busy. Why do you ask?"

"The state of your car."

Lucille's smile shifted direction, turning down at the corners. It looked more natural that way. Harriet recognized the expression: less a frown, more a face of concentration. She bet Lucille grew up doing crossword puzzles.

"Let me help you," the nurse said, easing his hands under her armpits.

Harriet settled into the cracked seat and shoved an empty Coca-Cola can and a burger wrapper aside with her foot. She was still nauseous from the anesthesia, and the smell of stale onions and pickles made her gag. She rolled down her window.

"You must really enjoy McDonald's," Harriet said.

"How'd you guess? Wait, don't answer that. I was being facetious."

"Oh, okay," Harriet said, though she'd never understand why anyone would waste time being facetious. It just complicated things. Les abhorred facetiousness, calling it 'a waste of precious energy.'

"Where to?" Lucille asked, pulling out of the parking lot.

"The disco," Harriet said.

Lucille stared at her. Not even a smile. See? Not worth it.

"My house, of course," Harriet said. "I'm not exactly up for much after this."

"Okay. Which way?"

"Make a right and head to Four Corners. I live near Monforton School," Harriet said.

Lucille nodded. An awkward silence filled the car. "So, what happened?" Lucille finally asked.

"That jerk with his obnoxious dog."

"The dog bit you?"

"No. A neighbor was walking around my neighborhood with his dog off-leash." Harriet raised her eyebrows. "Off-leash!" she repeated, more forcefully.

No response. They sat in silence for a bit. Lucille glanced at Harriet as if waiting for something. Lucille looked like she could use some lip balm, so Harriet searched through the side pocket of her purse where she kept her ChapStick. She used to have lipstick and lip gloss in there, but now even lip gloss was too much of a bother. Harriet found a tube and held it out to Lucille. She shook her head. Harriet shrugged and tucked it back where it belonged.

"So," Lucille said, glancing at Harriet, "I still don't understand how you hurt your foot."

"My ankle," Harriet said.

"Okay, your ankle," Lucille said, sighing.

"Well, that nasty dog tried to attack Bibbo, so we ran, but I tripped in a terrible divot in the grass and broke my ankle."

"Is Bibbo your son?" Lucille asked.

"Really? Would you name your kid Bibbo?" Harriet snorted at what Les would've said if she suggested the name Bibbo for a child.

"Les would never have allowed that. I had enough trouble getting him to agree to it for our dog. He's our Brussels Griffon."

"Oh, I see. Well, Bibbo is lucky to have you for his owner."

"Why's that?"

"Because you sacrificed yourself to save him."

Harriet allowed Lucille's words to sink in. They felt warm, and her heart swelled. "Turn left here. On Lemon Lane," Harriet said. "My house is that gray one there on the right."

"What a beautiful home you have. It's so…" Lucille paused, her gaze sweeping over the meticulously maintained exterior. Harriet stared, waiting. How would Lucille, with her messy car and relaxed demeanor, categorize Harriet's perfect house? "Tidy."

Harriet smiled. "Yes, it is."

Once parked, Lucille retrieved Harriet's crutches from the trunk. Pulling her to her one good foot, Lucille carefully positioned the crutches under each of Harriet's armpits. Harriet wobbled and nearly plopped back into the car. Lucille grabbed her under her arms and pulled her back upright. Harriet's cheeks flushed. It was almost a hug—more contact than she'd had in a while.

"Sorry, this is all new to me. It's going to take some getting used to, I suppose," Harriet said.

"Of course it will. Be kind to yourself," Lucille said, returning to the trunk to fetch Harriet's belongings.

"I'll take that," Harriet said, reaching for the small plastic bag.

"Nonsense! I'll help you inside and put your things where you'd like them."

"That won't be necessary. I'll manage."

"You sure? It's no bother," Lucille said.

Harriet pivoted to face Lucille as quickly as her crutches would allow. She sensed this woman's pity, sharp and unwanted, like a sudden draft. That was something she would never allow. Her rigid defenses snapped back into place. Her spine stiffened.

"I said I've got it, and I meant it. You can go now," Harriet said, her voice sharp, a barrier erected between them. As she turned and headed toward her house, her ankle throbbed in protest, but it only served to harden her resolve. Reaching the first porch step, she stopped and called over her shoulder, "Thanks for the ride."

CHAPTER 2

OPENING HER FRONT DOOR, Bibbo bounded toward Harriet and jumped on his hind legs, pawing at her shin. "Hey, watch it, mister. I wasn't even gone for a full day. No need to get all crazy." She bent down and rubbed him under the chin in his favorite way that made his back leg thump with pleasure.

Realizing there wasn't much she could do with a broken ankle, Harriet went to the couch and sank into its well-used softness. Harriet wasn't one to enjoy what people called "idle time," or "me time." She kept busy. As Les said, there was always something to clean, organize, or improve in some way. But she supposed returning home from ankle surgery was the one time she could allow herself a small break. Picking up Elizabeth Strout's latest novel, she relaxed back into the couch to read. Bibbo hopped up next to her and nuzzled his bearded face into her lap.

Outside, Harriet heard children shouting. Leaning forward, she peered out the front window. "School must be out." Bibbo went to the edge of the couch and barked. "I know. You'd love to play with them, wouldn't you?"

When Les and Harriet had toured neighborhoods twenty or so years ago to figure out where to build their forever home, the meticulous planning that went into The Orchards impressed them.

Of course, Les had laughed at the name. "We're in Montana, for Christ's sake! No one is growing citrus here. A few apples maybe, but that's about it."

Despite the name, Les liked how the plans included open space behind each row of houses for walking, playing soccer, or cross-country skiing in the winter. "Can't you see it, hon? You, me, and some little ones playing out here? We can bundle them up in the winter and build snowmen. I'll teach them to play football and baseball."

Harriet couldn't recall ever being happier. The sun had shone on the snow, illuminating individual flakes so they sparkled like glitter. The Bridger Mountains rose in the distance, their jagged peaks cutting into the azure sky like the serrated edge of a knife. That time of year, in early fall, the aspens dotted the mountainside with splashes of gold and orange. When the sun hit them just right, they glowed like embers against the darker pines. It was the perfect place to build their house and their life together. She had probably wiped tears from her eyes that day. Those were the times when happiness just spilled from her.

But not lately. The only thing spilling from her happened when she sneezed. She hated getting older. Her knees hurt, her arms weren't nearly long enough to hold her reading material far enough away so she could decipher it, and her neck looked like a turkey's waddle. She went to bed one day with knees that could walk for miles, a bladder that wasn't bothered by a sneeze, eyes that could read, and a taut neck, and woke as if she were ninety. Why hadn't anyone warned her that aging didn't happen gradually and certainly not gracefully? Age fell on you like gravel off a loader. Hard, heavy, and all at once. Suddenly, you were old.

Les hadn't cared about getting old. Harriet supposed she wouldn't either if its only effects were a few lines around the eyes and a bit of salt and pepper at the temples. Les loved to tease her about getting older. Once, he brought his index finger to her neck and jiggled the bit of skin that hung down. Some people were fortunate to have just one waddle, but others, like Harriet, were lucky enough to sprout two.

Les had fingered the two bits of wrinkled, sagging flesh and said, "Darling, what have we here? Your neck looks a bit like it has sprouted labia. Aren't I the lucky guy?"

Despite her complaints, there were some things about aging that weren't so bad. Her hair, typically styled in a smooth ponytail, now featured shimmering silver threads interwoven with her deep brown tresses, resembling the tinsel on a Christmas tree. Les had insisted she color it, but recently, she'd let it go natural. It was much easier that way. Time had etched subtle lines around her eyes and mouth, and the sun had dotted her cheeks with freckles. Well, they were probably sunspots, but she preferred to call them freckles. She didn't mind them. In fact, she thought they made her look a bit like Twiggy.

Turning back to her book, she was swept into the world of Olive Kittridge, living in a retirement home. Harriet hoped it wouldn't come to that for her. But she wasn't so sure what the future might hold for her now, without Les.

Harriet knew she wasn't supposed to drink while taking ibuprofen, but maybe one glass of wine instead of her usual two might help her relax and figure out how this broken ankle would affect her day-to-day. As she pushed herself from the couch, the doorbell rang. Bibbo barked and hopped like a Mexican jumping bean. He spun so fast his back legs slipped out from under him, and he splayed out on the tile foyer like Bambi on ice. Harriet chuckled. She would have had a proper laugh about it if she weren't so perturbed at someone visiting without calling ahead.

As Harriet bent to retrieve her crutches, she heard the door open. Her heart quickened its pace. Could it be a burglar? In the middle of the day? In this neighborhood? She pushed herself up to standing and raised one crutch overhead as high as she could. It would do for a weapon.

The librarian peered around the door. "Oh, dreadfully sorry. Did I scare you?"

"You certainly did. I couldn't imagine who would have the audacity to open the door to my home without my letting them in."

Lucille's face flushed. She avoided eye contact while pushing a grocery bag through the open door with her foot. "I came in because I figured getting to the door would be hard for you. You left this in my car."

"I'm sure I did no such thing. I never shop at Albertsons," Harriet said, lowering the crutch.

"It's your...um...unmentionables. I thought you'd rather I put them in a bag."

Harriet felt the blood drain from her face. She always carried an extra pair of underwear in her purse, just in case. She could hardly imagine the librarian finding them amongst all the crap in her car. And she must have handled them to put them in the bag. It was mortifying. How had they gotten out of her purse? It must have been when she was rooting around for the darned ChapStick the librarian hadn't even wanted. How could Harriet face her at the library knowing she'd handled her unmentionables?

"Well, since you mentioned them, they're no longer unmentionables, are they?"

Lucille spat a nervous chuckle. "I suppose not." She stood at the door, kneading her hands as though waiting for something.

Harriet raised her eyebrows. "Well?"

"I suppose I'll be going then. See you at the library." She turned and walked down the first porch step, then turned back. "You'll let me know if you need anything, won't you?"

"I'm fine. I can take care of things."

"Right," Lucille said, walking to her car.

Harriet shut the door and went back to the sofa. She reached into the bag and pulled out her plain white briefs. She was grateful, not for the first time, for her sensible choice of undergarments.

"At least she didn't find the lacy ones you bought me for our honeymoon, right, Les?" Harriet looked at the picture of his broad, smiling face and chuckled.

CHAPTER 3

THE NEXT MORNING, Harriet woke to the sound of Bibbo's whining. The clock said 6:07. It was the latest she had slept in...well, she couldn't remember when. Bibbo whined again. "All right. I'm working on it."

Harriet raised herself to a seated position at the edge of the bed. Bibbo climbed onto her boot, hopping on his back legs. He seemed to think it was some jumping apparatus built for his pleasure. She made her way to the window and peered out. Snow. As if it wasn't tough enough to walk a dog on crutches, she'd have to do it in the snow.

Catching sight of his leash, Bibbo jumped and squirmed like a stuck pig. "Hold still!" Harriet yelled.

Bibbo stopped. She rarely raised her voice. His tail stopped wagging. Leaning against the wall, she pulled his legs through the harness and snapped it shut. He squealed.

"Oh, Bibbo," she said, stroking his head and pushing his bushy eyebrows from his eyes. Tears threatened to spill from hers. "I'm so sorry. I didn't mean to pinch you. Things are tough with a broken ankle."

Unbidden, she heard Les's response. "You think an ankle is tough?"

The wind nearly ripped the doorknob from her hand as she opened it. She pulled her beanie further down over her ears and wrapped her scarf tighter around her neck. She thought about returning to the closet to get Bibbo's coat, but decided it was too much of a hassle with the crutches. He'd have to deal with it. Maybe he'd even want to head back early. She'd be okay with that.

"You're going to have to tough it out," she said to Bibbo. He looked at her, cocked his head, and if dogs could shrug, she knew he would have. He trotted down the street as far as his retractable leash would allow.

They made it halfway down their street before they spotted the darned off-leash Jack Russell terrier. Harriet stopped, heart hammering, blood boiling. She pulled Bibbo closer, and he growled his tiny, unmenacing growl. Harriet couldn't agree more. How dare he after what he'd done to them?

Off-leash-dog-man waved, as if he hadn't a care in the world. "Hey, Harriet! How's the leg?"

"How dare you!" she yelled.

He looked surprised. "What do you mean?"

"You know what I mean! You're the reason I'm in this predicament." She raised her right crutch and waved it, threateningly, she hoped.

"Geez," he said, hands raised, still walking toward them. His dog, who thankfully hadn't noticed them, was peeing on Gayle's rhododendrons.

"Don't come any closer! And get that dog on a leash!" Harriet said.

"Rocky? He wouldn't hurt a flea. You didn't need to freak out and run like that the other day. Here, let's have them meet, and you'll see. There's nothing to worry about."

"Get back!" Harriet poked her crutch at him. "You'll do nothing of the sort. You'll leash that dog at once. And I'm notifying the HOA. No dogs allowed off-leash. And I'm also notifying Gayle that your dog is the one ruining her rhododendrons."

"Fine. Be that way." He turned and walked away.

Harriet and Bibbo made it to the end of the street, not even a quarter of their usual walk, but Harriet's armpits were aching so badly that she had to turn around. Bibbo pulled at the leash, eyes pleading. It nearly broke her heart.

"I'm sorry. I can't do it, Bibs." She pulled at his leash, and he sat. "Come on, Bibbo. Enough of your stubborn behavior." Harriet yanked so hard this time that he spun around and slunk toward her, tail between his legs. "That's better. I wish you wouldn't make me do that. I love you too much."

Inching her way home gave her extra time to peer into her neighbors' houses. Bonnie was in the kitchen, most likely baking something for her kids when they got home from school. Lindsay's front porch was looking very stark. Didn't she used to have furniture, flowers, a welcome mat, or some accouterments that made her home inviting? A baby was wailing in Maggie's house. They had three little ones, all under the age of four. Harriet didn't want to imagine the mess that must've been behind those doors.

When she and Les had first moved into the neighborhood, Harriet made it her duty to call on each neighbor as they settled in, bringing a freshly baked pie as a welcome gift. It was Les's idea.

"Harriet," he'd said, sitting beside her on the couch. "This is to be our forever home. I've invested more money than I ever imagined to buy a home for you in this neighborhood, so I'd like you to get to know our neighbors."

Harriet had twirled a lock of her hair. "You know how shy I am, Les. I'll do my best, but I'm not really one to go out of my way to introduce myself."

Les had put his arm around her shoulders. "I believe in you. Sometimes it's worth it to get out of your comfort zone. You don't want any old slob or vagabond living next to you, do you? If you introduce yourself and learn a little about them, you'll know who you need to keep an eye on."

"Okay. But why does it have to be me? Can't you do it?" Harriet asked.

"I'll try, but I work longer hours than you, so I'm not around as much. Plus, women are usually better about the social side of things, you know."

"But you're so much better in social situations," Harriet said.

Les laughed. "What do you mean? We're rarely in social situations."

"The last company get-together you had a few months back, remember? You were so charming, talking to everyone and asking about their families. I just stood there awkwardly sipping my wine."

"That's different. I have to turn on the charm at work since I'm the boss. And those functions only happen a couple of times a year. This is where we live, so we need to make connections."

Harriet nodded and chewed on a hangnail. "Well, I work too. Not as many hours as you, but I won't always be here either."

He sighed. "I'd like you to take this house and this neighborhood seriously. Like we said, this is our forever home. Maybe you could take pies or casseroles to meet the new neighbors as their houses are finished and they begin moving in. It takes work to create a dream neighborhood."

Harriet swallowed. "I'm just not sure I'm comfortable doing that."

"I know, hon, but if this neighborhood goes downhill, that will be much more uncomfortable, won't it?"

Now, the house across the street made Harriet terribly uncomfortable. The for-sale sign had gone up a few weeks ago, which Harriet believed was a good thing, though the state of the property would surely lead to a lower sale price, reducing the average. Certainly, someone with better manners and a better ability to care for a lawn would move in. Janet, Bob, Burt, or whatever her husband's name was, were the laziest, most unkempt, beer-drinking slobs Harriet could ever have imagined. She believed these types of people, who no doubt held the Simpsons in the highest regard, lived only in trailer parks, not in upper-middle-class neighborhoods like The Orchards.

The unplowed driveway, always a source of agita for Harriet, was smooth and shimmering white, with no car tracks to be seen. Had they moved out? Did Harriet dare sneak over there and peek? It wouldn't do any harm to see the state of the place. That way, if any potential buyers inquired, Harriet could supply all the relevant information.

Three awkward hops landed her on the front porch. Thankfully, Bibbo patiently kept in step with her, finally seeming to understand her predicament. Putting her hand up to shield her eyes, she peered through the long window next to the front door. Harriet never understood these windows. Why even have a solid front door if the entire world could look in on the sides? She was grateful for them now, however, as they afforded a perfect view of the entire living room. It was empty and clean. They must've hired a professional cleaning company.

The ceilings were high, much higher than Harriet's, and vast windows stretched nearly from floor to ceiling. A surprisingly open great room was bright, light, and, well, inviting. Harriet felt an unexpected twinge of jealousy. Les had always liked a dark, cave-like house with the blinds drawn and the ceilings low. He said their lives weren't on display, so there was no need for large windows. Plus, they were terribly inefficient.

The rumble of a truck caught Harriet's attention. She pulled her phone from her pocket to check the time—7:28 a.m. Loud machinery was not allowed in the neighborhood before 9:00 a.m. She turned around to see who the offender was. It was a moving truck. And it was pulling into this very driveway.

Harriet's heart pounded. Bibbo, who had been content to sniff around the porch, now began barking maniacally. Even if she were adept at using crutches, and if the stairs weren't covered in snow, there would be no way to disguise the fact that she'd been here. Or, more correctly, that she was still here.

"Bibbo, knock it off. Sit down," Harriet said. Bibbo sat. Best to make it appear nothing was amiss.

"Hello." A woman's voice emanated from a red Suburban, which had been following the moving truck. "I'm Robyn Carter," she said, as though it was perfectly normal to have a stranger and a dog on the front porch of her new home. "You must be Dana," Robyn said, shutting her car door and walking toward Harriet.

"Who's Dana?" Harriet asked.

Robyn, who had been quickly approaching, stopped, and the smile fell from her face. She was curvy, a fact accentuated by her skintight sweater and jeggings. Harriet was skinny, and she still couldn't stand the things. There were leggings, which should be reserved for yoga and jogging, not worn instead of proper pants, and there were jeans. The two never should have mated.

"Well, who are you then?" Robyn asked.

"Harriet."

They stared at each other for a moment. Bibbo whined.

"Why are you on my porch?"

"I was just checking on things. The house looked empty, so I thought I'd take a peek. I was being neighborly, you know, monitoring things. Is there anything wrong with that?"

Robyn scratched her head. "It's just..." She paused, putting her hands on her hips. "I'm not accustomed to people feeling free to snoop around my house."

"Well, how could I possibly have known it was yours?"

Robyn chuckled. "I suppose you're right. Let's try again. I'm Robyn, and I'm moving into this house today. It's a pleasure to meet you."

"I'm Harriet, like I said."

"Do you live nearby?" Robyn asked.

"That's pretty obvious, isn't it?"

"Beg your pardon?"

"For what?" Harriet asked, pinching her eyebrows together.

"I'm sorry. I'm not following. Why is it obvious that you live nearby?"

"The crutches, right? I can't exactly jog over here from miles away, can I?"

"Of course not," Robyn said, wiping her hands on her jeans. "Forgive me," she said, putting her hand out. "Nice to meet you, neighbor."

Harriet took her hand even though she assumed it would be clammy, which it was. She wiped her hand on her coat after she let go.

"Well, we'll let you get to it." Harriet made her way down the steps. Robyn reached out to steady her.

"You got it?" Robyn asked. "That looks treacherous, using crutches on the steps in the snow."

"I can manage just fine on my own," Harriet said without turning around.

CHAPTER 4

BACK INSIDE HER OWN HOUSE, the darkness enveloped her like a cave. Les had insisted on wood paneling even though Harriet knew it was out of style, even twenty or so years ago when they built the house.

"My father had it in his study," Les had said. "Always felt regal, like a place a rich man went to smoke cigars and drink scotch."

"But you don't smoke cigars, and you hate scotch."

"Darling, it's the feeling I'm after. You don't always have to be so literal."

And so they had wood paneling installed everywhere but the bathrooms. Harriet hated it. Whenever she and Les fought, she'd get the courage to tell him. It seemed to be the first thing she flung at him, no matter the topic of the argument.

"And I hate these goddamn walls!" she'd yell. It had gotten so that it defused the argument. They'd both start laughing, no matter how mad they'd been just moments before. But the walls stayed.

Across the street, even though the sky was the color of a wet sidewalk, Robyn's house seemed to emanate light. It was a happy place where Harriet imagined people hummed while dusting the windowsills and played Scrabble in the evenings. Harriet's house felt like a dungeon where the inhabitants lived as if they'd already died. It had been over a year since Les's death, but Harriet still couldn't wrap her head around it. She certainly wasn't ready to get rid of his walls, no matter how much she hated them.

She shook her head—no sense indulging those thoughts. Jealousy was an evil beast best kept far away. It was time for breakfast and then yoga. Keep moving. It was better that way. Les hated when she got "all in her head."

Harriet counted out ten almonds, plopped them on top of her yogurt, and paused. How could she get her breakfast to the table while on crutches? Her shoulders drooped. She sighed. Tears pricked her eyes. Seriously? This wasn't worth crying over. But even as she tried to pull herself up by her bootstraps, a tear fell into the bowl.

She stood in her dark brown kitchen with the fluorescent light flickering overhead and ate her breakfast. "Quit looking at me like I've got a screw loose, Bibbo. I'm fine now, see?"

She googled "carrying things while on crutches." It seemed a silly search. She remembered the old days when people had to go to the library to find information. When she worked there, she'd never had anyone ask about maneuvering on crutches, but the students requested many odd things. One wanted to know how to care for her pet turtle, another wanted to know what Marilyn Monroe's measurements were, and yet another hoped to find the proper etiquette for accidentally sleeping with a friend after a drunken New Year's Eve party. That last one made her so flustered that she nearly forgot the Dewey decimal system.

She preferred the old days, yet Google had its uses. Like now, she was staring at pictures of people intelligent enough to think of wearing a backpack on their front like a kangaroo pouch to transport objects while on crutches. She would have to use water bottles with lids and Tupperware to transport food, but it would work. And, by crazy coincidence, Amazon was ready to ship her just such a contraption in only two days.

After breakfast, it was time for yoga. How was that going to work? Was there such a thing as one-legged yoga? She typed her request into the search bar and was astonished to see pages and pages of results. She could do this.

Years ago, Harriet belonged to a fancy yoga studio in town. She loved it. The instructor would come around and shift her into a better position. After a while, the instructor used Harriet as a model of how the poses were supposed to be performed. Harriet feigned embarrassment, but she loved it when everyone looked to her to see how it was supposed to be done.

When she started going to yoga nearly every day of the week, Les suggested she cut back a bit. He said it was getting expensive, and he liked having her at home more. His request saddened her, but since he earned most of the money, she figured she could honor it. And she was flattered that he wanted more time with her.

So, Harriet started doing yoga at home most days. She found she knew what to do and didn't need the direction of the instructor, so she ended up quitting the yoga studio entirely. Les had been thrilled. He even took her out to dinner more often with the money they saved. It was a win-win.

Now, in her dark living room, Harriet consulted the website to determine her next move. Three-legged downward-facing dog. She bent at the waist, placed her hands on the floor, and brought her leg with the boot up as high as she could, feeling a pleasant stretch in her good calf. The weight of the boot felt much heavier in this position. Her buttocks flexed with the weight, and she shifted to ease the pressure, but it was too far over her good leg. She twisted and fell onto her back. An awkward moan, not unlike the call of a howler monkey, escaped her as her breath left her body.

Bibbo scrambled to her side and began licking her face as she gasped, struggling to catch her breath. She pushed Bibbo away, but he wouldn't be thwarted. He whined with worry. Tears leaked from her eyes and tickled her ears. Bibbo licked those as well. She covered her face with her hands and wept.

"Pull yourself together," Harriet shouted. Startled, Bibbo stopped licking her face and began barking. "That's right, Bibbo.

Enough feeling sorry for myself. There are plenty of people who have it much worse than we do." Turning over onto her hands and knees, she rolled up her yoga mat, put it in the corner, where she hid it behind the hutch, and used the chair to pull herself upright.

The rest of the day passed in nearly the same manner as the next and the next and the next. She took Bibbo on a short walk, about which he made his disappointment known. If she left fifteen minutes later for their walk, she could avoid off-leash-dog-man, which was quite convenient. She ate her yogurt at the counter as she was still waiting for the delivery of her backpack—so much for two-day delivery. Montana was wonderful for many things, but on-time delivery was not one of them. She still did yoga daily, but kept at least one hand on the chair, watched TV, and read books. But that was it. The sum of her booted-foot existence. That was what it was. Existence.

Les would tell her to look on the bright side. She didn't have to worry about missing work or any kids' activities. She should look at it as a mini vacation, a stress-free life. He would tell her he'd happily switch places. He was probably right. But still.

As she settled onto the couch to watch the next episode of *The Golden Bachelor*, the doorbell rang. "Who is it?" Harriet called from the couch.

"It's me, Robyn."

What the heck did that woman want? Robyn had barely moved in, and already she was coming over whenever she felt like it. Ever since Harriet's efforts to make friends with the neighbors when they first moved in had failed, she'd gotten used to the idea of everyone keeping to themselves.

"I'm busy," Harriet called to the door, grateful she remembered to lock it this time.

"Oh, okay," Robyn said. "I'll leave this here, then."

Harriet rolled her eyes. It was probably an Amway catalog or some such crap. She pushed play on her remote, and that handsome old man started kissing one of the ladies. As much as Harriet enjoyed this show, she could do without all the kissing. She hoped people could still find love in their seventies, but she didn't need to see their wrinkles smashed together.

Another knock sounded at the door. "What!" Harriet shouted, hitting pause again.

"I'm really sorry, but I realized you probably won't be able to carry this on crutches."

"I probably don't need it then."

Harriet waited a few seconds and was about to press play when she heard Robyn's high-pitched voice yet again.

"It's a lasagna. I figured it must be tough to cook on crutches. Just trying to be neighborly," Robyn said.

Oh God. Now she was laying on the guilt trip. "Give me a minute," Harriet said, gathering her crutches.

She opened the door, and Robyn stared at her with eyes wide enough to belong to a lemur. Harriet wanted to tell her she didn't bite, but that might be all the woman needed to think they were friends.

"Can I bring this into the kitchen for you?"

"Sure," Harriet said, moving aside and opening her door wide.

"It's a lasagna," she said again. Harriet rolled her eyes behind Robyn's back. Robyn was darn proud of herself, wasn't she? "I wasn't sure if you ate meat, so it's a vegetable one. I've been told I make a good one."

"That's kind of you. Thanks," Harriet said.

"There's plenty for you and your husband for at least a couple of nights. You can always freeze some too, if you prefer. Stays good for at least a month that way. You should see my freezer! Of course, I need to get better at labeling things. I have no idea what most of it is," Robyn said, leaning against the counter.

"Okay," Harriet called from where she stood next to the open front door.

"Is this your husband?" Robyn asked, picking up a photo from a side table in the living room.

"Yes."

"You two look so happy together. My husband and I were happy like that once. At least, I think we were."

Harriet knew this woman wanted her to ask what happened. She also knew it was the polite thing to do. But the overwhelming desire for Robyn to leave overrode both these notions. Harriet said nothing.

"Well, I'll leave you to it. You can return the dish whenever. No rush," Robyn said, walking toward the door. "Oh, silly me. You can't carry a dish. How long will you be on those dreaded things?"

"At least four weeks."

"Goodness! That's a long time. How about I stop by in a week or so to pick up the dish?"

"That won't be necessary," Harriet said. "I've ordered a backpack."

Robyn knit her eyebrows together. "A backpack?"

"Yes. The internet says to wear it on my front and carry things like a kangaroo."

"Brilliant," Robyn said.

Harriet agreed, but didn't want to invite further conversation, so again, she said nothing.

"Well, take care. Holler if you need anything," Robyn said.

Harriet shut the door and left her palm pressed against it. She remembered when she was like Robyn, trying to get to know the neighbors. She baked a few pies with homemade crusts, the way her mom taught her. She peeled and sliced dozens of apples. Les loved apple pie. He would come into the kitchen and kiss her forehead as she worked the butter into the flour. She loved those gentle affections, which asked for nothing in return.

One such day, years ago, she'd donned her favorite sundress, the light blue one with the small daisies, and set out hoping to make a good first impression. Her mother told her about never having a second chance.

Harriet started with her closest neighbor, right next door. Watching discreetly from the dining room window, she'd learned they had two little girls, around two and four. They woke early and went out for much of the day, though Harriet didn't know where because the girls were much too young for school, and returned in the early afternoon. On the pie delivery day, Harriet waited until they'd been home for half an hour to let them settle in a bit. Then, she went to their front porch and rang the bell.

From behind the door, Harriet heard, "Elizabeth, how dare you! Get over here!" The smile she'd readied for the encounter slid from her face. Figuring this wasn't a good time, Harriet turned to leave. The door swung open. Harriet turned back around to face her neighbor. From her dining room window, this woman appeared around thirty and attractive, despite her rather frumpy clothing, but up close, she seemed to be closer to fifty. The creases on her forehead were so deep they didn't disappear even when she relaxed her scowl, which Harriet didn't think she did often.

"Can I help you?" the neighbor asked.

"Well, you see," Harriet said, "I've baked you a pie. I hope you like apple."

"Thanks," the woman said, taking the pie.

They stood staring awkwardly for a moment. Harriet assumed she'd be invited in and they would have a cup of coffee or tea, which could even become a glass of wine if they chatted long enough. Harriet thought this happened when you spent a day baking pies for your neighbors in a perfect neighborhood like theirs.

"I live next door. Just there," Harriet said, pointing.

"Okay," the woman said, running her hand through her messy hair.

Then nothing. A child yelled, "Mo-om, Katie pulled my hair again!"

The woman sighed. "Well, I've got to go. Thanks again!"

The door shut. Harriet stood staring at it. She hadn't even learned the woman's name.

The other three neighbors reacted similarly. One said dinner was on the stove, another was on the phone, and the last was a husband, who accepted the pie and explained that his wife was out of town on business. Harriet didn't think a woman who traveled for business would be interested in being friends with a part-time school librarian.

When she returned home, she sat at the kitchen table and stared out the window.

"What's for dinner?" Les asked.

She didn't answer.

"What's wrong?"

"No one even invited me in."

"Is that what you expected?" Les asked.

Harriet stared at him. "Of course. I thought that's what you said. That I should make friends."

He was smiling, almost laughing. "That's not what I said. I wanted you to meet them and keep an eye on them, not make friends. We have to be self-sufficient. It's never good to rely too heavily on anyone else."

Harriet nodded. She stood to go make dinner.

"If it's any consolation, I'd have eaten all your pies. And I'd invite you in." He kissed the top of her head and went back to the couch to watch the evening news.

Now, as she sat watching the golden bachelor ride a rollercoaster with one of the fawning ladies, her thoughts drifted to her mother. Harriet would have loved to watch this show with her mother. They would've laughed until they cried. Harriet's chest constricted in the familiar way that even thirty-four years couldn't erase.

Harriet missed her mother more than ever. She would've taken care of her with this broken ankle. How different her life would have been if she hadn't lost her parents when she was only eighteen. She'd probably still be talking to her brother, too.

As the latest episode of *The Golden Bachelor* ended, a heaviness settled upon Harriet. It happened from time to time. Les said she shouldn't indulge in these feelings. He said to keep moving, keep busy, and they'd pass. He was usually right. But this felt different.

Maybe she needed to eat something. Her heart lifted at the thought of the lasagna. She loved lasagna. Her mother had made one per week and frozen the leftovers, as Robyn had said to do. Harriet would come home from school and pop a small piece in the microwave. Her mom said it was too much for an afternoon snack, but Harriet didn't listen. It was like a warm hug after a hard day.

Though it was a bit more difficult to warm her lasagna in her current state, the feeling she got as she took the first bite was the same. Robyn wasn't kidding. She made a fabulous lasagna. Not as good as her mother's, but close. Standing at the counter, she inhaled the rich, cheesy scent and savored each bite. Bibbo let out a whine as he stared up at her, eyes pleading.

"Oh, all right. You can have a bite. It's too good not to share. But don't you go getting spoiled on me. I can't have you begging."

Bibbo swallowed his bite and barked. "I know, right? One more bite for you, but that's all. Understood?"

Bibbo swallowed and barked once again. "I said that was enough, and I meant it. No more." Harriet shooed him away with her hand. Tail between his legs, Bibbo obeyed. But the glare he shot her from his bed nearly knocked her over.

Dishes done, kitchen tidied, Harriet stood in her dark kitchen under the flickering fluorescent light and wondered what the heck to do next. She supposed she could head to bed early and hope for sleep to take her away from this dreary existence.

CHAPTER 5

THE SUN SHONE BRIGHTLY the next morning as she rose and got Bibbo ready for his walk. Opening the front door, the glare off the snow nearly blinded her. "You wait on the porch, Bibbo. I've got to get my sunglasses."

No sooner had Harriet turned her back on Bibbo than he was off like a shot, barking like a maniac. "Bibbo! Get back here!" Harriet yelled.

Of course, it was Rocky, running zigzag across the open area behind the houses where the walking trail meandered through the neighborhood. He flitted from one neighbor's yard to another, sniffing and lifting his leg wherever he pleased. Without time to grab her sunglasses, Harriet squinted against the glare of the sun and made out the tiny shape of Bibbo running full speed through the field and across the trail toward Rocky. Seemingly from out of nowhere, off-leash-dog-man scooped Bibbo up and came jogging toward Harriet.

"Looks like you forgot something," he said, setting Bibbo down and handing Harriet his leash.

"Not likely. I went in to get my sunglasses and he took off after your dog, of course. I can't even do a little thing like fetch sunglasses without your off-leash dog causing problems around here."

"Little good a leash does if there's no one holding the other end," off-leash-dog-man said.

"Can't you cut me some slack? Can't you see the predicament I'm in because of you?" Harriet asked.

He shook his head, a slight smile playing at the corner of his mouth. "Because of me, huh? You're still stuck on that? I think you have an entire world of problems, the least of which are me and my dog."

Harriet clenched her teeth and felt the heat rise to her face. "The nerve! You go around breaking rules, and you think you can judge me? You know nothing about me. I've had enough of cutting you slack. I'll be phoning Tammy today."

"Who's Tammy?"

"It figures you wouldn't know who she is. She's one of our neighbors and the head of our homeowners' association. That's what HOA stands for in case you were ignorant of those initials as well."

Harriet lifted her crutches, spun on her good foot, and made her way back to her house. Bibbo pulled at his leash, furious at being denied his walk, but Harriet kept him in tow. There was work to be done. This had gone on long enough.

"Yes. Hello, Tammy? This is Harriet at 466 Lemon Lane. I'm calling to report a repeat offender of the leash laws here in The Orchards."

"Hello, Harriet. Nice to hear from you again."

"Sure. Anyway, did you hear what I said about the repeat offender?"

"I did. Tell me more," Tammy said.

"Well, this man walks his dog without a leash every day. He caused me to break my ankle while saving my little Bibbo from his awful rogue dog. This has to stop."

"I see. Who is this man?"

Harriet stopped. She didn't even know his name. Nor did she know exactly where he lived.

"I'm not sure of his name. But I know he lives on Tangerine, near the school. His dog's name is Rocky. He moved in a couple of years ago, and that dog has been terrorizing the neighborhood ever since."

"Terrorizing? How so?"

"You know. Running willy-nilly all over the place. Doing his business on people's yards, chasing other dogs, that kind of thing."

"Has the dog bitten anyone?"

"Not that I know of, but I wouldn't put it past him."

"Unfortunately, Harriet, we need a name and address before we can follow up. We can't go knocking on doors, you know."

"Is that what you expect me to do?" Harriet asked.

"Heavens, no. Maybe ask his name the next time you see him," Tammy said.

"Really? You expect me to calmly approach the man who traumatized me and my dog and broke my ankle and ask for his information?"

"Well, if you're not comfortable doing that, maybe one of your other neighbors knows his name or where he lives?" Tammy asked.

Harriet sighed. "I thought the HOA was supposed to investigate these sorts of things. It's hardly common to ask residents to do your work for you."

"I can't go knocking on doors, either," Tammy said. "I'm sure you'll find a way. Is that all, Harriet?"

"I suppose it is." Harriet hung up—incompetence at its finest.

Computers weren't her friend, but she could usually cajole them into doing what she wanted when she absolutely needed them. However, in this situation, where she absolutely needed her computer to do her bidding, it wasn't. How hard could it be to make flyers, for goodness' sake?

"Have You Seen Me?" was bold and large at the top, sure to capture attention and tug at emotions. Then, at the bottom, Harriet typed, "If so, please call Tammy at 406-555-4356 and report me. Be sure to mention that I am off-leash." But she couldn't get it centered properly. If her flyer didn't look professional, she'd be the laughingstock of the neighborhood.

She fiddled with the font and the centering button until she had it perfect. Now, all she needed was a close-up of Rocky to put in the middle. She figured that wouldn't be hard since she saw him everywhere. Getting him to hold still long enough for a picture could be tough, however.

The next morning, she woke early to ensure she and Bibbo would be out at the same time as Rocky. Winding Bibbo's leash around her hand twice for safe measure, she opened the front door and braced herself for the tug on the leash she was sure would follow. As expected, Bibbo pulled on the leash and barked like mad when he saw Rocky traipsing around the neighborhood. Harriet knew he didn't think it was fair. It wasn't. And she was going to put a stop to it.

"Rocky!" Harriet called. The dog didn't even lift his head. He kept sniffing and marking every bush he came across. She'd have to go to him.

Navigating her way across the grass of the open space was harder than Harriet imagined. The ground was uneven, and her crutches kept landing in unlevel positions, lurching her from side to side. Bibbo pulled at the leash on her right side, further unbalancing her. That darned dog and his reckless owner were more trouble than they were worth.

"Hey, Harriet," off-leash-dog-man said as he jogged up beside her. He wasn't wearing a shirt. Granted, it was a warm day for April, but still. She wasn't sure of his age, but he had to be pushing fifty. Granted, he was in great shape, but weren't there rules about wearing shoes and shirts on neighborhood trails like there were for gas stations? "What are you doing out here?" he asked.

Harriet quickly turned her gaze to Rocky. "Trying to get a picture of your dog."

He raised his eyebrows. "Why would you want a picture of Rocky? I thought you hated him."

Harriet turned to glare at the guy. "I don't hate your dog. I hate you."

He chuckled and ran his hand through his thick brown hair. Harriet thought he was lucky to have all that hair still, and it wasn't even graying. "I could have guessed. But I thought we were a package deal," he said.

"Nope. It's not your dog's fault you're an idiot."

"Who says you're allowed to photograph my dog? I'm pretty sure I have to give you permission. And what's the purpose of wanting a picture of Rocky, anyway?"

"Dogs don't have rights. I can take his picture. And I need it for my flyer."

"Flyer? What flyer?" he asked.

"That's none of your business. You'll see soon enough."

Harriet stormed off, though it lost much of the desired effect on crutches. Rocky was running toward her. She pulled her phone from her back pocket, pushed the camera icon, and started pressing the red button. There had to be at least one good one in the bunch. Well, it didn't really need to be good. Just enough to identify his untethered self.

"That'll do," Harriet said, heading back toward her house.

"You really won't tell me what you're up to?" off-leash-dog-man asked.

"And ruin the surprise? You really don't know me at all," Harriet said.

• • • • •

If Harriet had anticipated the number of phone calls she would receive personally, she might have reconsidered her plan. How anyone knew she was the one to post the flyers was beyond her. Wasn't everyone tired of that dog running all over the neighborhood? Why was she the only one to do anything about the offenses?

The first call was from Bonnie. She could hardly get the words out from laughing so hard. "Harriet, you've really outdone yourself this time," she said. "Oh my, Tammy is going to be so mad at you if anyone really calls her."

"Well, if Tammy did her job, I wouldn't have to go to such lengths," Harriet said.

"I know the rules say dogs are supposed to be leashed, but he's just a little Jack Russell. Not a Pit Bull or a German Shepherd, or some big, scary dog like that. I don't understand why you get yourself in such a tizzy about these things."

"I'm sorry we don't see eye to eye on this, Bonnie," she said and hung up.

The next call was from Andy. "Harriet, are you trying to start a war here or something?"

"If that's what it takes."

"Come on. It's hardly worth all this. We're all friends here."

Harriet snorted. "That's a joke, and you know it. I'm simply enforcing rules no one else has the backbone to enforce."

"Some rules are better left unenforced between friends, Harriet," Andy said.

She hung up. The subsequent calls went unanswered until she saw Tammy calling in the afternoon.

"Hello, Tammy," Harriet said.

"What do you think you're doing, Harriet?"

"Getting you to do your job."

Tammy sighed. "It's not my job to help you carry out some grudge you have."

"Is that what you think this is? A grudge? He broke my ankle, and his dog wreaks havoc every day, and you think it's me with the problem?"

"Fine. Get me his name and address, like I asked, and I'll follow up, okay? And please take down the flyers. The calls I've received today have been highly entertaining, but they've distracted me from doing the rest of my job."

Harriet hung up the phone and plopped onto the couch. Bibbo jumped into her lap and licked her face. "How are we going to find out where he lives, Bibbo?"

Her doctor had forbidden her to drive for at least four weeks. It would be nearly impossible with her boot on anyway, and it still hurt too much when she took it off. Maybe, if she went slow and stayed in the neighborhood, she could do it just this one time. This mission had to be completed somehow.

CHAPTER 6

SITTING IN THE DRIVER'S SEAT in her garage, Harriet tried pushing the pedals without her boot, but the pain was too great to allow her to push down hard enough to operate her vehicle. She tried with her boot and thought she might manage. Pushing down with her thigh, she didn't have to move her ankle at all to press the pedals. Harriet realized she was breaking the rules set for her by her doctor, but he couldn't possibly know the importance of her task. Besides, she wouldn't leave the neighborhood. It would be like she hadn't really driven at all. Certainly, she would never attempt to drive to town or get on the highway, but this little sleepy neighborhood, with its 15-mile-per-hour speed limit, didn't really count as driving.

Strapping Bibbo into his safety harness in the passenger seat before fastening her own seat belt, Harriet adjusted her mirror and opened her garage. It felt like decades since she'd driven, even though it had only been a few days. Her heart hammered in her chest as if she was about to go for a bungee jump, for goodness' sake. What was wrong with her? It was no big deal. She had to get a grip.

Wrapping her right arm around the back of the passenger seat, she turned to look backward as she eased out of the garage. In no time, she was on the street. *You've got this, Harriet.* As she came around and exited her turn, her boot gave the car a bit too much gas, but when she attempted to maneuver her unwieldy boot onto the brake, it slipped, hitting the gas once more. Harriet screamed as the front of her car smashed into Robyn's mailbox and tipped down into the ditch in front of Robyn's house. Her boot finally found purchase on the brake as a frantic Robyn came running out of her front door.

"Harriet! My goodness, are you okay?" Robyn asked, opening her car door.

Harriet stared ahead, unable to move. Mortifyingly, a tear trickled down her cheek. She wiped it away quickly with the back of her hand. Bibbo whined. Robyn leaned into the car and put her hand on Harriet's shoulder. She flinched. Robyn stepped back. Harriet placed her hands on the steering wheel, laid her head on them, and sobbed.

"Harriet? Why don't I go to your house and get your husband? You seem in shock."

"He's not home."

"Well, is he at work? Can I call him for you?"

"No, you can't," Harriet said.

"Harriet, I don't think you should be alone right now."

"I'm not. You're with me."

"Yes, but—," Robyn began.

"He's dead, okay? He's been dead nearly a year now."

"Oh, Harriet!" Robyn's hand flew to her mouth. "I'm so sorry. I had no idea."

"No need to get into all that again. It's fine. I'm fine."

Silence filled the car like heavy fog. Harriet took a few deep, shaky breaths to calm herself. "I'm really sorry about your mailbox and your lawn," Harriet said.

"That's nothing. I'm worried about you. What were you doing driving with that boot?"

"It was an emergency."

"You can always ask me for help. I'm happy to help. I work from home, so I'm nearly always here."

"Thanks, but I need to handle this," Harriet said.

"What could be so urgent?"

"That off-leash dog started this whole mess, and I intend to end it. I was going to watch and see which house he lives in so I can report him to the HOA."

"Oh, Harriet. Is that worth all this?" Robyn asked, concern creasing her forehead.

"It wasn't going to be a big deal at all. But I suppose now it is. Hey, did you really mean you'd help me?"

"Of course," Robyn said.

"Then please go and watch on Tangerine Street and see which house Rocky's owner lives in. Then report the address to me, okay?"

Robyn folded her arms and took another step back from the car. "I suppose I could do that for you. But I was really hoping not to get involved. Was that you who put the flyers all over the neighborhood?"

"Yep. It would have worked, too, if people had called Tammy instead of me."

"All right. Well, let's get you out of the car. I'll have my husband get it out of the ditch for you when he comes home. He's got a truck and cables, so he'll have it out in no time."

Once out of the car, Harriet leaned on the hood and hopped around the front, looking for damage. Luckily, it appeared just the front wheel had gotten stuck, and her bumper might be dented, but it really wasn't terrible.

As she reached into the back seat for her crutches, Harriet heard a voice call out. "Oh goodness! What's happened here?"

Looking up, Harriet was horrified to see Bonnie running toward her.

"Nothing, Bonnie. Mind your own business, okay?" Harriet said.

"Doesn't look like nothing to me. Is this your car? Were you driving with that boot?"

"Again, none of your business. Head on home."

Robyn extended her hand in front of Bonnie. "Hi, I'm Robyn. I've just moved in here."

"Hi, Robyn. I'm Bonnie. I live across the street, two doors down from Harriet. This is quite a welcome you've received. It seems you've met Harriet."

"Yes. Fortunately, this wasn't our first encounter."

"Too bad what she did to your mailbox and lawn," Bonnie said.

"Oh, it's no big deal, really. I'm glad Harriet's okay."

"That's because you don't know Harriet very well yet." Bonnie covered her mouth as she laughed. "I'm kidding, of course."

"All right. I'm still right here, you know," Harriet said. "Why don't you mosey back to your house before we create more of a scene? Robyn here is nice enough to ask her husband to get my car out of the ditch, and I'll pay to have someone fix the mailbox. See? No big deal at all."

"You're lucky that's all that happened," Bonnie said. "What were you doing behind the wheel with that boot on your foot? You aren't one to break rules, Harriet. It had to be something important. Where's Les? Couldn't he help you?"

Harriet looked down and shook her head. Robyn's eyes went wide with surprise, but she kept quiet.

"What? Did I say something wrong? Les isn't the friendliest, but you'd think he'd help his wife, right? Is he out of town or something? Come to think of it, he's been even more scarce than usual."

"He's dead," Harriet said, still staring at the ground.

"He's what? My goodness, Harriet. I'm so sorry."

"Why does everyone have to say that? What does everyone have to be sorry about? It wasn't your fault. It wasn't anyone's fault. It just happened, okay? Let's move on."

"Was he sick?" Bonnie asked.

Harriet felt dizzy. Did she really ask that question? Sick doesn't begin to cover it. Tortured and dehumanized was more like it. ALS was a nightmare brought to this earth by some demon. No one deserved what Les had suffered. No one. But she didn't want to get into it with nosy Bonnie.

"Yep. He was. Anyway, let's deal with this situation and move on."

They stood staring at the car. Finally, Robyn opened the door on the passenger side, unstrapped Bibbo, grabbed his leash, and set him on the ground. "Let's get you inside, Harriet. I'll make you some tea, and we'll sort it all out. Bonnie, would you like to join us?"

Harriet shot Bonnie a warning glance. She took the hint. "No, I'd better get back to my chores. I really am sorry to hear about Les. Let me know if I can help." She turned and walked back to her house.

"I'm all right, Robyn. I'll wait for your husband to come home and see how I can help get my car out. Why don't you go on over to Tangerine Street for me and get that address?"

"Really, Harriet? That's all you can think about at a time like this? I'm sorry, but I won't do that today. I think you need to come inside and relax, and let me wait on you for a bit. It seems you've been dealing with quite a lot all on your own."

"I'm used to it."

"I don't care if you're used to it. You shouldn't have to be. Now, I'm not taking no for an answer. Let me help you up the steps."

Harriet disliked Robyn watching her struggle up the stairs. She wished she could borrow Hermione's wand for a quick *wingardium leviosa* to float her up the steps.

"Do you have to climb stairs to get to your bedroom in your house, Harriet?"

"No, but you'd think I'd be better at this by now, wouldn't you?"

"Absolutely not! Goodness, Harriet. You're much too hard on yourself. I ruptured my Achilles a few years back, and I never got the hang of stairs."

"Did your husband help you?" Harriet asked.

"Not really. He was upset with me for getting injured. I was playing tennis. He isn't thrilled that I play tennis," Robyn said.

"What's wrong with tennis?"

"Nothing. I got a bit obsessed. He said it was taking too much time from him and Audrey, our daughter. So, I've cut back, but that's a story for another day. Let's focus on you right now. Come on over to this chair at the table, and I'll get you some tea. What flavor would you like? I've got green, Earl Grey, chai, or rooibos."

"I hate tea," Harriet said.

Robyn choked out an awkward laugh. "Oh, well, no wonder you didn't accept my invitation right away, then. Is there something else you might like?"

"Do you have any coffee?"

"I do, but it's nearly 4 p.m. Won't it keep you up?"

"I'm often up no matter what. Might as well enjoy myself when I can," Harriet said, lifting her boot and placing it on the chair Robyn had set across from her for that purpose.

"I hear you. I swear, once I hit forty-five, I stopped sleeping through the night, couldn't read anything up close, and became completely uncool to my daughter. It happened overnight. So unfair."

Harriet nodded, looking around the kitchen. It was even brighter and airier than it looked when she had peered through the window. She thought she might be brighter and airier if she had a kitchen like this, too.

"Anyway, what's your obsession with this neighbor?" Robyn asked. "It must be something big for you to drive with your boot."

Harriet glared at Robyn, her brow furrowed. "Of course it's something big. His dog is always off his leash, running through the neighborhood like he owns the place. Peeing and pooping on any lawn he pleases. It can't be allowed to continue. It will be the end of the neighborhood as we know it."

Robyn chuckled. "It can't really be as bad as all that."

"I think I'd better head home," Harriet said, putting her boot on the floor and attempting to rise. "It seems we aren't as aligned as I thought we might be."

"Harriet. Please, sit back down. Let's talk about this. I didn't mean to upset you."

"Well, it is very upsetting to see how the rules are getting more and more lax around here. If Les saw what was happening, he'd be in an uproar. Probably best he's not here to see it. But I'm still trying, Les. I really am."

Robyn brought a cup of coffee and set it in front of Harriet. The mug displayed the face of a grumpy-looking orange cat with the words, "Cats make me happy. You, not so much."

Harriet studied it for a minute. "Do you have a cat?" Harriet didn't like cats. She rarely liked people who liked cats, either.

Robyn shook her head. "No, I've never had a cat. It's my daughter's idea of a joke. She's twelve going on twenty."

"I don't get it."

"Don't get what?" Robyn asked.

"The joke. Why is it funny?"

"Because my daughter was telling me she'd rather have a cat than me."

"Well, that's not very nice," Harriet said.

"No, it isn't, but she's nearly a teenager. Pretty typical, or so I've been told by my friends who have teenagers. Do you have kids?"

"No."

Robyn waited. Harriet didn't elaborate. They sipped their drinks in unison.

Robyn sighed. "Anyway, Chris will be home in a couple of hours, and I'll have him hook his chains to his truck and pull your car out. I'm sure it won't take him long. When he was in his twenties, you know, when he studied at Montana State – that's how we ended up here – he always wanted to come back. Well, anyway, where was I? Oh yes, Chris and his buddies used to drive the canyon between Bozeman and Big Sky during snowstorms, looking for people who had gotten stuck in the ditch. He'd pull them out, and they'd usually give him a tip for helping. He thought it was a great way to make some extra cash. So, he's pretty good at pulling cars out of ditches."

"Well, that's handy. People find all kinds of ways to make money, don't they? Seems cruel to take advantage of someone stuck in a ditch, but I suppose I could dole out twenty bucks tonight," Harriet said, sipping her coffee.

"Oh, Harriet. That was a long time ago. Chris won't be expecting any payment. He'll do it just to be neighborly."

"Good. It's nice to know some people still know what it means to be neighborly."

Robyn smiled. "Anyhow, do you have anyone, any family or friends, who can help you out around the house while you've got that boot on?"

"What makes you think I need help?"

"Well, it's tough to get around with that boot and those crutches. And I don't know how you can cook and clean with that thing. I think it might be nice for you to have some help. There's nothing wrong with asking for help, you know."

Harriet ran her finger around the rim of her coffee cup. "I've managed and I will continue to manage. I've ordered the backpack, remember? It should be here any day. That's all I need."

"A backpack isn't a substitute for a friend."

Harriet's eyes shot to Robyn's. "I'm fine. Les taught me all I need to know. We were a great team and didn't need anyone else. I can carry on the way he taught me."

"But why do you need to? Why would you want to?"

Harriet mulled over these questions. They swirled in her mind and made her dizzy. She hadn't thought about it. It was just the way it was for nearly thirty years with Les. He told her they were a team and didn't need others. Better to be self-sufficient. "I just do. It's what Les would've wanted."

Robyn nodded, but her mouth turned down. "I don't mean to pry or be rude, but I'm sorry, I'm not sure how to put this delicately..."

"Then don't," Harriet said.

Robyn snorted and her shoulders shook as she laughed.

Harriet stood. "Look, I'm glad I've been able to offer you some entertainment this afternoon, but I'll be going now. Have your husband come over, and I'll help get my car out of the ditch. Sorry to have inconvenienced you." She grabbed her crutches and turned toward the front door. "Come on, Bibbo."

Robyn and Bibbo followed her to the door. "Harriet, we're going to be living across the street from each other. I'd like to be, well, if not friends, at least neighborly. I don't want animosity between us. Life is tough enough without negativity in our own backyards."

"So mind your business and I'll mind mine and we'll be fine."

"I suppose that will have to work in this situation." Robyn opened the door. "I thought neighborly meant looking out for each other, helping when we can."

Harriet scoffed. "Yeah, I used to think that too." Harriet turned and made her way down the porch stairs.

"Take care, Harriet! Let me know if you need anything!" Robyn said.

Without turning, Harriet waved her hand over her shoulder.

Chapter 7

A FEW HOURS LATER, Harriet's recording of *America's Got Talent* was interrupted by shouting from across the street. "Honey, get me those damn tow straps, will you? I thought they were in my truck, but I must've left them in the garage."

Harriet thought the use of the word "damn" unnecessary. She was loath to go out there if that was how he was going to speak. He was doing her a favor, however, so she would have to go out and see if she could help or at least supervise. She didn't need any additional damage to her vehicle.

Harriet made her way to where Robyn's husband was lying on the ground behind his truck. "Hey, how's it going under there?" Harriet asked.

A man with orange hair that stood straight up on his head peered up at her, his mouth turned down in an almost comical frown. He looked a bit like Beaker from the Muppets. Was he frowning in concentration, or was that the normal set of his face? Harriet hated to think that was how he went about in the world, all frowny and clown-like.

"Going okay, I suppose. I assume you're Harriet?"

Harriet nodded. The man jutted his hand out toward Harriet from his position on the ground. She wasn't sure if he wanted to shake her hand or if he was hoping she would help him up. She shook his hand, since he didn't seem to be finished.

"I'm Chris," the man said. "Robyn said you were driving in that boot." He shook his head. "Not the best idea, if you ask me."

"Well, I didn't ask."

Chris laughed. "Robyn mentioned you were 'different.'"

"Aren't we all different? That's a silly thing to say."

Chris stared at Harriet for a minute, his mouth still frowning, though slightly less so. She wished she'd paid closer attention to what it was doing when he laughed. She still wasn't sure it could do anything other than frown.

"Anyway, I've almost got these chains hooked up, and I should be able to guide your car out in no time after that."

"Great. Thank you."

Robyn walked up beside Harriet. "Chris is so handy. Makes my life so much easier."

"Les wasn't. He said he worked hard at his desk to earn enough money to hire others to do manual labor."

"What did Les do?"

"He was a CPA. With his own firm."

"Wow. Good for him," Robyn said.

"I never enjoyed hiring help, though. I learned to fix most things myself," Harriet said.

"Amazing! I'm terrible with handyman stuff. Why didn't you like hiring help?" Robyn said.

"I hate having strangers in my house invading my privacy."

Robyn nodded and folded her arms across her chest. "Well, I appreciate the help. I'll have strangers in my house any day if it means things get fixed. Chris is great, but too busy most of the time."

The front door flew open, and a girl who looked to be around eleven or twelve stormed down the front porch steps. "I can't believe Mrs. Asher did this to us," the young girl said, not even glancing in Harriet's direction. Honestly, Harriet couldn't believe the lack of manners with today's youth. Robyn didn't seem like she'd be a bad mother, but Harriet supposed she couldn't tell from the few interactions they'd had. Obviously, based on this young lady's behavior, Harriet had given Robyn too much credit.

"Audrey, this is our neighbor, Harriet. Please say hello. Remember your manners," Robyn said.

"Oh, hi," the girl said, with a slight wave in Harriet's direction. Audrey had wavy auburn hair that framed a round face covered in freckles. Her fidgeting hands were adorned with colorful friendship bracelets that flitted up and down her arms as she conveyed her irritation.

"Anyway, Mom, Mrs. Asher is making us do all the practice problems at the end of the chapter AND the review section too! Can you believe it? It's too much. I mean, we're only in sixth grade, for God's sake!"

Harriet flinched. Robyn glared at her daughter. "I know you're frustrated, Audrey, but you don't need to get God involved. He has more important things to worry about. Now, if you'd like my help, I'll be in in a minute. Why don't you get some lemonade and a snack and give yourself a moment to calm down?"

Audrey stomped her foot. "Mom! Why do you have to be so annoying? Like lemonade will fix it."

"I'm with you there," Harriet said. "I hate lemonade."

Audrey turned to face Harriet. "I don't hate lemonade. But it won't fix my problem. Why do you hate lemonade?"

"The stands block traffic, and I hate that saying about making it out of lemons. It's so cliché. Everyone is trying to turn a frown upside down and all that. It turns my stomach. The sayings and the liquid are sickly sweet to me."

Audrey shrugged and started toward the house. "Mom, come in soon. I need your help," she called over her shoulder.

Robyn shook her head. "Not even a teenager yet, and she's full of attitude."

"I'd never have gotten away with speaking to my mother like that."

"Really? I didn't think that was too bad. You should hear Audrey's friends. No respect whatsoever."

"I don't think you should let her spend time with them, then," Harriet said.

"Please allow me to parent my child my way," Robyn said.

Harriet put her hands up, waving them slightly. "No need to get upset. I'm suggesting that maybe they aren't the best influence on Audrey if they aren't respectful."

"It's this generation. There isn't any way to avoid it."

"Sure there is. Just don't interact with people."

Robyn chuckled. "We can't all be pillars of solitary strength like you, Harriet."

Chris finally came out from under his truck. "That should do it. I'll slowly ease 'er out now."

Harriet held her breath as her car emerged from the ditch.

"You ask me, you got lucky this is all that happened. You driving in that boot and all," Chris said.

"I didn't ask. Here you go," Harriet said, extending a twenty-dollar bill toward him as he stepped from his truck.

"That's not necessary. We're neighbors. It's what we do. I'm sure if we need something, we can count on you, right?" He clapped her on the back, nearly causing Harriet to choke.

"Sure," Harriet said, though she hoped they wouldn't need things often. She went to her car and reached for the driver's side door handle.

Robyn rushed over and pushed herself between Harriet and the car. "Why don't you let me park your car in your garage?"

Harriet opened her mouth to protest, to say she had it covered, but in this instance, she thought maybe she didn't. That would be all she needed. To crash into her garage or something. The entire neighborhood would certainly know about that.

Harriet nodded and followed behind the car as Robyn pulled it into her garage. "Thank you again," Harriet said as Robyn exited the car. "I hope I won't trouble you any further."

Robyn put her hand on Harriet's shoulder. "It's really no trouble. Say, have you got that lasagna dish? I could grab it from you and save you the trouble of bringing it back over."

"I haven't finished it yet, but I suppose I could wash it quickly."

"Oh, heavens no! What was I thinking? I forgot it's just you." Robyn trailed off and looked at the ground.

"Yep. It's just me. Not to worry. I'll bring the dish back soon. I'll leave it outside your door, so I won't bother you. The backpack was delayed, but it should be here tomorrow. Then, I'll be nearly back to normal. Take care, and thanks again." Harriet went over to the door to her house and hovered her hand over the button to close the garage door.

Robyn opened her mouth, shut it, and turned and walked away.

"Oh, and please go find out off-leash-dog-man's address for me, would you? You wouldn't want me trying any crazy stunts again, right?"

Robyn turned to look at Harriet, a quizzical expression on her face. "Really, Harriet. You need to let this go. You've got bigger fish to fry."

"I don't even like fish."

Robyn shook her head and turned away again. Over her shoulder, she called, "If it will keep you out of trouble, I suppose I'll do it. But know I'm not happy about it."

"Well, I'm happy about it. Thank you," Harriet called after her.

Once inside her house, Harriet inhaled deeply and leaned against the wall. Bibbo barked and put his paws on her knee. "Yes, Bibbo. It's just us again."

CHAPTER 8

HARRIET WAS DREADING her checkup tomorrow at the doctor's office. She hated the doctor. She hated the personal questions they asked, the poking and prodding, and the smell. It didn't matter what kind of doctor she went to; OBGYN, gastroenterologist, or orthopedic surgeon, there was a smell that permeated them all. Part disinfectant, part cheap plastic, and all pungent, she gagged just thinking about it.

If she was honest with herself, she hadn't hated the doctor's office all that much before Les's diagnosis. She'd always been healthy, so a quick listen to her heart, a tap on the knee to check reflexes, and a tongue depressor in the mouth was usually the extent of it. When her parents died, she'd been spared any illness or hospitalization. They were pronounced dead at the scene of the car accident. It was horrific, but doctors weren't involved. Les's frequent visits ruined doctors' appointments for her.

Harriet supposed it wasn't really the office or the doctor, it was what each visit meant. After Les's diagnosis, they never left an appointment without at least a small dose of bad news. Before ALS, Harriet could go to the doctor, get some medicine, and know she would be better, usually in a matter of days or weeks. But there was no cure for ALS. It got worse and worse, so each visit was a list of things that would be taken away from Les's life. Every worst-case scenario was just the next scenario.

Les had a rarer form of the disease, which affected his speech and ability to swallow first. In fact, the first symptoms had been fun. Harriet knew how crazy that sounded, even when she thought back on it, but it really had been some of the best times they'd had. Les would start laughing. Hysterically, uncontrollably, until tears streamed down his face. It was impossible not to join him. Sometimes, a sitcom would set him off, but many times, it seemed nothing caused his bouts of irrepressible joy. How could something so wonderful be the harbinger of such a terrible disease? He'd had little sense of humor for most of his life, so Harriet welcomed this change. She thought maybe he was loosening up in the second half of his life. She couldn't say he was loosening up in his old age because he died at fifty-four, only a few years older than she was now. If only the laughing had lasted. If only he could have laughed himself to death.

It was a regular checkup that changed their lives. They hadn't gone in because of any complaints. Just his regular annual physical. He was a stickler about those. Harriet knew other women struggled to get their husbands to the doctor. Not Les. He was a rule follower, and going to the doctor was no exception. "Wouldn't you rather know what you are dealing with than pretend it's not there?" he'd say. Harriet wished they could have pretended a little longer.

Les liked Harriet to accompany him on his doctor's visits. He hadn't when they were younger, but ever since the doctor had found melanoma on his arm at age forty-eight, he'd wanted her support. She enjoyed feeling as though he needed her, since in most other aspects of their lives, she felt as though she was only along for the ride. So, on this visit, the doctor had just pronounced him to be in perfect health when Harriet said, "I love how he's started laughing lately. Sometimes, even the slightest thing will set him off, and he'll double over in hysterics. He was never much of a laugher before, so I'm really enjoying this. He must be loosening up a bit as he ages."

The doctor's bushy eyebrows furrowed, and his eyes nearly disappeared underneath them. He tapped his pen on his lower lip and leaned against the edge of the counter. "Has this been happening frequently?"

Les turned away from the doctor and scowled at Harriet. She shrank down into her turtleneck, wishing she could completely retract her head like a turtle. She hadn't realized she'd said anything wrong. How could laughter be bad?

Les turned back to the doctor and said, "Not really. Only about once a week."

"Hmmm." The doctor stood and paced across the room. "It's probably nothing, but I don't want to overlook anything. Early intervention can be helpful."

"How could laughter be a symptom of anything to worry about?" Harriet asked.

"It's called bulbar onset. I don't want to say anything further to scare you. Best to run some tests. Rule everything out. I'm exercising extreme caution."

"Bulbar onset? Like a bulb is going to form on him or something?" Harriet asked.

He huffed out a small laugh. "No. Nothing like that. I'll refer you to a neuromuscular neurologist. They'll be better able to ascertain whether anything is going on here."

It took months, not just a few tests. The laughter had been so wonderful. But it was nearly erased when things got bad. When he could no longer walk, or talk, or do much of anything. She hated how his eyes were still there, still seeing, still comprehending. It would have been better for Les if his mind had gone with his body, so he wouldn't have known how his body was failing him. He had been a rigid man, full of rules and consequences and commands. At times, he'd been controlling and unyielding. But this man, who had lost all control of everything, was so much worse.

So, doctors' visits were something that stirred up a bit of PTSD for Harriet. Not just that first visit, when they first had a notion that his irrepressible laughter wasn't a laughing matter. It was all the visits after that. Harriet believed this would be a routine checkup for her ankle, but that's what she and Les had thought before his diagnosis, right? Harriet supposed one never knew.

The problem was securing a ride. She didn't think she should ask the librarian, Lucille, again, nor did she like the prospect of riding in her disgusting car. Because of her broken ankle, she hadn't been to the library, which made her feel guilty. Lucille was expecting her. Harriet had told her as much, and she liked to be a woman of her word.

She didn't really have much of a choice, though. Retrieving her phone from her back pocket, Harriet found the library contact and dialed.

"Bozeman Public Library, how can I help you?"

"Lucille, please."

"May I ask who's calling?"

"It's Harriet."

"Oh, hi, Harriet. This is Susan. Lucille told me all about you. How's the foot?"

"Ankle."

"Oh, beg your pardon. How's your ankle?"

"Better. That's what I'm calling about. Is Lucille there?" Harriet asked.

"I'm so sorry, but she's not working today. Her son stayed home from school sick, so she's with him. Can I give her a message?"

"If her son's sick, then I guess it won't matter."

"Why's that?" Susan asked.

"The germs."

"Um, okay."

"Well, thanks anyway," Harriet said and hung up.

"I guess I'll have to call a taxi, Bibbo. Oh Les, why did you have to leave me?" Bibbo sat, turned his head to the side, and stared up at her. "Don't give me that look. I know he couldn't help it. I sure wish you could drive. I know you'd take care of me, wouldn't you?" she said, reaching down to scratch under his chin.

Harriet stared at her phone, gathering the gumption to call the taxi company. There weren't many cabs in Bozeman, so she'd need to reserve one in advance. A Google search for the phone number yielded an ad for Uber. She'd heard about it. Supposedly, you could reserve a ride completely on your phone without talking to anyone. Wouldn't that be fantastic? And you could pay on the app and everything.

She tapped the app store and downloaded Uber. A few more taps, and she had input her information, and it said she was ready to reserve her ride. Perfect. All done completely anonymously. She'd get in the back of the car, and off they'd go. Hopefully, she wouldn't get a chatty driver.

As she grabbed the remote, she felt a cool breeze that made her shudder. "Are you cold too, Bibbo?" She shivered. "It sure gets cold quick when the sun dips behind the mountains."

She went to the window to shut it, but stopped when she heard a shout. She couldn't make out what the guy said, nor could she tell where it was coming from, but it was obvious he was mad. The front door of Robyn's house opened, and Audrey came out onto the front porch, her hands over her ears.

Harriet watched Audrey as she shut her window. She heard more shouting, even with the window closed. It must've been that orange-haired Muppet yelling at Robyn. It didn't sound good, and Audrey obviously didn't want to hear it either. Heck, the whole neighborhood could probably hear him. It was not yet time for quiet hours, but still. He was disturbing the peace.

Harriet picked up the phone and called Tammy.

"Hello, Harriet. Are you calling with information about the man who doesn't leash his dog?"

"Not yet. That's not why I'm calling. My neighbor's husband is yelling at her, and it's disturbing the neighborhood."

"I'm sorry to hear that, but it isn't yet after hours, so I can't do anything about it. If you believe he's harassing her, you might want to call the police," Tammy said.

"Well, he's using a very derogatory tone. And their daughter's outside, pacing and covering her ears," Harriet said.

"Again, if you feel they might be in danger, you should notify the authorities."

Harriet hung up. She really didn't want to get involved, but he was disturbing the neighborhood. And he did sound quite angry. Harriet would never forgive herself if he were a violent man and she had stood by and done nothing. But shouting was a far cry from violence. Shouting didn't warrant a call to the police, did it?

Harriet heard another shout but couldn't make it out. Audrey paced across the front porch and rubbed her hands over her arms. Maybe she should check in with the girl.

Harriet threw her coat on and made her way across the street. Audrey froze when she caught sight of Harriet. "Everything okay over here?" Harriet asked.

Audrey shrugged. "Yeah. They're arguing, and I didn't want to listen. I'm sure it'll be over soon."

From upstairs, Chris yelled, "Goddamn it, Robyn! I can't believe you're stupid enough to fall for that."

"Does this happen often?" Harriet asked.

"Not more than my friends' parents from what I can tell."

"He sounds pretty worked up, and he shouldn't be calling your mom names," Harriet said. "Besides, he's disturbing the neighborhood."

Audrey shrugged again. "What am I supposed to do about it?"

"You're right. I guess there's nothing to be done."

"I swear, Robyn. I don't know how I could've been stupid enough to marry you," Chris shouted.

Harriet's eyes went to Audrey, who stared at her shoes. "I'm honestly not sure what to do. I feel as though I have a duty to intervene, but I'm not sure what I'd say," Harriet said.

"It'll be over soon, like I said. Don't worry about it," Audrey said.

Harriet didn't think it would be a good idea to interrupt the argument. She really didn't want to meddle in other people's business. But how would she know when she was required to interfere? The girl was probably right. They were arguing. It happened to everyone, even her and Les.

Audrey blew into her cupped hands. Even with her coat on, Harriet was cold. She couldn't imagine how cold Audrey must be in just a T-shirt. She couldn't leave the girl out here, could she?

"Do you want to come over to warm up?" Harriet said.

"Nah. I'm fine. Sounds like they might be done anyway," Audrey said.

"Suit yourself," Harriet said, relieved the girl said no so she could avoid any further involvement. "But come on over if you change your mind."

Audrey nodded. "Thanks."

Harriet was able to watch her shows with no further interruption that evening. Maybe it was only an argument. Les had been one to raise his voice when he was angry too. Harriet shuddered at the thought that maybe the neighbors had heard him. She was grateful no one ever came over or called the police on them. Either they hadn't heard, or they didn't have such a strong sense of civic duty. Harriet chose to believe they hadn't heard.

CHAPTER 9

THE NEXT MORNING, as the Uber app predicted, her driver arrived in a silver Jeep Cherokee. It was a little old, and the paint was chipped in a few places, but not too bad. The interior was clean and smelled faintly of Armor All, which was much more pleasant than stale McDonald's. Placing her crutches in ahead of her, she slid into the seat. She was about to tell the driver where she needed to go, but realized the app had already done that for her. She chuckled under her breath. This was the way to go.

"What was that?" the driver asked, peering at her in the rearview mirror.

"I didn't say anything," Harriet said, securing her seatbelt without looking up.

"Oh no," came his deep voice from the front seat. He had his head in his hands, so she couldn't see who was so dismayed.

"Is that how you greet all your clients? If so, I'm surprised you're still in business." Harriet folded her arms against her chest and sighed loudly.

"Hello, Harriet," he said, turning to look at her.

She jumped, and if the seatbelt hadn't restrained her, she might have hit her head on the ceiling. "Oh, God! What are you doing driving my Uber?" She picked up her phone and squinted at the tiny picture of the driver on the Uber app. How could she possibly have known from that itty-bitty picture?

"My job. Let's agree to table our disagreement for this ride, shall we? This car will be awfully small if we can't get along."

"Of all the people in this town, it had to be off-leash-dog-man who came to take me to my appointment. What have I done to deserve this?" Harriet asked. "If I wasn't going to be late for my appointment, I would get out now, but it seems I have no choice but to sit in this car with you."

"That's what you call me? Off-leash-dog-man?" He laughed, a slight coughing sound at first, but he kept laughing, and it gathered and grew.

"Quit that. Get a hold of yourself and drive already. I assume you can follow the rules of the road, unlike the rules of the neighborhood, which you are so intent on breaking."

He took a few deep breaths and calmed himself. "Fine. I'll drive and we'll keep silent. Deal?"

"I have one question first," Harriet said.

He dropped his hands against his thighs in exasperation. "Fine. What's your question?"

"What's your name and address? Oh, wait." She picked up her phone again and squinted at his name. "Kevin. Got your name, so I just need your address. Hang on. Let me find my notepad and pen before you answer," Harriet said, rummaging through her purse.

He spun around to stare at her. "Are you serious?"

Harriet nodded, pen poised above the paper.

He shook his head and pulled out onto the road. "You are a real piece of work."

"So, you won't answer my question?"

"No, I won't. I know why you want it. I've seen the flyers. Everyone thinks you are being ridiculous. Why can't you drop it?"

"Because rules are rules. Bibbo and I deserve to feel safe in our neighborhood."

He started laughing again. "You really haven't had much hardship in your life, have you?"

"You know nothing of my life. I refuse to be belittled by an Uber driver, of all people."

He pulled the car to the side of the road. "Get out."

Her mouth gaped open.

He got out of the car and leaned on the hood. "Shit," Harriet heard him say, rubbing his hand through his hair.

He climbed back into the car. "Despite how very much I would like you out of my car, I am a gentleman and will not leave you on crutches on the side of the road."

"A gentleman? Did you forget you are the reason I'm on these crutches?"

Shaking his head, he said, "I'm done talking."

"How do you afford to live in our neighborhood as an Uber driver?"

Shaking his head again, he drew in a big breath. "I'm a professor at Montana State. I do this on the side, in my free time, to make a little extra."

"You? A professor?"

"Yes. Imagine that. I'm more than just off-leash-dog-man."

"I really can't imagine it. What do you teach?" Harriet asked.

"Geology. I'm fascinated by rocks. I used to be a rock climber. I figured if I was going to risk my life scaling the things, I ought to know something about them."

Harriet nodded. In a small voice, she said, "I was a librarian, so I know a little about geology. Other things too. I knew teachers and professors. I respect them greatly."

His eyes sought hers in the rearview mirror. "Harriet? Did you pay me a compliment?"

Harriet felt her cheeks warm. "You might be the exception to all the wonderful professors I've known."

He laughed. "That's more like it. I was beginning to think you'd gone soft on me."

The doctor's office came into view, and Harriet breathed a sigh of relief. She couldn't stand another minute in his stuffy car. She was surprised when he opened his door and got out. Opening the door opposite her, he pulled her crutches from the car.

"Hey, what are you doing? I need those!" Harriet said.

He shook his head and came around to her side of the car and opened her door, handing the crutches to her. "Just trying to help you out," he said. "Though I'm not sure why I try."

Harriet blushed, hoping he wouldn't notice. Still holding her notepad and pen in her hand, she scooted out of the car awkwardly and let him help her situate her crutches under her armpits.

"Goodbye now. Thanks for the ride," Harriet said to his back as he walked to the driver's seat. He waved and slowly pulled away. Harriet waited and watched as he left the parking lot, quickly jotting his license plate number onto her notepad. She'd heard you could find addresses that way.

Her phone pinged with an invitation to rate and tip her Uber driver. As a rule, she was a decent tipper. She didn't particularly like how often people asked for tips, however. A tip was supposed to show appreciation for exceptional service, not for simply doing one's job. For example, she didn't understand how the person who merely poured and handed her a black coffee at the local coffee shop needed a tip for that. But if they were nice and offered a smile, she usually gave them a dollar even though she didn't feel she really needed to.

Anyway, the only tip Kevin deserved was how to leash his dog. But he was a professor, doing the Uber job on the side for some extra money. Harriet knew professors didn't make nearly what they should, and he had been prompt, his car was clean, and he got her to her appointment on time. Maybe she could manage a small tip.

Now, for the review. She'd give him four stars. One star would be deducted for the way he greeted her and for asking her to get out of the car. Plus, anyone who caused such a nuisance in his neighborhood was not a very good person, and only very good people deserved five stars. She pressed four stars and typed:

On time. His car was clean. He didn't greet me very kindly, but he did his job. If only he could do the same in his neighborhood. He is someone who refuses to leash his dog. I cannot fully recommend someone who blatantly defies rules in this manner. Otherwise, the ride was good.

CHAPTER 10

The doctor said she was healing nicely, and she'd only need to wear the boot for a couple more weeks. It was disappointing she hadn't gotten to see the handsome nurse, but she figured it was better that way since she didn't need to go complicating her life with a romance. Plus, he was too young to be good company for her. He probably spent his evenings in front of some shoot 'em up video game. Harriet shuddered. She'd rather be alone than listen to that or see a handsome man ruining his life in front of a game console.

In the waiting room, she was wondering how to get a ride home. Uber had seemed so perfect with the app and all, but now she'd always be in fear of who the driver might be. What if it was off-leash-dog-man again? Which was worse, off-leash-dog-man again, or germs from Lucille? Since she remembered Lucille's name so easily this morning, Harriet thought that was probably a sign.

"Bozeman Public Library," a cheery voice said after just one ring.

"Lucille, please."

"This is she."

"Oh, good. That saves a bunch of chatty baloney with someone else."

"Is this Harriet?" Lucille asked.

"Yes. How'd you know?"

"Just a good guess. How's your ankle?"

"It's better, but I still have to wear the boot, so I can't drive, so that's the reason I'm calling you."

"Do you need a ride again?" Lucille asked.

"Yes, but you're not sick or anything, are you? No scratchy throat?"

"No, why?" Lucille asked.

"When I called yesterday, they said you were home with a sick kid," Harriet said.

"I'm fine. So, you need a ride again?" Lucille asked.

"Yes. I also need your help finding someone's address. I have his license plate number."

"Goodness, Harriet. You can't look someone up by their license plate number in Montana without a valid reason."

"What makes you think I don't have a valid reason?"

"Oh, I'm sure you do, but I don't think I'm the one to make that determination," Lucille said.

"It's the guy in my neighborhood whose dog is always off-leash. He's the reason I broke my ankle, remember?"

Lucille hesitated. It sounded like she was doing some deep breathing exercise or something. "Okay. It's probably best if you contact the Motor Vehicle Department for that information. I'm not comfortable snooping like that. Would you like me to get you the number for the Motor Vehicle Department?"

Harriet sighed. "I can look it up. I'll have some time while I wait for you to pick me up, I suppose."

"Where are you and where do you need to go? I'll have to speak to my boss. I'm not allowed to leave whenever I'd like."

"How'd you do it last time?"

"I asked. I thought it was a one-time emergency-type situation. I didn't realize it would be a recurring thing. Don't get me wrong. I'm happy to help. I can't lose my job, is all."

"All right, I'll hold," Harriet said.

The phone clicked and started playing "Opus One." Harriet thought the jaunty tune with its trumpets blaring was better suited to a jazz club than the library. She turned the volume down on her phone when others turned to look at her.

"It's not my fault," she said to the mom waiting with her son, whose arm was in a sling. "It's the library's hold music. Terrible choice, if you ask me. I wish United Airlines hadn't ruined 'Rhapsody in Blue.'" The woman nodded and turned away.

The phone clicked again, and Lucille said, "All right, Harriet. My boss said it's okay, but not to make a habit of it."

"Well, tell your boss the doctor said I've only got two more weeks in this boot. I'll hold again."

Lucille chuckled. "Are you planning on hiring me as your chauffeur for the next two weeks? I'm not sure my boss would agree to my moonlighting."

"Moonlighting? It's not moonlighting if I'm not paying you."

Lucille laughed out loud this time. "Harriet, you really are something, you know that?"

Harriet didn't know what to say. What was "something"? Harriet was practical. "I'm not sure how to respond. I'm not sure what the next two weeks will bring, and I'd like to know that if I'm in a bind, you might help."

Lucille sighed. "It's not that I'm not willing, Harriet. I have to keep my job."

"Well, hopefully I won't need to go anywhere, then. So, when will you be here?"

"That depends on where 'here' is," Lucille said.

"I'm at my doctor's office. In the same building where you picked me up after my surgery."

"I'm on my way."

Harriet pushed the red button to hang up and then pushed the Google button to find the phone number for the Motor Vehicle Department. The woman on the other end of the line sounded both bored and as if she had smoked a pack of cigarettes a day for at least 40 years.

"Goodness. What a voice you have," Harriet said.

"Excuse me?"

"That can't be the first time you've heard that since your job has you answering the phone."

She cleared her throat. Harriet thought she probably needed to do that often. "How can I help you?"

"I need someone's address. I have the license plate number," Harriet said.

"I'm sorry, but driver records are not public in Montana."

"But I really need this guy's address, and I can't drive," Harriet said.

There was a long pause on the receiving end of the line.

"Hello?" Harriet said.

"Like I said, I cannot give you that information since those records are not public in this state. Is there anything else I can help you with?"

"Why would you say 'anything else'?"

"Excuse me?"

"You didn't help me in the first place, so how can you ask if there is 'anything else'?"

"If you have nothing further to discuss, I'm going to end this call."

"Fine. You weren't any help anyway," Harriet said, hanging up.

Turning to the mother next to her, she shook her head and said, "You can't get good, polite help anymore."

The mother stopped reading a book to her son, and they both stared at Harriet, saying nothing.

"Oh, look! There's my ride."

Lucille's car was slightly tidier than it had been that first time. No wrappers on the passenger side floor, at least. "You cleaned up a bit," Harriet said.

"Yeah, I tossed a few wrappers in the trash."

They rode in silence for a few minutes. Harriet took in the new construction as they headed west out of town. Since COVID, everyone wanted to move to Montana to get away from the crowds.

COVID and that show, *Yellowstone.* Harriet loved that show, but that's not how people lived around here. She laughed under her breath at the people who wore big belts, cowboy boots, and hats but lived in town. "All hat and no cattle," Les liked to say.

"So, what have you been up to?" Lucille asked, breaking the silence.

Harriet turned to look at her. "What could I possibly be up to?"

Lucille shook her head. "Oh, I don't know. Do you have any shows you like to watch?"

"I like *The Golden Bachelor.*"

Lucille turned briefly to look at Harriet. "Oh! I love that show! Isn't Garry dreamy? I never thought I'd have a crush on a man old enough to be my father, but I think I do. Who do you think he'll choose?"

"I really don't know. I hope he doesn't end up with the one who told Theresa to 'zip it.' That was rude. Jealousy does strange things to people."

"Why, Harriet. Don't take this the wrong way, but that seems like something you would say, don't you think?"

Harriet blinked and stared ahead. "Well, I'd never be dumb enough to go on a show like that."

"No, I suppose you wouldn't," Lucille said.

"I used to be a librarian, you know."

"Really?"

"Why are you so surprised?" Harriet asked.

"I-I'm not. Where were you a librarian?"

"The high school."

"That's odd. I thought I knew the high school librarians in the area. We work together sometimes," Lucille said.

"I know. I used to do it."

"Must've been a while ago, then. I've been at the library for five years now."

"It's been about ten years since I was the school librarian, so you wouldn't know me. I don't think anyone's still at the library who I used to work with. Maybe your boss. The one who doesn't want to let you help me out," Harriet said. "Is his name Richard?"

"Yes, it is. You knew him?"

"I suppose I still do. He's a good guy," Harriet said, glancing out the window as they came to the sign for The Orchards.

"Why did you leave your job?" Lucille asked.

"Les."

"Less? What does that mean? They paid you less?"

Harriet chuckled. "Les was my husband. Short for Leslie. Really chapped his behind that his parents gave him a girl's name, so no one ever called him by his full name. Not if they wanted to live to see another day."

"Really?" Lucille's eyebrows rose dramatically, and her eyes went wide as she turned to look at Harriet.

"It's a figure of speech. He never killed anyone. Not that I know of anyway." Harriet laughed and used the back of her hand to slap Lucille's shoulder. Lucille jumped.

"So why was Les the reason you left your job?"

"He needed me, even before he got sick. Since I didn't make much money, he said he'd rather have me home, keeping the house clean and having a warm meal ready for when he got home."

"Wow. A bit old-fashioned, don't you think?"

Harriet stared ahead. She hadn't really thought about it. "I don't know. It seemed a logical decision at the time."

"Do you miss it?"

"Cooking and cleaning for Les?"

Lucille laughed. "No. Do you miss your work?"

"Absolutely. I loved being a librarian. Even those obnoxious kids who would rather poke a sharp stick in their eye than crack open a book could surprise you once in a while. I loved opening their eyes to all the information to be found in a library. Of course, Google has interfered with some of its magic, but first-hand sources and the smell and feel of a good book can't ever be replaced."

"I couldn't agree more," Lucille said.

"I would think it would be hard to be a librarian nowadays. Everyone can Google everything and order books on Amazon. Who needs a library? What do you do all day? Sort and shelve books? Soon enough, they'll have robots for that."

"You are preaching to the choir. I help with research projects from time to time, assist people with the computers, help with job applications, put books on hold or take them off, ship materials to other libraries or schools, you know, the usual stuff. Not much has changed. People still need the library."

"Thank goodness for that," Harriet said.

They stopped in front of Harriet's house. "Nice chatting with you, Harriet," Lucille said. "I heard you say Les was your husband, so I assume he's passed?"

"Yes. It was pretty quick. But it's never quick enough with ALS."

Lucille put her hand on Harriet's shoulder. Her hand was warm and surprisingly pleasant. "I'm so sorry. That must've been terrible."

"It was," Harriet said, exiting the car and gathering her crutches from the back seat. "Thanks again for the ride. I'll let you know if I need another."

CHAPTER 11

LUCILLE HAD GOTTEN Harriet's mind turning about her time as a librarian. She really had loved her job. People needed her. Kids learned from her. She'd felt important. When she stayed home, she was only important to Les. Now, she was important to no one.

Harriet thought back to the early days when she fell in love with Les. He'd been so enthusiastic about starting a family. It was one of his most endearing qualities. She'd seen the way he interacted with his older sister's son, patiently playing peekaboo long after he'd grown bored with it. Airplane noises to get him to eat his mushy peas. He'd even changed his diapers. Harriet hadn't known other single men in their twenties who would do such a thing. Certainly, her father didn't. Her mother had trouble getting him to change his own children's diapers. Not that he was a bad father. He was devoted in many other ways, just not diapers.

Les splurged for their honeymoon. He surprised her with a trip to Hawaii. He'd been secretly saving for over a year, ever since they'd set the date for their wedding.

"Pack your bags, Harriet," he'd said. "Pack all your bathing suits and plenty of sunblock."

"Les! Where are we going?"

"It's a surprise, although I assume you'll find out at the airport, won't you?" he said, eyes shining, his mouth stretched into the widest smile she'd ever seen.

Harriet picked up the picture from the sunset whale-watching cruise they'd taken. She recalled how he'd come up behind her as she leaned against the railing, scanning the vast ocean for the telltale spray of a whale spouting. Wrapping his arms around her waist, he'd whispered into her ear, "I love you, Harriet. I'm so excited about starting our life together."

She'd turned and embraced him, not caring about the whales or what any of the other passengers might think. She was loved, protected, and safe with this man. She felt at home in his arms. Whatever life threw at them, they'd tackle it together.

That night, in the room he'd paid extra for to have a small sliver of a view of the ocean, they'd popped a bottle of champagne, and he'd kissed her with more tenderness than ever before. She was his. She felt it in his kiss.

"Let's not use any protection," Les said.

She pulled back from him, surprise lifting her eyebrows. "Really? So soon? Don't you want to get settled, find a house, get used to living together?" He'd always been so practical, so rational. Harriet was surprised he wouldn't make this choice in his usual pragmatic manner.

"We love each other. We know we want a family. Everything else will work out."

If only life were that simple. Harriet set the picture back on the side table and sighed.

Snapping herself back to the present, she focused on today's primary task. She needed groceries. Should she Uber to the grocery store? Did she dare take that risk? Wait. Off-leash-dog-man said he was a professor. Surely he'd be working in the middle of the day on a Tuesday.

Sure enough, the blue Subaru that pulled up in front of her house was driven by a man she'd never seen before. This was how the whole Uber situation was supposed to work. They said absolutely nothing on the drive. Perfect. Now, the only dauntingly embarrassing prospect was riding in that cart through the aisles of the store. Harriet prayed she wouldn't have to back up. That beeping was sure to draw the attention of every customer in the store.

Harriet hadn't imagined an even more mortifying situation, however. She'd barely rolled into the store when she heard a loud, "Hey, Harriet," coming from her left.

A tall, handsome man who looked vaguely familiar was headed toward her. As he came closer, she realized it was none other than the head of the library, Richard.

"Oh, h-hello, Richard," Harriet stammered, heat rising to her cheeks.

Richard's lips curled into a warm smile, his eyes crinkling at the corners in a way that Harriet had forgotten made her heart flutter. "Well, Harriet, fancy meeting you here," he chuckled, his gaze settling on her ankle boot. "Looks like you've had a bit of a mishap."

"Oh, it's nothing serious," she said. "Just a broken ankle."

"Well, I hope you have a speedy recovery. Lucille mentioned you'd been in an accident. Something about a rogue dog and a daring rescue?"

"That's right," Harriet said. "Some neighbors are terrible at following rules."

Richard nodded. "Well, it's nice bumping into you. I always enjoyed our collaborations back when you worked at the high school. You had such a passion for connecting students with the right books."

Harriet felt warmth spread through her chest. It was gratifying to know that he remembered her, that he valued her work. "Those were good days," she said.

"Well, I hope you'll be back in the stacks soon," Richard said. "In the meantime, if you need anything at all, don't hesitate to reach out. Lucille's been giving you rides, I hear? I'm happy to help out as well, if you need it."

Harriet's heart skipped a beat. Richard, offering to give her a ride? "That's very kind of you, Richard," she said, trying to maintain her composure.

"No problem at all," he replied.

"Any chance you could give me a ride when we're done here?" Harriet asked, her heart threatening to jump from her chest. She couldn't believe she was being this bold. "I took an Uber to get here, so it'd be great not to have to wait for another one to get home."

He pulled his phone from his pocket and glanced at the time. "I suppose I have time. I ran out to grab some cookies for our monthly meeting, so I need to get back, but they'll understand if I tell them I needed to help an old friend."

Harriet's heart did a little flutter-kick at his words. "An old friend? I like the sound of that."

"Well, it's true, isn't it? So, how about I help you with your shopping list? It can't be easy navigating in that thing."

Harriet started to decline, as she was accustomed to doing, but there was something about Richard. "That would be wonderful, thank you."

She pointed at what she needed, and he put the items in her basket. Harriet wasn't sure how she would have managed without him. And he wasn't only a great help with her grocery list. He was a great conversationalist. They chatted about their favorite authors, the challenges of keeping up with new releases, and the comforting familiarity of well-loved classics.

"Have you read anything by Katherine Reay?" Richard asked. "She's a local author, you know. Writes these wonderful contemporary stories with a touch of Austenian charm. More recently, she's been delving into historical fiction."

"I haven't," Harriet said. "But I'm always open to new recommendations. Especially from a fellow bibliophile."

On the drive back to Harriet's house, the conversation flowed effortlessly. They reminisced about their shared experiences at the library, the quirky patrons, and the challenges of keeping the Dewey decimal system in order.

As they pulled up to Harriet's house, she felt a deep sadness that her time with Richard was coming to an end. She couldn't believe how comfortable she felt with him. "So, are you still married?" Harriet asked.

Richard coughed. Well, it was sort of a cough and sort of a laugh. "As a matter of fact, I got divorced a couple of years ago. Did you know my wife?"

Harriet shook her head.

"How about you. Are you married?" Richard asked.

"Widowed."

"Oh, I'm so sorry," Richard said.

"Don't be. It wasn't your fault. Well, anyway, thank you for the ride, Richard," Harriet said. "And for the company. It's been nice catching up."

"The pleasure was all mine, Harriet," Richard replied. "Let's not let another decade pass before we do this again."

"Let's not," Harriet said, feeling her cheeks warm again.

As she watched Richard drive away, she felt a lightness in her chest. It was quite a foreign feeling. Perhaps this chance encounter was more than just a reunion with an old friend. She shook herself. What was going on? Why were these thoughts taking off like a runaway train? This wasn't like her. She needed to get a grip.

Groceries were put away, and meals were planned for the week. She looked around the house and saw a vast expanse of time unfold before her. There was so much less to do when she had only herself to look after. She hadn't realized quite how messy Les was. Well, he couldn't help it as his disease progressed. But that was different. Even in health, he'd needed a lot from her. He had high expectations, he'd said, and Harriet was the only one who could keep up with his standards.

Harriet's brother certainly did not live up to Les's standards. They'd been close growing up, but grew further apart as their distinct personalities took root in adulthood. Harriet was practical. Hank was a dreamer. They'd complemented each other as siblings only fifteen months apart. Hank started projects, and Harriet finished them. Harriet wanted to stay at home, and Hank dragged her out of the house. She was a ski racer, enjoying the precision and control required to shave off time, and Hank was a freestyle skier, soaring high in the air, twisting and turning in death-defying feats. Harriet couldn't watch Hank for fear he would end up paralyzed or dead, and Hank couldn't watch Harriet because he got bored and cold, waiting hours for his sister to fly by in seconds.

Skiing aside, they understood each other, balanced each other. When they'd gone off to college on nearly opposite sides of the country, Harriet at Montana State and Hank at NYU, not a week went by that they didn't check in with each other, fascinated by their different lives. They respected their contrasts and enjoyed seeing life lived differently through each other's eyes. They visited each other's campuses and shook their heads, knowing each could never live the other's life, but their respect was mutual.

Harriet missed her brother. She could admit it now. What had it been? Twenty years? Maybe more. With Les no longer here, maybe it was time to reconnect. She wasn't ready yet. But she was thinking about it.

CHAPTER 12

THE REST OF THE DAY passed languidly as Harriet reread *Mansfield Park* and sipped wine. As the sun began to dip in the sky, she went to bed early once again in an attempt to pass the hours.

She woke to a loud pounding at the door. Throwing on a robe, Harriet went to the door. "Who's there?" Harriet called.

No answer. Just more pounding. "Harriet?" A young girl's voice. Harriet peered through the peephole. It was Audrey. She was alone but kept turning to look behind her every few seconds. She hugged her arms around her as though trying to protect herself.

Slowly, Harriet eased the door open a couple of inches.

"I'm really sorry to bother you," Audrey said, wiping a tear from her cheek with the back of her hand. "My parents are arguing again."

"Okay," Harriet said, opening the door wider. "Come on in. Make yourself comfortable."

"I-I was hoping you would come over with me to try to get my phone back."

Harriet's eyes went wide. "You're kidding, right? You want me to go with you and interrupt your parents' argument to get your phone? What's wrong with teenagers today?"

"Please. My dad took my phone. And my mom's. He's really mad."

"Like last time, it will probably be over soon. If you don't want to be there, you can wait here, but I'm not getting involved," Harriet said.

Audrey's shoulders shook. She buried her face in her hands. "It's one of the bad fights," she muttered. "My dad's been drinking."

"It can't be that bad."

Audrey looked up at Harriet, tears trailing down her cheeks. "It is that bad." Her voice was nearly a whisper. "It doesn't happen like this very often, and she always makes excuses." She shook her head. "I don't think he means it, but sometimes when he drinks...he just, I don't know...goes crazy."

Harriet swallowed. "What do you think I can do?"

"I-I don't know. But I need my phone." Audrey started pacing. "And maybe if you interrupted him. Maybe if you knocked on the door or something, it would be enough for him to stop if he knew someone saw what he was doing."

Harriet thought this girl was probably being overly dramatic. Weren't all teenagers that way? She probably had her phone taken away for talking back. Harriet really didn't think she should be involved. Robyn would most likely be mortified that her daughter told Harriet about their business. But could she ignore this girl? What if it had been one of her students?

Harriet retrieved her phone from the coffee table and handed it to Audrey. "Here. Use my phone. Call 911 if it's that bad."

Audrey's mouth fell open. "You seriously want me to call the cops on my own dad?"

Harriet shook her head. She had no idea what to do. What if Chris was being violent toward Robyn? Shouldn't she call the police? It was her duty, after all. But this girl was an overly dramatic teenager who probably just wanted a ploy to get her phone. But Harriet had heard Chris shouting at Robyn. And it wasn't normal yelling. It was nasty. Derogatory, demeaning, and cruel. Recalling the tone of Chris's voice the other day made Harriet shudder. Damn it. She probably needed to do something.

"Well, if you won't call, I will," Harriet said, reaching for her phone.

"No!" Audrey said, pulling the phone against her chest. "You can't do that. My dad could go to jail!"

"Look, young lady. I'm not sure exactly what's going on here, but I know I'm not going to your house in the middle of your parents' argument. Not unless I know the police are on their way, at least. I don't get involved in other people's business unless it is absolutely necessary. And I am not in a position to determine if it is absolutely necessary based solely on a young girl's say-so."

"There isn't time to tell you everything. You have to trust me."

"If it's bad enough that you want me to go over there to interrupt whatever you think is happening, then it is bad enough to call the police. That is the only condition under which I will get involved."

"Fine," Audrey said, handing her the phone. "Call. But then we need to go right over there."

Harriet's heart sped up as they made their way across the street. Only one light was on in the kitchen. She heard more shouting. Honestly, Harriet couldn't believe the entire neighborhood wasn't out wondering about all the commotion. Maybe they had heard it. Maybe they were hoping to stay uninvolved, too.

"I hate that you're making me do this," Chris shouted.

"Stop, Chris. Please," Robyn said.

Audrey sniffed. "At least she's still yelling."

Harriet looked at the girl. What had she witnessed?

"So, we're going to barge in there? Don't we need a plan?" Harriet asked.

Audrey blinked and swiped at a tear. "I...I don't know. I just know my mom needs help."

"Maybe we should get Bonnie or some of the other neighbors to help," Harriet said.

"No!" Audrey grabbed Harriet's arm. "Please. You have no idea how hard it was for me to come to you. We don't need everyone in this neighborhood knowing all our problems."

"Do you think I should knock? Try to interrupt them?" Harriet asked.

Audrey nodded.

Harriet raised her fist and stopped. "Does your dad have a gun?"

Audrey shook her head. "Not that I know of."

"Not that you know of? We can't just knock on this door. He could shoot us both."

Audrey's shoulders shook. "Th-that's my d-dad. And this is my house."

"Goddammit, Robyn. Who do you think you are?" a male voice boomed from above. Harriet heard a loud thud, followed by a sharp squeal.

"They're upstairs," Audrey said. "They won't hear us if we knock. We should just go in."

"I-I," Harriet started. "This is a terrible idea. Let's wait for the police."

"Really? If that was your mom in there, would you wait?"

Harriet's shoulders slumped. She would've done anything to protect her mother. How many times had she rewritten the day of the car accident, shifting events forward and backward to find a way for her mother and father to escape their fate?

Audrey slowly turned the doorknob on the front door. She seemed like she had done a lot of sneaking around in her short twelve years of life. She pushed the door inward. Harriet winced when it creaked. They stood still, holding their breath.

It was silent. They exhaled, waiting.

"Mom?" Audrey said.

Harriet whipped her head around to stare at Audrey.

"Y-yes, dear?" Robyn's voice was strained.

"Everything okay?" Audrey asked.

Harriet heard the loud whisper of an angry man but couldn't make out what he said. Footsteps sounded on the stairs. Audrey grabbed Harriet's arms and crouched behind her.

Robyn's husband came barreling around the corner, eyes wild. He spotted Harriet and froze. Adjusting his shoulders from their aggressive, ape-like hunch, he leaned against the banister and smiled. "Hey, neighbor. What brings you to our house at this hour?"

Harriet's mouth fell open. How had he shifted so quickly? "I heard yelling," Harriet said.

"Yelling?" he asked, eyebrows lifting. "Maybe it was one of the neighbors."

"No, it was coming from this house. And it's not the first time I've heard it," Harriet said.

"Robyn," he called, not taking his eyes from Harriet. "Come down here. It seems Harriet has already made some assumptions about us. And she's gotten our daughter involved."

Robyn rounded the corner of the stairway and pulled her lips into a smile. It took some effort. A red mark stained her left cheek.

"Harriet," Robyn said, her voice trembling. "What a surprise." She stopped a little way behind her husband on the landing of the stairs and crossed and uncrossed her arms.

"Believe me. This is all a surprise," Harriet said. "Audrey was so concerned that she came to me and asked for help."

"Audrey," Chris said. "We've taught you better than that. What were you thinking?"

"That you might hurt Mom."

He laughed—a terrible cackle, like a cartoon villain. Harriet wondered if it was truly the sound of the laugh that seemed evil, or that it was so out of place in this situation.

"I'd never hurt your mother. You know that. Now, go on up to your room and let Harriet get back to whatever she was doing, and everything will be fine. Teenagers," he said, looking at Harriet and shaking his head.

Harriet started when a firm knock sounded from the front door.

In a few quick steps, Chris was at the door. "Evening, Officers," Chris said, his voice calm and confident.

"Evening, sir," the taller officer said. "I'm Officer Weise, and this is Officer Doyle. We're responding to a call from a neighbor about a domestic disturbance. Mind if we come in?"

Harriet peered at the officers from behind Chris and said, "That was me. I made the call."

Chris turned away from the officers and glared at Harriet. Turning back, he said, "It was all just a misunderstanding. Our neighbor is overly concerned."

"I beg to differ. The last thing I wanted to do was get involved. But here I am," Harriet said.

"Mind if we come in?" Officer Weise said again.

"It really isn't necessary," Chris said.

"It's just a formality, sir," Officer Doyle said. "If you'll let us in, we'll ask a few questions and then be on our way."

Chris pulled the door open and stepped back, allowing the officers to enter. Should one offer refreshments to officers who came on domestic disturbance calls? But it wasn't her house, so she supposed she wouldn't be the one to look rude.

To Harriet's surprise, the taller officer turned to her first. "Ma'am. You said you were the one who placed the call, correct?"

"Yes, but I didn't want to."

The officer smiled. "Well, no one wants to place a call to 911."

Harriet hadn't thought of that. She blushed.

"Not to worry. What prompted the call?"

"Audrey came to my house because she wanted her phone," Harriet said.

"Why would you call the police about that?" the officer asked.

"She said her dad took both her and her mother's phones, and Audrey wanted me to come with her to her house to get hers. I said absolutely not, so she admitted that she was worried about her mother," Harriet said.

The officer turned to look at Audrey. "I assume you're Audrey?" Audrey nodded and looked down at her folded hands. "What made you feel worried about your mother?"

Audrey's wide eyes went first to her mother and then to her father. Tears filled her eyes, and she swallowed hard. "My dad was yelling at my mom."

"Yelling doesn't mean you go to the neighbors, sweetie," Chris said, his voice sickly sweet.

"Please. Allow us to ask the questions," Officer Doyle said.

"I apologize, but that wasn't a question. I wanted my daughter to understand," Chris said.

Officer Doyle glared at Chris, pursed his lips, and looked back at his notepad. "Your dad was yelling at your mom, and you felt frightened?"

Audrey nodded, and a tear trickled down her cheek.

"Did anything else happen?" Officer Weise asked.

Harriet thought he was deliberately vague so he wouldn't lead the witness. She liked detective shows.

"Not yet," Audrey said, her voice barely above a whisper.

"What did you say, young lady?" Officer Weise asked.

Audrey looked at the floor.

Harriet asked, "Wouldn't it be better to ask these questions without her father's presence?"

"Ma'am, if you'll allow us to do our job, please."

"Well, I know little about abuse, but it's obvious her father's presence is making her uneasy. You'd probably get better information if he wasn't here."

All eyes turned to stare at her. Why did it bother people so much when Harriet stated what was patently obvious? "All right, I'll leave you to it, then. Obviously, my opinion isn't wanted." Harriet turned toward the door.

"Not yet. We have a few questions for you as well," Officer Doyle said.

"Okay, shoot. Well, not really. You know I don't really want you to shoot, right?" Harriet coughed a nervous laugh.

"Right." Officer Doyle looked at Officer Weise, then turned back to Harriet. "So, this young lady came to your house and said she needed help. Is that correct?"

Harriet nodded. "I told her I wasn't going to her house without calling the police first. Then we came over here, and I heard shouting. I heard it from outside, across the street, actually. It was that loud. This neighborhood is quiet, well-maintained, you see. I make sure of it. So, we don't get this kind around here." Harriet jerked her chin toward Chris.

"Now, hold on a minute. I don't like the implications you're making. You don't know me from Adam," Chris said.

Officer Weise stepped between them. "Let's not get off topic here. So, you came over to this house from... Where did you say you lived, Harriet? It's Harriet, right?"

"Yes, and I didn't."

"Didn't what?"

"I didn't say where I lived."

Officer Weise sighed. "Where do you live?"

"Across the street, which is why I said we could hear shouting from across the street." Harriet doubted this guy's competence. Hopefully, the other one was more astute.

"Anyway, as I was saying, I heard this jerk over here..."

Chris interrupted, but Officer Weise silenced him by thrusting a hand toward him.

Harriet continued. "This jerk was yelling something at Robyn about how he hated that she made him do this, and then I heard a loud thud and a shriek."

"You're sure that's what you heard?" Officer Weise asked.

"Of course I'm sure," Harriet said.

"Ma'am." Officer Weise looked at Robyn. "Is what she's telling us true?"

Robyn looked down at her hands and rubbed them together. Chris glared at her. Audrey looked from one to the other.

"Ma'am," Officer Doyle said, pointing at Robyn. "Could we have a word with you outside?"

As Robyn started toward the door, Chris reached out and touched her shoulder. Harriet wished the officers had seen the gesture, seen the warning in it.

Moments later, they reentered the house. With her arms folded across her chest, Robyn refused to make eye contact with anyone.

"Well, sir. Your wife says it was all a misunderstanding," Officer Weise said.

"But..." Audrey started.

"See? I told you," Chris interrupted. He turned toward Harriet. "Nothing to see here. Best if you head on back to your house and mind your own business." He moved toward the door but then stopped and turned back to Harriet. "Or maybe I should inform the officers of your little mishap with the car?"

The officers looked from Chris to Harriet.

Harriet's cheeks flushed. "That won't be necessary. I'll be on my way."

"No good deed goes unpunished," Chris said as Harriet made her way to the door.

"My thoughts exactly," Harriet said, turning to glare at Chris.

Robyn stared ahead as though she was a statue.

"Mom?" Audrey shook her mother's hand.

Finally, Robyn looked at her daughter. "We'll sort this out. We always do." Turning to Harriet, she said, "I'm sorry Audrey got you involved. All families have their struggles, as I'm sure you know." Robyn placed her hand on Harriet's shoulder and nudged her toward the front door. She thanked the officers and assured them everything was fine.

Harriet followed the officers outside. She turned back to look at the family, wondering if she was doing the right thing by leaving.

CHAPTER 13

From the street, ten sets of eyes stared at her. As if it couldn't get any worse. Of course all the nosy neighbors would come over to see what the police officers were doing in their quiet neighborhood.

"Nothing to see here, folks," Harriet said to the crowd. "Just head on back home. Mind your own business."

"What happened?" Bonnie called.

"Just a little misunderstanding." Harriet hated using that lie, but they didn't need the neighbors knowing their business. "Like I said. Just head home. Give the poor folks some privacy. Have you no manners?"

Whispering neighbors parted to allow her to pass, but Harriet didn't interpret their words. Who cared what they thought, anyway?

Once again, Harriet was glad Les wasn't around to see that. He would have told her to mind her own business, let that family deal with their own problems. But Audrey had come to her. Could she really turn a blind eye to what she'd seen and heard? It was her duty to help. That Chris was bad news.

· · · · ·

The next day dawned bright and sunny, and it was nearly possible for Harriet to believe last night had been a bad dream. Peering out her bedroom window, the patches of grass between the snow had grown considerably in the last few days.

"Well, Bibbo, it might be time to start the garden."

Harriet loved gardening, despite the challenges posed by Montana's climate. There were only 95 days between the last and first frost, which meant time was of the essence. She'd given up growing broccoli and beets since they needed to be planted in early April, and the snow was usually still deep then. She knew people who shoveled areas of their garden to plant broccoli and beets or started them indoors, but not Harriet. Those two vegetables weren't her favorite anyway, so why go to all the fuss? Of course, carrots and kale needed to be planted early as well, but they were worth a little extra effort.

Tomatoes were her most precious and most needy vegetables. The year before last, when Les required so much of her time, she'd taken to buying seedlings at Cashman's nursery. Both she and Les thought it was cheating, but that spring, when Les needed more and more from her, she'd forgotten to bring the poor baby plants in at night, and they froze, stiff and solid.

She'd cried at the sight of them the next morning. Even though Les said he could taste her nurturing in her homegrown tomatoes, he'd seen her despair and said it wasn't worth the effort anymore. Harriet knew then that he was truly sick. Effort was his most prized attribute in both himself and others. Harriet knew he'd never have let those words cross his lips if he wasn't dying.

"Come on, Bibbo. Time for your walk. It's a beautiful day. Don't you love it when spring arrives in Montana?" Bibbo whined. "I know. Spring hasn't really arrived. There will still be snow until June, but days like this need to be savored."

Through the living room window, Harriet peered out at Robyn's house. Nothing seemed amiss. It was as though nothing had happened. Harriet was certain that was how Chris wanted it. Harriet would have preferred not to know about what happened inside the light blue Victorian, but she supposed it was too late for that. As much as she didn't want to be involved, Audrey needed her help. And so did Robyn, even if she didn't want to admit it. She'd have to figure something out.

Returning from their walk, Harriet spied Robyn standing in the street between their houses, talking to someone. She was gesticulating and smiling as though all was right in the world. Compartmentalizing wasn't one of Harriet's strengths, but it was obviously one of Robyn's.

"Hi, Harriet," Robyn called as Harriet approached. "I'm sure you know Brittney, right?"

Brittney's long brown hair swung around as she turned to look at Harriet. Her exaggerated smile caused her eyes to squint and her teeth to protrude in a way that made Harriet's stomach turn. "Yes. I know Harriet. We moved in not too long after she did. We're some of the OG neighbors in The Orchards."

Harriet's blood boiled. It had been years, nearly decades, but she'd never forget what Brittney had done to her, how she'd dashed her hopes and stomped all over them.

"Unfortunately," Harriet said, sticking close to her side of the street, hoping to slide into her house without further interaction.

"What do you mean by that, Harriet?" Robyn asked.

"Brittney is the reason I stopped trying to make friends in this neighborhood. Now, if you'll excuse me. I have a busy day planned."

"Me?" Brittney said, putting her hand over her heart.

Harriet spun to glare at Brittney. "Yes, you. How dare you act like you don't know what you did? You were the only one to invite me in when I brought a pie. I'd nearly given up, but Les encouraged me to try one more time with you when you moved in, so I did. You invited me in. We talked for hours, and then you invited Les and me to dinner later that week. It was all I'd ever hoped for."

"I know. It was lovely. I never understood why you declined all my other invitations."

Harriet scoffed. "Please. You had the gall to have a party only a week or so after our dinner and didn't invite me. Les told me all about it. He saw all the cars parked outside, heard the laughing, and saw other neighbors walking into your house. Oh, and let's not forget your insults while I was in the bathroom."

"Honestly, Harriet. I have no idea what you are talking about. What party? I had barely moved in. I didn't know anyone other than you. And I have no idea what comments I could have made. I truly enjoyed your company," Brittney said, shaking her head.

Harriet waved her hand dismissively. "Whatever. I don't have the time or the energy to dig all that back up again. In fact, I should probably thank you. Because of you, I learned that Les and I were better off on our own." Harriet turned and went up the steps to her house.

"Well, it's never too late to try again," Robyn called to Harriet's back, her voice artificially bright.

Inside, Harriet leaned against the front door and tried to calm her hammering heart. All the years she'd imagined what she'd say to Brittney came gushing out. And Brittney had the audacity to look genuinely surprised. As if she didn't realize how she'd crushed Harriet.

Taking a few deep breaths, Harriet told herself to let bygones be bygones. She was better off not relying on anyone. What would Les have said? He'd tell her to mind her own business and keep busy, so that's what she would do.

Pulling her phone from her purse, Harriet phoned Lucille to ask for a ride to Cashman's nursery to buy her tomato sprouts.

"Harriet, I can't leave my job to take you wherever you want to go."

"Ask Richard. He'll understand. Remind him it's only for a couple of weeks."

Lucille sighed. "Harriet, it's a busy day here. Susan is on vacation, so I'm covering for her. I really can't leave."

"Lucille, please. I've got big plans for this beautiful day. It won't take long. Cashman's is only fifteen or so minutes down the road. The books can wait. They aren't going anywhere."

"Fine. I'll check with Richard."

The jaunty hold music didn't accost Harriet's ears as much as it had at the doctor's office. Was it because she was ready for it this time, or that the bright, beautiful day was more suited to the tune?

"You get your wish, Harriet. Richard says he'll help with some holds. He must really like you."

"Why do you sound so surprised?" Silence met Harriet's ears. "Hello?"

Lucille sighed. "I'm here. I'll leave now. See you in a few."

Harriet peered out her window, saw Brittney and Robyn were gone, and headed out front to wait. She wanted to savor every bit of sunshine on this glorious day. It was such a joy to feel the sun on her skin. Eyes closed, face tilted upward, a smile crept onto her face.

"Beautiful day, isn't it?" Lucille called from her car as she pulled up in front of Harriet's house.

"Sure is," Harriet said. "Say, before we head to Cashman's, would you mind circling around Peach Street? I haven't been able to do my usual tour of the neighborhood, you know. So, I'd like to have a quick look around."

Pulling onto Peach Street, Harriet surveyed the houses. Everything seemed in order. No dogs running rampant, she couldn't discern any brown mounds sitting atop the remaining snow, and no trash littered the trail. All was good. She sighed and sat back in her seat.

As they turned right onto Apricot Lane, however, Harriet sat bolt upright. "Lucille, stop the car."

Harriet fumbled in her purse for her phone. "Can you believe this? Are those plastic, light-up Easter egg decorations?" She snapped a few pictures.

Lucille craned her neck to peer out Harriet's window. "It appears so. Aren't they cheerful?"

"Cheerful? Are you serious, Lucille? This is an abomination! It is nearly May, for goodness' sake. This cannot be allowed." Harriet scribbled the address onto her notepad.

"At the risk of drawing your ire, Harriet, I don't think it's worth getting so riled up about. They probably have children who love those decorations. And they're probably busy and haven't found the time to take them down. Give them a break, please."

Harriet shook her head. "I won't allow it, Lucille. If they can't be bothered to take down their decorations in a timely manner, then they shouldn't put them up in the first place."

"I don't think you need to bother yourself with keeping everyone in line. Don't you get tired of it?"

"It's my job," Harriet said.

"Who says?"

"Les."

"But..." Lucille paused. "I don't mean to sound insensitive, but I thought you said Les had passed?"

Harriet nodded.

"So, you still need to do what he asked of you?" Lucille asked.

"Just because he's dead doesn't mean he wasn't right."

They drove on in silence for a few minutes.

"There is one neighborhood problem I'd rather not be involved with, but I don't think I have a choice," Harriet said.

"What's that?"

"My neighbor's husband is abusing her."

"That's terrible. How do you know?" Lucille asked.

"The daughter came to me for help." Lucille raised her eyebrows. "I know. I tried not to get involved, but how could I ignore the poor girl? She was so upset. Anyway, I thought maybe she was exaggerating, but I heard him screaming at the girl's mom. And I heard a thud, and a shriek."

Lucille's eyes went wide. "You're sure that's what you heard?"

Harriet nodded. "Positive. The police came, but my neighbor denied it. Now I don't know what to do. I keep telling myself to stay out of it, and I would if it weren't for the girl. The neighbor is old enough to choose to stay with that jerk, but the daughter has no choice."

"I agree with you about the girl, but I'm not so sure about the mother. It's never that simple. I volunteer at Harmony House, so I know quite a bit about it."

"Harmony House?"

"Our local domestic abuse center. We do talks and events for women at the library. Maybe you could convince your neighbor to come to one? And they have support group meetings every week."

"I suppose I'll have to give it a try," Harriet said, staring out the window.

Lucille reached over and turned on the radio. Harriet recognized the familiar sound of Taylor Swift's voice, but couldn't recognize the song.

"Can you believe how many songs this young lady has put out?" Lucille asked.

"She's quite prolific. I'll give her that."

"My daughter adores her. She'd love to go to a concert, but can you believe the price? I'd have to sell my car and refinance my house to go."

"Pretty sure a concert isn't worth all that," Harriet said.

"Have you been to many?"

"No, the only concert I attended was with my brother back in high school. I still can't believe our parents let us go. I was a senior, and he was a junior. The two of us went all the way to Red Rocks Amphitheater in Colorado to see U2."

"How fun. So, you grew up here in Bozeman, then?"

"Yep. I'm one of those rare people born and bred in Montana," Harriet said.

"Did you leave for college?"

"No, I went to Montana State. It was much different back then. So small and quaint."

"I can only imagine. I've only been in Bozeman for eight years now, and I can't believe all the changes I've seen," Lucille said.

"It's all those darned Californians."

Lucille smiled. "I'm afraid I'm one of them."

"You? But you don't have all that plastic surgery, and you aren't skinny. And you drive a crappy car."

"Thanks so much, Harriet."

"Well, let's say you don't fit the stereotype."

"Not all stereotypes are true," Lucille said.

They drove in silence for a few more minutes until the old wooden sign with yellow lettering announced Cashman's was right around the corner. Harriet opened her door. "I'll be as quick as I can."

"I'm not going to sit in the car and wait. I'm coming in."

"Suit yourself, but please don't distract me. I'm not one of those people who likes to shop with friends and get their opinions and all that. I don't dillydally. I get in and get out and get on with my day, as Les always said."

Half an hour later, Harriet spotted Lucille at the checkout area. Good. That would save her the trouble of looking for her. Harriet's wagon was full, and a salesperson seemed offended that she had asked him to pull it behind her as she shopped. She doubted he'd be happy following her around to find Lucille.

Lucille walked over to her. "Where will you put all of those?"

Harriet stared at her. "In my garden, of course."

"I meant, where in my car?"

Harriet blinked. "In the back seat, I suppose."

"Won't they topple over and spill?"

"I wouldn't think it would matter if they did. You'd hardly notice the dirt with all the other junk you've got in there."

"Seriously, Harriet. I've had about enough of you. Here I am doing you a favor, and you continue to insult me."

Harriet stared at Lucille, whose usually cheerful face was sullen. Lucille shook her head repeatedly as she stared at the ground.

"No need to get upset. I was only stating facts. I apologize if you took offense."

Lucille waved her hand in front of her face and started walking toward the car. "Never mind. We can put them in the trunk."

Harriet stopped. "We will do no such thing. These delicate sprouts will droop in the heat of the trunk. I will hold them on my lap if I must."

"Fine," Lucille said.

Harriet hummed along to a tune on the radio. Lucille turned up the volume. Arriving in front of Harriet's house, Lucille jumped out and ran around to open Harriet's door. She took the tray of plants from Harriet's lap and handed her the crutches. She seemed to be in quite a hurry.

"Where would you like these?" Lucille asked.

"Out back by my raised beds. I won't be able to carry them with these things," Harriet said, lifting her crutches. "Not even with my backpack."

Plants dropped off, Lucille waved and headed to her car.

"Thank you for the ride," Harriet called to Lucille's back.

CHAPTER 14

"LET'S GET TO WORK, BIBBO," Harriet said. Opening the sliding glass door to her back porch, she squinted against the bright sun and surveyed her yard. Just a few patches of snow and a few of Bibbo's poops remained, the ones that she hadn't picked up over the past few weeks since she'd broken her ankle. The snow on her garden boxes had melted, which would make planting much easier.

"Oh, goodness. I nearly forgot to call Tammy." Harriet pulled her phone from her pocket and dialed.

"Hi, Harriet. Let me guess. You got the address of the guy who walks his dog without a leash?"

"Unfortunately not. I've got another issue. I'm calling to report a neighbor who still has Easter decorations up."

Tammy exhaled in a long whoosh. Harriet moved the phone further from her ear.

"Could you move your mouth away from your receiver when you do that? It hurts my ears."

"Harriet, it's not even May. It's no big deal that someone has Easter decorations out."

"Isn't there a two-week policy on decorations? I know Christmas decorations are supposed to be taken down by January fifth, the Eve of the Epiphany. So there must be some sort of rule about Easter too."

"Those are guidelines, not rules. And I don't believe there are any guidelines about Easter decorations. I know there aren't any specifications in the HOA covenants. Can't you let this slide, Harriet? Is it really bothering you?"

"Those bright, unnatural colors are an assault on my eyes. And, as my husband always said, 'You can't go soft on any of the rules or it's a quick descent into anarchy.'"

"All right. Give me the name and address of the offending neighbor."

"I don't have a name, but I do have an address and pictures this time. It's 623 Apricot Lane. Right on the corner for all to see. She has a bunch of huge light-up Easter eggs. It's ridiculous."

"I'll send an email. Anything else I can help you with?"

"Have you done anything about off-leash-dog-man yet?"

Another sigh. At least it wasn't quite as loud.

"Harriet, you are the only neighbor who has complained. I'm sure it's not that bad."

"Not that bad! You're kidding, right? I broke my ankle, remember? I'm working on getting his address, but it's difficult with this boot on my foot. A boot he caused me to have to wear, mind you."

"Like I said last time, get me his name or address and I'll see what I can do."

"His name is Kevin. I found that out. Will that work?"

"Unfortunately, I'll need more than that. I know at least two Kevins in the neighborhood."

"This one's on Tangerine."

"I should be able to figure it out from that. I'll send him an email. Is that all, Harriet?"

"That's wonderful news, Tammy. If they haven't complied in a week, you'll send a formal letter, and then the fines begin, right?"

"Yes. You know the process well."

"All right, then. Thank you."

Harriet breathed a sigh of relief. Maybe now she and Bibbo could go out without fear of being attacked by a dog or assaulted by gaudy decorations. Heading to the side door of the garage, she gathered her gardening supplies, Bibbo following close at her heels. Harriet had begun clearing debris from the first bed when Bibbo started barking.

"Hush now," Harriet scolded. She turned to see what had gotten Bibbo so excited. It was Audrey coming around to the side gate.

"Hi, Harriet. Mind if I come in?"

"Why aren't you in school?"

Audrey smiled. "It's Saturday."

"Suit yourself, but I'm quite busy. I've got a bunch of seedlings to plant today. I don't want to waste this beautiful spring day. We never know what the next day will bring in Montana."

"Okay," Audrey said, shutting the gate behind her and reaching down to pet Bibbo. "What a cutie. What's his or her name?"

"Bibbo," Harriet said, not looking up.

"Bibbo?"

"Yes, Bibbo. I don't need any comments about it either. I've gotten enough of those in his six years of life to last a lifetime."

"Are you a ski racer?"

Harriet stopped and turned to look at Audrey. "How did you know?"

"I race. I figured no one else would know that term."

"Yes, as a matter of fact, I was," Harriet said.

"I always thought it was a silly abbreviation. As if bib order was really such a mouthful," Audrey said.

"I always thought it was a cute term. The way it bounces along your lips as you say it. Bibbo. Not to mention how amazing it feels when your coach calls you by that name."

"Bibbo. Bibbo. Bibbo," Audrey said, laughing. "I guess you're right. But why were you called Bibbo?"

"I was ranked near the bottom most of the time, so that part wasn't great, but I finished 16th in a big race of over 100 racers, so I suppose I deserved it."

"I'm confused. I thought it was short for bib order."

"I think it started that way, but my coach used it for those of us who did better in races than expected. I've heard it used on TV among the top racers, too."

"I'll have to ask my coach about it. I'm never seeded at the top, so if I do well, maybe I could win the Bibbo trophy."

Harriet returned to hoeing the soil, knowing she needed to ask about what happened after she and the police left Audrey's house last night, but dreading the answer. Steeling herself and keeping her eyes down on her gardening, she asked, "What happened after I left last night?"

Audrey squatted next to Harriet, so they were at eye level. "My dad yelled at me and said nothing was wrong, and my mom cried. Same as always. Do they really think I'm stupid?"

"I don't think either of them is thinking of you at all. That's the problem."

"What can I do?" Audrey's voice cracked. She sniffed.

"The librarian told me about an abuse shelter here in town called Harmony House. Maybe you could get your mom to call them?"

Audrey scoffed. "How am I supposed to do that when she won't even admit there's a problem?"

Harriet stopped digging. "I suppose you'll have to call then."

Audrey's eyes nearly popped out of her head. "Me? No way. What if my parents found out? I'd be in so much trouble."

"Has your dad ever been violent with you?"

"Not really. Just some shoving. He threw a shoe at me once and held me on my bed and shook me, but nothing major."

"That's good. Well, not that it's good he's done those things to you, but good that it wasn't worse. It sounds like it's been quite a bit worse for your mom."

Audrey nodded. "She always makes excuses for him. She gets black eyes, bruises, cuts, and when I ask her about it, she always says she's so clumsy. She makes up some stupid lie about running into the wall or falling down the stairs."

Harriet shook her head. Why would Robyn deny it? Harriet had heard about women staying with abusive men, but she never understood it. Weren't they strong enough to leave? Was it a financial decision? Did they really believe their men would change?

"So, if you won't call, I suppose I'll have to. Come on, let's go inside."

"Right now?" Audrey backed up a few steps.

"Why would we wait?"

Audrey folded her arms tightly. "I'm scared. What if they find out? What if it makes it worse?"

"Worse? It sounds like it's pretty bad to me. Calls to these places are anonymous, anyway. They'll never know. We'll get some information, is all."

Audrey nodded and followed Harriet into her house. Harriet sat at the dining room table and motioned for Audrey to do the same. Opening her laptop, Harriet googled the number for Harmony House, and a warning appeared at the top of the site. It said computer usage could be monitored. There was a big orange exit button to press if someone were to enter the room who couldn't know she was on the site. Shuddering again, she was glad she'd never had to visit before.

Harriet pressed the link to enter the site. There were two more orange buttons. One with a phone number and another that said, "Learn more about support services."

"Click the 'learn more' button, please," Audrey said.

There was a shelter, legal advocates, support groups, counseling, you name it. Harriet didn't know this existed in her little town. She picked up her phone and dialed the number, putting it on speaker so Audrey could hear. Audrey stood and began pacing next to the table.

"Don't tell them I'm here. Don't mention my name or my mom's, okay?" Audrey whispered as the phone rang.

"Harmony House, how can I help?"

"My neighbor's husband abuses her, and I'm wondering how I can get her out of that situation," Harriet said.

"I'm so sorry to hear about your neighbor. Has she spoken with you about the abuse?"

"No, I heard it. He was yelling at her, and I heard a thud and a shriek."

"A thud and a shriek? You're sure that's what you heard?"

"Why does everyone always ask me that? They are pretty distinct sounds. Yes, I'm sure that's what I heard. And she has a daughter. This girl doesn't need to live with that. So, I need your help to get her away from that terrible man."

Audrey stiffened.

"I see. That is a difficult situation. However, unless your neighbor is ready to leave and come to us of her own accord, there isn't anything you, or we, can do."

"What do you mean? She needs to get away from that man. Her daughter shouldn't have to deal with this."

"You are absolutely right. She shouldn't, but unfortunately, there isn't anything we at Harmony House can do to make someone leave an abuser. They have to come to that decision on their own. Is the child being abused as well?"

Audrey shook her head.

"Not that I know of, but hearing how that man spoke to his wife, I can't imagine the daughter's completely free from his wrath."

Audrey swung her body from side to side and chewed her fingernail.

"If the child is being abused, you or she can call Child Protective Services, but unless there are clear signs of abuse, that can cause more trouble."

"So, there's nothing I can do? I'm supposed to pretend it didn't happen?"

"You can talk to the mother, try to convince her to call us herself, or attend a support group. Sometimes it takes knowing she has support for a woman to have the courage to leave. There are many aspects to consider, especially finances. Many women don't leave because they are afraid they'll have nowhere to go."

"All right. Thank you," Harriet said, and hung up. "Well, that was no help at all."

Audrey sat down across from Harriet and continued to chew her fingernail. "I've tried to get Mom to leave before. Once, when he threw her against the wall so hard that it knocked the wind out of her, she said she'd call the abuse hotline. But she never did." She sniffed. "I always hide in the closet or go outside when they fight. She comes and finds me after, and we cry together. She tells me he doesn't mean it. And I don't think he does. He loves us, but he needs to stop."

"Have you talked to him about it?"

Audrey nodded. "He cries and says how sorry he is. He says he can't control himself, especially if he's been drinking. He stopped drinking for a while, and it was better, but he still screamed at her and called her names. He says he learned it from his father. I tell him that's no excuse, and he agrees with me, and things will be good for a while, but then he does it again."

"What about your school counselor? Have you told her?"

"Him, you mean. No. He'd tell my parents."

"I'm pretty sure he is sworn to secrecy. Confidentiality rules and all that."

Audrey shook her head. "No way. He's weird. He strolls the hallways, humming and whispering to himself. All he talks to us about is school stuff. Handling stress, bullying from other kids, that kind of thing. I'm not telling him what happens at home."

Harriet sighed. "Could you tell your mom we called Harmony House? Maybe you could convince her to call or go to a support group or something?"

Audrey folded her arms on the table. "I guess I could try." She stood and went to the front door. "Thanks for your help."

"Of course. We need to fix this for you."

Harriet shut the door behind Audrey and felt her shoulders slump. The sunshine streaming through the window seemed to mock the heaviness she felt. So much for a bright, cheery day spent in the garden. She felt as though an elephant was sitting on her chest. She wished Les were here. He would have advised her to stay out of it and let them handle their own issues. Without him, though, it was harder to shut off her feelings.

CHAPTER 15

HARRIET HEADED BACK out to her garden, trying to salvage the rest of a beautiful day. Her thoughts swirled about how to help Audrey, and their conversation about ski racing had gotten her thinking about her brother, Hank.

Maybe she should call him. Harriet still didn't fully understand why Les had had such a problem with him. Years ago, she and Hank and a few of their old friends had gone out for dinner and ended up at a karaoke bar. Karaoke is best done with a few drinks, so she'd come home drunk, and Les had been disappointed.

"You're a married woman now," he'd said. "It doesn't seem proper for you to be cavorting at all hours of the night."

"Geez, Les," Hank had said. "You sound like it's the Gilded Age or something. Cavorting."

She'd started giggling so hard she flew into the bathroom before she lost control of her bladder.

When Hank married Megan, things had gotten even worse. Megan was an investment banker and quite full of herself, Harriet had to admit. All conversations seemed to revolve around her: what stocks she was looking at, what brands she was wearing, what book she was reading. Everything she did had to be the best. Les didn't like her much at all.

"Did you hear how she went on about her new shoes? God, who cares where the company sourced the leather? And which celebrities are also wearing them? That woman is an egomaniacal, money-grubbing elitist, if you ask me."

"Well, no one asked, so you'd better keep your opinions to yourself. She has different ideas of what is important, is all," Harriet said.

"I sure hope you don't start thinking that superficial crap is important," Les said.

Harriet scoffed. "Of course not. I'm content with our little life right here in Bozeman."

"Little life?" His face fell, and he looked down at his hands.

Harriet's heart constricted. She'd offended him. "No, dear," she'd said, going to him and hugging him. "I meant that we don't need all those delusions of grandeur." He'd held her and kissed the top of her head.

Megan was the beginning of the end for her and her brother. Whenever Harriet suggested they get together, Les made excuses. He was working late that night; he had plans with an old friend from college; he wasn't feeling well. Harriet knew what he was doing, but arguing never helped.

"Les, you know we can't avoid them forever," she'd said.

"Why not?"

"He's my brother, for goodness' sake."

"Yes, but you are my wife." He'd come up behind her and wrapped his arms around her. "When you marry, you form a new family that takes precedence over your old life. Your brother was already driving a wedge between us with his comments about my being old-fashioned and the like. And since he married Megan, things have only gotten worse. Don't my feelings matter?"

She turned to face him. His forehead was creased, his eyes pleading. "You know they do. I understand your concern, but he means a lot to me. He's always been there for me."

Sadness filled his eyes. "Haven't I proven that I'll be there for you?"

She hugged him. "Yes, you have. Hold me. I love you."

She saw her brother infrequently after that. When she did, her brother's questions about why they never got together grew more and more difficult to answer. It was easier not to spend time with him. It was especially difficult when he told her Megan was pregnant. Harriet and Les had been trying for two years when she received the call from Hank.

"Guess what?" Hank said. "We're pregnant."

"Who's we?"

"Megan and I are pregnant."

"I'm pretty sure it's just her, unless there is some new science experiment I have yet to hear about."

Hank laughed. "Anyway, we got home from the doctor, and you were my first phone call. I know we've been busy, and we haven't seen each other often enough, but you were the first person I wanted to tell."

Harriet's heart squeezed in her chest. "I'm happy for you," she'd said, but she hadn't meant it. She loved her brother, but her jealousy was winning in this instance. She hadn't even known Hank wanted children. Harriet was the one who'd always gravitated toward them.

When Les came home that night, he'd found her sitting at the table, eyes red from crying, tissues strewn about the table. Harriet had lost track of time. She hadn't made dinner or even cleaned the dishes from breakfast.

"What's the matter?" Les had asked.

"Megan's pregnant."

He'd come to her side and put his arm around her shoulder. "I'm sorry, Harriet," was all he said. He didn't even mention the mess or the lack of dinner. He'd picked up takeout, and they ate in silence until he said, "Maybe now you'll listen to me and distance yourself further from your brother. He obviously isn't making you happy."

Harriet wanted to protest. He was her brother, after all. If she couldn't have children, why couldn't she find joy in being an aunt? And they hadn't given up trying yet. But since Les was opposed to accepting help with conceiving, the odds were against her becoming a mother after two years of trying. She knew the statistics.

"I'll have to be the best auntie ever," Harriet said.

"Do you think that's wise? Don't you think it will cause you pain to see your brother's children?"

Harriet didn't know what to believe. She supposed that's how it happened. Somehow, they stopped communicating, and time went by. That was that. It was surprising how easy it was, really.

"Well, that's the last seedling, Bibbo. Good thing too. It's getting chilly out here. Let's head in and figure out what's for dinner."

Inside, Harriet checked her phone. Only a notification from the Apple News app. She clicked on the weather app to see if it was going to freeze tonight. Hopefully not. She didn't feel like digging through the garage to find her tomato teepees.

"Darn it." Bibbo cocked his head at her words. "Looks like we aren't done yet. Going to get down to twenty-seven tonight. Those little seedlings won't like that."

Half an hour later, her plants all tucked in for the night, Harriet sighed as she looked in her refrigerator. She hadn't enjoyed cooking even when she'd done it for Les every night. Now, it was even tougher to get the motivation to make something healthy just for herself.

An organic vegetarian pizza from the new Whole Foods in town would suffice. Maybe she could even make this evening an enjoyable one. The frozen pizza meant she wouldn't have to cook or clean up. She chuckled to herself at how upset Les would have been with a frozen pizza. But now it suited her fine.

CHAPTER 16

IT WAS STILL CHILLY when she took Bibbo out the next morning. The melted snow from yesterday had frozen solid overnight, forcing Harriet to be extremely careful placing her crutches. She heard a garage door opening and saw Chris getting into his truck. She waited until he turned the corner and hurried across the street as best she could.

"Hello, Harriet," Robyn said as she opened her front door.

"I saw Chris leaving and figured it was my chance to talk to you."

"Look. I appreciate your stepping in to help Audrey, but you really don't need to be involved."

"Believe me, I don't want to be, but I can't help it anymore. I know what I heard and saw."

Robyn crossed her arms. "He's not always like that. It only happens once in a while. Usually when he's drinking. He feels terrible, and he says he'll cut back on the drinking. It'll be fine. You don't need to worry."

"Too late for that," Harriet said. "I googled Harmony House. They have all kinds of support, and it's completely anonymous."

"Harmony House? Is that a shelter or something?" Robyn's eyes were wide.

Harriet nodded. "Lucille, the librarian, volunteers there and says they do a good job. Audrey wants you to get help."

Robyn took a step back. "How do you know what my daughter wants?"

"She came by when I was out gardening yesterday. She helped me call Harmony House. She hopes you'll talk with them. She loves you both but wants this to stop. I don't blame her. She didn't choose this."

Robyn scoffed. "You think I did?"

"No. But you can do something about it. Audrey can't."

Robyn sighed and opened the door. "Come in. Do you want a cup of coffee?"

"No thanks. I already had some."

Robyn went to the kitchen and poured herself a cup of coffee. "Would you like anything else? Water at least?"

"No. I want you to agree to talk with the Harmony House people. When we googled them, we found that there are support group meetings on Monday evenings. You just have to call to get the location."

Robyn set her mug on the coffee table and ran a hand through her hair. "You aren't going to let this go, are you?"

Harriet shook her head.

"Fine. I'll go if it will get you off my back," Robyn said.

"Good. Now I can go back to minding my own business." Harriet turned to leave.

Robyn reached up and grabbed Harriet's arm. "You're coming with me, aren't you?"

Harriet's heart skipped a beat. "What are you talking about? Why would I go with you?"

"I'm not going alone. No way," Robyn said.

"Don't you have any friends or family who could go with you?" Harriet asked.

Robyn shook her head. "We just moved here, remember? And even back in Arizona, I didn't have many friends. Besides, I've never told anybody about any of this."

"What about your parents? Siblings?"

"I'm an only child, and my folks live in Seattle, but we aren't close. We haven't seen them in years. Chris doesn't get along with them, so it's easier to stay away," Robyn said.

"Darn. I guess you'll have to brave it alone, then," Harriet said, moving to the front door, Bibbo hopping at her heels.

Robyn didn't answer. Harriet hoped she'd go, but there was no way she was going to a domestic violence support group. She had to draw the line.

"Okay, then. See you around. I have to take Bibbo for his walk," Harriet said.

The sky had turned cloudy during the short time Harriet had been in Robyn's house. It looked like it might snow. When she used to ski, Harriet enjoyed spring skiing the most, with all the fluffy fresh powder, bluebird skies, and warm temperatures. But the end of April was too late for skiing, which meant it was too late for snow to be useful at all. It was a nuisance. It melted quickly and turned to mud. Cars were so dirty that it was impossible to read the license plates. Harriet assumed criminals used this to get away with things.

Bibbo trotted along, unconcerned with the weather. Up ahead, Rocky rounded the corner, followed closely by Kevin. As expected, Rocky came bounding over to Harriet and Bibbo. Thankfully, she had clutched Bibbo's leash in both hands to prepare. Rocky lowered his head and wagged his tail, signaling he wanted to play with Bibbo. Bibbo, accepting the invitation, bounced and pulled at the leash, twisting and tangling both dogs.

Finally, Bibbo emerged from the furball and ran behind Harriet, wrapping his leash around her legs and coming out on the other side. Kevin scooped Bibbo into his arms.

"Put him down! He isn't the problem," Harriet said.

"Well, unless you'd like to be on the ground again, I think I'd better untangle his leash from around you."

"Wait 'til Tammy hears about this. I take it you didn't get an email from her?" Kevin shook his head. "And wait, turn around," Harriet said.

Kevin cocked his head to the side and knit his eyebrows together. He set Bibbo down, raised his palms into the air, and turned around slowly. When he completed his circle, he said, "Care to dance?"

"You don't even have any baggies on you."

"Excuse me?"

"Poop bags. You don't even try to clean up Rocky's poop. Not that you could find it since he runs all over the neighborhood, pooping wherever he pleases. You could at least carry some baggies, in case."

"Guilty as charged." He placed his hands out in front of him as if waiting for handcuffs.

"Do you take anything seriously? Is life a big joke to you?"

"I believe it's best not to take life too seriously."

"Well, you're about to be in some serious trouble. Now get your dog out of here so Bibbo and I can finish our walk." Kevin called to Rocky and started walking away. "Wait. I have an idea," Harriet called after him. "Let's do a schedule at least until the HOA forces you to comply."

"A schedule?"

"Yes. A walking schedule. I don't want to worry about running into you every time I leave my house. I walk Bibbo in the morning around seven and again in the evening around seven. That should be easy even for you to remember. Seven and seven. So, be sure you aren't out for about half an hour at those times. Of course, once I get off my crutches in another week or so, I'll be out longer, more like an hour, so you stay away then, okay?"

He scoffed. "Sorry, Harriet. I'm not making any promises. My life isn't as structured as yours, and I prefer spending as much time outside as I can."

"You are incorrigible. If Tammy won't do anything, I'll have to get the police involved."

"That reminds me. I heard the police were at your neighbor's house. What was that about?"

"None of your business. Now get out of here so I can enjoy my day."

"Bye, Harriet. Always a pleasure."

"It'll be a pleasure not to have to run into you all the time," Harriet called to Kevin's retreating back.

Later that evening, a knock sounded at the door. Harriet opened it to find Audrey standing on her porch, arms folded across her chest, glancing frequently over her shoulder at her house.

"Did you talk to my mom about the meeting?" Audrey asked.

"Yep."

"So? Is she going?"

"No idea," Harriet said, turning to shut her door.

"What do you mean? Didn't you tell her about Harmony House? And that it's anonymous? And they have support groups and stuff?"

"Of course I did, but she said she wouldn't go if I didn't go with her."

"And you won't?" Audrey said, coming to stand in front of Harriet with her hands on her hips.

"No way. I have to draw the line somewhere. This whole thing is already too much for me. I don't want to be involved."

"Too much for *you*?" Audrey said. "How do you think I feel?"

Harriet blinked. "I can't imagine how you feel."

"Awful. Scared. Angry. You name it." Audrey ran a hand through her hair. "You're the first person I've ever talked to about this. Mom makes excuses and says it will go away, and I'm supposed to pretend like it never happened."

Harriet sighed. "There's no way I'm going to that meeting."

"Why? Is it really so terrible? It would be like an hour of your time. And if my mom gets some help, don't you think it would be worth it? What else am I supposed to do?"

Harriet stared at this girl, her eyes wide and pleading. A tear made its way down Audrey's cheek. She racked her brain for other ideas for how to help this girl and her mother, but nothing came to her. Again, she asked herself, wasn't it her duty to help them now that she knew Chris was violent?

"Okay," Harriet said, sighing. "I'll go."

Abruptly, Audrey wrapped Harriet in a hug. "Thank you. You have no idea how much this means to me."

Harriet stood, stiff and awkward, while this girl held her. She had to admit, even though it was unexpected, it felt nice. She smelled a bit like cherry blossoms and mint gum, which she remembered teenagers smelling like from her time in the high school library. It felt good to be needed again.

CHAPTER 17

MONDAY NIGHT CAME much too quickly for Harriet's taste. She'd have preferred it never came around at all, in fact. A domestic abuse support group was never on her list of things to do before she died; that was for certain. Robyn had better be thankful for this. It was quite a hefty repayment for the lasagna.

What did one wear to such a thing? She hoped for something that would make her disappear completely. Harry Potter's invisibility cloak would come in handy. Come to think of it, she wouldn't mind wearing it all the time.

She settled on her dark green sweater and black slacks. Bright clothing seemed too festive to wear to a place where everyone was most certainly depressed and uncomfortable. The meeting was at the old stone Episcopal church downtown, which was one positive aspect of the situation. She'd always wanted to see inside, but because she wasn't Episcopalian, she didn't think she'd be welcome there just to be nosy.

Hearing the garage door opening across the street, Harriet went out front to meet Robyn. "Hello, you look nice," Robyn said, as Harriet climbed into the car. Robyn was rubbing her hands up and down on the steering wheel and bouncing her left leg. Apparently, Robyn didn't mind looking festive for the occasion. She was wearing a nearly fluorescent flowery top that looked like she was on her way to a Mother's Day brunch on South Beach.

"My, aren't you colorful," Harriet said.

"Is it too much? I knew it was too much. I'll run back in and change."

"No way. You aren't getting out of this that easily. Maybe next time you'll be more subdued, but we're going right now, no matter what." As Robyn carefully eased the car onto the road, Harriet said, "I'm pretty sure a herd of turtles could beat us. You'd better speed it up a bit if we're going to make it on time. I don't want to cause a commotion coming in late."

"You're right. Maybe it's too late, anyway. Maybe we should wait until next week," Robyn said.

"As much as I'd love to forget the whole thing, I can't, and neither can you, so step on it."

They drove in silence. Nothing seemed to be amiss on Harriet's street, other than a lopsided basketball hoop that had seen better days. They made the left turn onto Huffine Lane, and they were bombarded with construction everywhere. Where there had once been fields of wheat and roaming cattle, now there were mounds of dirt and steel frames of huge commercial buildings. Did they really need a Town Pump on every corner? Couldn't people plan their gas station stops more than a block in advance? Or were people so lazy that they needed to drive just a block to pick up their beer, chips, and cigarettes? Modern society disgusted Harriet.

As they pulled into the parking lot, Harriet admired the quaint stone building she'd longed to explore since she was a child. The church she'd attended with her parents had been in a corner unit of a strip mall. They had plopped a cross on top and called it a church. Harriet and her brother dreaded going there. It was evangelical, so it felt more like a multilevel marketing scheme than a place of worship. Of course, Harriet made this comparison much later in life. At the time, she hadn't liked feeling pressured to tell everyone about Jesus in every conversation the way the minister asked them to.

Harriet might have stuck with religion if she'd gone to a place like this as a child. It invited her to relax and open herself up to possibilities. It felt sacred and loved, with its bell tower and copper cross. Built in the 1890s, it was a symbol of optimism for what Bozeman could become. Parishioners probably felt the same optimism for their futures in a place like this.

Harriet opened the car door and stepped outside. Pulling her coat closer against the wind, she waited for Robyn to emerge. Finally, she pulled the door open again to see what was keeping her. She was sitting there, staring straight ahead.

"Are you coming?"

"No, I don't think I can," Robyn said, her voice nearly a whisper.

"No way. Uh-uh. You didn't drag me all the way here to chicken out. We're going in there. Don't make me drag you out of that car. It would be difficult on crutches, but I'm stronger than I look."

Robyn emerged, looking like a deer in headlights.

"Isn't this little building gorgeous?" Harriet asked. "Look at the attention to detail. The masons laid the stones together perfectly, and the bright red door is so inviting. I've always wanted to go in."

Robyn nodded. "I bet you wish you were here under different circumstances."

"Yes, but I'm trying to ignore that."

Entering the building, Harriet's eyes took in the arched ceiling with gorgeous wooden beams, the art nouveau stained glass windows, and the intricate wooden altar. It was just as she expected. Inspiring and cozy all at once. Now that Les was gone, maybe she could convert and come here, if only to sit in this space. She felt as though hope lived here.

"Where do we go?" Robyn whispered. Harriet was glad she was whispering. It seemed like a place where one should whisper.

"How would I know?"

Just then, a petite, very young-looking woman emerged from a small side door. "Are you here for the Harmony House meeting?"

Her voice echoed off the tall, curved ceiling. She hadn't gotten the memo about whispering.

Nodding, they made their way in the direction the woman guided them. Robyn's boots squeaked, and the clank of Harriet's crutches echoed on the marble floors. "I'm sure there's an elevator here," the young woman said. "I've never used it, so I'll need to look around." She rounded a corner at the end of the hall. Peering back around the wall, she motioned for them to follow her. The elevator was small and slow. Harriet wasn't claustrophobic, but this tiny space made her understand the feeling. Exiting the elevator, they entered a narrow, dark corridor that smelled old and damp, the way Harriet imagined a wine cellar in France might.

The meeting room was an utter disappointment, like any other meeting room in any ordinary building. Four white walls and two round tables with cheap chairs circling them. At least there were grapes, cheese, and crackers on one table. But no wine. Harriet thought wine would be a good idea at a meeting like this, to take the edge off. But no. She'd have to get through this wineless.

"Come on in. Have a seat," the young woman said. "I'm Callie from Harmony House. I think we're expecting a few more, so we'll wait to get started. Have a snack and a seat while you wait."

Harriet had hoped to grab a seat at the back of the room, but the room was small, so there was nowhere to hide. Robyn still had a dazed look on her face, so Harriet took the lead. She put a few grapes on her plate and asked Robyn to carry it for her. She chose a seat furthest from the two other ladies who were quietly munching on snacks, staring at their plates.

The ladies looked normal, like Robyn. They didn't look like the disheveled, bruised, ragamuffins Harriet expected to see at a domestic violence support group. One was quite pretty, well-groomed, and professional, resembling a CEO rather than an abused woman. Maybe Robyn would feel more comfortable sharing her story with women like these instead of the stereotype Harriet had in her mind.

Two more women entered the room, chatting and giggling as if they had no worries at all. Harriet wasn't sure what she'd expected, but it definitely wasn't this. These women were so young, they looked as though they could be in college. Could they have gotten themselves roped into an abusive relationship already? And been mature enough to come to a support group to get help when they figured it out?

Harriet had met Les in college, so she supposed women that age were capable of serious relationships, and abusers probably started out that way. Isn't that what Harriet heard about them? They usually came from abusive families, so she supposed it started right away. Maybe they knew nothing different.

"Hello!" the young leader of the group said. "As most of you know, I'm Callie, and I'm a Survivor Advocate with Harmony House. I recognize most of you, but there are a couple of unfamiliar faces, so let's go around the room and introduce ourselves. Just say your name and your favorite food as an icebreaker. I'll start. I'm Callie, and I love ice cream."

Oh, God. This was going to be even worse than Harriet imagined. It was like the summer camps her parents forced her to go to up at Moonlight Basin. Now that she was older, Harriet knew her mother just needed to get her and Hank out of her hair for a few weeks over the summer. It wasn't about learning to ride horseback, rock climb, or use bear spray properly. Harriet hated that camp. Not only because she feared horses and heights, but also because the kids were mean. And it usually started when they teased her about whatever her choice had been for this type of icebreaker situation.

The woman to Callie's left stared at her hands and said, "I'm Melissa, and I like pizza." She looked even more miserable than Harriet felt, poor thing.

The two young girls went next. Giggling, the first one with the bright red hair like that arrow-shooting girl from the Disney movie said, "I'm Cora and I like lemonade."

Harriet rolled her eyes and flopped her arm onto the table. Everyone turned to stare at her. "Sorry," she said. "My hand slipped from under my chin." Her cheeks flushed. She needed to keep her irritation under control, for Robyn's sake. But lemonade? Really? That wasn't even food.

"I'm Morgan, and I love sushi."

It was Harriet's turn. "I'm Harriet, and I'm not really taking part. I'm here to support my neighbor here." She reached over to pat Robyn's arm.

"Wonderful. I'm glad you're supporting your friend, but you can still participate." Callie's eager eyes bored into her. Why did it matter what food she liked?

"Lasagna," Harriet managed, hoping Robyn would know she meant it as a compliment to her cooking.

It was Robyn's turn, but she wouldn't look up. She kept staring at the table. Harriet elbowed her gently, hoping to wake her from her trance.

"Hi there!" Callie said, coming around the table to stand next to Robyn. "I know this can be overwhelming, but we're all glad you're here. We aren't here to judge. We're here to support and listen. You don't have to say anything you aren't comfortable with. Are you comfortable telling us your name?"

"Robyn," she finally whispered.

"Welcome, Robyn. Do you have a favorite food?" Robyn shook her head. "That's all right. We're glad you're here."

Really? Why had Harriet been forced to name a food?

The CEO-looking woman said her name was Stephanie and that she liked pasta, and the silly game was over, thankfully.

"So, the way this works is that I share a bit of information about what abuse can look like because, as I'm sure you can see from our group here, the stereotype of the abused woman is a myth," Callie said. "We are strong, beautiful women who found ourselves in the wrong place with the wrong partner."

She strode over to a whiteboard and drew a giant circle. "Today, I'll be talking about the narcissistic cycle of abuse. Not all abusers are narcissistic, but it's pretty common, and they use emotional abuse tactics, which can be insidious because they don't always include physical abuse. It is purely emotional, so sometimes people don't recognize it. It's like you can't see the forest for the trees. For some of you, this might be a review, but that's okay. It's good to keep this fresh in our minds so we can recognize the pattern and try to extricate ourselves from it.

"Outsiders think we should recognize the abuse and leave, and if we don't, we're stupid or weak, but we know that isn't the case. It's much more complicated than that. Some can't leave because of finances, or children, or because we simply aren't ready to let go of what we thought our relationship could be. And, especially with emotional abuse, we don't even realize it's happening. I want you all to know that we understand. We all go through this process differently.

"So, the narcissistic cycle of abuse begins with what we call love bombing. How many of your partners completely swept you off your feet at the beginning?" Callie raised her hand and nodded as everyone's hand went up except Harriet's and Robyn's. Slowly, Robyn raised her hand as well. "Does anyone feel comfortable sharing a story of love bombing?"

The red-haired girl raised her hand. "When I met Jack, he couldn't get enough of me. We spent nearly every minute together. He took me out to fancy restaurants he couldn't afford, bought me dresses, and even took me on a weekend trip to Arizona after only knowing me for three months because he knew how sad I got during our long winters. He asked me to marry him there. It was so quick, and somewhere in my mind, I felt a red flag being raised, but I ignored it. I wanted to feel like a princess, I guess."

Harriet didn't think that sounded bad at all. Why were good things being twisted? Wasn't that the definition of falling head over heels? Wasn't that what little girls longed for and what Disney pushed? Harriet shook her head. This was going to be a long hour.

Looking up, Harriet noticed a crack in the ceiling. Her mind wandered to when this building had been constructed, and how different Bozeman was today.

Robyn nudged her. Callie was staring at her. "I'm sorry. I was thinking about something else. Did you need something from me?"

"We were talking about times our partners might have devalued us. That's the next step after love bombing."

"Oh, well, I'm only here to support Robyn. I'm not, or wasn't, in an abusive relationship," Harriet said.

"Okay, sorry. Robyn? Would you like to share something with the group? No pressure, it just helps us to see what's happening in our own relationships when we compare the experiences of others."

"Um, well, this is making sense so far. No wonder I'm confused. Sometimes Chris is amazing, so perfect, and then, the next day, I'll get the silent treatment, or he'll be angry that I didn't know he wanted eggs for breakfast, or something silly like that."

Heads nodded around the table like silly bobblehead dolls. Men were unpredictable. What was wrong with that? These ladies needed to toughen up. Physical violence was another thing altogether, but moodiness was part of being human.

The woman to Robyn's left said, "One minute my husband is telling me I'm the most beautiful woman in the world and he doesn't deserve me, and the next he says I'm disgusting and I'm lucky he stays with me. It's always when he's drinking, though, so I try to ignore those comments."

"Are you able to ignore them?" Callie asked.

She shook her head and sniffed. "Those comments stick much more than the kind ones. I think maybe that is his actual truth, and the alcohol makes the truth come out."

"This is very important, everyone. We hear people make excuses for abusive behavior because their partner had been drinking.

Listen closely. Alcohol doesn't make someone an abuser. It lessens their ability to control their abusive tendencies."

It was silent for a few minutes. Harriet could practically see the truth of that statement sinking into each woman's head.

"I'd like to leave a little time for us to chat and catch up, so I'll leave the instruction portion there. We'll continue filling in the circle next time." Callie came back to the table and sat down. "Who'd like to start? How was this week for you?"

The red-haired woman raised her hand. "I suppose I'll go. I've got some news." She shifted in her chair. "I've left Brett again. For good this time."

"Oh, Cora. I'm happy for you. Where are you staying? With your parents again?" Callie asked.

Cora shook her head. "I'm staying with Morgan this time. My parents don't get it. They were the ones to convince me to go back to him last time. They say I'm overreacting."

"I'm sorry to hear that. I'm glad you've found the support you need. It can be tough when family members don't see it, or they think only bruises and broken bones qualify as abuse."

"I thought that's what abuse was," Harriet said.

Callie snapped her head around to meet Harriet's gaze. "No. Emotional abuse is just as bad. Actually, it's often worse since there isn't a physical representation of the hurt to show others, or to remind yourself. That's why we are talking about this cycle of abuse. To show the other signs of abuse that aren't physical."

"I thought we hadn't gotten to the physical part yet," Harriet said.

"Well," Callie smiled, but it seemed to be stuck on like a sticker, "you're in the right place, then."

"Why's that?"

"So you can learn about abuse. It isn't just physical, like I said."

Harriet nodded but wasn't convinced. She hoped she wouldn't be back here anyway, so it didn't matter. She'd have to keep her mouth shut, no matter how hard it might be.

The CEO-looking woman said, "That was a hard one for me, too. I kept thinking I was overreacting. My ex didn't get physical often, but the emotional abuse had built up year after year, and I hadn't seen it. It's like the frog in the pot of water, you know?"

She looked at Harriet. Harriet blinked. She had no idea what this woman was talking about. Frog in a pot of water? Was this woman from France cooking up some frog's legs? What did that have to do with Chris hitting Robyn? More than ever, Harriet regretted her decision to accompany her.

"It's like this," the CEO woman said. "If you put a frog in a pot of boiling water, it will jump out because it's hot and it knows to escape. If you put a frog in a pot of lukewarm water, and slowly increase the heat, it won't notice, and it will cook. That's what emotional abuse is. They slowly increase the heat, and you don't realize you're cooking."

"That sounds like a crock of...you know what, if you ask me. How do you know what a frog will do? And who cares what frogs do anyway?"

The room was silent. A few women wiped tears from their cheeks. One sniffled. Robyn reached over and laid her hand on Harriet's arm. "Harriet, I'm sorry if the metaphor doesn't work for you, but it does for me. I've been cooking for quite a while now. Just hang in there with me, okay?" Robyn turned to the CEO woman. "Please continue."

"Well, that's the end of the metaphor, but for me, it was a lightbulb moment learning about how emotional abuse sneaks up on you. I'm a strong, educated, independent woman. How the heck did I end up with a guy who told me what a piece of shit I was? Even worse, how did I make excuses for him and believe what he said was true? It's this slow pattern of degradation and love bombing that keeps you off balance. You think, 'this person loves me more than anyone in the world, so if they feel this way about me, others must too. They're just too polite to say it.'" She shook her head and reached for a tissue at the center of the table.

"I'm so sorry that happened to you, but I'm so glad you see it now. So many women never see the forest for the trees and believe they deserve the treatment they are receiving. Thanks for sharing, Stephanie." Callie strode back to the front of the room and announced the meeting was over. "See you next week."

Robyn gathered Harriet's crutches and handed them to her. Before exiting the room, Robyn stopped and thanked Callie and nodded at the other ladies. Harriet was grateful she had to take the elevator, so she didn't have to chit-chat with the others.

"So, it sounds like you'll be leaving Chris, then. Have you thought about where you and Audrey will stay?" Harriet asked.

Robyn stared at her. She opened her mouth a couple of times, and nothing came out.

"Cat got your tongue?" Harriet asked.

"It's not that simple, Harriet." Reaching the ground level, Robyn exited the elevator much too quickly for Harriet to keep up. That was fine by Harriet. She took her time admiring the chapel once again.

Just like the ride to the meeting, the ride home was quiet. It was dark now, and Harriet rarely drove at night, so it surprised her how many lights speckled the mountains in the distance. Construction wasn't only happening in the valley. The mountains were being inundated too.

Stopping in front of Harriet's house, Robyn jumped out to grab the crutches from the back seat and hand them to Harriet. "Thanks for going with me," Robyn said. "It gave me a lot to think about."

"I bet. Leaving entails so much, like finding someplace to live, money issues, and splitting parenting time. I can't even imagine what must be going through your head."

"Thanks for the pep talk, Harriet. I'm not certain I'm leaving, though."

"You're kidding, right? Some other ladies left without physical abuse. You've endured much worse, and you still aren't sure?"

"Like I said. It's not that simple. Thank you again for joining me. Good night." Robyn walked back to the driver's side and climbed into her car.

Harriet stood on her front porch watching Robyn. None of it made any sense. As if it wasn't bad enough what Robyn was going through, she had Audrey to think about. How could she consider staying with that man? It was black and white. If a man hits you, you leave. Harriet shook her head as she inserted her key into the lock. Why did people make things so complicated?

CHAPTER 18

HARRIET HATED dull gray days but liked that the insulation of the clouds made the air warmer than on clear, cold days. Heading out to her garden, she uncovered her tomato plants. She was pleasantly surprised to find them looking quite perky. She'd been afraid the frosty nights would leave them droopy, but the tomato teepees seemed to work—such a simple invention, little plastic domes that fit over each plant. Someone probably got rich over something so simple. Harriet knew she'd had much better ideas and gotten nothing for them.

Glancing up, she spotted Rocky. Harriet squinted to be sure she was seeing correctly. No, it was true. Rocky was on a leash. Miracles did happen.

For once, she was eager to greet Kevin and call him by his real name. She stood and waved. Either he didn't see her, or he was ignoring her. Strange, he hadn't ever been one to shy away from a random conversation before. "Bibbo, you wait here. I don't have time to go get your leash."

Opening her back gate, she entered the open space and crutched down the gravel trail toward Kevin and Rocky. Rocky was still trying to run willy-nilly, which meant that poor Kevin's shoulder looked as though it was about to be yanked from its socket. He'd need to do a bit of leash training.

"Yoo-hoo! Kevin!" Harriet called. He kept walking. Harriet hadn't noticed that he was hard of hearing, but maybe he wore hearing aids, those little ones that hid down in your ear, so she hadn't seen them. Maybe he wasn't wearing them today. These darn crutches made it impossible for her to catch up to him. She called again, but he still did not respond.

Rocky stopped to do his business, and Harriet gained ground. She called to Kevin again, and this time he turned toward her ever so slowly. "Couldn't you hear me calling to you?" Harriet asked.

"As a matter of fact, I could, but I ignored you since I knew the only reason you'd want to talk to me is to gloat."

Harriet pursed her lips and looked down. "Well, I suppose you're right, but here we are. I can't tell you how happy I am to see this turn of events. Did Tammy finally get to you?"

Kevin nodded. "She threatened fines because you wouldn't leave her alone."

Tammy had finally come through. She'd send her some flowers or something.

"This is embarrassing, and please don't go on about reporting me again..." Kevin ran a hand through his hair and finally brought his eyes to meet Harriet's. "Do you have a baggie?"

"You still don't have baggies? Even after I caught you without them last time? You're the culprit." Harriet reached into her pocket, retrieved a baggie, and handed it to him. "Did you know we were discussing DNA testing of feces to determine who was not picking up after their dogs?"

He stared at her for a moment and then started laughing. Holding his stomach, he rocked back and forth on his heels and toes, laughing so loudly that Harriet turned to look at the surrounding houses, for surely the neighbors would peer out their windows to see what was so funny.

"You can't be serious," Kevin said, gasping for breath. "DNA testing? Let me guess. This was your idea."

"It was. And a brilliant one at that. It just wasn't in the budget."

"I see. Well, Harriet, you've gotten your wish." Rocky yanked the leash, nearly toppling Kevin to the ground. "And I must go. Take care."

Smiling as she made her way back to her yard, she was happy to see Bibbo sitting by the gate, waiting patiently, not barking like so many other dogs do at passersby. "Did you see that, Bibbo? Isn't it incredible? You don't have to worry about Rocky anymore. He's on a leash. Miracles do happen."

Harriet finished uncovering her tomato plants and went back inside. She sat on the couch and stared at the blank TV. What now?

Why hadn't she gotten Robyn's phone number in all their interactions? It hardly seemed necessary since they lived across the street. However, right now, she wanted to check on her, but she needed to be certain Chris wasn't there. Harriet was going to have to talk some sense into that woman. It was black and white. Your husband hits you, and you leave. Case closed.

Chris worked in construction or something, so he shouldn't be home in the middle of the day on a Tuesday. She'd have to risk it.

Harriet heard Robyn talking through her front door and went over to the window to peek in and see if she was talking to Chris. She was on the phone. She'd wait a minute until Robyn finished. What was it Robyn said she did again? Bookkeeping? Marketing? What did it matter? She worked from home, which meant she could do it anywhere. She could leave Chris and keep working. That was all that mattered.

"So, you'd like to host next month? Fantastic! Let's see, I have the 12th and the 23rd open. Will either of those dates work for you? Oh, and remember, as a host, you get sixty percent off when your guests spend two hundred dollars or more. You could finally get that nonstick grill pan and press set you've been wanting," Robyn said.

Oh God. She was a multilevel marketer. How had she not mentioned it to Harriet? That was usually the first thing these people said. They introduced themselves and said they were a rep for whatever. It came out as one sentence, as if it was on their birth certificate or something. She'd have to get in and get out of this relationship as quickly as possible—no overpriced grill pans for Harriet.

Robyn said goodbye, and Harriet pressed the doorbell. The door swung open, and Harriet whispered, "Chris isn't here, is he?"

"Hello to you too, Harriet," Robyn said, crossing her arms in front of her.

"Yeah, hi. Anyway, is Chris home? I'd rather not run into him, if you know what I mean."

Robyn sighed. "He's not home. You can relax. He also has good qualities, you know."

"What does that matter if he hits you?"

Robyn shook her head. "If only the world was as black and white as you see it. Life would be so much simpler."

"Why do you have to complicate it?"

"I'm not the one complicating it. It just is."

"Can I come in? It's not comfortable standing on one good leg, leaning on crutches," Harriet said.

"I suppose you can, but only for a minute. I'm swamped."

Harriet scoffed. "Sounded like it. Selling people overpriced things they don't need."

"Excuse me? Pampered Chef has the highest quality cooking innovations on the market."

"I see they've got you hook, line, and sinker. You've even memorized the vernacular."

"Honestly, Harriet. I think it might be better if you left. I'm busy and I'm in no mood to argue with you."

"I'm not arguing. I'm telling it like it is. But that's not why I came here. I came to find out when you are leaving Chris, and how I can help." Harriet nudged the door further open, went in, and sat on the couch. It was more comfortable than it looked.

"It's not that simple. He's not always mean. Most of the time, he's kind, helpful, and funny. There are many reasons I fell in love with him. Audrey doesn't like it when he gets angry. No kid does, but she needs her dad."

"Sounds like he's in the love explosion phase, or whatever they called it in the group. It's just a matter of time until the cycle happens again. Didn't you take anything in at that meeting? It wasn't my favorite thing to do, so if it doesn't help, we need to find something different."

"It's okay. I'm not your project. You don't have to come to any more meetings or worry about me," Robyn said.

"I'm afraid it's too late for that. I was a school librarian, and I care about kids. Audrey needs me even if you think you don't. Besides, now that I know abuse is going on here, it is my civic duty to do something about it."

Robyn sat opposite Harriet and put her head in her hands. "If you aren't going anywhere, I suppose I'll tell you everything. A few years ago, I cheated on Chris."

"You?" Harriet asked. Robyn looked like every other middle-aged mom. Harriet thought women who cheated were trying to recapture their youth with Botox, fake boobs, duck lips, and the like, not slightly dumpy moms with gray roots who sold Pampered Chef.

Robyn nodded. "I wish I could say it was just a stupid one-night mistake, but it was more than that. And it was one of Audrey's friends' dads."

Harriet inhaled and sat up straight. She shook her head in silence.

"I know. It's the reason we moved here. Audrey was mortified. Her friend's parents split up. Chris left initially, but we decided on the move instead."

"Well, you're no saint, but what he does is worse."

"How can you say that? I'm an adulterer. I should wear the big scarlet 'A' on my chest."

"He should wear an even bigger 'A' for abuser," Harriet said. "I bet the reason you had the affair was because of how terribly Chris treats you, so it's not really your fault."

Robyn sighed. Standing, she asked if Harriet wanted a coffee. Harriet nodded and settled her boot onto the ottoman. This might take a while.

From the kitchen, Robyn said, "It felt so good to be desired, you know? He wasn't even attractive, but he made me feel so special, so wanted. I hadn't felt that in years."

"My point exactly."

Robyn returned to the living room with a tray bearing a coffee pot that was not unlike the ones they had at fine hotels. There were two mugs, cream, sugar, and a couple of cute little spoons. Harriet lifted the tiny creamer pitcher and peered underneath, looking for the Pampered Chef label, but didn't see it.

"I'm not following," Robyn said.

"Chris is supposed to be the one to make you feel attractive. He obviously wasn't doing that."

Robyn scoffed. "Not really. Actually, it's really confusing. It's like that woman in the group said. Sometimes he tells me I'm the most stunning woman in existence. Other times, he says I'm repulsive and I'm lucky he chooses to stay with me because no one else would ever find me attractive."

"That's mean of him to say. Les used to joke about my flaws, too, but he never got physical. That's never okay," Harriet said.

"I know, but it doesn't happen often. He says he'll do better, and even though I know it's wrong, I can't help but feel I deserve it after what I did to him." Robyn sighed and flopped back against the couch. "Besides, where would I go? What about Audrey?"

"First of all, nothing you could ever do makes it okay for him to raise a hand to you. Second, you could go to Harmony House."

Robyn shook her head. "Nope. I'm not ready for that. Audrey can't live there with me, and there's no way I'm leaving her with him."

"I'm pretty sure kids go there too," Harriet said.

Robyn shot her a mean side-eye. "Really? You want to bring a pre-teen to a place like that? When her friends want to hang out, she'll have to tell them she's at an abuse shelter." Robyn scoffed. "She'd rather die."

"She was the one to come to me. She seems pretty desperate for you to leave."

"Not that desperate, I assure you." Robyn set her cup back on the tray and stood. "Look, I appreciate your concern, but I have to handle this myself."

"But you aren't handling it."

"Leaving isn't the only way to handle it." Robyn was nearly shouting now. Harriet needed to get out of here and devise a different plan.

"All right. I'll go." Harriet stood and headed for the door. She stopped and turned back. "Before I forget. Can I get your phone number?"

"Glad you remembered. I've been meaning to get yours too."

Numbers exchanged, Harriet turned to leave once again.

"I'll pick you up on Monday at 5:30," Robyn said.

Harriet spun back around as fast as possible on crutches. "You want me to go to that meeting again?"

"I thought you wanted me to go."

"Yes. *You* to go. Not me. But if it isn't helping..." Harriet trailed off

Robyn sighed and shook her head. "I don't know what to do, Harriet. If only Audrey hadn't come to you. I can figure this out. You don't need to be involved."

"That ship has sailed. I promised Audrey I'd go with you, so I suppose I have to keep going. And I'll go if it'll get you moving toward leaving that jerk."

Robyn's voice was small when she spoke to Harriet's back. "I don't have anywhere to go. Or any money. I can't leave."

Turning around to face Robyn, Harriet said, "You can, and you will. We will find a way. You deserve better. Audrey deserves better."

There might be hope if the logistics of leaving were percolating in Robyn's mind. Harriet needed to devise a plan.

CHAPTER 19

AS AN ACCOUNTANT, Les had been fastidious about his investments and his end-of-life planning. Even before he'd gotten sick, he had a generous life insurance policy and a myriad of short- and long-term investments. He'd even set aside a separate, highly liquid fund, a "future-proofing" account he called it, specifically for large, unforeseen opportunities or family needs, an accountant's version of a rainy-day fund. Harriet had been pondering what to do with this money for quite some time. Thus far, she'd lived on the interest and could continue to do so, but now she had an idea that might both solve Robyn's problem and afford her some extra income in the long term.

Real estate prices in Bozeman had been steadily increasing with the influx of newcomers. Harriet knew she wouldn't be able to buy a condo or townhome for $100,000 like she might have been able to do a decade ago, but she hoped she could get something in the $300,000 range. She could swing that. She knew people who had multiple condos and did short-term rentals with them. They did well, even with mortgages. Bozeman had been cracking down on zoning for short-term rentals, however, so she'd need to do her research. The prospect excited her.

A quick search on Trulia yielded depressing results. Robyn would need at least two bedrooms for her and Audrey, and those rented better than one-bedroom apartments for the long term, anyway. Harriet often prided herself on her financial acumen, even if Les had made all the final decisions. This felt like a tangible, sensible move, a way to put Les's well-managed funds to work, rather than letting them sit idly, simply accumulating interest. Harriet knew a bit about how this worked, since she'd tried to convince Les to buy a short-term rental when he was still alive. He hadn't seen the appeal.

"Why would we want to deal with renters? Do you know the wear and tear renters inflict on a house? No way. I'm not dealing with other people's messes," Les had said.

So that was that. But now, not only would she have something to do and make a little extra income, but she could also solve Robyn's problem.

She hated realtors. They were like multilevel marketers on steroids. Couldn't trust them as far as you could throw them, but they were a necessary evil. Who was that one with all the plastic surgery? Harriet hated plastic surgery, but for a realtor, it seemed a signal of success. They were fake anyway, so if they had the money to advertise it on the outside, they must be doing well. Her name was old school. Something from Jane Austen. Something the opposite of what she looked like.

Harriet googled realtors in Bozeman, and a waxy portrait popped up on her computer. Emma Barlowe. Such an old-fashioned name for such a modern lady. Filling out a contact form required no human interaction, which Harriet loved. She wished she could complete the entire transaction that way.

Just a few minutes later, her phone rang. Caller ID said it was Emma Barlowe. Someone was hungry for business. Not a good sign. If she was such a hot realtor, why was she waiting by her computer for the next deal? Harriet would have to be cautious with this one. Real estate agents were already difficult to trust, so one who portrayed herself differently than reality was cause for concern. However, Harriet wanted someone responsive, and this was certainly responsive.

It wasn't Emma Barlowe. It was an assistant, which was more in keeping with the image she portrayed. A promising sign, but Harriet still wanted attention from the boss. Hopefully, that would come as they got closer to a deal.

"I will need to see the HOA covenants of each property," Harriet said.

"Of course, when we put the offer in, we request them. Before the property is conveyed to you, you must sign and agree to them."

"I will need to see them sooner."

"Oh. Okay. When would you like to see them?"

"Before I look at the property. I'm not interested in a property that doesn't have adequate HOA covenants," Harriet said.

"That's rather unconventional, and it could hinder the process because it is a seller's market right now, and it can take time to gather the covenants in advance. I wouldn't want you to lose out on a property while we were waiting for HOA covenants."

"I require them before looking, nonetheless. Will that be a problem?" Harriet asked.

"N-no. I will get them. When would you like to view properties?"

"I'm free today, but I can't drive."

"O-okay. So, you'll need to be picked up. And you need covenants in advance."

Harriet didn't think she needed to respond. Were those statements or questions?

"All right. Let me see what I can do. I'll get back to you shortly."

It wasn't exactly shortly, at least not in Harriet's view, but the assistant, whom Harriet believed was named Kelsie, had emailed her the HOA covenants for five properties just on the outskirts of Bozeman city proper since the town had recently cracked down on short-term rentals. Harriet ruled out two of them for lax covenants. One allowed chickens. Granted, they had rules limiting the number of chickens to four, and they did not allow roosters or noisy breeds, but still. Even the so-called quieter breeds accepted by this particular HOA clucked and crowed from time to time, didn't they? And they were messy and stinky and attracted raccoons, coyotes, and all sorts of predators. Chickens were nonstarters.

The other lax HOA didn't have any rules about decorations. Harriet could imagine the mess of holidays strewn about. There would be the pastels of Easter overlapping with the greens and reds of Christmas and the orange and black of Halloween. Harriet shuddered.

•   •   •   •   •

Two days later, Kelsie arrived in a spotless Subaru Outback. A perfect, practical choice for this area, but not exactly the flashy mode of transportation Harriet would expect from an up-and-coming realtor at the most prestigious agency in town. Maybe Emma was stingy with her employees. Harriet would have to mention it to her. If she ever actually got to meet her.

As they approached the first townhouse, Harriet smelled a skunk. "My goodness. That skunk is truly prolific."

Kelsie laughed. "That's not a skunk. That's marijuana. There are quite a few marijuana growers here in the warehouse section. Many of the growers live above their grow facilities. It's very convenient for them to monitor their crops."

"Well, it is not convenient for me," Harriet said, pulling her shirt up over her nose. "Turn this car around. This was not disclosed in the HOA documents I received."

"No, it wouldn't need to be disclosed. Marijuana is legal, and this district has different zoning than the community I was going to show you."

"I don't care. I will not be subjected to this stench any time I visit my property."

The next property did not have a distinguishable odor, and the houses were tidy, and the backyard was a decent size. Harriet didn't appreciate the lack of organization she found in the kitchen drawers, however. The spatulas were on the opposite side of the island from the cooktop. Kelsie reminded her that the owners would take their things with them and Harriet could organize her kitchen any way she pleased, but still. Harriet wondered what could be wrong with the place if the current owners were so lacking in common sense. Kelsie also mentioned that it wasn't polite to rifle through the current owner's drawers when viewing a house, but

Harriet knew there was much to learn about the state of a property by the organizational habits of its occupants.

However, the vibrator in the bedside table drawer of the third property was a bit of a deterrent. Harriet thought she caught Kelsie chuckling behind her hand, but she couldn't be sure. Harriet knew they were quite popular devices nowadays, but she hadn't expected one to be lying completely uncovered in a top drawer. Harriet hoped she wouldn't have to meet this woman in person. She was sure she wouldn't be able to hide the flush on her cheeks.

Other than the unfortunate find in the main bedroom drawer, the third property was well maintained and in a pleasant location, so Harriet asked Kelsie to put an offer in on it.

"Oh! Already? You don't need to see anything else?"

"No. This one will do nicely. I'm on a tight timeline because I need to get my neighbor to leave her husband."

Kelsie stared at her for a minute, then opened her mouth, but said nothing. Harriet let herself out of the front door and headed over to Kelsie's car.

Despite Harriet's insistence on urgency, especially since she was a cash buyer, the whole annoying process of closing on the townhome would take thirty days. She wanted to tell Robyn right away, but thought she should wait until after Monday's meeting. Hopefully, a light bulb would go on, and she'd be ready to leave, so telling her about the townhome would be the icing on the cake.

What to do about furniture? She'd need it for when the townhome became a vacation rental, but she didn't want to spend too much on it. And Bozeman was terrible for furniture shopping. Either cheap or exorbitant. Nothing in between.

Another quick Google search led her to hundreds of furniture options in all price points. Many offered free delivery and installation. Problem solved. A few swift clicks of her mouse and she'd ordered basic furniture for the entire townhome. Scheduling delivery for the day after closing, Harriet sat back in her chair with a satisfied sigh.

CHAPTER 20

PROMPT AS ALWAYS, Lucille arrived in her beat-up car right at 9:30 the next morning to take Harriet to what she hoped would be her last follow-up doctor's appointment. Lucille didn't exit the car to help Harriet like she usually did.

"What's the matter?" Harriet asked, tossing her crutches into the back seat.

"Nothing," Lucille said, not looking at her.

"Must be something."

"I'm not thrilled to be your chauffeur. Especially after the way you treated me last time."

"Oh? What did I do?"

"You insulted me and my car while I was doing you a favor," Lucille said.

"Those weren't insults. They were the truth."

"Seriously, Harriet. Sometimes your thoughts are best kept to yourself. You aren't the judge and jury of everything, you know."

"I didn't mean to insult you, and I apologize if I offended you," Harriet said.

Lucille turned to look at her.

"What?" Harriet asked.

"I hadn't expected an apology from you," Lucille said.

Harriet didn't reply. She thought Lucille was being sensitive, but she probably wouldn't appreciate that insight. Lucille turned up the radio, and they didn't speak for the duration of the ride.

"We're here," Lucille said, as they pulled up in front of her doctor's office. "Text me when you're ready to be picked up."

Other than her sad, shriveled calf muscle, things were healing nicely. She was finally rid of the dreaded boot. The doctor said she'd need a few months of physical therapy, or PT, which Les said stood for pain and torture, but she figured she could handle it if it meant she could drive and properly walk Bibbo again. The doctor wanted her to keep the crutches for another week and ease her way into putting all her weight on her weak ankle. It was progress, at least.

Lucille said she'd pick her up in about ten minutes, which meant she had a few minutes to peruse *People* magazine. Les had never allowed that trash in the house, so she loved the guilty pleasure the doctor's waiting room afforded her. Les had always called it a "waste of brain cells." She remembered him saying it with a dismissive flick of his wrist, his gaze already back on the Wall Street Journal. At the time, she'd nodded, agreeing that intellectual pursuits were much more her style. But now, she found herself perusing the headlines, amused by the absurdities, sometimes even feeling a pang of sympathy for the public figures whose lives were dissected on the glossy pages.

A faint knot of unease tightened in her stomach. She was enjoying the "trashy" magazine. What was wrong with that? It was okay to enjoy something purely for the fun of it, right? For so many years, Les made his opinions known, and she'd always seen eye-to-eye with him. Of course, it wasn't just magazines. Les had strong opinions on everything: the coffee she bought was too bitter, her music was for "teenyboppers," and the food she liked was for rabbits.

She'd always deferred to him, telling herself it was just easier, or that his taste was simply "better." He was an accountant, precise, logical, always knowing the best way. So, naturally, his preferences had often become her own, his dislikes inherently hers too. The thought that she might now choose a magazine, a song, a meal, without that familiar internal alignment, felt both exhilarating and terrifyingly foreign.

The glass door swung open, and Lucille appeared, pushing her sunglasses to the top of her head. "Still on the crutches?" Lucille asked, walking toward Harriet.

"Only for a week or so, to ease into putting all my weight on my foot again."

"That's great news."

Lucille helped Harriet into the car, and they rode in silence to Harriet's house. "Thanks for the ride. I think I'm sorry I won't be needing many more rides now that my boot is off. The doctor said I'd be able to drive in about a week, once I've regained some strength in my ankle. I've enjoyed your company, and I rarely enjoy people's company."

"I suppose I've enjoyed your company as well, Harriet." As Harriet exited the car, Lucille said, "You really ought to consider going back to the work you love. We need people at the library who are passionate about books. We're a dying breed."

"I don't think so. Les made sure I'd be comfortable and not need to work."

"It's not about needing to work. It's about wanting to work. Just think about it."

Harriet wanted to tell Lucille to mind her own business, but since she was so sensitive about what Harriet had said last time, she kept her thoughts to herself. She watched Lucille's beat-up car pull away, then hobbled inside. *Wanting to work?* The phrase snagged in her mind. Les had indeed made sure she'd be comfortable, and financially, she didn't need a job. But the days often felt like an expanse of perfectly clean, perfectly quiet hours, waiting to be filled. The meticulous polishing of every surface, the careful cataloging of her book collection, the precise planning of meals for one. These activities, once comforting in their predictability, just weren't enough.

She thought of Lucille, a woman who clearly didn't earn much, yet radiated a quiet contentment. Lucille genuinely loved books. Harriet loved books too, enough to organize them by the Dewey Decimal System in her own personal library. Was it really just about "needing" to work, as Les had framed it? Or was there something more, a satisfaction that came from applying oneself, from being part of something larger than her own meticulously curated solitude? Harriet pushed the thought away, telling herself it was simply Lucille's romanticized view of employment, not something that applied to her own life.

There must've been too many physical therapists in the world, or at least in Bozeman, because they'd scheduled Harriet for later that very same afternoon. Did it mean the physical therapist her doctor had recommended wasn't any good, so she didn't have any clients? Or maybe she was new? Or maybe she hurt people more than usual? Harriet's mind was spiraling, threatening to send her anxiety through the roof.

The worst part of the situation was that she still couldn't drive. Should she call Lucille again? Maybe she should see if Robyn was free. After all, she was doing Robyn quite a favor, accompanying her to her annoying meetings. Why hadn't she thought of Robyn before? Probably because she didn't want her to think she was a friend or something. But it was too late now. She was stuck with Robyn, so she might as well be useful.

Robyn answered after the first ring, sounding out of breath. "Hey, Harriet. Sorry, I'm panting. I'm on the treadmill."

"Interesting. I didn't figure you worked out." Harriet heard the hum of the treadmill and voices from the TV. "Robyn? Are you still there?"

Robyn exhaled sharply. "Yes, I'm here. Just not sure how to respond. I suppose I'll choose not to."

"Suit yourself. Anyway, I need a ride to PT this afternoon, and I was hoping you could help me out."

"I have a party tonight with a new host, so I have to be sure to be back in time to get ready. What time is your appointment?"

"Three. Those people are usually very prompt when ending the sessions. Working overtime is not their forte. Not that I mind. I don't need any extra pain and torture. Get it? PT? Pain and torture? Les loved that saying."

"He's not wrong. PT is tough, but necessary. Okay, three o'clock will work."

"Great. Thanks."

Now. What to do until her appointment? She called Lucille. Thankfully, Lucille answered, so she didn't have to chat with anyone else.

"Could I ask for a favor? I was hoping you might bring me some books," Harriet said.

"Now, that is a task I'm happy to help with. Are you feeling more in the mood for some Jane Austen or E. L. James?"

"Goodness! Do you have to bring that up? I didn't even know what it was. I heard someone on TV mention the Fifty Shades trilogy and thought it was real literature. I was sorely mistaken. I never even finished the first one," Harriet said, exhaling with a huff.

"I'm sorry. Lots of people love those books. Nothing wrong with that. So, what are you feeling like?"

"Oh, I don't know. Women's fiction, mystery, psychological thrillers. Surprise me with a mix."

"That I can do. I'll drop them by after work today."

"Can't you do it sooner?" Harriet asked.

Silence.

"Hello? Did you hang up already?" Harriet asked.

"Gosh, Harriet, you really are something."

"Okay. So, can you bring them soon?"

"I'll see what I can do. You're lucky Richard seems to like you," Lucille said.

"Yeah, he's a good guy. So glad he's not still married to that bimbo with the bleach blonde hair."

Lucille snorted.

"Are you sick?"

"Why do you ask?"

"That noise you made," Harriet said.

"I was shocked by the way you described Richard's ex-wife. Did you know her?"

"No, but I saw a picture once."

"Well, they got divorced a few years back when she cheated on him with one of his friends. He was a mess for a while. He's okay now, thankfully," Lucille said.

"He deserves better. Like I said, he's a good guy. So, I guess I'll see you soon with those books," Harriet said before hanging up the phone.

For once, Harriet was glad to hear the knock at the door. Bibbo didn't share her enthusiasm, so he yipped and barked like he was ready to tear the intruder limb from limb. He didn't know he was only twelve pounds. Harriet admired that about him.

"Hello, Harriet. I came as soon as I could. It wasn't hard to find books I think you'll like. Can I come in?" Lucille asked. Harriet moved aside, and Lucille carried the books over to the coffee table. "I chose a Kristin Hannah because I've seen you check out historical fiction, and a Jodi Picoult because most people like her books, the Matthew Perry biography, in case that's your thing, and have you read anything by Katherine Reay? She has a house near here, and she writes about Jane Austen differently. I think you'll like her work."

"Richard mentioned Reay the other day. I'm excited about that one. I'm not sure about Jodi Picoult or Matthew Perry. I used to like Picoult, but her recent stuff pisses me off. And I couldn't care less about pop culture."

Lucille stared at her hands as she said, "Sorry. I wanted to give you a variety."

Remembering how she'd upset Lucille, Harriet's face flushed. This woman was so sensitive. "I'm sorry, Lucille. I appreciate the effort. Thank you."

Lucille looked up and beamed at Harriet. Geez, not that big of a deal, but from the look on her face, you'd have thought Harriet gave her two round-trip tickets to Australia.

"Okay, well, I guess I'll leave you to it," Lucille said, backing toward the front door. She reached down to pet Bibbo, whose tail wagged like a wind-up toy that had been wound too tight.

"He really seems to like you. Dogs are good judges of character. Better than humans."

Lucille nodded. "I couldn't agree more."

"Want a cup of coffee? Or tea?" Harriet wasn't sure why those words escaped her lips, but they had, and she found herself hopeful that Lucille might say yes.

"Oh, thank you for the offer. That's very kind of you, but I have to get back to work." Lucille walked to the door and put her hand on the doorknob.

"Of course. That was silly of me," Harriet said, waving her hand dismissively. Her cheeks flushed, and her heart pounded—such a trivial thing to get all worked up over.

The door shut behind Lucille, and the house was quiet once again. What was wrong with her? Harriet had always looked forward to the quiet of her house after Les left for work. She delighted in her routine and her solitude. It must've been because she knew Les would come home. The loneliness wasn't so lonely when the promise of a partner was there. She felt a sense of belonging even when alone that was gone without Les. Since he'd passed, the lonely feeling kept increasing, and she didn't like how vulnerable it made her feel.

The worst was that she suddenly couldn't sleep at night, either. She fell asleep without a problem but woke somewhere around 3 a.m. with the weight of the world on her shoulders. It was then that every little thing that seemed insignificant during the day threatened to crush her chest with its weight. A dish forgotten in the sink, a missed pill for Bibbo, an appointment for an oil change, something she wished she'd said to Les, or her parents, or her brother. It was then that she scolded herself and vowed to call her brother because he was the only one for whom it wasn't too late.

The sun would rise, and the weight would lift, and she'd put the dish in the dishwasher, Bibbo would get his pill, she'd make an appointment for her car, but she still hadn't called her brother. She really couldn't put her finger on what was stopping her.

Most likely, it was because Hank had been critical of Les, and Harriet tired of sticking up for him. Even though Hank wanted the best for her, he didn't know what that was. He thought he did, and he had when they were younger, but not as they got older. Les had a much better understanding of what she wanted from her adult life.

Harriet thought back to her courtship with Les. They'd met in English class during Harriet's sophomore year. Harriet was so lonely without her brother. They'd always been close, but after they lost their parents, he'd become her confidant and best friend. They'd stayed with their father's parents until they went off to college. But Harriet and Hank were shells of their former selves. Their grandparents tried, but they still felt like boarders whose hosts took pity on them. They retreated to Harriet's room and played cards on the evenings Hank wasn't playing basketball with his friends. He was popular. She was an outcast, but at home, they were best friends. When he left for college on the East Coast, Harriet felt unmoored. She'd always struggled socially, but it was bearable when Hank lived nearby. When he was accepted to his dream school in New York, she never let him know how devastated she was.

Les had come up behind her as they were leaving the lecture hall that day in her sophomore year at Montana State, startling her when he spoke. "Hey there. I liked your analysis of the eye in 'The Tell-Tale Heart.'"

Harriet turned to see a tall man, his hair impeccably parted and smoothed to the side, wearing an old-fashioned button-up shirt and khakis. He looked as out of place as Harriet felt.

"Thanks," Harriet said.

"I noticed you on the first day of class. I like how you color-coordinate your notes. What do the different colors mean?"

Harriet's cheeks burned. She hadn't thought anyone would notice her note-taking techniques. Her brother had teased her about it, but it made sense to her, and it made the lecture less boring.

"Oh, it's silly, really. Just a way to pass the time," Harriet said.

"I don't believe that. I think you've got a method there," Les said.

"I suppose I do, but it's not worth mentioning."

"I'd like to hear about it. I need help to stay awake in that class. English isn't my thing," Les said.

"What is your thing?"

"Accounting. I like things to be black and white, neat and tidy, right and wrong. None of this abstract theme and metaphor stuff."

Harriet chuckled. "I agree with you there. I'm doing well in this class, but most of the time I think I'm making things up. I like order and reason."

"Sounds like we have quite a bit in common. Are you busy, or do you have time for a coffee before your next class?"

Harriet hesitated. She'd planned to study before her library science class that afternoon. He seemed nice, though. And she could use a friend.

"All right. I can spare a few minutes, I suppose."

That was how it started. They'd been inseparable from that moment on. Les showered her with small tokens of his affection: a teddy bear with an MSU T-shirt, tickets to a theater production of *Little Shop of Horrors*, and a dress he saw downtown that he thought she'd look nice in. Their meetings shifted from a coffee shop to the library to common rooms to one or the other's dorm room when their roommates were out. Quickly, Harriet couldn't imagine her life without Les.

After a wonderful dinner off campus, Les told her he planned to marry her. It startled her since they'd only been dating a few months, and they were still so young. But her heart quickened its pace. She'd never had a boyfriend before, and thoughts of becoming a spinster with a house full of cats had entered her mind. It was flattering to be wanted and for a man to be so sure about her. Les was a senior, which meant he was a bit more mature than she was, so maybe that was why he was positive she was the one for him.

Hank hadn't been thrilled when she'd told him. "But Harriet, it's only been a couple of months. How can he possibly want to marry you? It takes time to get to know someone."

"We know each other, Hank. We've spent nearly every minute together since we met. The only time we're apart is when we're sleeping. And we never argue. We agree on everything. He's my soulmate."

"Ugh. I hate that word. And not fighting *is* a red flag. You can't possibly agree on everything. I don't like this, Harriet. I wish I was there to meet him."

Harriet wanted that more than anything, and her throat had constricted at the thought. She swallowed hard so Hank wouldn't know she was close to tears. "I wish that, too, Hank, but you're busy and you've got a life out there. Don't worry about me."

"I can't help it. You're my sister. And your heart is too big for this world."

Harriet took a long, deep breath and bit her lip. "That's not true. You think my heart is so big because I've given it all to you. It's time I shared it."

He sighed. "I suppose you're right, but there's no need to rush."

Harriet had heeded his words, more out of necessity than caution. Les graduated that spring and wanted to get married right away, but they didn't have the money for a proper wedding, and Harriet preferred to graduate first. They saved, Harriet graduated, and they were married just weeks later, and they'd been married for nearly thirty years.

Harriet knew she'd been lucky to find the right one so quickly. She felt bad for these women who'd been love torpedoed or whatever it was called. She and Les had defied the odds. They'd still be happily married if ALS hadn't swooped in and taken him much too early. It really wasn't fair. Despite Hank's hatred of the word, Les was her soulmate. She'd never find another one. Whenever she felt sad about losing him, however, she reminded herself that she'd had what so many spent their whole lives searching for. So, even if it had been cut short, she'd known true love, which was more than many would ever experience.

Still, did that mean Harriet would never talk to Hank again? Even now that Les was gone? She shook her head, picked up the phone, saw his tiny face smiling next to his name in her contacts. It would be so easy to push the button. But then what? Would he be angry? Maybe he had a bunch of kids and a high-powered job, and he'd be too busy to talk to her. Maybe he didn't want to talk to her. Setting her phone back on the kitchen table, she sighed. Maybe tomorrow.

CHAPTER 21

THE WAITING ROOM at the physical therapist's office was empty except for a young couple sitting on the couch. Harriet didn't know couples did physical therapy together. Maybe one was just there to support the other? She scoffed, imagining asking Les to come and sit and watch her do physical therapy. He'd rather watch paint dry.

Harriet, tucked into a corner chair, pretended to read a magazine while she eavesdropped on the couple's conversation. The woman, with a messy mop of blonde curls, was gesturing emphatically.

"I just don't understand why you packed the hiking boots and not my sneakers! You knew we had to come here before we headed out of town."

The man, a burly figure with kind eyes, winced. "My bad, honey. Completely spaced it." He reached over and squeezed her arm. "Look, my fault. Want me to run home and grab them? It'll only take twenty minutes."

The woman let out an exasperated sigh, yet a smile fought its way to her lips. "No, it's fine. I shouldn't expect you to remember my schedule and everything I need. Besides, Jodi can probably tailor my exercises to be more hiking-focused." She nudged his chest playfully. "But seriously, remind me to always make a packing list. My brain is just as scattered as your packing skills."

He chuckled, drawing her closer. "Deal."

Harriet watched, a strange tightness in her chest. *He'd offered to go back.* The very idea felt alien to Harriet, an indulgence Les would have swiftly dismissed as illogical. Les would never have offered to drive back home for a forgotten item. That kind of spontaneous accommodation simply wasn't part of their marital ledger. It was inefficient, a complete waste of precious time. Yet, this man had offered without hesitation, without a lecture.

And they had argued. Not loudly, not cruelly, but openly. Harriet and Les never argued. Not since those early days, before he made it clear that confrontation was "unproductive" and "unnecessary." Harriet would state her point, Les would state his, and then, invariably, Les's point became the conclusion. It was efficient. It was peaceful. But watching this couple—so openly annoyed, so quick to forgive, so willing to compromise or even inconvenience themselves for each other—Harriet felt suddenly off balance. The couple's messy give-and-take, a chaos she and Les had avoided at all costs, contained an unfamiliar energy, one that quietly clashed with the pristine, unwavering quiet of her own marriage.

The peculiar sensation lingered, a faint unease lurking beneath her perfect memories. Her mind was increasingly swirling with conflicting thoughts and emotions, which seemed to enhance the pervasive loneliness that had settled since Les's death. Her grief over losing Les had just begun to loosen its grip, and she'd thought she might be able to move on, alone, with her rules and memories of their perfect life intact.

But the loneliness was proving far more unsettling than the grief that had consumed her immediately after Les passed. It was as though grief had been an unwanted guest that somehow kept the loneliness at bay. Odd to think one might miss grief, but it was a tangible thing to point to as the reason for her sorrow. It was heavy, yes, a suffocating blanket, but it was discernible. She could acknowledge it, curse its presence, and recognize it as the source of her sorrow. Grief was a monument to Les, a constant reminder of what she had lost, and therefore, of what she *had* had. It was a physical ache, a well-defined pain she could understand. She missed Les, the physical presence, the routine, the shared history, and grief was the natural, if unwelcome, manifestation of that loss.

But as grief slowly receded, a new, far more unsettling void had emerged. This loneliness wasn't about missing Les's physical presence as much as it was about the chilling absence of a purpose his presence had once provided. It was a hollow echo in rooms that suddenly felt too large, in days that stretched out endlessly without a schedule dictated by his needs or preferences. It was a profound, existential emptiness that whispered, "Who are you without him?"

She had lived her entire adult life orbiting Les, defining herself through their shared existence. His opinions had shaped hers, his desires had become her goals, and his careful financial planning had become her security. He had filled every corner of her life, and in doing so, had inadvertently masked a more profound solitude within her she'd never known existed.

Harriet shook herself to dislodge these desperate feelings. She needed to keep busy, to keep these nagging, depressing thoughts at bay. Maybe that was why she was actually looking forward to Monday's meeting with Robyn. Plus, she couldn't wait to tell Robyn about the townhome.

•   •   •   •   •

On Monday evening, as she and Robyn entered the basement room where Callie held the meeting, Harriet spied the same people as last time sitting in the same seats. Why did people do that? Like they were all in second grade and had to sit in assigned seats. Maybe it was a comfort thing, that somehow a bit of routine cut down the anxiety of the unknown.

"Hello again, everyone," Callie said. "Good to see you all. Harriet, Robyn, glad you two made it back this week. It's usually a good sign when people come to consecutive meetings."

"I'm the support team, remember?"

"Yes, Harriet. I remember. It's good of you to be so supportive." Callie walked over to the whiteboard. "Does anyone have anything to share before I begin?"

The red-haired one raised her hand. "I texted Jack." She looked down and sniffed.

"Oh?" Callie asked, eyebrows raised.

"I know. I shouldn't have. I-I was feeling lonely, and I'd had a few drinks. It's no excuse, but he didn't respond anyway, so it doesn't matter."

Her friend put her arm around her shoulder as she wiped a tear from her cheek. "Thank goodness he didn't respond. I think you should delete his contact from your phone and call me next time instead."

"Yes, that's excellent advice, Morgan. It's common to go back, even when we know they are bad for us. We remember the good times and convince ourselves this time will be different. But it won't. You're much better off texting a friend."

Harriet raised her hand. Since it felt like school, it seemed the right thing to do.

"Yes?"

"Can't these guys ever change? It seems harsh to say it won't ever be different. Especially for the ones who you say are abusive, even if they aren't physically violent." Harriet said.

"I'm glad you asked that," Callie said. "I have a quote I printed off from TheHotline.org right here in my paperwork." She shuffled through a stack of papers on the table. "Aha. Here it is. 'In discussing why abusers abuse, it's clear that a lot of the causal factors behind these behaviors are *learned* attitudes and feelings of entitlement and privilege, which can be extremely difficult to truly change. Because of this, there's a *very* low percentage of abusers who truly do change their ways.'" Callie looked up from reading. "I believe I read somewhere that only around two percent of abusers change, but don't quote me on that. For change to happen, abusers have to admit they are wrong and take steps to change. We can't ever make someone else change. And admitting they're wrong is not an abuser's forte."

Callie walked back over to the whiteboard and drew another piece of the pie. She wrote "discarding" inside the triangle.

"Who can tell me what discarding looks like?"

Everyone's hands went up except Robyn's and Harriet's.

"Stephanie, go ahead."

"It's when they make you feel like crap, like you can't possibly live without them, like every problem in the relationship is all your fault, like they are going to leave you, and no one will ever love you again."

Callie nodded. "Exactly."

The room was silent while everyone let out a collective sigh. Even Harriet. It was infectious.

To Harriet's surprise, Robyn started speaking. "Maybe that's what happened last night. Chris came home after grabbing a few beers with his buddies and got angry that I'd cleaned the kitchen and not left him a plate. He got in my face and poked my chest with his finger. Hard. I fell back against the wall. Then he said I never thought about anyone but myself."

"What the hell are you still doing with that man?" Harriet glared at Robyn.

"Harriet, please. Let her continue," Callie said.

"I ran upstairs, knowing Audrey would be upset. I went to find her, to comfort her. She was hiding in the closet. He found us and apologized. He cried and said he was no good for us, and said he was no good for anyone. He grabbed his keys and started for the front door. I grabbed his arm and begged him to stay. I was afraid he might hurt himself. Audrey is the one who told me to let him go."

Harriet opened her mouth, but before she could give Robyn a piece of her mind, Callie said, "Please, Harriet. Keep your thoughts to yourself for the moment."

Turning to Robyn, Callie continued. "I assume Audrey is your daughter?"

Robyn nodded.

"What would you tell your daughter if she were you?"

Robyn's eyes widened. She opened her mouth. Shut it. Stood and grabbed a tissue from the box in the middle of the table and dabbed at her eyes. "I'd tell her to get away from him."

"What is Audrey learning from you?" Callie asked.

Robyn dissolved into hysterical sobs. She put her head on her arms as her shoulders shook. Harriet put her hand on Robyn's back. This Callie was better than Harriet had given her credit for. Questions worked better than telling her what to do, it seemed.

"You're teaching her it's okay to be treated that way," Callie said.

Robyn looked up. "I make excuses for him. I say he doesn't mean it, that he's sorry, that he loves us."

Callie nodded. "Is that what you want for her?"

Robyn shook her head.

"I hope you don't think I'm being mean," Callie said, "but sometimes when we look at things through the eyes of our children, our treatment becomes clearer. We accept things for ourselves that we would never want for our children. We stay in relationships for our children, but we are teaching them to accept that type of behavior.

"So, when your husband said he was leaving, that was discarding. He was saying he was no good, but he was making you feel guilty about his feeling badly about himself. He was attempting to manipulate you by saying he wasn't any good for anyone. Threatening suicide is often a last-ditch attempt to regain control over a partner when they aren't responding the way abusers want them to. Was anything different about your behavior during your fight last night, Robyn?"

Robyn nodded again. "I didn't apologize like I usually do. I said nothing. I didn't really react at all."

"I figured it was something like that," Callie said. "When abusers don't get the reaction they seek, it enrages them further. They then try different manipulation tactics."

"But what if he really killed himself? I could never live with that." Robyn put her face in her hands and shook her head.

"It rarely happens. Like I said, it's a way to make you feel guilty and come back to them, and to instill that fear in you. It can be a dangerous time, however. When they threaten suicide, it can mean suicide, homicide, or both," Callie said, putting her hand on Robyn's shoulder. "But you can't allow him to control your life. Like we talked about earlier, is this the life you'd want for your daughter? You have to be careful if you leave. File a restraining order, although they aren't often helpful, but at least your situation is on the police's radar. And don't let him know where you and your daughter are."

"Oh, I don't think I can do this," Robyn said. "It's terrifying. If anything happened to my daughter, I couldn't forgive myself. Or even if something happened to him. You know, he's not all bad. We've been together for sixteen years. We've had some great memories."

Callie went to the front of the room and turned to face Robyn. "Of course you have. If they were all bad, we'd have left right away. But that's why it's important to learn about this cycle of abuse. It keeps happening, over and over again. It's no way to live, in fear of the next episode, because we all know there will be another episode, no matter how great it seems at the moment. How many of you have been having a wonderful time with your partner, going out to dinner, on a trip, or even a quiet night at home, but you can't fully relax and enjoy the moment because you know it won't last? You wonder what you will do that might set him off. The anxiety in the good moments can be worse than the bad. In the bad moments, at least you know where you stand."

Everyone nodded in silence. Robyn's confession hung heavy in the air, a raw wound exposed for all to see. Harriet's heart quickened its pace, and she rubbed her palms against her thighs to dry them. But didn't these things happen in all relationships? People did things that pissed off their partners all the time, so it was only a matter of time before another fight happened, right? Didn't everyone deal with that?

As Callie continued to speak about the cycle, about the subtle manipulations, the feeling of walking on eggshells even in "good" moments, the constant anxiety of the next episode, Harriet noticed a peculiar tightness blooming just beneath her sternum. It wasn't pain, not exactly, more like a tiny, coiled spring suddenly tense. She cleared her throat, a little too loudly. The room felt stuffy. She shifted, tugging at the collar of her blouse, wondering if the air conditioning was working properly in this old building. It must be her age, she thought, that darned menopause wreaking havoc again. She focused intently on Callie, nodding along to her general points, determined to dismiss the inexplicable flicker of unease.

Callie walked over and put her hand on Robyn's shoulder. "Robyn, know that if you decide to leave, we're here for you. Harmony House has resources to help protect you and get you on your feet."

Harriet blurted out, "And I have a townhome for you. I haven't closed on it yet, but I will in a couple of weeks. I asked for a fast close, hoping you'd be ready for it soon."

All eyes stared at Harriet. Her cheeks burned. "What? Why are you staring at me like that?"

Callie cleared her throat. "Harriet, you bought a townhome for Robyn?"

Harriet nodded. "I knew she needed a place to stay, and she wanted to stay in the school district for Audrey. I have some money my husband had squirrelled away that I was wondering what to do with, so it was the logical conclusion."

"Wow, my parents didn't even do that for me when I left my husband. I mean, they probably would have if they could've afforded it, but still. That's amazing, Harriet," Stephanie said.

"It wasn't completely altruistic, you know. It's an investment. If and when Robyn moves out of the townhome, I will rent it as a source of income, and it will appreciate. Hopefully, once Robyn gets on her feet, she'll be able to contribute as well."

"That's incredible of you, Harriet, but that's a lot of pressure on me," Robyn said.

"I'm being practical. Just solving a problem. Audrey came to me and asked for my help, so that's what I'm doing," Harriet said.

Robyn sighed. "Thank you, Harriet. I don't know how I can ever repay you, but I appreciate it."

"So, you'll leave that asshole, then?" Harriet asked. Everyone chuckled, even Callie.

Robyn's mouth gaped open as she stared at Harriet.

Callie said, "Harriet, give Robyn a minute. This is a lot to take in."

Harriet was dumbfounded. She'd bought the townhome and solved the problem. Why weren't they all telling Robyn to take the townhome and get away from Chris? Harriet stood to leave. She'd had enough of this nonsense.

CHAPTER 22

Harriet heard Callie tell the group to wait a moment before following Harriet into the hall. "Please, Harriet. Come back inside. I realize how frustrated you must be since you did something so incredible for your friend, and she didn't immediately accept it. You have to be patient. Give her time to let the idea fully sink in," Callie said. "Don't ruin a good thing by turning your back on her now. Come back inside and continue to support her. Support doesn't mean forcing someone to do something. It means meeting them where they are and being there for them no matter what."

Harriet shook her head but obeyed Callie's request and went back into the room.

"I'm glad you came back," Robyn said.

Harriet nodded and slid back into her chair.

"And...I don't mean to intrude on your life, or seem at all ungrateful, but the little you've told me about Les..." Robyn trailed off and looked at her hands.

"What do you mean by that?" Harriet asked, glaring at Robyn.

"I don't know. It seems like he had a lot of rules for you."

"He did. We did. I still do. There's nothing wrong with that. He was old-fashioned and Catholic. Our vows included obeying. It's not a crime. And we aren't here for me."

"You're right," Robyn said. "Forget I said anything."

Harriet turned away from Robyn, folded her arms across her chest, and leaned back.

"Just a few more minutes, Harriet. We're nearly finished." Callie returned to her pie chart and said, "So, the last piece of the pie is something we were talking about. It's called hoovering."

"Like the vacuum?" Harriet asked.

Callie pointed at Harriet. "Exactly. It's named after the vacuum. Because this is the phase when they suck you right back in."

One of the young ones nodded. "Yep. Dave starts love bombing again. Gifts, expensive dinners, trips, you name it. It worked so many times."

"You're lucky," the red-haired lady said. "I got guilt trips. He'd tell me that if I loved him, I wouldn't leave, or that I was cruel because he was going through a tough time, or he'd even threaten suicide. I didn't think I could live with that, so I'd take him back. I'd much rather have gifts and trips. But then maybe I wouldn't have left, so it's for the best."

Callie nodded, taking in everyone's words. "Yes, hoovering can take different forms, but the underlying intention is the same: to draw you back into the cycle of abuse. It's important to recognize these patterns and to understand that they are not acts of love, but manipulation tactics."

As the meeting drew to a close, Callie offered some final words of encouragement and support. "Remember, you are not alone in this. Harmony House is here for you, and we will continue to support each other through the challenges ahead."

Everyone stood to leave except Robyn. "Are you coming?" Harriet asked.

"I suppose I have to leave. For Audrey," Robyn said.

Callie came over to Robyn and wrapped her arm around her. "It might be for Audrey now, but hopefully it will be for you at some point."

"We're proud of you, Robyn," the red-haired one said.

Robyn stood up, her resolve clear in the determined set of her jaw. "Thank you, Callie. And thank you, everyone, for your support."

As they made their way out of the meeting room, Robyn turned to Harriet with a grateful smile. "Thanks for sticking around, Harriet. And for the townhome. Well, for everything. I honestly have no idea how to thank you."

Harriet offered a tight-lipped smile in return, unsure of how to respond. "Well, you know. Audrey asked for my help, so I'm helping." Harriet turned away from Robyn and hurried to the car as fast as her crutches would carry her. She didn't like the lump forming in her throat and certainly didn't want Robyn to notice.

Later that evening, as she stared blankly at the TV, her mind wandered to one of her most memorable dates with Les. The sun had dappled through the leaves of an ancient oak tree, casting a warm glow on the picnic blanket spread beneath its branches. Harriet leaned against Les's shoulder, her hand resting comfortably in his.

She'd baked a fresh apple pie, her third in her recent attempts to make a good one since he said they were his favorite. The smell of cinnamon and apples mixed with the fresh spring air, and she thought that life surely didn't get any better than this. Sitting with the man she loved in the shade of a tree on a beautiful spring day was pure magic.

She turned to look at him, his profile outlined against the vibrant blue sky. His strong jaw, his gentle eyes, the way his hair fell effortlessly across his forehead—in that moment, she felt an overwhelming sense of love and gratitude. This was her happily ever after, her own true love story.

"I love you, Les," she whispered, her voice filled with a tender sincerity.

Les turned to face her, his eyes sparkling with adoration. "I love you too, Harriet. More than words can say."

He leaned in and kissed her, their lips meeting in a gentle, lingering kiss that spoke volumes of their love and devotion. In that moment, under the shade of the ancient oak tree, Harriet remembered feeling a sense of completeness, a feeling that she had finally found her place in the world, nestled safely in the arms of the man she loved.

Then, without warning, as though she was watching a movie that flipped rapidly from one scene to the next, her mind flew to another time when she was lying in Les's arms.

"Les," she'd said. "It's been two years. We want a family so badly. I think we need to see a doctor about infertility treatment."

He shoved her off his arm and leaped to his feet, anger flashing in his eyes.

"I've explained to you many times that I am not about to play God. I thought we were on the same page with this, yet you insist on bringing it up time and time again. Are you trying to make me feel guilty? Do you want me to be the bad guy here?"

Harriet had stared at him. Even though they'd been married for over two years, she still couldn't predict his outbursts. They seemed to come from nowhere.

"I-I'm sorry, Les. I didn't mean to upset you."

He scoffed. "Really? You had to know how this whole topic upsets me. You think I like that you aren't pregnant yet? Do you think it makes me feel like a man? But there is no way we're going to the doctor so he can tell us all the things that are wrong with us and poke and prod. No way. If God has decided we aren't going to have children, so be it."

"But, Les," Harriet said, her voice soft and kind. "So many people need help conceiving. Good Christian people, like us."

He smacked the bed with his hand. "Damn it, Harriet! They aren't good Christian people if they're interfering with God's wishes. How can you not see that? This conversation is over, and you are never to bring it up again. Understand?"

The sudden memory of Les's fury, the sting of being shoved off his arm, left a raw, exposed feeling in its wake. She'd dismissed it then, smoothed it over with explanations of his deep faith and her own overzealousness. But now, the sharp image of his contorted face, the booming command, "Understand?" resonated with the persistent, low hum of anxiety that had begun to bubble up within her.

Harriet pinched the bridge of her nose tightly, a small, sharp pain that momentarily displaced the unwelcome thoughts. There was a reason she'd neatly tucked away those memories. That was where they should stay. Why focus on things that couldn't be changed? She shook her head to clear the memory and started getting ready for bed.

CHAPTER 23

THE DAY OF THE CLOSING on the townhome dawned bright and clear, the sky painted with hues of pink and gold as the sun peeked over the horizon. For Harriet, however, the morning brought with it a sense of unease, as she'd remembered another of Les's outbursts during the night. She didn't like how these memories she'd deliberately buried were forcing themselves to the surface. Well, since Robyn would be moving into the townhome, hopefully that meant Harriet wouldn't have to attend any more meetings with her. So, these unwanted memories would go back to being buried where they belonged.

Though Harriet was cleared to drive, Robyn had offered to take Harriet to the title company for the closing. "Are you ready for this, Robyn?" Harriet asked as she climbed into the car.

Robyn wrung her hands and slowly nodded. "I'm excited to have my own place. But I'd be lying if I said I wasn't nervous."

Taking her seat at the table, Harriet watched as the real estate agent reviewed the documents spread out before them. Each signature was a step closer to Robyn getting away from that jerk and toward a new life for Audrey.

"I can't thank you enough, Harriet," Robyn said.

"I hope it's enough," Harriet said.

Robyn tilted her head in confusion. "There isn't much more you could do."

"I don't mean that. Did you get the restraining order?"

Robyn shook her head. "I'm afraid it might make him even madder. I'm trying not to upset him."

"I think he's going to be furious no matter what. You need to do everything you can to protect yourself and Audrey."

Robyn sighed. "I suppose you're right. So far, he's been understanding, but it seems he thinks this is temporary. He's on his best behavior."

"Don't be lulled into that again," Harriet said, rolling her eyes.

"I know, I know. I'll be strong."

Exiting the building, Harriet inhaled the fresh spring air. "So, we'd better hurry home so you can pack. The furniture is being delivered between nine and noon tomorrow, so you can start moving in right away."

"Right away?" Robyn asked, opening the car door.

"Of course," Harriet said, settling into the passenger seat and pulling the key to the townhome from her purse. "Here's the key. Let's get moving."

"I-I'm not sure I'm quite ready," Robyn said. "I thought I'd have a week or so to pack and let the idea settle with Chris."

"I think that's what you need to avoid. You don't want any settling to happen under your feet or in Chris's mind. Act with stealth."

As Robyn turned into their neighborhood, the car came to a stop behind a row of other cars. "What's the holdup?" Harriet asked.

Robyn craned her neck to see around the cars in front of her. "It looks like some kids set up a lemonade stand." Reaching into the back seat for her purse, Robyn pulled out her wallet.

"You aren't going to encourage them, are you?" Harriet asked.

"What do you mean?"

"They're clogging up the neighborhood selling that rotten stuff. Look at this. No one can even get to their houses."

Robyn's lips curled into a slight smirk, and a soft chuckle escaped her. It started as a gentle rumble, barely audible, but soon her laughter bubbled up uncontrollably. Her shoulders shook, and tears welled up in her eyes as she laughed out loud.

Harriet asked, "What's so funny?"

Robyn could barely speak as she laughed. "Oh, Harriet. What will we do with you?"

"Explain what's so funny, that's what."

"Only you would find fault with some adorable kids trying to make a little money."

Harriet opened her mouth, an angry retort about to spill from her, but she stopped. "So, it doesn't bother you that they're clogging up the road? Causing traffic to slow and making people feel guilty if they don't buy some of that foul-tasting stuff? What if you had cookies in the oven? Or you were going to be late for an appointment? Or..."

Robyn put her hand on Harriet's arm. "Harriet. A few minutes won't make or break anything. It brings joy to the children and teaches them about entrepreneurship. Most people smile to see them out trying to earn a little money."

They pulled up to the stand, and a towheaded boy of about seven asked if they'd like some lemonade, his bright blue eyes wide with hope. "We'll take two cups, please," Robyn said, handing him a five-dollar bill. Another girl with equally blonde hair hurried to pour the lemonade as the boy opened the metal box to make change. "Keep the change."

"Really?" The boy and girl both turned to look at each other, wide grins stretched across their faces. The boy was missing his two front teeth, and the gap-toothed smile made Harriet chuckle.

"See, Harriet? It's sweet. Let yourself enjoy these little moments instead of getting all worked up about everything. Ultimately, our lives are comprised of little moments like this. You don't want to miss them."

"I suppose you have a point," Harriet said. As they drove away, Harriet turned to Robyn and held out her cup. "Do you want mine?"

"Why? You don't want yours?"

"No way. I hate lemonade."

Robyn chuckled. "No one hates lemonade, Harriet."

"I do."

"When was the last time you tried it?"

"Who knows? But every time I tried, I felt like I was being personally attacked by citrus."

"I think you should try it again sometime," Robyn said.

Harriet ignored her. Enough about lemonade. What was the big deal? It was a stupid drink. Why did people take it personally that she didn't enjoy the taste of lemonade? It wasn't a personality flaw, just a personal preference. People didn't get all bent out of shape if you said you didn't like anchovies or brussels sprouts.

Pulling up in front of Harriet's house, Robyn said, "Well, I guess we need to pack." Robyn's exaggerated exhale made Harriet think maybe she wasn't looking forward to what was next.

"I can help you move. I'm much more mobile now. When should I come over? Saturday? That'll give you a couple of days to pack up, and Audrey will be around to help."

"U-um," Robyn said, clearing her throat. "We're going to need more time than that. I've barely started packing."

"I think time is of the essence here," Harriet said.

Robyn nodded. "Okay. I'll make Saturday work."

"Perfect. I'll be over bright and early Saturday," Harriet said as she opened the passenger door. She wouldn't allow any excuses. This had to happen.

That night, as she was eating her delivery from Thai Basil, Harriet chuckled at the memory of the time she tried to make pad thai noodles from scratch for Les.

"What the hell is this on my plate?" Les had said. "It looks like something Bibbo might have vomited."

"I'm trying something new. Don't you want something other than meat and potatoes from time to time?"

"No."

"Well, I'm bored with cooking the same things week after week."

"People get bored with their jobs all the time, but it is what it is. Cooking for our family is your job. I go out and earn the money, and I come home to a meal I enjoy. That's the deal."

Harriet sighed and sat at her place at the table. She hoped he'd like the pad thai, so he'd allow her to try new things in the kitchen more often. She held her breath as he took a bite.

Spitting the mouthful into a napkin, he'd stood and taken his plate to the trash. "God, woman. Are you trying to kill me? If so, I can think of kinder ways to do it."

"It can't be that bad," Harriet said, taking a bite.

It was. It was fishy and salty and mushy and absolutely disgusting. Running to the kitchen, she spat her mouthful into the sink. She wouldn't face Les for fear of the tongue-lashing she knew was coming.

Instead, a low chuckle rumbled in his chest. They'd started laughing and had trouble stopping. She'd laughed so hard tears had leaked from her eyes.

"Can we agree to leave the exotic cooking to the experts?" Les asked.

She'd nodded and wiped her eyes. From then on, she'd stuck to the dinner rotation of meatloaf on Monday, tacos on Tuesday, steak on Wednesday, pork chops on Thursday, and chicken or fish on Friday. Weekends varied, and occasionally they dined out, but that had been her routine for nearly thirty years. For the first few weeks after Les passed, she'd stuck to the schedule, more from habit than anything. But as time wore on, she realized she'd only been doing it for him. She hated the monotony of it, and those were not her favorite meals. She'd started mainly eating vegetarian food and found she felt better that way. Les would have been horrified if she'd suggested being a vegetarian to him. But it didn't matter anymore. She had only herself to please.

•   •   •   •   •

Entering Robyn's house on Saturday, Harriet found Robyn and Audrey already bustling about, packing boxes and sorting through their belongings.

"Good morning, Harriet," Robyn greeted her, a forced smile on her face. "We've made a bit of progress, but there's still so much left to do."

Harriet nodded, rolling up her sleeves and diving into the fray. Together, they worked methodically, packing boxes, labeling them with colored markers to denote their contents, and organizing them in neat stacks in the living room.

"So, what's next?" Harriet asked, wiping sweat from her brow as they finished packing up the last of the boxes.

"We'll need to load everything into my Suburban," Robyn replied. "Since we're making this move so quickly, I didn't have time to hire movers or a van. Not that I could have afforded that, but it sure would've been nice."

"We can use my car as well," Harriet said. "Let's get started then."

Arriving at the new townhome with the first load, Audrey bounded up the stairs. "I'm so happy this townhome is even closer to school. Izzy thinks we'll be on the same bus. I sure hope so."

"Chris doesn't know this address, right?" Harriet asked.

Robyn shook her head. "We're still very close, though. I'm sure he'll eventually figure it out. I don't know how long I can keep him at bay with my story about needing space."

"You're giving him time to calm down, let the dust settle. Then, when he's less emotional, you'll tell him you're leaving for good," Harriet said, lifting a box from the back of the Suburban.

Robyn nodded but looked unsure. Harriet pretended not to notice and headed into the townhome. After what seemed like forever, Robyn set the last box on the kitchen counter and exhaled. The weight of the moment pressed down on them. The decision to leave Chris was made, but the reality of what lay ahead loomed large.

"Can I call Izzy to come over?" Audrey asked.

Robyn sighed. "We haven't even unpacked yet."

"Please, Mom? She can help me get my room set up."

"Oh, all right. She can keep you occupied while I work on the kitchen."

"Want to join us for dinner, Harriet?" Robyn asked.

Harriet nearly blurted, "Yes," before catching herself. She couldn't intrude on them more than she already had. They were starting their new life, and she'd already spent the whole day with them. She'd bought the townhome, moved them, and now they needed to each live their own lives. As much as Harriet didn't want to face her own, she couldn't avoid her lonely life forever.

CHAPTER 24

Back at her own house, Harriet turned her attention to her garden. She was thrilled to find yellow flowers blooming on her tomato plants, and the frilly green shoots of her carrots were already a few inches tall.

"The garden is coming along nicely, isn't it, Bibbo?" He spun and hopped on his two hind paws. She loved how he read her moods. He had no idea what she was talking about, but the tone of her voice must have pleased him. That, or he thought she might be getting ready to give him a treat.

When she'd finished tending her garden, Harriet went inside to face the rest of the long day with nothing on the calendar. She thought again about what Lucille said about working at the library. Maybe Lucille was right. Maybe it wasn't just about the money. Yet again, another memory popped into her head.

The night Les asked Harriet to quit her job as a librarian, she'd gotten home later than usual because she'd stayed to help a young girl with a research project about Stuart's Stranglers, a well-known group of vigilantes in Helena, Montana in the late 1800s. Harriet became fascinated by this group and delved deeper than she intended, and deeper than the student needed, but neither of them minded. Les minded, however.

"How come I don't smell anything cooking?" Les said, removing his coat and hanging it on a hook by the door to the garage.

"I'm getting to it," Harriet called. "Just running a bit behind, is all. Grab a drink and make yourself comfortable."

"I don't want a drink. I want food."

"Sorry, hon. Working on it now," Harriet said, chopping zucchini with vigor. "How was your day?"

"It's almost April 15. Did you forget what I do? How do you think my day was? I need to come home and relax and have an enjoyable meal waiting for me. I work hard enough for both of us. Your piddly salary is not worth my coming home, stomach rumbling, to a wife who is full of excuses."

"I really am sorry. I got caught up in a research project. I'll watch the time better from now on." Harriet hurried to the pantry and put some smoked almonds in a bowl. She set the bowl on the coffee table and backed away.

"What the hell is this? Am I a squirrel? I don't want to come home to some nuts!" With the back of his hand, Les whacked the bowl and sent almonds flying across the living room and under the kitchen table. Silently, she swept the almonds and plucked the rest from the carpet and hurried to check on the Italian-style chicken and vegetable sheet pan recipe she had put in the oven. She wrung her hands as she watched the food, willing it to brown.

"Dinner's ready!" Harriet announced, trying to use her everything-is-normal voice.

"About time," Les said, standing from the couch and going to the dining room table.

Harriet set his plate in front of him, and he began shoveling forkful after forkful into his mouth.

"Shouldn't we say grace?"

Les glared at her. "No time for grace when you make me wait."

They ate in silence except for the sound of forks scraping plates. In no time, Les's plate was empty. Harriet wasn't even halfway through hers.

"That's better. You know I'm a bear when I'm hungry. I'm sorry to have been so grumpy, but you did that to me when you didn't have dinner ready."

Harriet looked down at her plate, unsure how to reply. She thought his anger had abated, but sometimes, if she said the wrong thing when he was in one of these moods, he could erupt again.

"I think we should discuss this job of yours," Les said. "Before we got married, you said you planned to stay at home."

Harriet's eyes shot to his. *How dare he?* "Les, you know why that changed. We don't really have to bring all that up again, do we?"

"I know it's hard for you, but this," he gestured to the table and the kitchen, "this is hard for me. We don't need your income. Whereas I need to count on you."

"Les," Harriet started, feeling the prick of tears in her eyes. "I said I would stay home to raise our children. What would I do all day without children to raise?"

He stood abruptly. "It's not my fault you couldn't have children, but that doesn't mean my needs have to suffer!"

He'd gone to bed and left her sitting at the table. Tears trailed from her eyes. She stared at her half-uneaten food and pushed the plate away.

The next day, at the high school, she'd moved about like she was in a bog of thick mud. The things she'd loved about her job felt hollow. The kids' requests felt meaningless and trivial. Her left arm was constantly swiveling up so she could check her watch to ensure she had plenty of time to get home and prepare a meal Les would enjoy. Maybe this job wasn't so important. It certainly wasn't about the money. And if it didn't bring fulfillment, and caused problems at home, why was she doing it?

She'd quit that very afternoon.

Her eyes filled with tears once again as the memory replayed before her. He simply wanted her home, where she belonged. He needed her there. It was his way of protecting her from the stress of the world, of ensuring their peace. Wasn't it? She'd successfully pushed so many painful memories into the deepest recesses of her mind that they almost didn't seem real. She supposed her desire to keep the peace and her caring for him through his illness had helped to squash these memories, but there didn't seem to be any stopping them now. At the time, when he'd gotten angry and asked her to quit her job, she'd been sad and scared, but she'd done his bidding because she'd seen the logic in it. But now, the neat, orderly narrative of her life with Les began to fracture, revealing uncomfortable seams she'd never allowed herself to see.

Without his weighty presence anchoring her life, a question formed in her mind. Such a simple question, but one she'd been too afraid to ponder. *What if?* What if she had stood her ground that night? What if she'd refused to quit, defying his demands for her constant presence, his need for her to remain a silent, domestic fixture? She pictured a different path, one where she hadn't quit, where she'd continued to do the job she adored, surrounded by the students she loved. The possibilities stretched out, a vast, unexplored country she'd foregone.

The thought stung with a pain that was too raw, too disloyal. Harriet quickly pulled her mind back from that forbidden path, seeking refuge in the familiar. So much of the time he'd been so loving, and he'd been such a wonderful provider, always making her feel safe and secure. They'd built their life around rules and routine, and it had been a good life, hadn't it? Sure, she'd longed for children, but as Les said, a family needn't be big to be a family. It only had to have love. They'd had love, hadn't they?

Another time, she'd gotten up the courage to broach the subject of adoption. Les hadn't yelled or been cruel, but he had shut her down immediately. He'd said he knew he could never love someone else's child the way he'd love his own, and he didn't feel that would be fair to the child. As much as it crushed her to hear this, she'd valued his honesty and his insight into himself. But now, she wanted to ask him, what about my feelings?

Had he ever asked about her feelings? She couldn't remember a time now. He must've, right? And when had she stopped considering her own feelings? The sheer effort of sifting through decades of memories, each one now tainted with a new, unsettling possibility, left her head throbbing. It felt like her brain was short-circuiting, trying to compute a new reality that defied everything she'd believed.

And then there was his illness. During that horrible time, if she'd had any lingering whispers of individual desire or any flicker of her own needs, they'd been instantly extinguished. It would have been utterly selfish to think of herself when his life was so clearly defined by illness and fear. Her role was simple - to care for him, to provide comfort, to maintain the order he so desperately craved in his suffering. She'd married him in sickness and in health, and they'd enjoyed over two decades of health, so she'd done her duty during his sickness without question. Her feelings simply hadn't factored into the equation.

Early in his diagnosis, she'd attributed his irritability to the disease and his fear of what was to come. Harriet cocked her head to the side as another memory came to her, one from soon after his diagnosis, as she realized how many of their arguments had been about the food she prepared for him. She'd taken his criticism to heart since cooking him dinner was, arguably, her most important job. But, yet again, she hadn't stopped to consider what she might have liked for dinner, or whether she wanted to cook for him at all. She'd accepted his demands as gospel.

That particular evening, they'd just sat down to dinner, and he exploded. He'd taken one bite of his taco, since it was Tuesday, and spit it into his napkin. "What's this?" he'd demanded, his voice booming across the room.

Harriet's heart sank. She'd added some different spices to the meat she thought he'd enjoy. But his words, delivered with such disdain, stung like a slap in the face.

"I'm sorry," she'd said. "I read about some different spices in a magazine. I thought you'd like them."

"You're a terrible cook. I've tried to encourage you to make simple meals to avoid telling you the truth, but enough is enough. I might not have that many meals left on this earth, and I'm not wasting them on this crap."

Harriet's eyes filled with tears. She felt humiliated, degraded, worthless. "I'm sorry," she repeated, her voice barely audible. "I'll try harder."

"Don't bother," he said, waving her away. "Just go clean up this mess."

Harriet stood there for a moment, her eyes fixed on his barely touched plate, her heart heavy with a sense of despair. She knew Les was struggling. His outbursts, his anger, his frustration—she'd attributed it all to the disease, to the fear and uncertainty that gnawed at him. She cleaned up the mess in silence, her movements mechanical, her mind trying to rationalize his behavior. He wasn't himself, she'd told herself.

She picked up the picture of them on their honeymoon again. She traced his smiling face, recalling the effortless joy of those early days, the feeling of being utterly cherished and protected. *This was the truth of their marriage, wasn't it? The love. The security. The good outweighing anything else.* But then, the image of the flying almonds, the cruel words about her cooking, the sting of being called "worthless" by the man who had promised to love her forever, flickered behind her eyes. It wasn't *only* after his diagnosis, was it? He'd done similar things throughout their marriage, and she'd made excuses for him, time and time again. He never laid a hand on her. So it couldn't have been that. It couldn't have been anything truly wrong. Not in the way Robyn experienced. *Could it?*

She threw the picture across the living room, sending glass shattering across the floor as it hit the wall. "Damn you, Callie! I was perfectly fine living with my version of my life. Why did you have to dig up all these memories?"

Burying her face in her hands, she sobbed. She gasped and hiccoughed and sniffed as her shoulders shook. She howled so loudly that Bibbo came to her and put his paw on her leg, his eyes concerned. She never let herself go like this, and he knew it. She felt as though she was coming completely undone, her insides spilling from her as though she'd been stabbed. She didn't try to stop herself, nor did she think she could if she tried.

When her sobs subsided, the house felt as though it was caving in on her. She took short, shallow breaths as though she was breathing through a straw. She had to get out of there.

The drive to Robyn's new townhouse wasn't far, but Harriet's swollen eyes and the tears that kept welling up in them made it a bit treacherous. Robyn opened the door before Harriet finished knocking.

"My God, Harriet," Robyn said, pulling her into a hug. "What's happened? You look awful."

From some deep well Harriet never knew she carried within her, the tears began to flow yet again. They went inside, Robyn brought her a box of tissues, made coffee, and told Harriet to sit.

"Tell me everything," Robyn said.

Harriet, her body still trembling with the aftershocks of her emotional breakdown, took a shaky sip of the coffee Robyn offered. The warmth of the mug in her hands and the comforting aroma did little to soothe the turmoil raging within her.

"It's Les," she choked out. "I've been remembering things. Ever since you made me go to those meetings with you, these memories come out of nowhere. My mind just conjures things up. So many memories I'd pushed down are bubbling up. I try to keep busy, gardening, reading, walking Bibbo, but it doesn't matter where I am or what I'm doing, my brain has a mind of its own. I feel like I'm going crazy. These flashbacks, I can't stop them."

"I'm guessing these aren't nice memories," Robyn said.

"Gee, you think?" Harriet said, blowing her nose into a tissue.

"Tell me about them. Why are they so upsetting?"

Harriet's gaze fell to the floor, her hands fidgeting with the tissue, shredding it slowly. "I... I guess I'd suppressed a lot. Of Les being... not very kind. And sometimes... sometimes he was mean. Or maybe even... manipulative." The words were hesitant, tasting foreign on her tongue.

Once Harriet started, the dam seemed to break, but the flow was still hesitant and painful. She recounted the instances, not in a torrent of accusation, but as if discovering them anew as she spoke. "He'd belittle me. Not always with shouting, but with those dismissive gestures. The way he'd chip away at my self-esteem."

She took a ragged breath. "He made me quit my job." Saying it out loud made it real. Her voice hitched. She swallowed, her throat raw. "He made me give up my friends, my hobbies, my dreams. He made me believe I was nothing without him." The words hung in the air, heavy with a fresh layer of understanding. It wasn't just *control*, as Callie had defined it. It felt deeper, more insidious than that.

Robyn listened intently. "Harriet," she said softly, "I'm so sorry."

"I made excuses for his behavior. So many excuses. And I suppose over the years, I... I accepted the way he treated me. I convinced myself I deserved it. It was like his voice became my own." She looked up, her eyes pleading for understanding, for confirmation that she wasn't losing it.

Robyn nodded. "I know exactly what you mean."

Harriet shook her head. "I thought I was happy. I thought we had a good marriage." The assertion was weak, a question rather than a statement.

"But you weren't happy, were you?" Robyn asked gently.

Harriet hesitated, the question hanging in the air like a judgment. She searched inside herself, past the decades of rationalization, past the ingrained loyalty. A sob escaped her lips, small at first, then growing into a shuddering release. "No," she gasped. "I wasn't. I was lonely, isolated, and miserable. But I didn't know any better. I thought that was how marriage was."

Robyn reached out and took Harriet's hand, her touch warm and reassuring. "It's not, Harriet. You deserve so much more than that."

"I don't know who I am anymore. I've spent my whole life living for him, according to his rules. Now that he's gone, I feel…lost."

"It's a journey, Harriet. The first step is this realization. Like they said in the group, you're seeing the forest through the trees. Believe me, I know how it feels. It's sad and scary, but now you can start to figure out who you are, without Les and his controlling rules. Maybe the walls you've built around you aren't really yours."

"What do you mean?" Harriet asked, using another tissue to wipe her cheek. But even as she asked the question, her mind began to latch onto this new, terrifying possibility.

"Well, if Les was controlling and manipulative, some stories you've told me about the rules he laid out for you, including not allowing you to work at a job you loved, might not be correct. Maybe you were living his life, and not yours."

More memories flooded her mind, and Harriet felt dizzy. Les telling her she was "too sensitive to handle the real world" when she expressed discomfort with a social gathering he insisted they attend. The time he dismissed her excitement over a new hobby, saying it was "childish" and "a waste of time" as she tried to explain her passion. The time he put his finger in her face as she backed against the wall and told her he didn't understand why he'd been dumb enough to marry her.

Leaning forward and putting her head in her hands, she said, "I can't believe I was so stupid."

Robyn put her arm around her. "You weren't stupid, Harriet. I'm sure he was wonderful, much of the time, if not most of the time. That's how they do it." She scoffed. "Do you think I'd have married Chris if he had hit me early on? It's like Callie said. At first, he was the most amazing, romantic guy I'd ever met. I bet that was true of Les as well."

Harriet nodded, remembering their early college days. The way he waited outside her classroom to walk her from class to class or back to her apartment. The way he held the door for her and brought her flowers for no reason. It was as though he had read a book on what to do to win a woman over. Now that she thought about it, he probably had.

Harriet sat there, her mind a whirlwind of conflicting emotions. How could she have been so blind to Les's true nature all these years? How could she have missed the signs of his manipulation and control?

Robyn's words echoed in her mind. *"Maybe the walls you've built around you aren't really yours."*

"I wasted my whole life on a controlling, demeaning, manipulative asshole," Harriet said.

"You still have plenty of life left, Harriet. You don't have to live the way Les wanted you to anymore," Robyn said.

"But I don't even know who I am. Is it his voice in my head or my own?"

"You're preaching to the choir. It might be a bit of the blind leading the blind here, but we'll work through all this together. I'm glad I have you, Harriet."

Harriet felt tears prick her eyes again, but this time, her heart swelled with the realization that she had Robyn, Audrey, Callie, and, she was loath to admit, she was glad she had the Harmony House support group to help her through this as well.

But a controlling, demeaning asshole? The words felt harsh, too definitive, even as her memories confirmed them. He'd been so loving, too, so generous with his time and resources, always providing. He made her feel safe, secure. It wasn't all bad. No one was perfect, after all. Was she simply exaggerating now, swinging to the opposite extreme out of raw pain? It felt so disloyal to him, now that he was gone and couldn't defend himself. He'd done his best, hadn't he? He'd loved her in his own way. Perhaps she was just seeing things through Callie's jaded lens or Robyn's painful experience. *My life wasn't wasted,* she insisted silently, trying to shore up the collapsing walls of her past. *It was a good life. Mostly.*

Later that evening, after she was back in her own quiet house, the emotional hangover settled in with a vengeance. Harriet felt utterly and completely drained. It wasn't just the residual ache of tears or the lingering tremor in her limbs; it was as if her mind was performing an exhausting, psychological surgery. Confronting those buried memories, pulling them from the depths, and holding them up to the light had taken an immense toll. Even simple tasks, like preparing a cup of coffee or letting Bibbo out, felt like monumental efforts. She flopped onto the couch, hoping the television would offer some escape from the relentless onslaught of unwanted realizations.

When her stomach eventually rumbled, Harriet reached for her phone. Pad thai, her mind offered. Then, just as quickly, Les's voice, sharp and dismissive: *"What the hell is this on my plate?"* She flinched, pulling her hand back. She loved pad thai, but had only ever ordered it when Les was out of town. Tonight, the memory of his disgust, his spitting it out onto a napkin, soured the thought. *But did it? Or was that still his disgust, echoing in her head?* Eventually, with a sigh of weary defiance, she ordered the pad thai.

CHAPTER 25

THE NEXT MORNING, when she woke, Harriet couldn't bear the thought of being alone. Once again, she made the increasingly familiar drive to Robyn's place.

"How about I help you unpack?" Harriet said when Robyn opened the door to her townhome. "It'd be good for me to have something to do."

"Sure," Robyn said, going into the kitchen to open a box on the counter.

Harriet pulled open a drawer next to the stove. "Oh no. This can't be."

"What?" Robyn asked, hurrying over beside Harriet.

"You can't put your silverware here. Silverware goes over near the dishwasher. Didn't anyone teach you at all about organizing a kitchen?"

Robyn chuckled. "Harriet, I thought there was something truly wrong. You scared me."

"Well, you scared me with this obvious lack of organization. Silverware is the most annoying thing to unload from the dishwasher, right? So, put the silverware next to the dishwasher, then you don't have to walk all the way across the kitchen with the blasted things."

Robyn shook her head and went back to the box she was unpacking.

"No, no, no," Harriet said, taking the coffee mug from Robyn's hand. "You can't put the mugs all the way over there. Your coffee maker goes here, on this side of the counter, so you need to have the mugs above it."

Robyn covered her mouth to stifle her giggle. "What if I don't want my coffee maker there?"

"Of course you want your coffee maker here. It's next to the sink. Don't you know how often you have to refill the water on these Keurigs?"

"Seriously, it's not that big of a deal. So what if I have to take a couple of extra steps? Probably good for my step count."

Harriet shook her head. "You aren't taking this seriously. Organization is the key to running a successful household. Do you want people to think you don't care about keeping a nice home?" Harriet was nearly shouting now.

Robyn looked stricken. She slowly leaned her hip onto the counter. "Harriet, you don't need to get so worked up about it."

Harriet's face went pale, her lips parting in a silent gasp. She ran a hand through her hair and pressed her fingers to her temples as if trying to push unwanted thoughts away.

Robyn took two steps toward Harriet and put a hand on her shoulder. "What is it?"

"I...I sounded just like him," Harriet whispered, her voice breaking. "Like Les. I scolded you exactly how he used to scold me."

"You're not him, Harriet. It's natural to have moments where his words creep into your thoughts. I mean, you were married to him for what, like thirty years?"

Harriet nodded slowly, feeling a surge of conflicting emotions— anger at herself for echoing Les's demands, and sorrow for the years she'd spent internalizing his harsh judgments. "I don't think I even know who I am," Harriet said. "He was the one with the rules for how the kitchen had to be organized. He had the rules for the neighborhood, for how I dressed, how I wore my hair, how much makeup was appropriate, and how to speak on the telephone. He had rules for everything. When did that become normal for me?"

"I have no idea, Harriet, but I think it's amazing that you are realizing it wasn't you."

"I wish I could have a glass of wine right now."

"I've got a few bottles in a box somewhere. Let me look," Robyn said.

"Oh, heavens no," Harriet said. "I couldn't, really. It's much too early. Wine can't be drunk before at least 4 p.m."

"Who says? Les?"

Harriet opened her mouth and stopped. She had no idea whose rule this was. "Isn't it a general rule? For health and to keep us all from becoming alcoholics?"

"I suppose if you were drinking all day on a daily basis, it would be a problem, but when you're facing an existential crisis, maybe you can bend the wine rule a bit."

"I'm not good at bending rules," Harriet said, walking to the living room and flopping onto the couch.

"I give you full permission to break all the rules," Robyn said, waving her arm in the air as if she were the fairy godmother from Cinderella.

Harriet giggled. "Okay, but not drinking wine before noon isn't the first one I'm going to break because I'm pretty sure I wouldn't stop until I drank all your wine. And then I'd ask you to get me more. Drunk driving is not a line I'm willing to cross."

"Good call," Robyn said, unpacking a box of books and placing them on the bookshelf. "You know, Harriet, this whole moving thing is exhausting, but it feels good to start fresh."

"Yeah, it's a lot of work," Harriet replied, sitting up and folding an empty box with precise, methodical movements. "But it's worth it."

There was a pause before Harriet drew a deep breath. She had sounded just like Les, scolding Robyn about the silverware and coffee mugs. The realization had been a punch to the gut. But as

Robyn moved around the kitchen, humming softly, Harriet found herself trying to soften the blow of her own self-condemnation. It was just kitchen organization, after all. A preference, a logical system for efficiency. Like how she preferred a certain brand of coffee or found lemonade entirely unappealing. Surely, expressing an opinion on where the mugs should go wasn't akin to Les's deeper manipulations. It was just Harriet, being Harriet. Right? "Robyn, would you mind if I took Bibbo for a quick walk? Maybe I could even bring him here with me?"

Robyn looked up. "Of course, Harriet. Bibbo is welcome anytime. After all, it's your place. But you don't have to stay all day and help. I'm grateful for any help you can offer."

"It's okay. I like helping. I need to keep busy. Plus, I need to get to know this townhome, too. I'll be back soon."

Back at home, Harriet gathered Bibbo and put on his leash. As Harriet stepped outside, the cool air hit her, refreshing and invigorating. She walked down the quiet street, letting her thoughts wander. After a few minutes, she arrived at the small park, the bench inviting her to sit and rest.

Her mind raced. Harriet realized how isolated she had become over the years, slowly alienated from friends and family. Was it Les's doing? Had his constant criticism and control made her feel unworthy? Or was his disdain for nearly everyone his reason for cutting them off from the world? Her mind wandered to her brother. She'd gotten used to life without him, but why? Maybe it was time to rebuild those bridges.

When Harriet returned, Robyn was in the middle of unwrapping a lamp in the living room. "Feel better?"

"Yes," Harriet replied, nodding. "I think I needed a moment to clear my head." She removed Bibbo's leash, and he went about sniffing the living room.

Robyn placed the lamp on a side table. "Harriet, can I be honest with you about something?"

"Of course," Harriet said.

Robyn hesitated, then spoke. "I'm scared, Harriet. What if Chris stops being understanding? I mean, this isn't a very big town, and he'll find out where Audrey and I are living quickly. What if things get ugly again?"

Harriet felt a surge of protective anger. "If he comes near you, we'll handle it. File that restraining order. We'll make sure you're safe."

Robyn nodded, but her eyes were still filled with worry. "But...what if it's me?"

"What do you mean?"

"What if I'm tempted to take him back? I know he's bad for me, but sometimes I miss him. The good moments, the promises he made..."

Harriet's eyes widened. "Don't be ridiculous. You tell me not to put up with Les's mean voice in my head, and you think you might go back to an even worse guy?"

"I don't really know if you can say he's worse. Don't downplay emotional abuse. Sometimes it's worse because you don't even realize it's happening."

Harriet let the words sink in. She hadn't really thought of it like that, but maybe Robyn had a point. Maybe if Les had hit her, she would have realized it much earlier, before he brainwashed her completely.

She shoved the thought aside. "Well, anyway. We aren't talking about me right now. You have to promise not to take that jerk back. If you can't be strong for you, do it for Audrey, remember?"

Robyn's eyes welled up with tears, and she nodded. "I know, but it's hard sometimes."

"That makes absolutely no sense to me. It shouldn't be hard. He's bad for you and Audrey. End of story."

Robyn wiped her eyes and took a deep breath. "Thank you, Harriet. I needed to hear that."

"Anytime," Harriet said, her voice calm and steady. "Now, let's get this place in order."

CHAPTER 26

HARRIET WOKE to a dreary Saturday morning, wishing she could disappear. Working on the townhome with Robyn had given her purpose, but now, with the work mostly finished, Harriet felt unmoored. The lonely weekend stretched out before her like a book full of blank pages. Before, when she still believed in the beauty of her marriage, she had felt Les's warm presence, and it had comforted her. She'd felt as though she understood the world and her place in it. Her rules were a roadmap for her life, and she didn't care if no one else joined her journey. Now, she was on a path full of forks and dead ends in the middle of a dark forest. The weight of it was crushing.

As Harriet sat up, she heard the rain pounding against the windows. The sky was a uniform gray, and the steady downpour blurred the world outside. It matched her mood perfectly. With a resigned sigh, she decided there was nothing else to do but indulge in a day of wine and mindless television. Robyn had said to break all the rules, right?

She dragged herself out of bed and padded to the kitchen. Opening the cabinet, she pulled out a bottle of wine and a glass. "It's five o'clock somewhere," she muttered to herself, pouring a generous amount of wine into the glass. She carried it with her to the living room and collapsed onto the couch, remote in hand.

Flicking through the channels, she landed on a documentary about ancient civilizations. Les would have approved. He'd often said, "Now that's intellectual stimulation, Harriet, not that drivel you sometimes gravitate toward." But the dry narration, the long-winded explanations of pottery shards, felt tedious. Her finger twitched on the remote. Reality TV. The plastic surgery show. *Trash, Les would have called it. Lowbrow. Brain-rotting.* But was her disinterest in the documentary authentic, or was she just tired of conforming to what Les considered "intellectual?" And was her fascination with the reality show a true personal preference, or just a defiant lean into something he would have despised? Finally, with a sigh that was more surrender than conviction, she pressed the button, returning to the chaotic world of questionable aesthetics. It was easier to watch something mindless today.

The hours crawled by as Harriet alternated between sips of wine and bites of leftover southwest quinoa bake. The rain showed no signs of letting up, creating a constant background noise that was both soothing and depressing. She could feel the alcohol warming her from the inside, dulling the edges of her anxiety and self-doubt.

By the time the afternoon rolled around, Harriet was on her second bottle of wine. The television droned on with melodramatic arguments and over-the-top reactions, but she barely registered it. Her thoughts drifted back to her conversation with Robyn. Maybe she should reach out to her brother, Hank.

She picked up her phone and stared at it for a long time, her finger hovering over Hank's contact. The last time they had spoken was a blur of tension and frustration. But maybe things could be different now. With a deep breath, she typed out a message: *Hi Hank, it's Harriet. It's been a while. I'd like to catch up if you're free sometime.* She hesitated, then hit send before she could second-guess herself.

The wine continued to flow, and Harriet found herself laughing at the absurdity of the show she was watching. People were crying over poorly installed countertops and mismatched paint colors. It was all so trivial, yet in her hazy state, it seemed almost profound.

Maybe she had spent too much time worrying about rules and organization when life was really a series of chaotic moments.

As evening approached, Harriet felt a wave of exhaustion. She glanced at the clock and realized she had been drinking and watching TV for nearly ten hours. The rain outside was still relentless, and the house felt colder and emptier than ever.

Opening the sliding glass door for Bibbo, a gust of wet wind hit her face, sobering her slightly. Bibbo walked over to the door, his fur flying back from the force of the wind, and then turned around to climb back into his bed.

"I don't blame you," Harriet said. "I'm not venturing out there either."

Harriet finished her last glass of wine and set it down on the coffee table. She turned off the TV and sat in silence for a moment, listening to the rain. Maybe tomorrow would be better. Maybe tomorrow she would find her way out of this dark forest. But for now, sleep seemed the only escape.

Stumbling to her bedroom, Harriet collapsed onto her bed, fully clothed. The room spun slightly, and she closed her eyes, willing the world to stop moving. As she drifted off to sleep, she hoped that reaching out to Hank was the first step toward rebuilding her life. But tonight, she would let the wine and the rain lull her into oblivion.

. . . . .

Harriet woke the next morning with a headache and a sense of regret over the previous day's wine-fueled binge. Had she really texted Hank? She couldn't decide if she hoped she had or hadn't. She reached for her phone, looking for a reply from Hank, but there was nothing. The disappointment she felt must've meant she was glad she'd reached out. But now, facing the possibility of rejection, her stomach churned. She supposed she couldn't blame him if he didn't want to reconnect.

Another long, lonely day ahead of her, Harriet pulled herself up to a seated position on the side of the bed and looked out the window. Still raining. She flopped back down on the bed and put her pillow over her head.

"Make it go away," Harriet moaned.

Bibbo whined. "What? You need to go out? Okay, but you aren't going to like it any more than I do." Harriet threw on her robe and repeated the scene of sliding back the glass door and Bibbo recoiling. This time, however, he had to do his business badly enough to brave the terrible weather.

Contemplating another day like yesterday, Harriet's head throbbed. She took it as a warning. Maybe a good book could whisk her away from the mess of her life. A trip to the library would do her some good. Maybe she'd bump into Richard again. The thought sent an unexpected flutter through her chest. What was happening? Her heart thudded more quickly. Did he work on Sundays? Probably not, but she could still stop by.

She headed back to her room and went to the closet. Her hand hovered over a sensible navy blouse and a crisp pair of khaki pants, her usual "library attire," what Les would have deemed "appropriate" and "respectable." He'd always had an opinion on her clothing, from the cut of a dress to the length of a skirt. "That's a bit too flashy, isn't it, Harriet?" he'd say. But today, the thought of the stiff fabric, the muted color, felt like a constraint. Her gaze drifted to a bright fuchsia sweater with flowers sewn on it, one she'd bought on a whim years ago but rarely wore because Les had once commented it made her look "a bit ostentatious." Did she genuinely dislike the sweater, or was it simply Les's judgment still dictating her choices? Was she dressing for herself today, or for the ghost of his approval? A tiny sigh escaped her lips as she reached for the sweater. She could always change if it really was too much.

Inside, the library was warm and inviting, filled with the soft murmur of patrons and the aroma of old books, a blend of musty paper and aged ink that conjured memories of countless stories read and cherished. Harriet glanced around, spotting Richard behind the circulation desk, engaged in conversation with a young woman checking out books. His dark hair was neatly combed, and his glasses perched perfectly on his nose. His khakis had an ironed crease in them, and his pink polo shirt appeared to be starched. He looked like a member of a high school golf team. Harriet found it adorable. And he did work on Sundays. It must be a sign.

Lucille was nearby, organizing a cart of returned books. Not wanting to call attention to her presence, Harriet hurried past Lucille and went straight to Richard. Harriet felt her heart racing in her chest as she approached the desk as soon as he was finished with his customer.

"Hi, Richard," she said in a high-pitched tone. "Long time no see."

Richard looked up and smiled. "Good to see you, Harriet. Great to see you walking without assistance. Is your ankle all healed?" he asked, smoothing the back of his hair with the palm of his hand.

"Yep. Good as new," Harriet said, her heart thrumming in her ears so loudly she could barely hear him.

An awkward silence passed.

"So, how can I help you?" Richard asked.

Harriet fidgeted with the strap of her purse. "I was wondering if you...Well, I mean, if you might want to...maybe get coffee sometime?"

Richard's smile faltered, and he glanced briefly at Lucille, who had stopped her work and was now watching their interaction.

"I'm sorry, Harriet," Richard said. "I'm really flattered, but I'm actually seeing someone."

Harriet felt her face grow hot. "Oh, I see. I didn't know. But that's not what I meant, anyway. It's just a cup of coffee, not a marriage proposal."

Richard smiled apologetically. "Of course not. Forgive me. I suppose a cup of coffee would be no big deal."

Harriet forced a smile, though she felt like sinking through the floor. "Never mind. I'll, um, check out a book."

She turned away quickly, feeling the sting of embarrassment. Lucille's eyes followed her as she moved toward the fiction section. Cheeks burning, she pretended to browse the shelves, trying to collect herself. As she pretended to read the back cover of a novel, she heard Lucille's voice behind her.

"Don't let it get you down," Lucille said. "Takes a lot of courage to put yourself out there."

"You heard that? That makes it even worse. I thought my shame was just mine."

Lucille patted her arm. "It's fine, Harriet. You can count on me as a friend. Friends don't judge about things like that. We're there for each other."

Harriet stared at Lucille. She thought of her as a friend. And Robyn was now a friend. How long had it been since Harriet had friends? Probably not since college. Before Les found fault with every single person she tried to bring into her life. Even the people at yoga. She opened her mouth, but she didn't know what to say, and she was worried her voice would waver, giving away her fragile emotional state.

"I'd be up for a coffee sometime," Lucille said.

Harriet smiled. "That sounds great. How about tomorrow?"

"Sure. Meet you at Cold Smoke at eight?"

Harriet nodded, her heart swelling. She had friends. Harriet checked out her book and left the library, the cold, damp air a stark contrast to the warmth inside. As she walked back to her car, she found she wasn't as sad or embarrassed as she should've been given Richard's rebuff, thanks to Lucille. And she had plans for tomorrow. Coffee with Lucille and the Harmony House support group in the evening. Was she actually looking forward to it? Maybe. Like everyone said, she had to give herself grace as she was figuring out what the rest of her life was going to look like. She'd thought she was an introverted, grieving widow, and that was hard enough. But it seemed there was much more to it than that.

The initial relief provided by Lucille's friendship began to wane as Harriet settled back into the quiet of her own home. The cheerful buzz of the library, the comforting presence of Lucille, receded, leaving her alone with the echoing silence and the lingering sting of Richard's polite rejection. *He's actually seeing someone.* The words, so innocuous, twisted into something sharper in her mind. It wasn't just a simple "no"; it was a reinforcement of a deeper, more insidious message.

Les. He hadn't outright forbidden her from interacting with other men, but his subtle criticisms of potential male friends, his possessiveness, the way he subtly conveyed that no one would ever quite measure up to him, had instilled a quiet conviction within her: she was only truly desirable or interesting through his lens. Richard's rebuff, despite her initial brave front, pricked at that old wound. It ignited a familiar, creeping sense of unworthiness, a feeling that she simply wasn't enough, not vibrant enough, not interesting enough to attract genuine connection on her own merit.

She felt a pull toward her old habits. The precise folding of laundry, the meticulous dusting of shelves, the rigid adherence to her established routine – these were her comfort, her defense against the chaotic emotions now stirring within her. If she just kept everything ordered and controlled, perhaps these vulnerable, exposed feelings would retreat. The temptation to isolate herself, to pull back from the messy prospect of new connections, was strong.

But then, she thought of Lucille, waiting for her tomorrow morning. A promise, a shared cup of coffee. It was a tiny thread, but a thread nonetheless. A connection that didn't involve Les or his judgment. For now, it was enough to keep her from retreating entirely into the rigid solitude she had once mistaken for contentment.

CHAPTER 27

PEERING OUT THE WINDOW the next morning, Harriet found a fresh blanket of snow on the ground. It was much prettier than the previous gray, rainy day, but by mid-May, she was over snow. Sighing, she made her way to the kitchen, the house still and silent. Her heart lifted at the prospect of coffee with Lucille in a couple of hours.

Sirens blaring outside interrupted her thoughts. Harriet frowned, glancing out the window. Police cars were pulling up in front of Robyn and Chris's house across the street. Harriet's heart quickened with worry.

She grabbed her cardigan, slipped on her Bogs, and stepped outside into the crisp spring air. Across the street, a small crowd was gathering, their curious gazes fixed on the flashing lights and the commotion. She hurried across the street, her brisk pace betraying her growing anxiety.

As she approached the house, she saw two police officers standing near the front door, talking in low, urgent tones. Harriet's stomach knotted. She spotted Bonnie in the crowd.

"What's going on?" Harriet asked.

"I don't know. I just got here. It looks serious, though," Bonnie said.

Harriet's heart raced. She pushed through the crowd, making her way toward the officers. "Excuse me," she called out. "What's happening? I know Robyn. I've been helping her. She's finally leaving her jerk of a husband."

One officer turned to her, his expression somber. "Ma'am, I'm sorry, but we can't disclose any information at this time. Please step back."

Harriet's anxiety surged. "Please, I need to know. Is Robyn all right? Is Audrey okay?"

The officer hesitated, then nodded toward a third officer who was emerging from the house. The man approached Harriet, his face grave. "Ma'am, are you Harriet?"

"Yes, I'm Harriet. What's going on?"

The officer took a deep breath and led her away from the crowd. "I'm very sorry to have to tell you this, but Robyn was found dead in the house early this morning."

Harriet felt the world tilt beneath her. "What? No, that can't be. She moved out. She wasn't supposed to be here."

The officer's eyes softened with sympathy. "We believe she came back to collect some belongings. It seems her husband showed up. There was a confrontation, and...she didn't make it."

Harriet staggered back, the words hitting her like a physical blow. "No, no. This can't be happening."

"I'm very sorry for your loss," the officer said. "She scribbled a note up in the bedroom. We found this on the bedside table. It's tough to discern since the handwriting is so shaky, but I believe that is your name at the top." He pointed to the top of a small pink piece of paper and handed it to her.

With trembling hands, she took it, her mouth gaping in disbelief.

Harriet,
I don't have much time. Chris found me. I'm so scared. I locked myself in the bedroom. I don't know how long the door will hold. If you find this, please take care of Audrey. You've been a true friend to us. Tell Audrey to be brave and live life fully. Tell her I LOVE HER. Take care of her. She has no one.
Love, Robyn

Harriet's legs gave way, and the officer caught her before she hit the ground. Her mind was unable to process the horror of what she had read. The officer asked, "Is there anyone we can call for you? Someone who can be with you right now?"

Harriet shook her head, numb with shock. "What about Audrey? Where is she?" Harriet asked.

"Robyn was the only one here. We've checked the house."

Harriet gasped. "Did her dad take her?"

"We don't know anything yet, but we'll find her."

Harriet stared straight ahead, seeing nothing, as tears streamed down her face.

As the officers continued their work, Harriet's mind raced with guilt and grief. She had encouraged Robyn to leave, to start a new life, and now look at what had happened. It was her fault. She hadn't believed the Harmony House people when they told her about the danger of leaving. Robyn hadn't believed it either. The enormity of the situation was suffocating.

But Harriet had to pull herself together. She had to be there for Audrey, assuming Audrey was safe. The note said it was Harriet's duty to protect Audrey from the nightmare that had taken her mother. It was the only thing she could do for Robyn now.

Harriet's heart felt like it was being crushed by an invisible hand as she drove to Audrey's school. She prayed Audrey would be there. Robyn said she had a best friend, and the two of them were inseparable. Maybe she'd been there last night. The school came into view, a place meant to be a safe haven, now the site of a heartbreakingly difficult conversation, if Audrey was even there.

She parked the car and took a deep breath, wondering how the heck she was going to get through this. The school office was quiet, the receptionist smiling warmly as Harriet approached.

"Good afternoon. How can I help you?" the receptionist asked.

"I'm here to pick up Audrey Carter," Harriet said. "It's an emergency."

The receptionist's smile faltered. "Are you on the emergency contact list?"

Harriet hesitated, then shook her head. "No, but I'm a...friend. There's been a family emergency. I need to take her home."

"I'm sorry, but I can't let you take her unless you're on the list or we have parental permission," the receptionist said. "It's for the children's safety."

"So she's here?" Audrey asked.

"I'm confused," the receptionist said. "You came here asking to take her, and you don't even know if she's here?"

"It's a long story. A terrible, tragic story, and I need to know if Audrey is safe."

"I'm sorry, but I can't give you that information if you aren't on the contact list," the receptionist repeated.

Harriet's mind raced, searching for a solution. "Please, you have to understand. Her mother... Something terrible has happened. Can I show you my ID? Can you check with the principal? Or the police?" An idea came to Harriet. She reached into her pocket and pulled out the crumpled pink note. A lump formed in Harriet's throat as the receptionist looked at the jagged and uneven letters. She handed it over wordlessly.

The receptionist swallowed hard. "I'll call the principal."

Harriet's stomach churned as she waited. Every second felt like an eternity. Finally, the principal, a tall woman with piercing eyes, walked into the reception area.

"Hello, I'm Principal Reynolds." She extended her long, thin hand toward Harriet. It felt like it might break if Harriet squeezed at all as she shook it. "I understand there's an emergency?"

"Yes, there is," Harriet said, her voice cracking. "Audrey's mother was...was killed last night by her father. The police have taken him, but Audrey doesn't know yet. This note," Harriet handed the small pink piece of paper to the principal, "explains that I am to take care of Audrey."

Principal Reynolds' eyes widened. "Oh, my goodness. That's... I'm so sorry. I don't mean to cause unnecessary grief given this terrible situation, but I can't hand a child off to someone who is not on any of Audrey's contact lists." She brought her hand up to her chin and furrowed her brow. "We've never dealt with a situation like this. Audrey doesn't have any other family nearby?"

"Do you really think Robyn would scribble this note to a neighbor across the street if she had other options?"

The principal raised her hands as if in surrender. "I'm just doing my job."

Harriet quickly pulled out her driver's license. "This is me. You can photocopy it or whatever."

"Tell you what. I'll call the police to verify everything," the principal said.

"I bet they're a little busy right now," Harriet said, folding her arms across her chest.

"Please. I'm not trying to be difficult. I have to cover all my bases. Give me a minute."

Moments later, Principal Reynolds emerged from the back office and nodded. "I'll bring Audrey to you now."

"Oh, thank God. She's safe," Harriet said, sighing as new tears filled her eyes.

Seeing Audrey's sweet, unsuspecting face coming down the hallway, Harriet forced a smile, her heart aching. "Hey, sweetheart. We need to talk. Let's go to the car, okay?"

Audrey nodded, sensing the seriousness in Harriet's tone. They walked to the car in silence, the sound of their footsteps echoing in the quiet corridor. Once they were inside, Harriet gathered her courage and turned to Audrey.

"Were you home last night?" Harriet asked.

Audrey shook her head. "I stayed at Izzy's. What's wrong?"

"A lot has happened, Audrey," Harriet began gently. "There's no easy way to say this. Your mom...your mom is gone."

Audrey blinked rapidly. "What do you mean? Where did she go?"

Harriet reached out and took Audrey's hands in hers. "Your dad...he hurt her, Audrey. Very badly. The police took him away, but your mom didn't make it."

Audrey's face went pale, her eyes filling with tears. "What? Didn't make it? What does that mean?"

"I'm so sorry, sweetheart. She's passed on," Harriet said, pulling Audrey into a tight hug as the realization took hold. "I'm so, so sorry."

They sat there for a long time, Harriet holding Audrey as she sobbed. Finally, when the tears had subsided a little, Audrey spoke again.

"H-how did it happen?"

"No one knows exactly. All we know is your mom went back to your house for some reason, and your dad was there, or he showed up while she was there. He was angry." Harriet reached into her pocket and handed the note to Audrey. "She left this note."

Audrey's chin quivered as she read. Covering her face with her hands, she howled like a wounded animal. A pang of anguish pierced Harriet's heart, sharp and unrelenting. Harriet remembered her own pain at the loss of her parents. Her pain had receded over the years, but it was always there, surging back like the rush of the tide at unsuspecting moments. But seeing Audrey's pain, her own was dwarfed in comparison. She would do anything to take away Audrey's suffering.

"I lost my parents, too. I was a few years older than you, but I lost them both in a car accident. I can't know exactly how you feel, but I can empathize."

Audrey sniffed. Harriet reached into the glove box for a tissue and handed it to her. Audrey blew her nose and dropped her hands into her lap.

"You'll stay with me for now, Audrey," Harriet said. "We'll be safe at my house because the police have your dad. We'll figure things out together, okay?"

Audrey nodded weakly, her eyes red and swollen.

Harriet started the car, her mind racing. She couldn't believe this had really happened. Things like this didn't happen in real life. Robyn and Audrey were so happy to be starting a new life. A tear streamed down her cheek, and she swiped it quickly.

CHAPTER 28

THEY DROVE IN SILENCE to the new townhome to gather Audrey's things. Audrey climbed the stairs in slow motion, her feet seemingly filled with lead. Harriet waited in the kitchen, remembering how just days ago she and Robyn had laughed as they unpacked her things. Harriet pulled open the drawer next to the dishwasher and found the silverware. That was all it took for Harriet to start sobbing again.

Sitting on the kitchen floor, Harriet forced herself to take deep, calming breaths. She had to pull herself together for Audrey.

A cold emptiness settled in Harriet's stomach as she and Audrey made their way back to her house. Harriet felt an overwhelming sense of responsibility for the young girl beside her. She glanced over at Audrey, who stared blankly out the window, her eyes puffy and red.

When they arrived at the house, Harriet guided Audrey inside. "Let's get you settled in the guest room, okay?" Harriet said, trying to muster a comforting smile.

Audrey nodded, clutching her backpack. Harriet led her to the guest room, a cozy space with pale blue walls and a quilted bedspread Harriet had made herself during her quilting phase. "This will be your room for now," Harriet said. "You can unpack whenever you feel like it."

Audrey sat on the edge of the bed, looking lost and small. Harriet's heart broke for her. "If you need anything, I'll be in the kitchen, mustering up something for lunch."

"Okay," Audrey said, her voice barely a whisper.

Harriet left the room, giving Audrey some space to process everything. Opening the pantry and then the fridge, Harriet tried to come up with something comforting to eat. She found a box of macaroni and cheese and some leftover rotisserie chicken. It wasn't much, but it would have to do.

Harriet set the table with two plates and called down toward the guest room. "Audrey, lunch is ready!"

Audrey appeared at the end of the hall, her steps slow and hesitant. She joined Harriet at the table, her eyes still glazed with grief.

"I know it's not much," Harriet said. "Mac and cheese and chicken. Comfort food."

Audrey nodded, taking a small bite of macaroni and cheese. She set her fork down after just a few bites, put her head in her hands, and sobbed. "I can't believe it," she choked. "She can't really be gone."

Harriet stood and went behind Audrey and wrapped her in an awkward hug. It was all she could think to do. She racked her brain to remember how she felt when she lost her mom, but all she remembered was being angry and numb. She must have blocked this torturous, painful part from her memory.

"I know, sweetheart. It's awful. No one should have to go through what you are right now. I'm so sorry."

Audrey cried for what seemed like ages, but eventually, her tears dried, and she wiped her nose with the back of her hand. Harriet brought her a tissue.

"I don't think I can eat," Audrey said.

"Understandable," Harriet said, clearing their plates and setting them in the sink. "How about we watch something on TV? Take our minds off things for a bit?"

Audrey shrugged but followed Harriet into the living room. Harriet flipped through the channels until she found an old sitcom rerun. They settled onto the couch, the familiar sound of canned laughter filling the room.

Harriet picked up her phone and saw three texts from Lucille. She'd completely forgotten they were supposed to meet for coffee. Of course she had. Lucille would understand. She typed off a quick apology and explanation and put her phone away.

As the show played, Harriet glanced over at Audrey, who was staring at the TV but not really watching. Her gaze drifted to the window, and she could see Audrey's old house in the distance. Harriet's heart ached for her.

"Audrey," Harriet said softly, "I know this is really hard, but we're going to get through it together. You're not alone."

Audrey turned to Harriet, her eyes filling with tears once again. "I already miss her so much. How can she be gone forever?"

Harriet pulled Audrey into a tight hug, holding her close. "I know, sweetheart. I miss her too." She was getting used to all this hugging. It was terrible something this awful had to happen for her to enjoy hugging, but she found she enjoyed the warmth and comfort in it. It felt good to hold Audrey, her body a cushion against their mutual grief.

They sat there for a while, holding each other. Eventually, the emotional exhaustion caught up with them. Audrey's head drooped, and she curled up against Harriet, her eyes fluttering closed.

Harriet reached for the remote and turned off the TV, the room falling into a heavy silence. She leaned back against the couch, her own eyes heavy with fatigue. She knew there were many tough days ahead, but for now, she was content to hold Audrey close and offer her what comfort she could.

·　　·　　·　　·　　·

The next morning, Harriet opened the front door quietly so as not to disturb Audrey, who still slept soundly on the couch. Bibbo bounded out the door and nearly pulled Harriet down the front porch steps as he barked at the police officers still examining the house across the street.

"Can you believe this, Harriet?" a voice called out from down the street. "I heard something happened to Robyn."

Harriet turned to see Rocky pulling Kevin by his leash. Harriet nodded, her throat tight with emotion. "Yes, it's...it's awful."

"What happened?" Kevin asked.

Harriet paused, taking a deep breath in an effort to compose herself. "Chris, her husband..." Harriet's voice broke, and her chin trembled as she struggled to say the words she wished more than anything were not true. "He killed her."

Kevin's head jerked back in shock. "Oh my God. I can't believe it. I hadn't gotten to know her well, but Robyn seemed like such a kind woman. They had a daughter, right? How is she handling it?"

Harriet glanced back at her house. "She's devastated, of course. She's staying with me for now."

Kevin shook his head, his face filled with sorrow. "If there's anything I can do to help, please let me know."

Harriet forced a small smile. "Thanks. I appreciate that."

As Kevin continued his walk with Rocky, Harriet turned her attention back to the activity across the street. She watched the officers moving about, feeling a mix of sadness and anger. This tragedy had shattered so many lives, and it all felt so senseless.

Back in the house, Harriet found Audrey stirring on the couch. She blinked sleepily, her eyes still puffy. "Good morning, Audrey," Harriet said. "How did you sleep?"

Audrey rubbed her eyes and sat up, looking around as if trying to remember where she was. Her eyes met Harriet's, her face crumpled, and she shook her head and cried. Harriet went to her, wishing there was something she could do. She had to let her cry.

Finally, after what seemed like an eternity of sobbing, Audrey said, "Is my dad still in jail?"

Harriet nodded, sitting down next to her. She didn't know for sure, but she figured and hoped he was.

Audrey's shoulders sagged with relief. "Good. I don't want to see him ever again."

Harriet reached up and awkwardly patted Audrey's hair. "You're safe with me," Harriet said, hoping that was true too.

Harriet and Audrey spent a quiet day at home. Harriet busied herself with small tasks around the house, trying to keep her mind occupied. She knew they both needed some semblance of normalcy. Later that afternoon, as Harriet was folding laundry, there was a knock at the door. She opened it to find an officer standing on the porch, his expression serious but kind.

"Good afternoon, Ms. Henderson," he said. "I'm Detective Lawson. I wanted to check in on Audrey and see how you both are holding up."

Harriet stared at the imposing man, unsure of what to say. How did he think they were doing? "We'd be doing a lot better if Robyn was still here, if none of this had happened."

Detective Lawson cleared his throat and nodded, glancing around the living room where Audrey sat on the couch, clutching a stuffed animal. "I understand. I also wanted to let you know that Chris has been charged with first-degree murder. He won't be getting out anytime soon."

Harriet felt a wave of relief wash over her. "Thank goodness someone got that right."

Detective Lawson nodded. "We've contacted Robyn's parents in Seattle, and they're flying out here as soon as they can. It seems Chris's parents passed some time ago, so Audrey's only surviving relatives appear to be her maternal grandparents. So, I hope it's okay if Audrey remains with you for a while."

"Of course it's okay," Harriet said. "I'll do everything I can for Audrey. I can't help but feel guilty for convincing Robyn to move out so quickly."

"Don't blame yourself. We'll keep you updated as the case progresses. In the meantime, I suggest you both try to take it one day at a time. And remember, there are resources and support groups available to help you through this."

Harriet nodded. "We'd started going to Harmony House. They warned us, but I didn't think it was really as serious as this."

"No one ever does," the officer said, returning his hat to his head and turning to leave.

Closing the door behind the officer, Harriet returned to the living room. Audrey looked up at her, her eyes filled with silent questions.

Harriet forced a smile. "It's good that your grandparents are coming to see you."

Audrey pulled her knees to her chest and rested her chin on them.

"What's wrong?" Harriet asked.

"I...I don't really know them. We hadn't seen them in years. My dad didn't like them."

Harriet caught the snarky reply in her mouth. Of course Chris didn't like them. He'd isolated Robyn like Les had isolated her. Anger rose in her chest, and she paced in front of the couch to release some of it.

"Well, I'm sure they're nice people." Harriet didn't know what to say. She had no idea if they were nice people. But they were Audrey's family. Apparently, the only family she had.

Audrey nodded, but Harriet could see the lingering fear and confusion in her eyes. Harriet had always wanted to be a mother, but not under these circumstances. She had no idea how to be a mother, and now she had to be one, at least for the time being, and try to make up for the loss of the other.

CHAPTER 29

EACH DAY PASSED slowly as Harriet and Audrey settled into a quiet routine. Audrey spent some days in bed, unable to gather the strength to do much of anything. Harriet brought her food and tried to read to her. When she got out of bed, they played board games, watched TV, and did puzzles, attempting to distract themselves from the looming shadows of grief and fear. Harriet watched Audrey closely, her heart aching with every sad, vacant look.

Harriet focused on the practicalities. She called the school to ask how long Audrey could be absent, given this horrific situation. Thankfully, the school was understanding and said she could take as much time as she needed. Her teachers would email to check in and keep her up to date, and it would be at her discretion to complete the assignments. She then called Harmony House, seeking guidance and support from Callie.

Harriet told Callie about Audrey staying with her. Taking a deep breath, she asked the question that had been creeping into her mind. "Do you think there's any chance they'd consider me as her guardian?"

"It's possible, Harriet. Courts typically prefer placing children with family members, but given the circumstances and Robyn's trusting you with Audrey, they might consider it. It's important to show that you can provide a stable, loving environment for her. Support from other people in your life will be crucial."

Harriet's breath caught in her chest. *What other people?* The question screamed in her mind, a cold panic clutching her throat. Robyn was her first friend in what felt like forever. Maybe Lucille was becoming a friend, but it was too soon to count on her to have Harriet's back. Why hadn't Hank responded to her text? A tremor of raw vulnerability threatened to ripple through her voice, but she swallowed it down. She had to be seen as stable, well-connected, a pillar of support. No cracks. Not now, when Audrey's entire future rested on her shoulders.

"Thank you, Callie. I want to do what's best for Audrey."

"I know you do. We'll help you through every step. One more thing, Harriet. Document everything. Keep records of all communications, any interactions with authorities, and anything related to Audrey's care. That will be important for the legal proceedings."

Harriet hung up the phone after scheduling counseling sessions for herself and Audrey, feeling a small sense of relief at having some instructions as to what to do next. Then, determined to keep trying, she typed an email to Hank. Maybe he'd changed his phone number, and that was why he hadn't answered her text. She'd been missing Hank in her solitude, but she hadn't realized how much until now. And it wasn't only because she needed to show the court she wasn't completely alone.

Out for Bibbo's morning walk, she rounded the corner onto the main path of the neighborhood park and spotted Kevin walking Rocky.

"How have you been holding up?" Kevin asked, concern creasing his forehead.

Harriet felt a lump in her throat and managed a quick nod. "It's been tough. Just attempting to handle each day as it comes."

Kevin reached out and gently squeezed her shoulder. "I'm sure you're doing a great job."

Harriet had no idea how he could possibly know this, but she appreciated the sentiment nonetheless. Harriet felt warmth spread through her at his touch. "Th-Thanks," Harriet stammered, looking quickly to the ground, hoping to hide the flush in her cheeks.

They continued down the path, enjoying the sunshine, dogs trotting side-by-side, tongues lolling. Eventually, Kevin asked, "Did you hear about Tammy?"

"No. What about her?"

"I heard she's going through a nasty divorce. Supposedly, her husband cheated with someone like twenty years younger, and he's trying to take everything. He kicked her out of the house and everything."

"That's terrible. No one deserves that. Not even Tammy."

Kevin stopped. "Really, Harriet?"

"What?"

Kevin shook his head. "How can you say that about Tammy?"

"I had to do her job for her, remember?"

Kevin sighed. "You seemed different. I thought you'd let go of your..."

"My what?"

"Your bitter and angry ways."

Harriet's mouth fell open. Kevin thought she was bitter and angry? She was taking care of the neighborhood, keeping things in order. "I-I didn't realize that's what you thought about me."

Kevin sighed. "Don't you remember how mean you were when you thought of me as off-leash-dog-man?"

"That wasn't mean. That was enforcing the rules. There's a difference. Now that Rocky's on a leash. You can get to know the real me."

"Huh. I thought you'd changed. But it was just the leash." He looked so sad, like a little boy whose scoop of ice cream had gone splat on the sidewalk.

Harriet looked down at the ground. "I honestly didn't realize I was mean. I was being practical, keeping the neighborhood from going to hell in a handbasket, as Les used to say."

Practical. That summed it up. She valued order. Les had valued order. It was a shared trait, a foundation of her entire adult life. Kevin, with his loose leash and easy smile, probably just didn't understand the importance of boundaries, of maintaining standards. He was a free spirit; she was a woman of good sense. It was simply a difference in personality, not a character flaw on her part. She hadn't been "mean," she'd been correct. He just hadn't seen it that way.

"Maybe there are more important things than following the rules," Kevin said.

Harriet felt the instinctive indignation rise, sharp and hot in her chest. *More important?* What could be more important than order, than proper conduct, than ensuring things didn't descend into chaos? Her mouth opened, ready with a crisp retort, but she caught herself. She remembered the look on Kevin's face, like a deflated child. And Robyn's struggles, the raw, messy reality of her life, where rules hadn't protected her from anything. Harriet's throat tightened. The words remained unspoken. She stared straight ahead. They began walking in silence for a few minutes, the quiet stretching between them, thick with her unspoken thoughts.

"Maybe you're right," Harriet finally said, almost under her breath, the admission tasting like ash on her tongue.

"What was that?" Kevin asked, cupping his hand behind his ear.

"You heard me."

Kevin turned and shot a sideways smile at her. Heat surged through her. She took a few more deep breaths. "I have an idea," Harriet said. "But I'm going to need your help."

"Okay..."

"Robyn was living in a townhome I bought for her."

"You bought a townhome for Robyn?" Kevin's eyes were huge.

Harriet waved her hand dismissively. "It wasn't that altruistic. I bought it with the money Les left me, and it's an investment. I planned to turn it into a vacation rental. Anyway, maybe Tammy could stay there. Just until she gets things figured out."

Kevin turned and wrapped Harriet in a hug. Harriet's breath caught in her chest. She was too stunned to respond or even move.

"I knew there was kindness under that harsh exterior. That's amazing. How can I help?" Kevin said, into her hair.

"I'll have to move Robyn's things out." She pulled away from the hug and peered sideways at him to gauge his reaction.

He smiled. "No problem. Happy to help."

As they reached a bend in the path, Kevin said. "Hey, would you like to grab a drink sometime? I know things are crazy right now, but maybe it would be good to take a break and...relax a bit."

"You want to get a drink? With me? I thought you hated me."

A nervous chuckle escaped Kevin's lips. "Hate's a strong word. I didn't understand why you were, or maybe still are, such a stickler for all the rules, but I suppose I understand why it makes sense to have Rocky on a leash. He was getting more and more rebellious about going into people's yards, and he wasn't listening to me like he should have."

A smile spread wide across Harriet's face. "I told you so."

Kevin laughed. "I didn't think people actually said that. I thought they just thought it."

"If you know people are thinking it, what difference does it make?"

"Good point." He ran a hand through his hair. "Anyway, how about that drink?

"Sounds good, but I have to think about Audrey now, so I'm not really sure of my schedule. Why don't you come over for coffee?"

"Works for me. Let me know when you're free."

"I'm free now."

Kevin smiled. "All right. I'll drop Rocky at home and be over then."

"Rocky can come. Audrey loves dogs."

"Let's go then," Kevin said, pulling Rocky closer and turning toward Harriet's house.

Inside, Harriet went straight to the kitchen, setting out coffee mugs and pulling out the box full of an array of different K-Cups. Les only drank dark roast, but she liked to mix it up. The habit stuck. Thankfully, she always had hot chocolate as one option, so she figured Audrey would be happy with that.

"Kevin, what kind of coffee do you like?" Harriet called from the kitchen.

"Oh, anything is great. I'm not picky."

Wow. What a change from Les. Harriet was certain those words had never come from his lips.

Audrey looked up from the book she was reading on the couch at the sound of Kevin's voice. The sadness that clung to her lifted enough for her to flash a small smile at Kevin. "Hi," she said softly, setting her book aside.

"Hey, you must be Audrey," Kevin said, giving her a friendly wave. "I'm your neighbor. I heard about your mom. I'm so sorry." He strode into the living room and sat across from her on a chair. "How are you holding up?"

Audrey shrugged. "Okay, I guess." She leaned over to pet Rocky.

Rocky seemed to sense Audrey's need for comfort and went closer to her, nuzzling her hand with his wet nose. A small giggle escaped her. Harriet's heart lifted at the sound.

The aroma of hot chocolate and coffee filled the air, mingling with the faint scent of vanilla from a candle she'd lit on the counter. Harriet poured the coffee, her hands shaking slightly. She inhaled deeply and reminded herself that this was just coffee with a neighbor. Nothing more. Carefully, she carried the mugs into the living room.

"Here you are."

Kevin grabbed a mug and took a sip. "This is great, Harriet. Thanks for having us over."

"It's no problem," Harriet replied, hoping to sound like she did this kind of thing all the time, even though this was the most people she'd had in her living room in years. Maybe decades.

Kevin leaned forward in the chair, his posture relaxed and open, a stark contrast to the rigid formality Harriet was accustomed to. He wore a pair of well-loved jeans, a far cry from the crisp suits and starched collars of Les's wardrobe. He held his coffee mug loosely in his hands, his fingers occasionally drumming a gentle rhythm against the ceramic.

An awkward silence settled over the room. Harriet glanced at Audrey, who was now resting her head on Rocky's back, looking more relaxed than she had in days. She turned her attention back to Kevin, searching for something to say.

"So, Kevin, how are things at the university?" Harriet asked.

Kevin's face lit up. "Busy as always, but I love it. It's nearly the end of the semester, and we're gearing up for a new field study in the fall, which should be exciting."

"That sounds fascinating. What kind of study is it?"

"We're looking at some rock formations in the Bridgers. It doesn't matter how many times we study the area; there's always something new to find. It's amazing to see the story the Earth can tell."

Harriet found herself drawn to his enthusiasm. "I've always admired people who can read the earth like that."

"Do you ever take younger students on those trips?" Audrey asked.

"Absolutely. It's a great learning experience for them. There's nothing like seeing geology in the field. Would you be interested in that sort of thing, Audrey?"

Audrey nodded. "I like learning about rocks in science class."

"That's great," Kevin said. "If you ever want to learn more, I'd be happy to show you some of the work we do."

Audrey smiled. "Thanks. That sounds cool."

Another pause filled the room, but this time it felt less awkward, more like a comfortable silence shared among friends.

"Do you have any kids, Kevin?" Audrey asked.

Kevin shook his head. "No. But I have Rocky, and he keeps me plenty busy."

"Do you live alone?" Audrey asked.

"Of course not. I have Rocky," Kevin chuckled. "And we live in this great neighborhood, so it never feels too lonely."

Rocky, with a mischievous glint in his eye, grabbed one of Audrey's pink socks that had been lying on the floor and darted across the room. Bibbo, not wanting to be left out, immediately joined the chase, barking excitedly.

"Hey, that's my sock!" Audrey laughed, jumping up to chase them.

Rocky dodged around the coffee table, with Bibbo hot on his heels. The two dogs weaved through the furniture, causing delightful chaos. Audrey giggled as she tried to catch Rocky, who seemed to enjoy the game immensely.

Kevin shook his head, chuckling. "Rocky, you little thief. Give that back!"

Harriet couldn't help but laugh as well. "Bibbo, you're supposed to help catch him, not join in!"

The dogs continued their playful antics, knocking over a few cushions and causing a bit of harmless mayhem. Finally, Audrey managed to corner Rocky by the couch and retrieved her sock, holding it up triumphantly.

"Got it!" she announced, smiling.

Kevin sipped his coffee and looked at Harriet thoughtfully. "So, Harriet, do you work?"

Harriet hesitated for a moment. "I used to work as a high school librarian. I absolutely loved it."

"I imagine you were great at it," Kevin said.

A wistful smile crossed Harriet's face. "I like to think so."

"So, what happened? Why did you stop?"

Harriet took a deep breath, her gaze dropping to her coffee cup. "Les, my late husband, insisted I quit. He wanted me to be home more to cook and clean for him. He had very specific ideas about what a wife's role should be, and working outside the home didn't fit into that."

Kevin frowned. "That must have been tough, giving up something you loved."

"It was," Harriet said. "I missed the interaction with the students, the energy of the library."

Kevin reached out and gently touched Harriet's hand. She flinched at the unexpected touch, and he pulled back, his eyes emanating concern. "I'm sorry you had to go through that. It sounds like you were an amazing librarian, and it's a shame you had to give that up."

Harriet looked up, meeting Kevin's gaze. His sincerity and kindness were palpable. Yet again, a warmth spread through her chest. He was just being polite. Men often said things like that to grieving widows, didn't they? A simple gesture of sympathy, nothing more. Still, the warmth in her chest lingered.

"Thank you, Kevin. It means a lot to hear that."

Audrey, who had been quietly listening, looked up at Harriet. "Maybe you can be a librarian again someday."

Harriet's heart lifted at Audrey's words, but she swiped her hand in front of her face and said, "Nobody wants an old fuddy-duddy like me anymore."

"You aren't old, and that's not true," Audrey said.

"It's never too late to go back to what you love, Harriet," Kevin said.

Harriet's eyes lingered on Kevin, his words echoing what Lucille had said. Maybe she could go back to work. The idea was beginning to feel like a real possibility. It was exciting.

Kevin stood. "I should probably get going. But Harriet, if you need anything, don't hesitate to ask. And Audrey, Rocky and I are always around if you need some cheering up."

Audrey smiled. "Thanks. I like having Rocky around."

Kevin nodded and turned to Harriet. "Take care. I'll see you soon."

Harriet walked him to the door. "Any chance you'd be interested in making this a weekly thing?"

"I think that could be arranged." Kevin shot her a mischievous half-smile as he turned and walked down the front steps.

Returning to the living room, Harriet sat down next to Audrey, who had wrapped a blanket around her legs and was holding her book but staring absently out the window.

Not wanting to lose the positive energy permeating the house after Kevin's visit, Harriet said, "How about we bake some cookies?"

Audrey's eyes lit up. "Yeah, I'd like that."

They headed to the kitchen, Harriet feeling a renewed sense of purpose. Between Kevin's visit and having Audrey around, Harriet could imagine a new life filled with impromptu get-togethers, children laughing, and a messy house. Was this truly what she wanted? The thought of embracing chaos was both terrifying and exhilarating.

A messy house. The phrase tripped her up. Could she really deal with a messy house? She pictured sticky fingerprints on her pristine counters, books askew on shelves, muddy shoe prints trailing across her polished floors. The image sent a faint shiver down her spine. Was the warmth she felt just now a fleeting emotion? Perhaps this messy, spontaneous life was simply a fantasy, a childish rebellion. Order was safety. Predictability was peace. Hadn't she always thrived in that? It was a beautiful thought, this free-spirited existence, but could she really do it? Or was it an idea she was trying on, like a costume that didn't quite fit?

CHAPTER 30

THE NEXT MORNING, as Harriet poured herself a cup of coffee, she heard a notification from her phone. She picked it up and saw an email from Hank. Her heart skipped a beat as she opened the email, hoping he'd still be willing to be there for her.

```
Subject: Re: Urgent - Need to Talk
Hi Harriet,
I got your message. I can't believe what I'm
reading. I'm so sorry about Robyn. That's awful. I
hear about things like that in the news, but it
doesn't seem real.
It's been too long since we last spoke, and I'm
sorry for that.
Anyway, the reason you couldn't reach me by phone
is that I have a new number. We moved from NY to CT
a few years ago. My new number is (203) 555-4441.
Call anytime.
I want to help in any way I can. If you need me
to come to Montana, I'll be on the next flight. I
want to meet Audrey and be there for both of you.
Please let me know what you need.
Love, Hank
```

Harriet's eyes welled up with tears as she read the email. She felt a mixture of relief, guilt, and hope all at once. Even after all these years, her sweet brother's words were like a balm to her aching heart.

Picking up the phone, she punched the numbers from the email and heard the phone ring. Her heart felt as though it might jump completely out of her chest. Excitement, nervousness, joy, fear, every emotion she had worked so hard to control for Les was bubbling over in anticipation of speaking to her brother again.

"Hello?" Hank's voice was thick with sleep, barely audible.

"Hank, it's Harriet," she said, her voice trembling slightly.

There was a moment of silence on the other end, and she could almost picture him trying to clear the fog of sleep from his mind. "Harriet? My sister?"

"Unless you have another one."

Hank chuckled. "Yep, that's my Harriet."

Harriet couldn't hold back the tears. "Hank, I've missed you," she whispered.

"It's been a long time," Hank mumbled, clearly still groggy. "Uh, what time is it?"

"It's early, I know. I'm sorry."

Hank sighed, and she could hear the rustling of sheets. "It's fine. What's going on? Your email was...a lot to take in. I'm sorry we lost touch. Les always made it hard."

"Yes, he did. I'm figuring out so much. We can talk about that later. Right now, I'd love some help. I mean, I've never been a mother."

"Tell me what you need. Do you want me to come to Montana?"

"Yes, please," Harriet said, her voice breaking. "I don't know how to do this alone. Audrey needs a stable environment, and I...I need my brother."

"You've got it," Hank replied without hesitation. "I'll book a flight today and be there as soon as I can."

"What about Megan and your kid or kids? I can't believe I don't even know how many kids you have."

"We have a lot of catching up to do. I have three, and Megan will understand. She knows how sad I've been not having you in my life."

"Okay," Harriet said, wiping away her tears. "Thank you, Hank. I can't tell you how much this means to me."

"We're family, Harriet. It's what we do," Hank said. "I'll call you with my flight details. Hang in there, okay?"

"I'll do my best. I can't wait to see you."

"Me too, sis. See you soon."

Harriet hung up the phone and sat down at the kitchen table, her coffee growing cold as she stared out the window, lost in thought. *Les always made it hard.* Hank's words echoed in her mind. But it wasn't entirely Les's fault, was it? Hank lived so far away, busy with his own life. And it had been hard for Harriet to accept her brother was starting a family when she couldn't. Les was protecting her. And then, time went by, and their lives had drifted apart. Les had simply preferred a quiet life, just the two of them. And she'd agreed to it, hadn't she? Some decisions in life were difficult. People these days were too emotional about everything, making mountains out of molehills where simple choices were concerned.

She shook her head. None of it mattered now. Les was gone, and her brother was coming to visit.

Hearing footsteps in the hall, Harriet went to greet Audrey. "Good morning, sweetheart. How did you sleep?"

Audrey blinked sleepily, clutching her stuffed animal. "Okay, I guess."

"That's good. How about I get you some breakfast?"

Audrey nodded, her eyes filling with tears. "I miss Mom."

"I know, sweetheart," Harriet said, pulling her into a hug. They stood holding each other while Harriet waited for Audrey's tears to run their course. Harriet remembered how, when she lost her mother, waves of sadness would overwhelm her, and there was nothing anyone could do to make it better. She had to wait for it to pass. Audrey needed space to mourn her mother, just as Harriet had.

When Audrey pulled away, Harriet said, "I have what I hope will be good news."

"What is it?"

"My brother is coming all the way from Connecticut to visit."

Audrey stared at her. Of course she wouldn't care about his visit. She had no idea who he was.

"I haven't seen him in many years, but he was my best friend growing up. If he's half as kind as he was back then, I bet you'll like him."

"Why haven't you seen him?" Audrey asked, her eyebrows pinched together.

"It's a long story. I don't fully understand it either. I'm just glad he's coming."

Audrey nodded, still looking confused. "Do you think I could invite Izzy over today?"

Harriet's breath caught. She had no idea how to entertain another child. She knew what to do at the library, but in her house? What would she feed her? How would she entertain her? What did twelve-year-olds like to do? "Um. I'm not sure..."

"Please. I miss her. I think it would help me stop thinking about my mom."

"I don't know how to host kids," Harriet said.

Audrey laughed. "It's not a formal thing. She'll come over and we'll hang out in my room for a while. You won't even know she's here."

"So, I don't need to make her food and entertain her?"

"No. We can grab snacks ourselves if we're hungry."

"Okay, then. I suppose it's all right," Harriet said, biting her fingernail. As much as she was beginning to enjoy having other people in her house, it was still an adjustment.

Joy lit up Audrey's face, and Harriet's heart melted. "Thanks, Harriet. I'll text her to come over after school."

Later that afternoon, the doorbell rang, pulling Harriet from her cleaning. Audrey leapt from the couch. "That must be Izzy!"

Harriet went to the door and found a smiling girl with bright blonde ponytails and emerald green eyes standing on the porch. "Hi!" she said, shyly twisting from side to side.

"You must be Izzy. Come on in," Harriet said, stepping aside to let the girl in.

Audrey and Izzy walked down the hall, their sweet voices echoing through the house. Audrey was right. It was good for her to have a friend close by, someone who could help distract her from the pain.

For a few precious hours, the house vibrated with their youthful energy, a welcome reprieve from the quiet sorrow that clung to the house. After Izzy left, the silence descended once more, but it felt softer, less suffocating. Audrey emerged from her room. "What's for dinner?"

"Hamburgers and fries. How does that sound?"

Audrey nodded in reply, looking down at the floor.

"Want to help me?"

Audrey sighed. "I guess so. I always cooked with my mom. She wanted to be sure I knew how. I can't believe I'll never do that again."

"I know," Harriet said. "Maybe you can show me how you and your mom did things?"

Audrey nodded, a tear traveling down her cheek.

After dinner, she and Audrey settled on the couch to watch some TV before bed. "I think I want to go back to school," Audrey said.

"Are you sure you're ready?"

Audrey nodded. "I don't want to stay home and feel sad."

"Okay. It's your call. How about Monday? Your grandparents will be here the day after tomorrow, and they'll want to spend some time with you, and my brother will be here as well."

Audrey nodded again and looked down at her hands.

"What's wrong?"

"My grandparents won't try to take me, will they?"

Harriet put her arm around Audrey's shoulders. She wanted to reassure her that she'd be allowed to stay with her, but Harriet knew she couldn't. "Whatever happens, I'll be here for you."

Audrey laid her head on Harriet's shoulder and put her arms around her waist. Harriet's eyes burned, and her heart ached with love for this sweet girl. She hadn't known her long, but she already couldn't imagine life without her.

CHAPTER 31

THE NEXT MORNING, Harriet checked her phone for updates from Hank. He had texted that his flight was on time, and he would land in Bozeman in a couple of hours. She'd offered to pick him up, but Hank insisted on renting a car. He didn't want to be a burden. Harriet wasn't surprised. She knew how independent he was.

As his car pulled up, Harriet burst through the front door, desperate to see her little brother. He was taller and a bit grayer than she remembered, but unmistakably her brother.

"Hank!" she called out, waving.

Hank's face lit up when he saw her. He hurried over to wrap her in a tight hug. "Harriet, it's so good to see you."

"You too, Hank," Harriet replied, feeling awkward and stiff in his arms, but happy. "It's been too long."

Hank pulled back slightly and smiled down at Audrey, who'd come up beside Harriet. "And you must be Audrey. I'm Hank, Harriet's brother."

"Hi," Audrey said.

"It's nice to meet you. I've heard a lot about you," Hank said.

"Let me help you with your bags. Come on in. We have a ton of ground to cover," Harriet said.

Inside, Hank sat on the couch, and Harriet poured them each a cup of coffee. Audrey went to the fridge, helped herself to a Capri Sun, and sat cross-legged on the oversized chair next to the couch.

"So, Hank," Harriet began, "how's life been for you? I mean, where do you work now? And Megan, how is she? And tell me about your kids."

Hank chuckled softly, glancing over at Harriet. His eyes were like looking into a mirror. They shared the same warm brown eyes that glowed in the sun. "I'm a marriage and family counselor. You probably could have guessed that since I was a psychology major. Megan is great. She's still in banking but at a local branch now, so no more crazy hours. And, like I said before, we have three kids. After our first son, Cole, the one you knew about, we had twins. A boy and a girl. Cole is a senior in high school this year, and the twins are in eighth grade."

Harriet smiled, feeling a pang of guilt for not knowing these basic details about her brother's life. "Twins. Wow, that's...that's a handful, I bet."

"It is, but it's also wonderful," Hank replied. "What about you, Harriet? What have you been up to all these years?"

"Nothing much," Harriet said. "I mean, Les kept me busy at home. He liked things a certain way. Well, you know how he was. Or maybe you don't." She stopped herself before she said more.

"I'm sorry, Harriet. I wish I could've done something."

Harriet waved a hand in front of her face. She didn't want her churning thoughts about Les and the overactive emotions they brought with them making Hank think she'd lost it entirely. "So," Harriet said, changing the subject. "As you can see, this is the living room," she said. "And the kitchen is over there, and there are three bedrooms down the hall. It's not much, but it's home."

"It's...very brown," Hank said. "What's with all the wood paneling? It doesn't seem like you. I remember your lavender room with all the flowers everywhere when we were growing up."

Harriet sighed. "Les wanted it to feel cozy, like a smoking room."

Hank's eyebrows rose. "Was he a smoker? I don't remember that, and the house doesn't smell like I expect it would if he had been."

Harriet shook her head and let out a small chuckle. "It was the vibe he was after."

"Well, I suppose he nailed it." Hank gestured to the walls and asked, "How do you feel about it?"

"I hate it. I always have. It's depressing," Harriet said.

Audrey looked up from her book. "I agree. I wanted to say something, but I didn't want to offend you, Harriet."

"Let's do something about it," Hank said. "Megan and I have done a couple of fixer-uppers, and I'm no expert, but I think I can help give this place a facelift. What do you say?"

"Sounds great, but aren't you only here for a couple of days?" Harriet asked.

"Yeah, but we can pull the paneling off, at least in one room, and get it patched and painted if we all work together. If we can't get it all done on this visit, we'll get it done the next time I visit. How does that sound? Audrey, you game?"

"Absolutely," Audrey said, jumping to her feet.

"Where should we start, living room or kitchen?" Hank asked.

"Kitchen," Harriet and Audrey said in unison.

"Great. It's settled. There's no time to waste. I'll run to the hardware store to get some tools. I'm assuming you don't have a pry bar, drywall saw, or joint compound, Harriet?"

"Are you speaking another language?" Harriet asked.

Hank laughed. "Exactly as I expected. I'll be back in a bit."

Just a few hours later, the dreary kitchen quickly became a battlefield of transformation. Sunlight streamed through the windows, illuminating the dust motes dancing in the air as Harriet, Hank, and Audrey embarked on their demolition project. Drop cloths covered the countertops and floor, and a toolbox lay open with an arsenal of pry bars, hammers, and pliers ready for the task at hand.

Harriet, her hair tucked into a bandana, ripped away a piece of paneling, just as Hank had instructed. A mischievous glint sparkled in her eyes as she revealed the faded wallpaper beneath. "Look at this hideous pattern," she said. "I forgot we'd initially used this wallpaper when we built the house. Les said it was a 'timeless classic.'"

"Really, avocado green with psychedelic swirls was a 'timeless classic'?" Hank asked.

Harriet chuckled. "He changed his mind pretty quickly. He covered it with the paneling after a few months. I suppose he needed something even more classic."

By late afternoon, the walls were bare, revealing decades-old plaster and patches of avocado green. The room, stripped of its dated paneling, felt brighter and more spacious, a blank canvas awaiting a fresh start.

Harriet surveyed the scene with a satisfied smile. "It's amazing what a little demolition can do."

Audrey nodded in agreement. "It already feels like a whole new kitchen."

Hank, leaning against the counter, wiped his brow with the back of his hand. "Just wait until we're finished," he said. "It'll be beautiful."

As the sun began to set, casting long shadows across the room, they gathered their tools and surveyed their progress. The kitchen held a promise of renewal, but not a promise of dinner.

"How about I take you two out for dinner tonight?" Harriet asked. "It's the least I can do to repay you for all your hard work."

"Audrey, what's your favorite restaurant?" Hank asked.

Audrey was silent for a moment. Her bottom lip began to tremble. "My mom and I used to go to Sidewinders to celebrate a good grade, a great ski race, that kind of thing."

"Would you like to go there again, or is that too difficult?" Hank asked.

Audrey hesitated. "I think I'd like to go. It was a special place for us, and maybe it will help me feel close to her again. Is that okay?"

"That's more than okay. It's brave of you. Let's grab our coats and head over there," Hank said.

During dinner, they chatted about Audrey's school and her favorite subjects. Harriet liked how easily Hank talked with Audrey. It was so wonderful to have him here.

"Are you sure you can't stay longer than just a couple of days, Hank?" Harriet asked. "I mean, it's been so long."

"I wish I could, but the twins are in a play Friday and Saturday, and I promised I'd be there."

Harriet's heart sank. "Just when we're getting to know each other again. I need more than a few days."

"I know. I guess you and Audrey will have to visit us in Connecticut. It's only a short train ride to New York City."

Audrey's eyes lit up. "Can we, Harriet? I've always wanted to go to New York."

"I suppose we can," Harriet said. She worried whether she would still have Audrey by the time they could plan a trip, but shoved that thought out of her mind for the time being.

Returning home from the restaurant, Harriet said, "Well, young lady, it's bedtime."

"Do I have to?"

"Yes, sweetheart." Harriet hugged her, and Audrey walked down the hall to the bathroom to get ready for bed.

Harriet poured two glasses of wine and joined Hank in the living room. He took a sip of his wine and said, "Harriet, there's something I've been meaning to talk to you about."

Harriet had been bringing her glass up to her lips to take a sip, but stopped halfway. "What is it, Hank?"

Hank sighed. "Over the years, I tried to get in touch with you so many times. I didn't give up."

"I didn't know," Harriet said.

"I sent letters and emails, and even called your house and cell phone. Every time, Les intercepted them. He'd respond to my letters pretending to be you, saying you didn't want to talk. Emails went unanswered, or I got replies that sounded nothing like you. When I called, he always had an excuse— 'She's not home,' 'She's busy,' 'She doesn't want to talk.' It was always something. It was strange how he always answered your phone."

Harriet pursed her lips together. "He screened my calls. He said it was for my safety. He convinced me there were so many crazy people out there with all the new technology. He said having a cell phone was a privilege, and he needed access to everything so he could ensure that I was safe."

Hank nodded. "I figured something like that was going on. I even came to visit once. I showed up at your house, and Les answered the door. He told me you were out of town and made it clear I wasn't welcome. I felt so helpless. I wanted to be there for you, but he made it impossible."

"He always said you didn't care, that you were too busy with your own life," Harriet said.

"That's exactly what he wanted you to believe," Hank said. "He isolated you, Harriet. It's a classic tactic to control someone."

A tear trickled down Harriet's cheek. "I never knew any of this."

Hank continued. "So, I wrote you one last letter. I poured my heart out, telling you how much I missed you and asking why you weren't responding. A few weeks later, I got a letter back, but it wasn't from you. It was from Les. He wrote that you didn't want to have any contact with me and that I should stop trying. The letter was cruel. He said things that made me think you really didn't care anymore."

"I never saw any letter from you, Hank. Never."

"I know that now," Hank said. "But back then, it crushed me. I thought I'd lost you. But I still didn't give up. I tried calling again a few years later, thinking maybe things had changed. This time, Les threatened me. He said if I ever tried to contact you again, he'd make sure I regretted it."

Harriet's heart ached with every word. "What'd he mean by that?"

"He said he knew where I lived, that he could make things very difficult for me. He mentioned my kids by name, even though I hadn't told him about the twins. It was like he was watching us, Harriet. It was terrifying."

"He never told me any of this. I can't believe he did that to you. To us," Harriet said, tears trickling down her cheeks.

Hank nodded. "I didn't want to put Megan or the kids in danger, so I backed off. But I never stopped thinking about you. I'm so sorry."

"It's not your fault. He controlled everything. Les also convinced me it didn't matter, that I didn't need anyone other than him." Harriet set her wine on the coffee table and grabbed a tissue to wipe her eyes.

Hank leaned forward. "Harriet, Les was a master manipulator. He knew exactly how to keep you isolated and dependent on him. I don't know if you want to hear this, but I think you need to." He took a deep breath. "Harriet, I think Les was abusive. Emotionally, at least. Obviously, I don't know if anything else was going on. The isolation is a common tactic. They make their victims feel worthless and alone so they can maintain control."

Harriet flinched at the word "abusive" coming from her brother's mouth. Her first instinct was to rail angrily against her brother's assertion, to defend Les, to protect the very foundation of her past. But hadn't she begun to see it herself? The word felt too harsh, too ugly for her meticulously constructed life, for the man she had loved. *Abusive?* That was for Chris, for the monsters. Not for Les, who had provided and cherished their quiet life. Yet, the memories, so recently unearthed, flickered behind her eyes: the control over her job, the dismissal of her desires, the subtle, biting criticisms that chipped away at her spirit. It was a cold, creeping realization, the pieces of a puzzle she'd carefully ignored now assembling into a horrifying picture. The truth felt like a betrayal, not just of Les but of herself for having been so blind. "I can't believe he did that. All this time, I thought I was better off relying only on Les."

Hank reached over and took her hand. "I've missed you every day. I'm here now, and I'm not going anywhere."

A sob escaped from Harriet, and she covered her mouth to tamp it down. Her swirling thoughts came pouring from her, "I can't believe I was so blind to what Les was doing. Even after he died, I didn't see it. I still mourned him and the life we built. I'm still struggling with it. What was real and what wasn't? Sometimes, I think I'm being too harsh, and other times, too lenient. Ultimately, it seems I lost myself in him. I don't seem to know what I want without him." She shook her head. "These memories just keep popping into my mind of him being, well, a jerk. I can't believe I didn't see it. I can't believe I stayed and let him control me like that."

"It's the strong ones who stay," Hank said.

Harriet turned to stare at him. "What do you mean?"

"Strong people think they can overcome the situation, fix it. They think it's weak to leave and give up on a relationship, even when they are being taken advantage of or manipulated."

Harriet's eyebrows knit together as she took this in. "I never knew that. I've been beating myself up for being so stupid and blind. And I thought I was weak for staying, not strong."

"If you're anything like the girl I grew up with, you're definitely not weak," Hank said.

Harriet looked at him, truly seeing him for the first time in decades. Not just her little brother, but a man who understood, who saw a strength in her that she had buried under layers of self-doubt and Les's pronouncements. The tears came again, but this time they were different—less about sorrow, more about a profound, almost dizzying, sense of revelation. She was tired of crying, but she couldn't stop it.

"But what do I do with all of this now?" she asked.

Hank offered a small, knowing smile. "You start by accepting it. And then, you decide what kind of life you want. One that's truly yours." He paused. "You don't have to be 'stupid' or 'blind' anymore,

Harriet. You just have to be Harriet. And she's pretty formidable, from what I remember."

Harriet managed a small smile in return. The room didn't exactly brighten, but the oppressive weight in her chest eased a bit. Maybe she was stronger than she thought.

CHAPTER 32

OVER BREAKFAST the next morning, Hank shared stories from their childhood. "Harriet, do you remember our ski racing days?"

Harriet laughed. "Oh, do I ever! You always wanted to race me down the hill."

Audrey's eyes lit with curiosity. "Who usually won?"

"Most of the time, Hank. He was younger, but he was a natural on skis and usually beat me. But there was one time when things didn't go as planned."

"Oh, this is a good one," Hank said, leaning in conspiratorially to tell the story. "We raced down the steepest run. I was way ahead, but I hit a patch of ice and went flying, skis and poles in all directions."

"Yard sale," Audrey interjected.

Hank laughed. "It sure was. Thankfully, it was a powder day, and I just ended up face-first in a soft snowbank."

Harriet shook her head, chuckling. "I was so worried. I was sure he'd broken something. I hurried to help him, and as I was pulling him up, he yanked me into the snowbank with him. After sputtering and spitting snow from my mouth and wiping it from my goggles, I started burying him in the snow. He pummeled me with snowballs, and we laughed so hard we couldn't get up."

"It sounds like you guys had some fun times," Audrey said.

"We did," Harriet said. "We were lucky to have each other."

"Why are you using the past tense? We still do," Hank said.

Harriet smiled and sipped her coffee to swallow down the lump forming in her throat.

"Mom and I used to go skiing every winter," Audrey said. "She taught me everything I know. She signed me up for the race team, even though I was scared."

Hank reached out and patted Audrey's hand. "Maybe Harriet and I can take you skiing sometime."

"Oh no. You aren't getting me on skis again. Much too dangerous at my age," Harriet said.

Hank turned to stare at Harriet. "What are you talking about? You are one of the most beautiful skiers I know."

Harriet blushed. "You really think so? Les said it was a sport best left in childhood since we tend to break so easily as we get older. We're asking to end up in the hospital."

"Sounds like that's what Les thought. What do you think, Harriet?" Hank asked.

Harriet paused. What did she think? She'd loved skiing, the feeling of speeding down the mountain, the wind whipping against her cheeks, poles tucked in against her sides, skis swishing, the rooster tail of snow flying out behind her. Was it really as dangerous as Les said? Tons of older people skied. What did they know that she didn't?

"With your technical foundation, it'll be like no time has passed since you last skied. You can take it as slow," Hank smiled a conspiratorial smile at her, "or as fast as you'd like."

"I'd love to go with you guys," Audrey said. "I can't believe I'll never go with my mom again, though." She looked down at the table.

Harriet put her arm around Audrey, and they sat in silence for a few minutes. "Do you feel like sharing any stories about fun times with your mom?" Harriet asked.

Audrey thought for a moment, then smiled. "Well, there was this one time my mom, dad, and I went camping. Dad went to sleep, and

Mom and I brought our sleeping bags outside to see the stars. My mom studied a little astronomy, so she told me all about the constellations. We lay there looking up at the sky until we fell asleep under the stars."

"That sounds magical," Harriet said.

"It was," Audrey said. "I've loved stargazing ever since."

"How about we go stargazing tonight?" Hank said.

Audrey's face broke into a wide smile. "I'd love that."

"Well, until then, let's get back to work on the kitchen," Hank said.

The kitchen was thrown into cheerful chaos. Hank, tools clanking, tackled a stubborn patch of drywall. Harriet meticulously taped off the trim around the window, and Audrey hummed as she smoothed rough edges with sandpaper. Dust hung in the air like fog, and Harriet waved her hand in front of her face to clear it.

By late afternoon, their muscles ached, but the kitchen walls were stripped, ready for a fresh start. They ordered takeout, devouring it amidst drop cloths and paint cans, then collapsed onto the couch for a movie. The easy camaraderie of shared effort and simple pleasures settled over the house, warm and comforting, a feeling all too foreign to Harriet.

That night, under a canopy of stars, sprawled out on a blanket in the backyard, the vastness of the universe seemed to dwarf their troubles. In the quiet moments between pointing out constellations, Harriet's heart filled with a love she hadn't realized she craved so deeply.

$\bullet \quad \bullet \quad \bullet \quad \bullet \quad \bullet$

The following morning, the kitchen was a whirlwind of activity once again. "You're quite the handyman, Hank," Harriet said.

Hank, pausing his work, grinned back at her. "Just a few tricks I picked up over the years. It's satisfying to give things a whole new, fresh look."

Just as they sat down to take a break, an unfamiliar sedan with Washington plates pulled into the driveway. Harriet felt a pang of anxiety; she knew Robyn's parents were on their way, but she still wasn't ready.

Audrey froze. "Who's that?"

Harriet placed a hand on Audrey's shoulder. "It's probably your grandparents, honey."

Audrey sat upright in her chair. "But...I haven't seen them in forever. And..."

"And what, sweetheart?" Harriet asked.

"I don't want to go to Seattle with them. I want to stay here. I don't want to go to a new school. I want to be where Izzy is. And even though I haven't known you long, it's nice here."

The doorbell rang, punctuating the tense silence in the kitchen. Harriet drew in a long breath and opened the door.

"Hi. You must be Harriet." An older woman with shiny gray hair styled in a neat bob extended her hand. Harriet shook it. "I'm Linda, Robyn's mother, and this is Carl, her father." She lifted her arm in his direction, and Harriet took in a tall, slightly stooped man with kind eyes, despite the somber expression on his face. "We never liked that guy, but we didn't think it would come to this."

Harriet nodded. Every muscle in her face felt taut, as she forced a smile. She hoped to hide the churning protectiveness and burgeoning fear rising within her. She was not just a grieving neighbor; she was Audrey's champion, and she needed to appear utterly unflappable. "Please come in."

After a brief exchange of condolences, Linda turned to Audrey. "Audrey, sweetheart, it's so good to see you. We've missed you so much."

Audrey managed a weak smile, but her eyes remained wary. "It's good to see you too."

"This is my brother, Hank," Harriet said. "He's a psychologist and a dad, so he's a great help for us."

Hank shrugged. "I try. Nice to meet you. Can I get you a coffee or something? Sorry about the state of the kitchen. We're doing a little updating, but the coffee maker still works."

"That would be nice, thank you," Linda said.

Harriet escorted them to the couch, and she and Audrey sat in chairs opposite them. Linda said, "We'll get to the point. As I'm sure you know, we're here to make arrangements to bring Audrey back to Seattle with us."

Audrey pulled the pillow from behind her and hugged it tightly to her chest. "But I don't want to go," she said. "I want to stay in the same school as my friends. And Harriet's taking good care of me."

A tense silence filled the room. Harriet looked at Robyn's parents, remembering what Callie told her about the strong claim they had for guardianship since they were Audrey's next of kin. However, Harriet knew that Audrey's wishes were important too, and she was determined to fight for her.

"Audrey's been through a lot. I lost both my parents when I was just a few years older than she is. It's terrible. I really needed my friends during that time. Moving away would've made it harder. I'm prepared to care for her here if that's what she wants," Harriet said.

Linda and Carl exchanged a look. After a few moments of awkward silence, Linda said, "This is unexpected. We're her grandparents. There shouldn't be a fight."

"I want what's best for Audrey," Harriet said.

"We do too," Carl said. "And she should be with her family."

"I don't want to go!" Audrey shouted.

Each of them held their breath as they stared at each other.

"Well, this isn't the time or the place. Audrey doesn't need to be upset any further," Hank said. "This isn't something that will be solved here and now."

Harriet nodded. "I've already reached out to Harmony House, the women's shelter, where Robyn and I participated in a support group. They have a legal advocate who can help us through this process."

They agreed to set up a meeting with the advocate to discuss the legal aspects of guardianship. Audrey's grandparents stood to leave. "Can we get a hug, Audrey?"

Standing slowly, Audrey went to them and put her arms around them.

"We'll be in touch with details about the funeral." As they opened the door, Carl turned back to Audrey and said, "Maybe we could take you to the Museum of the Rockies?"

"Maybe," Audrey said.

"Think about it, sweetheart. We've missed you, and we love you," Carl said, his eyes glistening.

After Robyn's parents left, Harriet and Audrey shared a worried look. "I didn't think they'd try to make me go. I don't want to."

"I know, sweetie. We'll work through this."

"In the meantime," Hank said, "let's finish the basecoat in the kitchen. Then we'll be ready for paint tomorrow."

By the time the sun sank below the mountains, the kitchen was nearly finished. Harriet leaned against the wall, taking in the scene before her. Hank, whistling softly, worked diligently next to Audrey, who worked slowly and steadily to make sure the primer didn't drip. Harriet's thoughts drifted to Les and how he would've hated all this - the mess, the noise, the laughter, the people in his space. Her throat tightened with emotion as a wave of gratitude washed over her for these people who had suddenly filled her empty house with life and purpose. Now that she had them, she couldn't imagine life without them.

CHAPTER 33

THE NEXT MORNING, rollers in hand, they attacked the blank canvas of the kitchen walls with a shared enthusiasm, each stroke a vibrant splash of sunshine. The scent of fresh paint mingled with the shimmering rays of the morning sun, sending Harriet's heart soaring.

"I really can't thank you both enough," Harriet said. "I knew I hated those dark walls, but I had no idea the effect they were having on my mood. I can't imagine ever being sad in this bright kitchen."

"Yeah, butter yellow is the perfect color," Audrey said.

"Agreed," Hank said. "Once we finish this coat, we'll need to let it dry, so how about we take a break? I've noticed you reading quite a bit, Audrey. Maybe we can go to the library this afternoon?"

"That would be awesome."

Just a few hours later, leaving the kitchen glowing in its new paint, they were browsing the library shelves for new books. As Audrey excitedly picked out a stack of novels, Harriet wandered over to the historical fiction section.

Suddenly, a familiar voice called out, "Harriet! Is that you?"

Harriet turned to see Lucille approaching her with a wide smile. "Yep, it's me."

They stared at each other for a few minutes. Harriet wanted to be Lucille's friend, but her nerves were getting the best of her.

"Well, I'm glad you found the time to stop in. I wanted to talk to you about something I thought you might be interested in," Lucille said.

Harriet raised an eyebrow, intrigued.

"We have an opening for a part-time assistant librarian," Lucille explained. "I think maybe it might be good for you to get back to doing something you love."

Harriet's eyes widened. She'd just begun to settle into the idea of going back to work, and here was the perfect opportunity falling into her lap. Her heart sped up and thrummed loudly in her chest. But what about Audrey? "I'd love to apply, but I'm the temporary guardian for that cute girl over there. She's my neighbor's daughter," Harriet said, pointing to Audrey. "So, it would have to be when she's in school."

"Well, the job is part-time, so it shouldn't interfere with caring for her."

"But what about Richard?" Harriet asked.

"What about him?" Lucille asked, her brows knit in confusion.

"Would I have to see him much?"

Lucille cocked her head to the side. "Probably. Is that a problem?"

"It certainly is. Have you forgotten my embarrassing episode with him the last time I was here? How can I face him again?"

Lucille laughed. "Harriet, I'm sure he's forgotten all about it. Water under the bridge."

"I hope I might be more memorable than that. I did 'put myself out there' like everyone tells me to do. Some good it did me. All I ended up with was a red face and a bruised ego. I don't know if I can face him."

"It isn't worth giving up on something once again. You've already had to put yourself last. Don't let a little embarrassment allow you to miss out on this," Lucille said, putting her hand on Harriet's shoulder.

"All right, I suppose I'll apply, but I'll have to do so with the caveat that Audrey comes first. And maybe my hours can be when Richard isn't here."

"I'm sure we can work things out with Audrey, but Richard comes and goes as he pleases. I'm afraid you'll have to get over it. Who knows? When he sees you here, doing the wonderful job I'm sure you'll do, maybe he'll change his mind. You never know."

Harriet folded her arms across her chest and sighed. "Doubtful, but I guess I'll have to put on my big girl panties."

"You crack me up. I never know what will come out of your mouth."

As they left the library, Harriet was carrying not just the books she hoped would entertain her over the coming days, but the hope that maybe she could get back to the job she loved.

Back at Harriet's house, the first coat of paint had dried, so they each took a section of the kitchen and applied the second coat. The yellow was subtle, but still bright and cheery.

"I love this color," Audrey said. "It'll be like the sun is shining all the time in here."

When they were finished, they stood back to survey their work. "It's perfect," Harriet breathed, turning in a slow circle to admire the transformation. The kitchen seemed to glow from within, no longer the dark, claustrophobic space Les had insisted upon. She felt a weight lifting from her shoulders with each passing moment.

Hank wiped his hands on a rag and nodded approvingly. "Amazing what a fresh coat of paint can do for a room, and a person's spirits."

"Can we do the living room next?" Audrey asked.

"One room at a time," Harriet laughed, surprising herself with how light she felt. "But yes, eventually we can tackle the living room too."

Later that evening, the aroma of chicken pot pie filled the air as Harriet and Audrey settled onto the couch, plates balanced on their laps. Hank had gone out to run an errand he said was a surprise for them, and Harriet and Audrey decided to enjoy a casual meal in the living room.

As they ate, the local news came on, the anchor's face grave as she announced the top story: "Chris Carter, accused of murdering his wife, Robyn Carter, appeared in court today for a bail hearing. The judge denied bail, citing the severity of the charges and the potential flight risk. Carter remains in custody at the Gallatin County Detention Center, awaiting trial."

The screen flashed to a photo of Chris, his face grim and haggard, his eyes downcast as he was led away in handcuffs. Audrey's fork clattered against her plate, the sound echoing in the living room.

Harriet's heart sank as she reached out to grab the remote from the coffee table. "Oh my. You don't have to watch this."

Audrey shook her head, her eyes fixed on the screen. "No, I want to know what's happening. He took my mom from me. He deserves to pay."

When the segment ended, Harriet turned to Audrey, not knowing what to say. She couldn't imagine how it would feel to have your dad kill your mom. She finally managed, "That must be tough."

"I hate him."

Harriet pulled Audrey tight against her chest. "That's understandable."

They sat together in silence for a long time. Eventually, the front door creaked open, and Hank stepped in, a white box in his hand. "Hey," he said, closing the door behind him. "I'm back. Everything okay?"

Harriet looked up, but continued holding Audrey. "We were watching the news. The story about Audrey's dad came on."

Hank's expression turned grim as he crossed the room and sat down on the chair facing them. "I see," he said, his gaze shifting to Audrey, who continued to stare vacantly at the TV screen. "How are you holding up, Audrey?"

Audrey shrugged. "I don't know."

Hank nodded. "It's okay not to know. It's okay to feel whatever you're feeling. Anger, sadness, confusion…it's all valid. Your mom would want you to be kind to yourself."

Audrey pulled away from Harriet and leaned back against the couch, a single tear escaping her eye and rolling down her cheek. Harriet was grateful her brother was here to help with these difficult emotions.

"Do you want to talk about it?" Hank asked.

Audrey shook her head.

"That's okay," Hank reassured her. "We're here for you whenever you're ready." Setting the white box on the table between them, Hank said, "I went to the bakery we used to love when we were kids. I'm so glad it's still there. Not everything has changed in Bozeman. I thought we could all use a little something sweet after a long day."

"What'd you get?" Harriet asked.

Hank grinned. "Well, I know how you love a good cannoli, Harriet, so I got you a chocolate chip and a chocolate. I wasn't sure what you liked, Audrey, so I got a little assortment. There's a slice of chocolate cake, some macarons, and a couple of eclairs to share."

As Hank opened the box, the sight and smell of the pastries brought a momentary distraction from the heaviness that had settled over them. Audrey reached for an eclair, a small smile returning to her face.

"Thanks, Hank," she murmured, taking a bite.

The shrill ring of Harriet's cell phone startled them. Harriet reluctantly got up to answer it, hoping it wasn't bad news.

"Hello?" she said.

"Harriet? It's Kevin."

"Kevin? What time is it? Isn't it nearly eight at night? Do you usually call people so late? Or is something wrong?"

Hank was making a motion with his hand across his throat. She put the phone against her chest. "What are you doing, Hank?"

"Telling you to cut it out. Be nice. It's not that late."

"Oh," Harriet said, bringing the phone back up to her ear. "Sorry. Anyway, why are you calling?"

"I was wondering if you and Audrey would like to go for a hike tomorrow. Maybe up to the M? That is, if your ankle is up to it. We could take the easy way and turn around if you're uncomfortable. It's supposed to be a beautiful day for it. And..." He hesitated.

"And what?"

"Dogs aren't required to be on a leash."

"Well then, I don't think I'll be interested in that hike."

Hank came and stood in front of Harriet, motioning for her to stop her conversation again. "Why are you being mean to whoever is on the phone?"

Harriet held the phone against her chest once again. "He's suggesting a hike where the dogs don't have to be on a leash. The absurdity! I'm just recently able to walk, let alone hike, because of what his dog did," Harriet said.

A small smile crept across Hank's face. "So, Kevin is inviting you on a hike, and you are being mean to him because it happens to be a leash-free hike for dogs?"

Harriet nodded.

"Harriet," Audrey said, coming to stand next to her. "Remember how much fun Rocky and Bibbo had when Kevin visited? I think they'd like to run around together."

Harriet looked from Hank to Audrey, who was nodding emphatically.

Slowly, Harriet brought the phone back up to her ear. "That sounds lovely," Harriet said. "But don't you have to work tomorrow? It's Thursday, isn't it?"

"Not anymore," Kevin said. "Classes finished last week. I'm officially done for the year."

"How nice. Such a wonderful thing about working in education. Especially when you live in Montana, summer is a time to be outdoors."

"I couldn't agree more," Kevin replied. "So, what do you say? Are you guys up for a hike?"

Harriet glanced at Audrey, who nodded again. "We'd love to. Would it be all right if my brother joined us?"

"Of course," Kevin said. "I'll pick you up at 10 a.m. tomorrow, then. See you soon."

Harriet hung up the phone, a smile spreading across her face, unbidden. "So, I guess we're hiking the M tomorrow."

"The M?" Hank's eyebrows shot up. "That's quite a hike. Are you sure you're up for it, Harriet? With your ankle?"

"I'll be fine," Harriet reassured him, a hint of defiance in her voice. "Besides, Kevin's a geologist. He'll take care of us."

"What does his being a geologist have to do with your ankle being okay on a hike?" Audrey asked.

"He knows about rocks, so he can tell me the best places to step," Harriet said.

Audrey and Hank exchanged a glance. "Whatever makes you comfortable, Harriet," Hank said.

The following morning, Kevin arrived promptly at 10 a.m., cheerful as always. Rocky was peering out the open rear window, tongue lolling to one side. He seemed to smile too. The three of them, along with Bibbo, climbed into Kevin's car, and Rocky jumped onto Audrey's lap.

Audrey giggled.

"Sorry about that," Kevin said. "Just shove him off if he's bothering you."

"He's good," Audrey said.

When they arrived at the trailhead, Audrey leapt from the car and skipped up the trail with the dogs, who were already sniffing everything they encountered. Harriet had to admit, she enjoyed seeing the dogs running and exploring. Their joy was nearly palpable. Bibbo seemed to thank her with his eyes each time he looked at her. She didn't remember how happy dogs could be off-leash.

After a few minutes, Kevin turned back and said, "How's the ankle holding up, Harriet?"

"It's a little sore, and I'm a bit slower than usual, but with my brace, it's holding up just fine."

When they reached the summit, they stopped to catch their breath and admire the view. The entire valley was on display, surrounded by rugged peaks and verdant meadows.

"It's beautiful," Harriet said.

"It is," Kevin agreed, his gaze fixed on the horizon. He turned to look at Harriet, a slight smile tugging at the corners of his mouth. Harriet blushed and turned away, so neither Kevin nor Hank would notice. She really didn't need her brother teasing her about the strange feelings bubbling up within her.

CHAPTER 34

LATER THAT AFTERNOON, Hank appeared in the kitchen with his luggage trailing behind him. The dreaded time of his departure had arrived.

"I wish you didn't have to go," Audrey said. "It's been so much fun having you here."

Hank leaned down to embrace Audrey. "I'll miss you too, kiddo, but I promise I'll be back soon. And you and Harriet are more than welcome to visit me and Megan anytime. I'd love for you to meet my kids. The twins are in eighth grade, so not much older than you. I think you'd really get along."

"I'm the worst aunt ever. I haven't even met my niece and nephews," Harriet said.

"You're family, Harriet. Always have been, always will be. They'll be happy to see you, no matter what."

With one last round of hugs and promises to stay in touch, Hank drove off toward the airport, leaving Harriet and Audrey standing on the porch, waving goodbye.

•　•　•　•　•

Just a few short days later, tension hung thick in the air as Harriet, Audrey, Linda, and Carl gathered in the cozy meeting room, which felt more like a living room, at Harmony House. Sarah, one of the legal advocates, joined them. Harriet was grateful for her calm and professional demeanor despite the palpable unease in the room.

"Thank you all for coming," Sarah said. "I understand this is a difficult time, and I want to assure you that my goal is to help find the best possible solution for Audrey." She then outlined the legal process for establishing guardianship, explaining the different types, the factors the court would consider, and the documentation required.

"Now, I'd like to hear from each of you about your desired outcome. Linda, we'll begin with you," Sarah said.

Linda's lips tightened into a thin line. Her hand, resting on her knee, trembled almost imperceptibly. Carl, beside her, visibly swallowed hard, his gaze drifting to a point beyond Harriet, lost in his own sorrow. "With all due respect, we're Audrey's grandparents. We've raised a family of our own, and we're more than capable of providing a stable and loving home for her," Carl said.

Linda nodded in agreement. "We're grateful for Harriet's kindness, but we believe Audrey belongs with her blood relatives."

Harriet bristled at their words. She felt the familiar indignant heat rise, but this time, a new, cold calculation swept over her. She couldn't afford an outburst, not here, not now. Every glance from Linda, every quiet note Sarah took, felt like an appraisal. She was on trial. Harriet forced her shoulders down, smoothed her expression into one of polite concern, and spoke with a measured calmness that surprised even herself. "Audrey is family to me too already, and she's made it clear she wants to stay in Bozeman, with me."

Linda sighed. "We told Robyn for years she could come back home. Offered her a place, a fresh start." Though she spoke softly, her bitterness came through loud and clear. "He had her so twisted, wouldn't let her come home for holidays. We barely saw Audrey for years. And now... now this. It just seems like the natural thing for her to be with us, her own."

An awkward silence descended upon the room as everyone looked at Audrey, who sat quietly, her hands clasped tightly in her lap. "I don't want to go to Seattle," Audrey whispered. "I want to stay here."

Linda softened, her voice taking on a pleading tone. "Honey, we understand you're comfortable here, but wouldn't you like to be with your grandparents, your own flesh and blood? We have a nice house with a big yard, and the school near us is excellent."

Audrey shook her head, tears welling up in her eyes. "I don't care about your yard or your school. I hardly know you, and I want to stay in my same school, with my same friends. Especially Izzy."

"And I'm the only one who knows how to make my special grilled cheese sandwiches with the crusts cut off just the way Audrey likes them," Harriet said.

Everyone stared at her. Even Sarah, the seasoned professional, raised an eyebrow in surprise. The tension in the room eased slightly.

"We're grateful for you stepping up to help, Harriet. But you've done quite enough. Audrey is still young, and she'll adapt," Linda said.

Audrey stood up abruptly. "No, I won't!" she cried. "I won't adapt! I want to stay here in my school with my friends!"

She ran out of the room, slamming the door behind her. Harriet started to go after her, but Sarah gently restrained her.

"Let her have a moment," Sarah advised. "She needs to process her emotions."

Turning to Linda and Carl, Sarah continued, "As you can see, Audrey's wishes are very clear. The court will take her feelings into account, especially since she is old enough to express her preferences." Sarah paused. "One other option for you both to consider is relocating to Bozeman so Audrey can stay here."

Linda sat up straight and folded her hands together. Carl turned and looked at her. After a moment, Linda spoke. "We've discussed that option. It would be tough for us. Our house is paid off, and Bozeman is so expensive. We have our friends and our church. We aren't as spry as we used to be. And our doctors..." Linda shook her head. "I think it would be tougher for us to relocate than for one young girl."

Carl nodded. "She's young. She'll adapt better than a couple of old folks."

"It's more than just the house," Linda added, looking down at her hands. "Carl's back isn't what it used to be, and my sister is just down the road for my appointments. Our doctors, our entire life is there. It's a lot for two old people to uproot."

"A young girl in a normal situation could adapt, but not one who's been through what Audrey's been through," Harriet said, folding her arms across her chest.

Sarah said, "Harriet makes a good point."

Linda sighed and put her head in her hands.

"And what about her father?" Carl interjected. "Will that bastard have a say in this?"

"Well, typically, the father would have parental rights. However, given Chris's current incarceration for Robyn's murder, his parental rights are automatically suspended pending the outcome of his trial."

"So, what happens next?" Linda asked.

"If you can't come to an agreement, the next step is for both parties to file petitions for guardianship," Sarah explained. "The court will then conduct a thorough investigation, including background checks, home studies, and interviews with everyone involved, including Audrey."

The meeting concluded with a curt nod from Linda, reciprocated by Harriet. This wouldn't be easy, but Harriet was up for the fight.

Finding Audrey sitting on a bench in the hallway, Harriet went and sat next to her. "I'm sorry you have to deal with all this. As long as you want me to, I will fight to keep you here, in Bozeman, with me."

Audrey nodded and wiped the tears from her cheeks. They walked out of the building in silence, the weight of the situation heavy on their hearts.

CHAPTER 35

THE NEXT MORNING, under a bleak spring sky, Sunset Hills Cemetery was filled with mourners gathered to say their final goodbyes to Robyn Carter. Everyone shared a sense of shock and sorrow over the untimely and tragic death of such a wonderful woman.

The Bridger Mountains loomed in the distance, their rugged peaks dusted with remnants of winter snow, defiant against the warming spring air. Wildflowers had begun their tentative emergence through the green grass surrounding the cemetery, dots of purple lupine and yellow arrowleaf balsamroot creating a bittersweet tapestry of life amidst the markers of those who had passed. The mountains stood as silent sentinels, unchanging and eternal against the backdrop of human grief. The scent of pine and fresh earth mingled in the cool breeze that swept down from the slopes, a reminder of the respite the mountains offered even on the hottest days.

Harriet clutched Audrey's hand tightly. They stood at the front of the crowd, trembling with barely suppressed sobs. Audrey twirled a single white rose between her fingertips. Harriet looked down at her. She was still a child, yet she, like Harriet, would have to grow up in a world without her mother. Her life would be filled with confusion and a deep-rooted sorrow that words could not express.

Harriet knew only Linda and Carl amid the many mourners. The cemetery was full of people sharing tearful embraces and whispered condolences. Harriet's arm remained wrapped protectively around Audrey's shoulders, hoping to offer at least a bit of comfort on this terrible day.

As the service concluded, Audrey stepped forward to place the rose on her mother's casket. Her fingers traced the smooth wood, her tears falling silently onto the polished surface. Harriet put her hand over her mouth to stifle a sob. Fearing her legs might give way, she shifted to lean against a tree.

At the conclusion of the ceremony, Harriet put her arm around Audrey's shoulders and led her to the parking lot. The poor girl moved stiffly and stared vacantly ahead, as though sleepwalking through a terrible nightmare. Harriet recognized that vacant stare. She had worn it herself at her parents' funeral.

"Are you ready to go to the reception?" Harriet asked softly.

Audrey shook her head. "I can't. I can't face all those people telling me how sorry they are."

Harriet nodded. "We don't have to go if you don't want to."

Linda approached them, her eyes red but her posture rigid. "We should all head to the community center now."

"I think Audrey needs some time," Harriet said. "This has been overwhelming for her."

Linda's expression hardened. "I understand she's upset. We all are. But there are people who've come a long way to pay their respects."

"Audrey," Carl said, walking toward them. "Your grandmother's right. These people loved your mother. They're here for you too."

Audrey's shoulders slumped further. "Please, I can't."

Linda put her hand on Audrey's shoulder. "This is what family does, Audrey. We honor the departed, even when it's difficult."

Harriet felt a surge of protectiveness. "She's already honored her mother by being here today. If she needs space, we should respect that."

"With all due respect, Harriet," Linda said, her voice taking on an edge, "you're not family. You don't get to make these decisions."

The words stung, but Harriet stood her ground. "Robyn trusted me to take care of Audrey. That's exactly what I'm doing."

"Enough!" Audrey said. "Please stop fighting over me like I'm not even here."

The adults fell silent, startled by her outburst.

"I'll go to the reception," Audrey said. "But only for a little while."

Linda's expression softened. "Thank you, sweetheart. It will mean a lot to everyone."

The community center was filled with people sharing stories about Robyn, plates of barely touched food scattered across tables and countertops. People approached Audrey, offering awkward hugs and well-meaning platitudes. The girl nodded politely, but Harriet could see her withdrawing further with each interaction.

After an hour, Harriet noticed Audrey sitting alone in a corner, her face pale and drawn. Harriet made her way over, carefully balancing two cups of punch.

"How are you holding up?" she asked, offering one of the cups to Audrey.

"I want to go home," Audrey said. "Your home, I mean."

Harriet nodded, setting the cups down on a nearby table. "Let me tell your grandparents we're leaving."

Linda and Carl were deep in conversation with an elderly couple when Harriet approached. "Excuse me. Audrey's exhausted. I'm taking her home."

Linda frowned. "We were hoping to spend some time with her this evening. We're flying back to Seattle tomorrow afternoon."

"She's been through enough today. And after our meeting with Sarah, I don't think you are her favorite people," Harriet said.

Linda's eyes widened, and Carl placed a restraining hand on her arm. "We understand, but please, can we at least say goodbye to her properly? She's our granddaughter, and we've missed her."

Carl's plea softened Harriet. "I suppose. She's over by the window."

Harriet followed Carl and Linda to where Audrey was standing. Audrey allowed herself to be enveloped in their embrace, her arms hanging limply at her sides.

"We love you, sweetheart," Linda said.

Carl squeezed Audrey's shoulder gently. "And we'll be back soon to visit. Maybe next time we can go to the dinosaur museum."

Audrey nodded, her eyes fixed on the floor. "Okay. Bye."

The ride back to Harriet's was steeped in a heavy silence. Audrey, hunched in the passenger seat, stared out the window, her jaw set. At Harriet's house, she retreated. She didn't rage or cry, but moved through the rooms like a ghost, a quiet, almost deliberate sulk clinging to her. Harriet offered small comforts—her favorite stuffed animal, a silly sitcom, a quiet presence—but Audrey remained distant, walled off by the fresh wound of the funeral.

It was a tense quiet for most of that first day, but as time wore on, Harriet's attempts to pull Audrey from her shell began to work. Eventually, Harriet's invitation to play a board game was met with a hesitant nod, and a shared quiet evening of mindless TV offered a fragile truce with her pain.

On Monday, Audrey returned to school. Harriet kept busy by cleaning the house, preparing for the upcoming home study, and making a list of all the documents she would need for the guardianship hearing.

Later that afternoon, she received a call from Sarah. "Harriet, I just got off the phone with the court," Sarah said. "Your hearing is scheduled for next week."

Harriet's heart pounded with a mixture of excitement and anxiety. "It's going to be a fight, but I'm like Mike Tyson when I need to be."

Sarah chuckled. "Just gather what you need and stay positive. Your lawyer will take care of the rest. And keep caring for Audrey."

Harriet loved having Audrey around. When she came home from school, Harriet was happy to help with homework, even though Audrey was a great student and didn't need much help. She got a bit frustrated with math, and Harriet had forgotten how to do most of it, so they'd had a few tense moments at the kitchen table with both of them ready to tear their hair out over problems that made no sense at all.

"How many more small dogs are signed up to compete in the dog show than large dogs? Who cares?" Harriet said, standing and pacing next to the kitchen table.

"I think I've got it," Audrey said. "I'm pretty sure it's 42.5."

"How can you have half a dog competing in a dog show?" Harriet exclaimed, putting her hands on the table and leaning over to look at Audrey's paper. It seemed right. "As if math isn't hard enough, they have to make impossible situations. When would anyone use this in real life? I swear, common sense has gone right out the window."

"Maybe that's where the other half of the dog went too," Audrey said, giggling.

Not every night ended so happily. The smallest things, the way Harriet loaded the dishwasher, the oatmeal Harriet sometimes tried to sneak in her chocolate chip cookies, Harriet's insistence on keeping things neat and tidy, could make Audrey cry. Harriet's heart broke for her. It was hard to feel so completely helpless in those moments. She wished she could wave a magic wand and fix everything for her.

As the days passed, instead of the lonely, pointless expanse of hours that made up Harriet's days before Audrey, she smiled as she picked up Audrey's cereal at the grocery store, or sniffed Audrey's favorite blue shirt when it came out of the dryer and folded it so it looked as though it belonged on a display shelf at the Gap. She loved finding Audrey's books strewn about the house. She'd read a page or two to get a peek into her mind.

Yet, there were still so many hours that Audrey was in school. There was only so much grocery shopping and laundry to be done. Harriet peered out the window nearly half an hour before she expected Audrey to be home because she couldn't wait to see her.

When Izzy came home with Audrey, which happened frequently, Harriet set about making snacks for them and inquiring about their day. She sat at the kitchen table with them, hoping they would linger there with her all afternoon. When they retreated to Audrey's room, Harriet's heart sank, and she had that old middle-school feeling of being left out. She knew it was silly. She was happy Audrey had her best friend, but she couldn't help longing to have more time with both of them.

One day, after Izzy had left, Audrey said, "Harriet, you don't have to entertain us when we're here, you know."

"Oh, I don't mind."

"It's a little...I don't know, weird?" Audrey said, staring at the floor and shifting from foot to foot.

Harriet's cheeks flushed. She was both embarrassed and a touch angry all at once. She liked doing things for them, being a part of their world, but they didn't want her. She was crushed.

"Okay," Harriet said, turning back to the chicken she was dicing for dinner to hide the tears that threatened to spill over her eyelids.

Audrey came up beside her and put her hand on her arm. "Don't take it the wrong way. We're so happy you're so nice to us, but we're almost teenagers, so, you know, we need to do teenage stuff without adults around."

Harriet inhaled, pasted a smile on her face, and turned to face Audrey. "Of course, sweetheart. You're right. I'm just so happy to have you with me."

"That's sweet, Harriet. Thank you. Maybe you could take up a new hobby or something, so you have something to do too?"

Harriet's mind went to the library. She'd filled out the application but hadn't brought it in to Lucille. Maybe Audrey was right. As much as Audrey added to Harriet's life, she couldn't be expected to be her entire world, especially since she could end up having to go live with her grandparents.

•   •   •   •   •

The next morning, Harriet stood outside the Bozeman Public Library, a nervous knot tightening in her stomach. She'd been thrilled when Lucille told her over the phone yesterday that she should come in right away for an interview. But it had been years since she'd had a formal job interview, and the prospect of working under the watchful eyes of Lucille and Richard was both exciting and daunting. Especially considering her recent impulsive attempt to ask Richard out.

She took a deep breath, smoothed down her blouse, and pushed open the heavy wooden door. The familiar scent of old books and polished wood greeted her, a comforting reminder of the countless hours she'd spent here as a child, and in her career, escaping into the pages of books.

Lucille, perched behind the circulation desk, looked up with a surprised smile. "Harriet! You're early," she said. "Richard's just finishing up a meeting. Why don't you have a seat?"

Harriet nodded, her nerves momentarily eased by Lucille's friendly demeanor. She took a seat in one of the plush armchairs by the fiction section, her eyes scanning the familiar shelves lined with books. Lucille took a seat next to her.

"We need to reschedule that coffee," Lucille said.

"Absolutely," Harriet said. "Although, if I end up working here, you might get sick of me."

"Not likely. You're always entertaining," Lucille said.

"Glad to be of service," Harriet said.

A few minutes later, Richard walked toward them. He greeted Harriet with a polite smile and led her and Lucille into his office. "Well, Harriet, I'm so happy you've reconsidered going back to work."

The interview began with the usual formalities before Richard expressed his condolences for Robyn's passing. "I hear you're a temporary guardian for her daughter."

Harriet nodded. "Yes, as sad as I am to have lost my newfound friend, and as horrific as it is for Audrey, I'm happy to be there for her. But I guess I've been there for her too much lately. She told me I need a life of my own, so it's about time I went back to work."

Richard smiled. "I know your qualifications are second to none. You've been out of the workforce for what? Twenty or so years now, right?"

Harriet clutched her hands together in her lap. *Was this a reason not to hire her?* "Oh, Lucille, why did you let me get my hopes up about this job?"

Lucille's mouth dropped open. "Whatever do you mean, Harriet?"

"Well, Richard is saying I've been out of the workforce for too long. Les was right. I'm old and washed up." Grabbing her purse, she stood to leave.

Richard leaned over and put his hand on her arm. "I meant no such thing, Harriet. I'm sorry to have upset you. I meant that you must be eager to get back to doing what you love."

Harriet blinked and lowered herself back into the chair. "Really? You still want me?"

Richard chuckled. "As I recall from our years working together, there is no one better, or more passionate about books and the library, than you. It would be an honor to have you working here."

Harriet turned to see Lucille nodding. "You're certainly not washed up. There isn't a genre you don't know. Heck, I bet you know your way around this library nearly as well as I do."

"Possibly better," Harriet said.

Richard cleared his throat, his gaze darting between Harriet and Lucille. "So, Harriet," he began, his voice slightly hesitant, "how about that cup of coffee? As coworkers?"

Harriet's cheeks flushed with embarrassment. "You really had to bring that up?"

Richard waved his hands in front of him. "Yet again, I didn't mean to upset you. Just wanted to let bygones be bygones and start fresh."

Harriet let out a long exhale and said, "I'd like that."

CHAPTER 36

THE SOCIAL WORKER ARRIVED promptly at 3 p.m. on Wednesday, her clipboard clutched in her hand and a stern look on her face. Harriet had spent the morning meticulously cleaning the house, ensuring every surface gleamed and every room was impeccably organized. She was more grateful than ever to have her new cheery kitchen. She was sure the social worker would agree that a happy family could live in this house.

"Hello, Ms. Henderson. I'm Carly Jenkins, and I'll be conducting your home study today," she said, extending her hand. "It's a pleasure to meet you. Thank you for welcoming me into your home."

Harriet shook her hand, her own palms slightly damp with nerves. "Please, come in," she said, leading the way into the living room.

Audrey, who had been anxiously awaiting the social worker's arrival, sat on the couch, her fingers nervously twirling a strand of her hair. Bibbo sat quietly at her feet, his tail thumping softly against the floor.

"You must be Audrey," Ms. Jenkins said.

Audrey offered a small smile and nod in return.

Ms. Jenkins settled into a chair, opened her clipboard, and scanned the documents within. "I'll be asking you some questions about your home environment, your daily routines, and your relationship with Audrey," she explained. "It's important for us to understand how you would provide for her physical, emotional, and educational needs."

Harriet nodded, her hands clasped tightly in her lap. "I understand."

The interview began with questions about Harriet's background, her employment history, and her financial stability. Harriet answered each question, but her anxiety began to make her twitchy. She crossed and uncrossed her legs, then leaned forward to splay the magazines on the coffee table into a perfectly symmetrical fan.

Ms. Jenkins, observing this, couldn't help but raise an eyebrow. "You seem to have a penchant for order, Ms. Henderson."

"Yep. It is important to keep order. In your house and your neighborhood. Can't have things going to hell in a handbasket."

Ms. Jenkins jotted something in her notebook.

"Is that a problem?" Harriet asked, her hand going to her neck where she felt her pulse jumping.

"Not as long as it doesn't interfere with your ability to be flexible and understanding when it comes to the needs of a child."

"Oh, it doesn't," Audrey interjected. "Harriet is kind and helpful. She just likes things a certain way sometimes. It's no biggie."

Ms. Jenkins then turned her attention to Audrey, asking about her school, her friends, and her hobbies. Audrey, initially hesitant, gradually opened up, sharing her love for reading, her passion for skiing, and her close friendship with Izzy.

"Ms. Henderson," Ms. Jenkins said gently, "I understand that this is a challenging time for both of you. Audrey's loss of her mother was a devastating blow, and adjusting to a new living situation can be difficult."

Harriet nodded. "I'm committed to providing a safe and loving home for Audrey," she said. "I want her to feel secure and supported, and I'll do everything in my power to make that happen."

Ms. Jenkins smiled. "I don't doubt that, Ms. Henderson. You've already demonstrated your dedication and love for Audrey. And it's clear that she feels safe and happy here."

Harriet exhaled a long, loud breath. "That's a relief."

Ms. Jenkins chuckled, stood, and went to the door. "I wish you the best," she said as she closed the door behind her.

"Well, I guess that went as well as it could," Harriet said.

"Do you think she'll let me stay here with you?"

Harriet went to Audrey and embraced her. "I hope so."

Harriet loved their new routine. Audrey woke and got ready for school while Harriet made her breakfast. Audrey wasn't talkative in the morning, so they moved about silently as they prepared for the day ahead. Harriet waved as Audrey walked to the bus stop, and then Harriet headed to her new job at the library. Harriet felt a sense of purpose and belonging in the world she'd never felt before.

The day of the guardianship hearing, Harriet was up before the crack of dawn. She'd barely slept, worrying about what would happen. The thought of losing Audrey made her physically nauseous, so she did her best to shove that thought from her mind.

The Gallatin County courtroom, stark with its white walls and stiff wooden benches, felt stifling as Harriet, Audrey, Linda, and Carl shuffled in and took their places at tables on opposite sides of the aisle, their lawyers flanking them. Linda looked paler than at the funeral, her neat bob slightly disheveled, and Carl's shoulders seemed to sag more heavily. The initial rigidity had given way to a weary, almost hollow-eyed determination. They were fighting, but the fight was clearly taking its toll.

Sitting down to wait for the judge, Harriet glanced around the nearly empty room, imagining what it might be like if this were a jury trial, with eyes inspecting their every move, searching for hidden meaning. She shuddered at the thought and hoped she'd never have to feel that heavy gaze upon her. Harriet gave Audrey's hand a quick squeeze, and they stood as the judge entered the room.

Judge Morrison asked everyone to be seated, then began. "The court recognizes the tragic circumstances surrounding this case. The untimely death of Robyn Carter has left a void in Audrey's life, and we must ensure her well-being and future."

He paused. "Audrey, I understand this is a difficult time for you, and I appreciate your bravery and willingness to participate in these proceedings."

Audrey nodded, her eyes wide and scared.

Harriet and Audrey's attorney rose to her feet and addressed the judge. "Your Honor, my client, Harriet Henderson, hasn't known Audrey Carter long, but they've bonded quickly since her mother's tragic passing. Ms. Henderson has provided a stable and nurturing home, ensuring Audrey's physical, emotional, and educational needs are met. Furthermore, Audrey has expressed a clear desire to remain in Bozeman with Ms. Henderson, where she has established a strong support network of friends and familiar surroundings. Additionally, we would like to submit into evidence a note written by Robyn Carter on the night of her death, expressing her wish for Ms. Henderson to care for Audrey."

The lawyer representing Linda and Carl stood and countered, "Your Honor, while we acknowledge the note's existence, we believe it was written under duress and cannot be considered a legally binding testament of Ms. Carter's wishes. Had my clients lived closer, Ms. Carter would most likely have expressed her desire for them to care for Audrey. My clients are Audrey's maternal grandparents. We believe Audrey should be with her next of kin. My clients deeply love their granddaughter and wish to provide her with a loving home in Seattle, where they have lived for nearly thirty years, and have a network of friends and family to support them. They understand Audrey's wish to remain in Bozeman, but circumstances make it impossible for them to relocate. The cost of living is prohibitive, and at their age, uprooting themselves from their established medical care and support network in Seattle would be detrimental to their health."

The judge paused and pulled at his wiry, gray beard. Finally, he addressed Audrey directly. "Audrey," he said gently, "I'd like to hear your wishes, but understand that while I'd like to hear what you have to say, I can't guarantee your wish will be granted. There are many factors to consider. That said, can you tell me, in your own words, where you would like to live and why?"

Audrey took a deep breath and stood. "I want to stay in Bozeman, with Harriet," she said, standing straighter. "She's taking good care of me, and I feel safe and happy in her home. And even though I just moved here recently, I don't want to leave my friends or my school. Moving to Seattle would be like starting all over again, and I don't think I can handle that right now."

Each side argued back and forth while Audrey squirmed in her chair, her arms wrapped around her. Harriet wanted nothing more than to hug her and take her home. She hated seeing her so upset. Children shouldn't ever have to deal with a situation like this. No one should.

The judge listened intently to each argument, his brow furrowed in contemplation. "This is not a decision to be made lightly, and I wish it was possible to make everyone happy. While the court acknowledges Ms. Henderson's dedication and Audrey's wishes, it is generally best to place children with blood relatives. Additionally, the note presented, while heartfelt, was written under extreme duress and cannot override the legal precedence of placing a child with their closest living relatives," he paused, folded his hands, and frowned. "As I said, I understand Audrey's wish to remain in Bozeman, but she has only been in Bozeman a short while, and she hasn't lived with Ms. Henderson long. She's young and will adapt. I believe the precedent set in this courtroom and those around the country for placing children with their closest living relatives is the most important consideration in this matter. Therefore, guardianship of Audrey Carter is granted to Mr. and Mrs. Thompson."

Harriet's stomach lurched. Audrey's face crumpled, and she pulled her knees to her chest as her small shoulders shook. Harriet couldn't believe her ears. She sat and put a stiff arm around Audrey, too stunned to speak. Just when she thought her life was going to improve, to have meaning, Audrey was being taken from her. She should have known better than to get her hopes up.

The judge cleared his throat. "Since the school year is almost over, Audrey will complete the year in Bozeman with Ms. Henderson and then move to Seattle with Mr. and Mrs. Thompson in the summer so she can start fresh at her new school in the fall."

The judge turned and addressed Audrey directly. "I realize this is not what you wanted, but you will adjust. Your grandparents raised your mother, so they know how to parent you as well. They are your family, and it is always best to be with family. Especially in tragic times such as these."

Audrey, who had briefly looked up when the judge spoke to her, put her head back on her knees and sobbed even louder.

Sarah leaned over and whispered, "I'm so sorry. I really hoped the judge would put more weight into Audrey's wishes."

"Well, you were wrong. And you got both of our hopes up," Harriet said, turning away from her.

Linda and Carl came over to Harriet and Audrey's table. Carl put a hand on Audrey's shoulder. She pulled away. "Sweetheart, I know this isn't what you wanted, but the judge knows what's best for you. We're your family. We love you."

"I don't even know you. I don't want to go. You can't make me," Audrey yelled.

"You'll adjust, Audrey. We have a nice home and the school is nearby. You'll make new friends," Linda said.

"No, I won't! I'm not going!" Audrey said as she ran from the courtroom.

Harriet found Audrey sitting against a wall in the hallway. Harriet cleared her throat. She had to be strong, even though her heart was breaking. "Audrey, the judge has made his decision, and there's nothing we can do. You'll visit me whenever you want. I'm always here for you."

"I can't. I-I won't go," Audrey said, barely choking out the words between sobs.

"Come on. Let's go to my house, where it's more comfortable. You still have some time here in Bozeman," Harriet said, holding her hand out for Audrey.

As they drove back to Harriet's house, the car was silent. Harriet had no idea what to say. She wanted to scream at the unfairness of it all. For herself and Audrey. Why did the world have to be so cruel? She had put herself out there, opened her heart. For what? Only to have it crushed to pieces. She was better off the way she'd been. Alone was much better than devastated.

Audrey broke the silence. "I can't believe I really have to go to Seattle."

"I know. But your grandparents love you, and you'll visit me and Izzy. It'll be okay. You'll see," Harriet said, swallowing hard so Audrey wouldn't hear the devastation in her voice.

Later, Harriet was in the kitchen, pretending not to eavesdrop on Audrey's conversation with Izzy, who had come over soon after they'd arrived home. "My grandparents are moving me to Seattle," Audrey said.

"But didn't you tell them you don't want to go?" Izzy asked.

Audrey sniffed. "I did. But they didn't listen. They say I have to be with family. Even though I don't even know them. They didn't care at all about what I wanted."

Harriet turned away so Audrey wouldn't see her trembling chin and the tears leaking from her eyes. Straightening her shoulders and wiping her tears, she turned back around and set a bowl of Goldfish crackers on the coffee table between them. "It's going to be okay. Audrey's grandparents promised to let her visit, so you girls will still see each other all the time."

Audrey shot Harriet an angry glance. "That's not true, and you know it. They say they'll let me visit, but once I'm there, I'll be their prisoner."

"You don't know that. They love you, Audrey. They want you to be happy," Harriet said, hoping it was true.

Audrey scoffed. "If that were true, they wouldn't force me to go with them."

"When do you have to go?" Izzy asked.

"When school is out," Audrey said.

"So you have a couple of weeks to spend time together. You can get together every day after school and on weekends," Harriet said.

A horn honked outside, signaling Izzy's mom had come to pick her up. The girls embraced. "You're the best friend I've ever had," Izzy said.

"Mine too," Audrey said.

"Well, then a friendship like that will last no matter what," Harriet said, again hoping it was true.

CHAPTER 37

THE DAYS LEADING UP to Audrey's departure felt like a slow, agonizing countdown. Audrey, determined to make the most of her remaining time with her best friend, spent nearly every waking moment with Izzy. They explored the trail behind Harriet's house, giggling and sharing secrets as they walked. They huddled together on the couch, devouring books and whispering late into the night.

On the day of Audrey's departure, Harriet felt as though she was moving underwater, the weight of a world without Audrey suffocating her. Methodically, she helped Audrey finish packing her bags, carefully folding each item and placing it in the suitcase.

"I don't want to go," Audrey whispered. "I'll miss you and Izzy so much."

Harriet pulled her into a tight hug, her own tears threatening to spill over. "I'll miss you too, sweetheart," she said. "But your grandparents love you, and I'll be here for you, always. And you and Izzy can talk or text every day."

Audrey nodded, her bottom lip quivering. "I know, but it's not the same."

As they drove to the airport, the silence in the car was punctuated by Audrey's sniffles and Harriet's attempts at reassurance. Harriet filled out all the forms so she could accompany Audrey to her gate, wishing each minute could last a lifetime.

As Audrey turned to say goodbye, her eyes met Harriet's, and a silent understanding passed between them. "Thank you, Harriet."

Harriet nodded, her tears flowing freely now. "You take care of yourself, sweetheart. And remember, you're always welcome at my house. It's your home too."

Audrey smiled weakly, then turned and walked down the ramp, her small frame dwarfed by the other passengers. Harriet watched her go, a sense of loss and longing washing over her. She had grown to love Audrey like a daughter, and the thought of her being so far away was almost unbearable.

Returning to her empty house, Harriet felt the silence close in around her like a suffocating shroud. The echoes of Audrey's laughter and the warmth of their shared moments lingered in the air, mocking the stark emptiness that now filled her home. The carefully organized rooms suddenly felt sterile and devoid of life, each perfectly placed object a reminder of the void Audrey left behind.

She wandered aimlessly from room to room, the once-familiar routines and rituals that had given her life structure now feeling hollow and pointless. Initially, she tried to cling to some semblance of normalcy by going to her job at the library. The quiet hum of activity offered a temporary distraction, but the joy she once found in her work had faded. Her interactions with patrons felt forced, her smiles strained. Even Lucille's cheerful presence couldn't penetrate the fog of despair that had settled over her.

Eventually, Harriet found herself making excuses, calling in sick, or simply avoiding her shifts altogether. The thought of facing the world, of pretending to be okay when her heart was crumbling within her, became unbearable.

In the evenings, she found solace in the bottom of a wine bottle, the familiar burn of alcohol offering a temporary escape from the gnawing emptiness. The carefully measured four-ounce pours became generous refills, the once-strict rules of her life dissolved in the haze of intoxication.

Her phone buzzed with calls from Hank, but Harriet, ashamed of her weakness and inability to face the world, ignored his calls, letting them go to voicemail. Invitations from Kevin went unanswered. The thought of attempting a normal conversation seemed overwhelming.

Weeks passed, and Harriet's isolation deepened. She neglected her garden, letting the weeds encroach upon her carefully tended plants. The house, once a model of order and efficiency, was littered with dirty dishes, dust covered most surfaces, and Harriet couldn't remember the last time she'd done laundry.

A listlessness permeated her every move. She spent her days curled up on the couch. The world outside her window seemed distant and gray, and Harriet couldn't believe she'd begun to reengage with that world. She'd almost started to believe there was goodness and kindness in the world. Les had been right after all. The world was cruel.

In the depths of her depression, Harriet felt like a ghost haunting her own home. The echoes of Les's control still lingered, but the lines between right and wrong, good and evil blurred, whispering doubts and insecurities into her mind. She was lost, adrift in a sea of sorrow, unsure of how to find her way back to the shore.

All Harriet thought about was Audrey. She wondered how she was spending her summer, if she'd made any friends, if her grandparents were treating her well. It was killing her not to know. It was taking all her strength not to call her. Sarah had said she should try to give Audrey some time to adjust to her new life, but Harriet couldn't hold out any longer.

The line rang just once before a robotic voice told Harriet the number was disconnected.

"That's odd," Harriet said to Bibbo, who lifted an eyebrow in response. "Thank goodness I have Linda's number."

Pressing the contact button for Linda, Harriet held her breath as the phone rang. When Linda answered, Harriet's breath left her in a quick gust, and she rushed to get her words out. "Linda, it's Harriet," she said, trying to keep her voice steady. "I wanted to check in on Audrey. How is she doing?"

A long pause followed. Harriet could hear Linda's breathing and a dog barking in the background. "She's...adjusting," Linda finally replied. "It's been a difficult transition, but we're doing our best."

"Is she okay? Can I talk to her?"

Another pause, this time filled with a heavy sigh. "Harriet, I'm afraid that's not possible right now. Audrey's new counselor has advised against any contact with you or Izzy for a few weeks."

Harriet's heart sank. "What? Why?"

"He believes Audrey should focus on settling into her new life here," Linda explained. "It's like the strategies used for kids at summer camps or boarding schools. They need time to adjust without distractions from their old life."

Harriet's frustration bubbled to the surface. "But she's not at camp! She's lost her mother, and I quickly became like family to her. She needs her friends, her support system."

Linda's voice remained firm. "I understand your concern, Harriet, but we're following the counselor's advice. It's for Audrey's own good."

Harriet's anger flared. "Her own good? You're isolating her! She needs connection, not separation."

"We're doing what we believe is best for her," Linda said, her voice rising. "Please respect our decision."

The line went dead, leaving Harriet staring at her phone in disbelief. She stood and paced the kitchen, her anger simmering. She couldn't understand how anyone would think isolating Audrey was the answer. Should she go there and try to talk to her in person? What if she was doing well and didn't want to see Harriet? As much as she hoped Audrey was happy, her heart stung at the thought that she didn't need her. She'd lost her. She had to wait for her to reach out. There wasn't any point in trying. Harriet pulled another bottle of wine from the fridge and filled her glass.

That evening, Harriet was startled awake on the couch by a knock at her front door. Combing her fingers through her tangled hair, she called, "Who is it?"

"It's Kevin. Are you okay?"

"I'm fine. Just a little under the weather," Harriet slurred. "You'd better not come in. I don't want to give you anything."

"Are you sure? I haven't seen you in quite a while. Is there anything I can do for you?"

"Nope, I'm good," Harriet said, lying back on the couch. Thankfully, he didn't press the issue. She heard his footsteps as he headed down the stairs and off her front porch before she fell back into a hazy state of near unconsciousness.

Night and day blurred while Harriet did little more than move from the couch to the kitchen to her bed. She hadn't showered in days, or maybe weeks. What did any of it matter?

Harriet's phone vibrated on the coffee table, waking her from a fitful sleep on the couch. She glanced at the unfamiliar number, a frown pulling down the corners of her mouth. With a hesitant hand, she answered the call.

"Hello?"

A hushed voice, choked with emotion, whispered on the other end. "Harriet? It's me, Audrey."

Harriet's heart skipped a beat. She sat up straight on the couch. "Audrey! Oh, sweetheart, how are you? Are you okay?"

"No, I'm not." Audrey's voice cracked. "I'm miserable here, Harriet. My grandparents are so strict. They won't let me do anything. They took away my phone. I can't even talk to Izzy. I feel like I'm suffocating."

Harriet's protective instincts launched her into overdrive, waking her fully from her drunken, fogged sleep. "Where are you calling from?"

"I'm at a girl in my neighborhood's house," Audrey replied. "I'm using her phone. I'm running away, Harriet I can't stay here any longer."

Harriet thought her heart might leap from her chest. "Audrey, no! You can't run away. It's not safe. What about your grandparents? They'll be worried sick."

"I don't care," Audrey said. "I'd rather be anywhere but here. I'm coming back to Bozeman."

Harriet closed her eyes, her mind whirling. She knew she couldn't let Audrey wander the streets of Seattle alone.

"Audrey, listen to me," she said, her voice firm but gentle. "I understand how you feel, but running away isn't the answer. It's dangerous. Seattle is a big city. Anything could happen to you. Can you stay where you are for a while? Until I can get there?"

"I don't know... I haven't known Isla long..."

"You have to be somewhere safe. Either stay there or go to your grandparents. Just until I can get there."

Audrey didn't respond.

"Audrey? Promise me."

"Fine."

Harriet hung up the phone, questions flooding her brain. Could she really go get her? Was she sober enough to drive? Glancing at the clock, it seemed she'd slept quite a few hours, and she felt okay. She had to go to her. But would she get in trouble? Was it kidnapping if Audrey was going to put herself in danger?

As Harriet picked up her phone to call Hank, it rang. It was Sarah. "Harriet, I just got off the phone with Linda and Carl's attorney. They're frantic. Absolutely beside themselves. They called every number they had, the police, us... they just wanted to know she was safe. Do you know where she is?"

"Yes," Harriet said. "She's safe for the moment. I'm going to get her."

"What do you mean you're going to get her? Where is she?" Sarah asked.

"She's at a friend's house. She says she's running away," Harriet said. "I can't have her wandering the streets of Seattle. I have to go to her."

Sarah exhaled. "Harriet, Audrey's grandparents have legal guardianship. You can't just go get her. I don't know the law fully in Washington, but if you take Audrey out of the state, you could face legal consequences."

"I understand. But Audrey's safety comes first. I'll face whatever legal consequences that come my way later."

CHAPTER 38

HARRIET GRABBED HER KEYS and paused at the mirror by the front door, taking in the sight of her neglected body. Running back to the bathroom, she took the fastest shower in history and emerged refreshed and ready for action. Throwing wine bottles into the recycling and dishes into the dishwasher, she grabbed Bibbo and ran out the door, determined to find Audrey before she got herself into a situation she couldn't handle.

Harriet's hands gripped the steering wheel, her knuckles white as she navigated the winding mountain roads. The endless expanse of highway stretched before her, a monotonous ribbon of asphalt cutting through the vast Montana landscape. Just over ten hours of driving lay ahead, but it was a small price to pay to be certain Audrey was safe.

Her thoughts churned as she drove. She had no concrete plan and no way to contact Audrey directly. All she had was the address where her grandparents lived, but Harriet didn't know if she'd be there or at her friend's house, or, God forbid, somewhere in the maze of Seattle city streets.

Dialing Hank, he answered in his usual jovial manner, and Harriet quickly filled him in. He said he'd research what he could about the laws on guardianship in Washington State, but agreed with Harriet that Audrey's safety was the most important consideration at the moment.

The hours dragged on, the monotony broken only by the occasional truck rumbling past or the distant lights of a passing town. It began to rain, and huge, fat drops fell and splattered on her windshield like ripe tomatoes hitting pavement. As the windshield wipers thrummed a frantic beat, Harriet's mind scrolled through scenarios like a never-ending movie. What if she couldn't find Audrey? What if something terrible happened?

Just as despair threatened to consume her, her phone vibrated in the cup holder. Harriet's heart skipped a beat as she answered the call.

"Hello?"

"Harriet? It's me, Audrey."

Harriet exhaled. "Audrey! Oh, thank God. Are you okay? Where are you?"

"I'm... I don't know," Audrey sobbed. "I'm somewhere downtown. I ran away. I had nowhere to go. I'm so scared, Harriet."

"It's going to be okay, honey. I'm almost to Seattle. Can you tell me anything about where you are? Any landmarks or street names?"

Audrey's voice was barely a whisper. "I... I'm near the market with all the stinky fish."

Harriet had been to Seattle a handful of times and knew enough to recognize that Audrey must be near Pike Place Market. "Audrey, stay where you are. I'll find you. I promise."

The neon lights of Pike Place Market reflected on the rain-slicked streets, creating a disorienting maze of colors and reflections. A wave of adrenaline surged through Harriet as she scanned the crowds.

"Audrey!" she called out. "Audrey, where are you?"

Despair gnawed at her as she navigated the labyrinthine streets, each corner offering a new wave of disappointment. Finally, she spotted a huddled figure on a bench near the waterfront.

Harriet slammed on the brakes, switched on her hazard lights, and ran to Audrey. Relief washed over Harriet like a tidal wave, and she enveloped Audrey in a tight embrace.

"Oh, sweetheart," she whispered into Audrey's soaked hair. "I'm so glad I found you. You're safe now."

Audrey clung to Harriet, her sobs echoing in the quiet night. They found refuge in a nearby hotel, where they changed into dry clothes. Audrey had stuffed her backpack with as many of her belongings as she could, a small vessel for all she held dear in the world.

"I took Isla's phone. I have to give it back to her," Audrey said.

"No problem. We'll get it to her tomorrow."

The trill of Harriet's phone made Harriet jump. "Harriet, I've found a ton of great information online," Hank said. "It seems there might be a way to expedite the process and potentially get Audrey back to Bozeman quickly."

Harriet's heart leaped with hope. "Really? What did you find?"

"Well, it seems that Washington law gives significant weight to a child's wishes in custody cases, especially when the child is over twelve years old," Hank explained. "If Audrey expresses her wish to remain with you in Bozeman, it could sway the court in your favor."

Harriet's brow furrowed. "But Audrey already did that at the initial hearing, and the judge still ruled against us."

"I know," Hank said. "But this time we have a stronger case. I don't know the law in Montana, but like I said, Washington takes the child's wishes seriously. Plus, Audrey ran away from her grandparents' house, so she must not be happy. And her safety will be a priority as well."

Harriet's spirits lifted. "That's good news, Hank. Thank you. So, can I take her back to Bozeman, or do I have to stay in Washington to wait for a hearing?"

"Contact Sarah and get her advice. I would think you need to stay there, but I really don't know."

Sarah was adamant that Harriet stay in Seattle since moving Audrey across state lines without a court order could jeopardize her chance for guardianship.

"I want to get her out of here. She's so upset," Harriet said.

"I'd imagine so, given what the poor girl has been through," Sarah said. "But I want you to have the best chance possible of settling her guardianship with you for good. I'll call domestic abuse shelters in Seattle and get a recommendation for a lawyer, and explain the situation. Usually, the court will set an emergency hearing within a few days, or maybe even within 24 hours."

Harriet sighed. Sitting in a crappy hotel for a few days was not what either of them needed. "But since Audrey ran away, her safety is in jeopardy," Harriet said. "Surely the court will understand if I take her home."

"I would hope so, but there are no guarantees. Plus, you'd have to come back for the hearing anyway, since her current guardianship with her grandparents is in Washington State. Just stay put and love her up. I'll call you back when I have more information."

The next morning, Harriet woke to find Audrey sitting at the edge of the bed, staring at the dreary sky outside the window. Harriet didn't understand how people could live in Seattle. She needed the sunshine to feel sane. Although Harriet was beginning to feel as though she didn't know how that felt anymore. Or if she ever had.

"Hey, sweetie," Harriet said, sitting up. "Let's try to make the best of our time here."

"I just want to go back to Bozeman. Why do we have to stay here?"

"Because we have to do things the right way. It's our best chance of you getting to be with me in Bozeman forever," Harriet said.

Audrey nodded, then sat bolt upright, eyes wide. "My grandparents can't come get me, can they?"

Harriet shook her head. "They don't know where we are at the moment, so that can't happen."

Harriet's phone rang. She didn't recognize the number. Before she even said hello, a voice shouted, "You encouraged her to run away! You're undermining our authority! We'll be taking legal action."

Harriet held the phone away from her ear. "I can only assume this is Linda. You have no right to call me and threaten me."

"You took Audrey! You are the one who is wrong here," Linda said. "We have a life, a proper home here, a community. We know what's best for a child, for her stability and upbringing. What kind of chaos are you creating?"

"Audrey is safe with me," Harriet said, forcing her voice to remain calm. "And that's all that matters right now."

Harriet hung up, her hands trembling and her breath shaky.

"See? I told you. She's going to take me," Audrey said, burying her face in her hands.

"No, she won't. We'll get this figured out." Harriet racked her brain for something they could do to keep their minds off things for the moment. "What do you think about a trip to Elliot Bay Bookstore? We'll drop Isla's phone at her house and head over there."

"Okay," Audrey said, mustering a slight bit of enthusiasm.

When the lawyer Sarah found for them called later that day, Harriet filled him in on the situation, and he said he'd file for an emergency hearing before the end of the day. He was confident they'd have a hearing set within 48 hours.

Each hour felt like an eternity while they waited. Even books, which had been Harriet's saving grace all her life, couldn't pull her from her worry. She paced, flipped through the channels on the TV, trying to find something they would like, and bit her nails down to a nub. Audrey was sullen and distant, a shell of her usual spunky self.

"How about we give Izzy a call?" Harriet asked.

Audrey leaped from the bed. "Can we?"

"Of course. Here's my phone. I'll go for a little walk so you two can chat. I'll be back in a few minutes."

Harriet was thrilled to see a small spark back in Audrey's eyes. Hopefully, the court would see that Audrey needed to be in Bozeman with her. The thought of going back to the routine they'd just begun to fall into filled Harriet's heart. But then the next minute, the thought that she could lose again in court sent her anxiety spiraling out of control. A drink would help calm her nerves.

The hotel lobby had a small bar with a limited selection of overpriced alcohol. As the bartender came to take her order, she opened her mouth to order a glass of cabernet sauvignon and stopped. What was she thinking? How could she expect to win custody of Audrey if she ran to grab a glass of wine every time things got stressful?

"Nothing to drink for me. I'm looking for some kid-friendly restaurants around here for dinner," Harriet said, summoning a quick reason for standing at the bar.

The restaurant the bartender recommended was decent, but neither of them had much of an appetite. The nerves they felt about the future swirled and churned in their stomachs, leaving room for little else.

Back at the hotel after dinner, Harriet and Audrey were getting ready for bed when Audrey's face suddenly crumpled and she dissolved into tears. "I'm scared," she said, her breath hitching.

"I know, sweetheart," Harriet said, wrapping her in a tight hug. "Our lawyer believes the judge will listen to you this time, given what has happened. We have to have faith."

Audrey sniffed and cried silently for what felt like hours. Harriet held her and rocked her, wishing she could take all her pain and worry away. Finally, exhaustion overwhelmed Audrey, and she fell asleep. Harriet climbed into bed beside her, but sleep did not come.

As the sky turned purple, then pink the next morning, Harriet's phone buzzed, and her lawyer told her the hearing was scheduled for the following morning. He wanted them to come to his office to prep. Harriet's heart pounded in her chest, and her stomach lurched. This was happening. And it had to go their way this time.

CHAPTER 39

THE MORNING OF THE TRIAL dawned bright and sunny, which Harriet hoped was a good sign. They both tried to eat breakfast, but they did more pushing food around on their plates than actual eating. Driving to the courtroom in silence, Harriet felt as though the entire car was reverberating their mutually pounding hearts.

The courtroom was bigger than the one in Bozeman had been, which was immediately intimidating. Harriet felt small inside the cavernous room that held her fate. Her lawyer shook her hand and offered a reassuring nod, but Harriet still felt as though she might faint.

They all stood as Judge Williams entered. "This is an emergency hearing regarding the guardianship of Audrey Carter," he said. His bespectacled eyes scanned the courtroom, taking in Linda and Carl at one table and Harriet and Audrey at the other. "I've reviewed the case file and the emergency petition. Let's proceed."

Harriet's attorney rose to his feet. "Your Honor, my client, Harriet Henderson, wants only what is best for Audrey. During their guardianship hearing in Montana, the judge took note of Audrey's wishes but decided to place Audrey with her grandparents despite her desire to stay in Bozeman with my client. Audrey states that her grandparents were unduly strict and did not allow her to contact my client or her best friend in Bozeman, leaving her feeling isolated and alone. This is the last thing a child who lost her mother needs.

Her distress at her grandparents' home was so great that she ran away. Audrey has never run away before, so this is a clear indication of her unhappiness and distress in that environment, and it is obviously not safe for Audrey to wander the streets alone. After receiving a distressed call from Audrey, Ms. Henderson drove immediately from Bozeman to Seattle, found Audrey near Pike Place Market, and stayed with her at a local hotel. If Audrey were ordered to return to that environment, the likelihood is high that she would run away again. We hope the court will find that Audrey's safety and well-being are best served by granting permanent guardianship to Ms. Henderson in Bozeman."

Linda and Carl's attorney stood up, his voice booming with indignation. "Your Honor, Ms. Henderson should have contacted Audrey's legal guardians immediately when she learned of Audrey's whereabouts. She had no right to pick Audrey up and take her to a hotel without informing her grandparents. Ms. Henderson has undermined the court's authority and caused my clients significant distress. They have not mistreated Audrey. Rather, they have provided a loving home where Audrey is learning to adjust. These things take time. If Harriet swoops in and takes Audrey every time she gets upset with the rules of her new home, Mr. and Mrs. Thompson will be robbed of their ability to parent her entirely. We request that the court reaffirm the guardianship of Mr. and Mrs. Thompson and order Audrey's immediate return to their custody."

Harriet's lawyer stood and countered, "Your Honor, Audrey is a good kid. It is not like her to run away unless circumstances are dire. This is not just a matter of learning to adjust. Audrey says they took her phone and wouldn't allow her to contact Ms. Henderson or her friends. Audrey didn't know her grandparents well before she moved in with them, so it is only logical that she would need access to those she holds dear. As I said before, she felt completely isolated and alone. She ran away because she felt she had no other alternative. Audrey's safety is first and foremost. I also ask you to refer to the note Audrey's mother wrote just before her death, leaving Audrey in Ms. Henderson's care. Her mother knew what was best for her daughter. If Ms. Carter wanted Audrey to be cared for by her parents, wouldn't that have been the direction in her note? I ask the court to do right by Audrey by considering her safety, her mother's wishes, and Audrey's wishes, and return her to Bozeman in the care of Ms. Henderson."

The judge removed his glasses and turned to Audrey. "Audrey," he said gently, "can you tell me why you ran away from your grandparents' home?"

Audrey's voice was strong as she replied, "I was miserable there. They were so strict, and I felt trapped. I missed Harriet and my friends. I couldn't bear the thought of staying there. I thought what I wanted mattered. And my mom said she wanted Harriet to take care of me. What's wrong with that? Harriet has taken good care of me. I was happy with her. Or at least as happy as I could be after what happened. Why did the judge make me move to a new place with grandparents I hardly knew? They were mean to me and took my phone. I had no one to talk to. It was awful. Please, let me go back to live with Harriet and back to my old school in Bozeman with Izzy."

The judge nodded, his gaze landing on Harriet. Her heart thrummed wildly. "Ms. Henderson, can you tell me in your own words your relationship with Audrey and why you believe your home is the best place for her?"

Harriet's breath hitched in her throat. She stood on wobbly legs and met the judge's gaze, her voice trembling as she spoke. "Your Honor, I've been told I am very blunt. This seems like a time when that might come in handy. I love Audrey. She was doing great with me. Her mom, moments before she passed, chose me for Audrey. I certainly didn't expect that, but she trusted me with her daughter, so I'm begging the court to do the same. My husband died a little over a year ago, and I didn't even realize how lost and alone I was. Audrey has brought such joy to my life. I would do absolutely anything for her. Even though I haven't known her long, she's like a daughter to me. It's an honor to do my best for her."

Harriet paused, took a deep breath, and continued, "Audrey called me from a friend's phone because her grandparents, for some reason unknown to me, took her phone from her. They wouldn't allow her to contact me or her best friend, Izzy. How ridiculous is that? If they want what is best for her, why in the world would they cut her off from the only people she has left who care about her? This poor girl has had to endure the most horrific of tragedies, and her grandparents think it's best to isolate her? That makes no sense, and they certainly don't care about what's best for Audrey.

"Anyway, when Audrey used her friend's phone to call me, she was crying and pleading for me to come and get her. She told me she was running away. So, I got in my car and went to her. They're upset I didn't call them? Why the heck would I do that? She wanted to get away from them. I wanted to keep her safe. She was alone, terrified, and far from the support she knew. I was horrified at the thought of a young girl lost and alone on the streets of Seattle. When I found her, I took her to safety. I can't, for the life of me, understand how there could be a problem with that. Heck, I wanted to grab her and take her right back to Bozeman. It was my brother and the legal advocate from the domestic abuse shelter who talked me out of it."

Harriet's gaze shifted to Audrey, who sat beside her, her eyes wide and pleading. "I know I haven't been in her life long," Harriet said, a lump forming in her throat. She cleared it and attempted to swallow down the lump. "But I love her as if she were my own. She wants to be with me, in Bozeman, with her friends and the life she knows. I believe that's where she truly belongs."

Harriet turned back to the judge. "Your Honor," she began, but she had to stop because she couldn't hold back the tears any longer. Her tongue felt thick, and her voice was hoarse as she said, "I understand the importance of family ties, but sometimes family is more than just blood. It's about love, connection, and the people who show up for you when you need them most. I'm asking you to consider what's truly best for Audrey, to look beyond the legal technicalities and see the bond we share, the home we've created together in such a short time. Please don't send her back to a place where she feels unsafe and unhappy. Let her come home with me, where she can heal and thrive."

A tear escaped Harriet's eye, tracing a path down her cheek. She brushed it away, her gaze unwavering as she met the judge's stare once more. "I'll do whatever it takes to be the best parent I can be for Audrey. I won't let her down."

The judge tapped his bottom lip with his finger and leaned forward, resting his elbows on his desk. After what felt like an eternity, he said, "The court made its initial decision based on the belief that it is best to award custody to next of kin. However, there are circumstances where this is not the best placement for the child. Audrey's actions and her clear testimony demonstrate that the court may have erred in its judgment."

He looked at Linda and Carl. "Mr. and Mrs. Thompson, while the court respects your love for your granddaughter, it seems clear that Audrey's well-being is best served by returning her to Bozeman with Ms. Henderson. Her actions, though drastic, were motivated by a desperate need to be in an environment where she feels safe, loved, and supported."

Harriet held her breath and squeezed Audrey's hand in both of hers as the judge prepared to deliver his verdict. "Therefore," he declared, "the court hereby grants permanent guardianship of Audrey Carter to Harriet Henderson."

A wave of relief and joy washed over Harriet as she embraced Audrey, tears streaming down both their faces.

"I can't believe it," Audrey said.

"Me neither. You're mine, officially and forever. It's going to take a while for that to sink in fully."

Audrey pulled back, her eyes sparkling with happiness. "Can we celebrate?"

"Absolutely," Harriet replied. "What do you have in mind?"

"Ice cream!" Audrey declared. "And pizza! With Izzy!"

"Sounds perfect. Let's go home and throw a party. We definitely have something to celebrate."

The courtroom doors swung open, and as Harriet and Audrey stepped out into the bright sunlight, Carl came up behind Audrey and tapped her shoulder.

"Audrey," Carl began, "we're sad things didn't work out at our home, but we want you to know we don't hold any hard feelings about what you did."

Harriet bristled. "How dare you blame Audrey?"

Carl turned to Harriet. "You've never raised a child. Discipline is a virtue. You cannot allow a child to run away anytime they don't agree with something."

"I agree with you, but these are extenuating circumstances. Sometimes you have to be flexible. That's something I've recently learned and I'm still getting used to it," Harriet said.

Carl nodded. His expression, however, held a stubborn conviction, a quiet certainty that despite the judge's ruling, his fundamental truth about parenting remained unassailable. He wasn't convinced, merely compliant. Harriet's eyes narrowed, an angry retort to his quiet defiance about to spring from her mouth, but she bit it back. "We thought we were doing the right thing," Carl said.

Linda turned to Audrey. "We love you and are always here for you, no matter what." They bent down and gave Audrey a stiff hug, sniffling and wiping tears from their eyes.

Harriet and Audrey watched as Carl and Linda made their way to their car. "I'm sure they did what they thought was best. We need as much love in this world as we can get. Like they say, it takes a village."

Audrey rolled her eyes. "I didn't know you could be so corny, Harriet."

Harriet laughed. "Me neither. I didn't know much about myself, apparently. But I do know I'm thrilled you will be with me forever, and I'll do my best to care for you even if it means breaking some of my rigid rules from time to time."

"I'll believe that when I see it," Audrey said, earning her a light punch on the arm from Harriet. She hoped Audrey would see it. Because "breaking rules" and "embracing chaos" were still new languages Harriet was learning, and the old, rigid grammar of her past felt stubbornly comfortable at times. It would be a conscious effort, every single day.

They passed the hours on the long drive back to Bozeman listening to music. Audrey filled Harriet in on the latest gossip about Taylor Swift, Sabrina Carpenter, and Chappell Roan. Harriet made a silent vow to try to get Audrey to a concert at some point in the near future, even though concerts were not her favorite form of entertainment.

Exhausted and relieved, they went right to bed when they finally arrived home. Harriet fell asleep with a smile on her lips and a heart full of gratitude.

CHAPTER 40

THE NEXT DAY, as they readied the house for their celebration, Audrey said, "I think we should invite Kevin and Rocky, too."

Harriet's heart surprised her by fluttering at the mention of Kevin's name. "I bet they're busy."

"Well, I still think you should invite them, even if they can't come. Kevin's been nice about inviting you to hike and bringing Rocky over. We need to be nice, too."

"You sure have a lot to teach me, young lady. All right, I'll text him." Harriet pulled out her phone. "Maybe we should invite Lucille from the library. And maybe even Tammy." Harriet sighed. "And I suppose if I invite Lucille, I'll have to invite Richard."

"What's so terrible about that? And who's Tammy?" Audrey said.

"Tammy runs the HOA," Harriet said, glancing at Audrey, whose eyebrows had scrunched together. "That's the homeowner's association. I didn't used to get along with her when I thought she wasn't doing her job enforcing the rules in the neighborhood. But she's been living in the townhome you and your mom were in because she's been going through a rough time. Kevin arranged everything for me. He says she's nice."

"We definitely should invite her then," Audrey said.

Harriet, unaccustomed to party planning, found herself meticulously orchestrating the gathering. She had to have healthy appetizers to balance the pizza, ensure ample seating for everyone, and select just the right background music. Should she indulge Audrey's pre-teen tastes or cater to the adults? It was undeniably stressful, yet the very act of planning offered a familiar security. This meticulous organization, this need for everything to be "just so," was a habit so deeply ingrained, she couldn't distinguish where Harriet ended and Les's influence began. But now, it wasn't solely for the sake of order; it was for joy, for connection.

A few hours later, the house was bustling with activity. Rocky and Bibbo were bouncing and playing, Izzy and Audrey had put on music, and they were dancing around the living room. Kevin was sitting on the couch with a huge smile on his face, taking in the scene. Lucille and Richard introduced themselves to Tammy, and they discussed the latest Mel Robbins book.

Harriet, after a brief internal debate, stepped forward. "Tammy, I hope you're finding the townhome comfortable. It's a, well, it's a good place for a fresh start." The words felt clumsy, too personal for someone she'd previously only viewed through the lens of HOA infractions, but she pushed through the discomfort.

Tammy's eyes, though still holding a trace of wariness, softened. "It's been a lifesaver, Harriet. Truly. Thank you."

Harriet felt a warmth spread through her, a different kind of satisfaction than from a perfectly organized drawer. Harriet brought the pizza over to the kitchen table and announced it was time to eat. The flowers Kevin had brought brightened the room and emanated a fragrance of spring, setting the mood perfectly.

Harriet held her glass of water aloft and said, "To new beginnings and found family."

"Absolutely," Kevin said, toasting everyone at the table.

Audrey and Izzy giggled and clinked their glasses. "I wish we were sisters," Audrey said.

"Me too," Izzy said.

"Well, I believe that's the meaning of found family. The people you care about most become your family," Harriet said. "I'm learning all of this along with you, but if this gathering is any indication, it seems those can be the most meaningful relationships in your life."

"Here, here!" Lucille said.

"Is it time for cake?" Audrey asked.

"Of course. It's your favorite. Red velvet with cream cheese frosting. I wanted to make it myself, but I've been known to ruin a good meal, so I ordered it."

"You've never ruined a meal for me," Audrey said.

"Yeah, your cookies are the best," Izzy said.

"Well, Les would have disagreed," Harriet said.

"No offense, Harriet, but who cares what Les thought?" Kevin said.

A choked chuckle escaped Harriet. "Good point. I guess I'll have to start experimenting in the kitchen again."

"I'm happy to be your guinea pig," Kevin said, putting a forkful of cake in his mouth.

Just then, Bibbo, in a playful leap for a dropped crust, accidentally nudged Kevin's elbow, sending a dollop of cream cheese frosting splattering onto his cheek. Harriet's immediate instinct was to grab a napkin, to apologize profusely, to restore order. But Kevin merely chuckled, swiping the frosting with a finger and offering it to Bibbo, who licked it eagerly. Audrey and Izzy erupted in giggles. Harriet found herself laughing too, a genuine, unforced sound that rippled through her. It was messy, unexpected, and utterly delightful. A few months ago, a minor incident like this would have sent her into a quiet frenzy of mortification and control. Now, it was just life.

Later, as the evening began to mellow, Harriet found herself leaning against the kitchen counter, a half-empty glass of wine in her hand, taking in the scene. Richard, normally so buttoned-up, was still deep in conversation with Lucille and Tammy, his tie slightly askew, a smile plastered across his face as he recounted some anecdote. Lucille laughed and gestured animatedly, seeming to truly enjoy the conversation. There was an effortless quality to their interactions, a comfortable back-and-forth that felt utterly authentic. Harriet realized that these were people capable of navigating the messy, unpredictable currents of life with a grace she was only just beginning to grasp. They were real, and they were here, in her once-impenetrable home.

After everyone left, Audrey and Harriet listened to music and danced while they cleaned up. Harriet couldn't remember ever feeling so fulfilled and happy.

As Harriet was tucking Audrey into bed, Audrey said in a small voice, "Harriet?"

"Yes, sweetheart?"

"Is it bad that sometimes I'm happy?"

"Of course not! I'd love for you to be happy all the time," Harriet said.

"It's just...I feel guilty being happy when my mom's gone and my dad did what he did."

Harriet leaned down and pulled her into a tight hug. "That's understandable, but don't you think your mom would want you to be happy?"

Audrey tilted her head to the side for a moment and then nodded. "She would. She always said she was happiest when I was happy. Do you think she can see me?"

"I don't know for sure, but I believe she can. If she can, I'm positive she's incredibly proud of you."

"Good. I want to make her proud," Audrey said, snuggling into her pillow. But even though she seemed content, a shadow of lingering sadness passed over her face, a fleeting reminder that the path of grief was not linear, and Audrey's joy would always carry the faint echo of loss.

"Good night, sweetheart. I hope you have many more happy times to come. I know your mom wants that too," Harriet said, kissing Audrey on the cheek.

In the hall outside Audrey's room, Harriet slumped against the wall, and the tears she'd been holding in began rolling down her cheeks. She hadn't imagined she could love someone so thoroughly and so quickly. It was scary, feeling as though your heart was walking around outside your body, but it was worth it.

CHAPTER 41

THE SUMMER DAYS WERE LONG and peaceful, with Audrey and Izzy and a few new friends they'd found in the neighborhood spending nearly all their time outside. They camped in the backyard, made s'mores over the small firepit Harriet had installed, and rode bikes until the sun started to set, which in Montana wasn't until around ten at night. Audrey had resumed her counseling sessions and seemed to be coping as well as could be expected. Harriet contacted Lucille and explained everything, and asked if there was still room for her at the library. Lucille said she would be welcomed back with open arms.

Harriet often found herself smiling, even as she looked around the living room - a discarded blanket, a puzzle piece under the coffee table, Bibbo's chew toy abandoned in the middle of the rug. A faint, almost involuntary twitch of her eye still accompanied the sight of disarray. Then, with a conscious effort, she'd let it go. Messy, yes. But alive. It was a constant, small battle to unlearn decades of rigid order, but the joy it brought was slowly outweighing the discomfort. It almost seemed as though they might be able to put the terrible events of the past, if not completely behind them, at least out of the way a bit.

As Harriet and Audrey strolled through the park one afternoon, laughing at Bibbo's enthusiastic antics with Rocky, Harriet noticed Mrs. Gable, who lived across from the park, quickly pull her terrier closer and avert her gaze. A fleeting prickle of the old defensiveness rose in Harriet, a reminder that not everyone had forgotten her "off-leash-dog-man" days, or the woman who enforced the rules with a zealous grip. It was a fleeting thought, but it unsettled her nonetheless. It would take a while for people to realize she wasn't that rigid person anymore.

Harriet and Audrey were resting on the park bench when Harriet's phone rang from an unknown number. "Ms. Henderson, this is Devin Hartshorn. I'm the prosecutor in Chris Carter's murder trial."

Harriet's heart stopped. Why was he calling her? Had something happened in the case? Wouldn't Harriet have seen something on the news? Why did she still have to be involved? "Why are you calling me?" Harriet asked.

"I am hopeful you will be willing to testify against Mr. Carter."

Harriet wanted nothing more than to slam the phone down on the cradle in the satisfying way one did back before cell phones. As her finger hovered over the red hang-up button, she heard his voice again.

"I understand you'd like to stay uninvolved, but we need you to be a voice for Robyn. Obviously, she can't speak for herself, so you and Audrey are the next best thing she has."

Harriet exhaled and brought the phone back up to her ear. Gesturing to Audrey to wait for her on the bench, she walked across the park where she hoped Audrey couldn't hear. Her mouth had gone completely dry, so she had to lick her lips to say, "I'll do it. But don't you dare try to drag Audrey into this."

"Your desire to protect Audrey is understandable and commendable, but she could be our best chance at a conviction since she can attest to her father's violent pattern of behavior," the lawyer said in a practiced, flat voice.

"What nerve you have. Asking a young girl who lost her mother to testify against her own father. What he did was absolutely abominable, but he's still her father. I can't imagine how she feels, knowing she shares DNA with a man who murdered her mother. And, of course, she has positive memories of him as well, as she should. I understand it might help the case, but at what cost to Audrey? No. The poor girl has been through enough. I will do it, but I will not put her through that."

Thankfully, he didn't persist further, and Harriet hung up the phone. She'd have to meet with him a few times over the coming weeks to prepare. As much as she dreaded every time she met with him, she knew she had to get this right. That man had to pay for what he did. And Audrey had to be safe from him.

The week of the trial, Harriet was careful not to turn on the news on TV. She didn't want Audrey to know that the trial was happening. Once it was over, Harriet would sit Audrey down and, hopefully, if there was any justice in the world, deliver the news that her dad would be locked away forever.

Harriet requested that she only be present in the courtroom for her testimony. She'd be in and out and hope for the best. Reliving the nightmare, hearing his excuses, worrying what the jury was thinking, would be much too much for her nerves.

Harriet had arranged for Audrey to stay at Izzy's the night before Chris's trial, so she awoke to a silent, heavy house. She readied herself in quick, stiff movements, conjuring her inner warrior.

"Ms. Henderson," the prosecuting lawyer said, "Please tell me, in your own words, what you know about the events leading up to the night Robyn Carter was murdered."

Harriet spoke clearly and confidently as she recounted how she and Robyn grew to be friends, and how Audrey had begged for her help. Her heart beat loudly in her ears, and she had to struggle to hear her own thoughts, but she made it through, doing her best to paint the picture of a loving mother, devoted friend, and good neighbor, whose life was stolen from those who loved her. She glanced in Chris's direction just once, saw the smug look on his face, and her determination grew.

"He was supposed to love and protect both Robyn and Audrey. Instead, he was the monster. I hope he never sees the light of day," Harriet concluded.

Days went by with no word from the lawyer. With each day that passed, Harriet's anxiety increased. She'd read that a quick verdict often meant guilty, so that was what she'd expected. The wait was excruciating.

Finally, the lawyer's number was displayed on the screen of her phone. With a trembling hand, she brought the phone to her ear. "Chris Carter has been found guilty of deliberate homicide, or murder in the first degree. He's been given life without the possibility of parole."

All the air whooshed from Harriet's body. "Oh, thank God. There is justice in the world."

Harriet hung up and leaned back against the couch. Now, to tell Audrey. Harriet figured she'd be relieved, but she wasn't sure. The whole situation was just so awful.

"Audrey," Harriet began, "your father's trial was last week."

Audrey sat up straight. "What? And you didn't even tell me?"

Harriet shook her head. "I thought it was best for you not to know, not to be involved at all. You've already dealt with so much. They asked you to testify, but I said no."

"Thank God for that," Audrey said.

"He was found guilty. He's going to jail forever."

Audrey nodded, but said nothing. Silence hung thick in the air while Harriet bit her tongue and waited. Hank and Sarah counseled her to tell Audrey the facts and to wait for questions. It was best not to fill her in on too many details of the case. She only needed to know her father was not going to be around to bother her anytime soon. They'd also warned her that there could come a day when Audrey would want to visit her dad, and Harriet had to be open to that. After all, he was still her father. Harriet couldn't imagine that day, but she'd take Audrey to him if that's what she wanted. She'd promised to do anything for her, so she needed to live up to her word.

After a few minutes, Audrey said, "So, I don't have to worry that he might try to take me like my grandparents did?"

"Definitely not. For better or worse, you're stuck with me," Harriet said.

Audrey scooted closer to Harriet and put her head on her shoulder. "It's definitely for the better."

Harriet held her close, knowing that while this moment was a triumph, the healing for a girl who had seen such darkness would be a long, winding road. There would be good days, and hard ones, and the love she was building with Audrey would have to be strong enough for both of them.

Harriet's chin quivered, and that annoying lump crept up her throat again. "I love you, Audrey," she croaked.

Audrey squeezed Harriet tighter. "I love you, too."

CHAPTER 42

HARRIET STARED at her phone, her thumbs hovering over the keyboard. She'd been drafting and deleting texts to Kevin for the past ten minutes, wondering why she was texting him one minute and why not the next.

Hey, Kevin. It's Harriet...

He knew it was her. Caller ID, remember? Delete.

Hey, Kevin, what do you say we walk the dogs together?

Duh. That's how she broke her ankle and why they had all their earlier problems. Delete.

So, funny thing, I saw you out with Rocky this morning. Beautiful day for a walk, huh?

Was she really going to admit she'd been watching him? Delete.

She sighed, running a hand through her hair. Why was this so difficult? She'd invited him to Audrey's celebration without a problem. Maybe it was because that was for Audrey, and this was for her. But it was just a simple invitation for a dog walk, nothing more. Yet, her heart pounded in her chest like she was about to confess her undying love.

Taking a deep breath, she finally typed a message that seemed rational:

Hi Kevin, remember how we talked about walking the dogs together weekly? Things got crazy, so that didn't happen, but maybe now we could walk them together sometime?

She hit send, then immediately tossed her phone onto the couch as if it were on fire. Her face flushed as she replayed the message in her head, dissecting every word for any hint of desperation or hidden meaning.

"It's just a dog walk," she muttered to herself, trying to calm her racing heart. "Just two neighbors being neighborly. Nothing more."

She picked up her phone. No reply. She went to the kitchen and tried to find something to do. She rechecked her phone. Nothing. She sat down at the kitchen table and attempted to read a magazine. Still nothing. She went to her bedroom and got dressed, and finally her phone buzzed and there it was, a new message from Kevin:

Hey Harriet, that sounds great! How about tomorrow morning around 9?

Relief washed over her. He said yes. And he used an exclamation point. Maybe, just maybe, he was happy about this arrangement too. She replied:

Good. I'll meet you at the fork in the trail off Tangerine at 9.

He was already there when she arrived. Bibbo and Rocky strained against their leashes in their excitement to greet each other. Harriet felt nearly the same way about seeing Kevin.

They fell into step, the dogs trotting happily ahead. The morning air was crisp and invigorating, the sunlight filtering through the trees, casting a warm glow on the path.

"So," Kevin began, breaking the initial silence, "how's Audrey doing?"

"Okay, I guess. I don't know how much is a tough act, or how much is true resilience. Even though her dad being given a life sentence was a huge relief, this all has been too much for anyone to handle."

"I can't even imagine what she must be going through."

Harriet nodded and tried to think of something else to say. "So, have you been giving many people rides lately?"

Kevin chuckled. "A few. Bozeman's not exactly a hotbed for Uber. Still a bit too small of a town, but I can do it on my time and earn a few extra bucks, so it's worth it. Are you back to working at the library?"

Harriet nodded. "Lucille is very good at giving instructions and not bothering me too much while I accomplish my tasks, so it's going well."

Harriet's feet crunched in the gravel, and birds twittered overhead. She was once again at a loss as to what to say. "So, are you excited for Bobcat football?" She finally managed.

Kevin smiled. "Absolutely, I love the Bobcats."

"It'll be different without Tommy. I'm sad he's moved on. Good for him, of course. You know he was drafted, right? Went to Las Vegas. They're turning him into a wide receiver."

"Wow, you are quite the Bobcat fan," Kevin said. "We'll have to go to a game this fall."

Harriet felt her cheeks flush once again. "It's been years since I went to a game in person. Les said..." She stopped. "Never mind what Les said, I'd love to go to a game." A part of her still heard his disdainful chuckle, picturing the rowdy crowds, the spilled beer. The old voice insisted it was 'unseemly.' But another, newer voice, fragile but persistent, told her to try new things, to figure out what she wanted without any of Les's judgment.

"Wow," Harriet breathed, taking in the view of the Spanish Peaks as they rounded the corner. "This view never gets old."

Kevin stood beside her, his shoulder brushing against hers. "It sure doesn't," he agreed, his voice barely above a whisper.

Their eyes met, and for a moment, time seemed to stand still. A shared smile flickered between them. Heat rose throughout her body, and she thought she might hyperventilate.

"Um, I'm not sure how to say this, but I'm feeling a little...overwhelmed right now. I'll head on home." Mumbling a small apology, she turned and walked toward her house as quickly as her long legs would carry her. As she rounded the corner onto her street, she dared to peek back to where she'd left him. He was still standing there watching her. Her breath caught, and a fresh wave of heat washed over her. Of its own volition, her hand came up beside her and offered a little wave. A grin lit up his face as he returned the gesture.

Later that afternoon, Audrey and Izzy came bounding through the door, smelling of sunbaked skin and a slight hint of sweat.

"Hi, Harriet! Guess what? We rode our bikes to the mall and went to Barnes & Noble. There is a new book in the Keeper of the Lost Cities series that we absolutely have to have."

"I'm happy to give you money for books. I am a librarian after all. Of course, you could borrow books from the library."

"That's not the same. I have every book in the series. I'm collecting them," Audrey said.

"How much do you need?"

"Harriet, I'd rather earn the money myself. It would be more special that way."

"Maybe we could babysit?" Izzy said.

"That's a good idea, Izzy. However, even though you ladies are quite grown up, you're still a little young," Harriet said.

The girls' shoulders slumped. Harriet hated to see their enthusiasm draining from them.

Leaning against the kitchen counter, Harriet put her finger to her lips. "I have an idea. How about we do a lemonade stand?"

THE END

ACKNOWLEDGEMENTS

If I had known all the incredible people I would meet on this writing journey, I would have done it much sooner in life. While the hours spent crafting a novel happen in solitude, the revising and critiquing can't be done without a group of amazing people you trust when your writing is in its most infantile and vulnerable state. These are people you bare your soul to way before you are truly ready to do so.

Thank you to my incredible group of beta readers and fellow authors: JB Harris, Diane Dickinson, and Rhonda Wiley-Jones. Your thoughtful and insightful critique in the early stages of this novel made it so much more than the story I initially tried to tell. And to my fellow Black Rose Writing authors who are always ready with words of wisdom and sound advice, I am truly grateful to you all. In such a competitive publishing environment, I feel truly blessed to have landed in this supportive and helpful group.

To my someday-to-be husband, Brian, thank you again for listening to the same passages over and over, for dealing with my stress, and for hearing me ramble through thoughts that make no sense to you. Your kind words of encouragement never go unnoticed or unappreciated. You make me better every day.

To my dad, to whom this book is dedicated. I am in awe of you. There is no challenge you cannot overcome, no obstacle too great for you to conquer. You are my hero. To anyone who would count you out, I say, "Just watch him." I am grateful for our at least weekly phone calls, your wisdom on life, politics, and parenting. You've made this world a much better place for me. Thank you.

And my children. Aidan, Harlan, Brielle, Riley, and Dean. I am so proud of the wonderful humans you are becoming. Watching you soar and take on the world is my greatest joy. Thank you for your words of encouragement about my writing and your interest in this journey. I love you all.

ABOUT THE AUTHOR

Kim McCollum graduated from Barnard College with a major in Japanese and was soon navigating the hustle and bustle of Wall Street. When her first child was born a few years later, she stayed home to raise her children. Once they headed off to school, Kim finally found time to pursue her passion for writing. Her award-winning, debut novel, *What Happens in Montana,* was published in January 2024, and her short stories have appeared in several publications. She lives in Bozeman, Montana, with her supportive husband, Brian, and their blended menagerie of five kids and three spoiled pets.

OTHER TITLES BY KIM MCCOLLUM

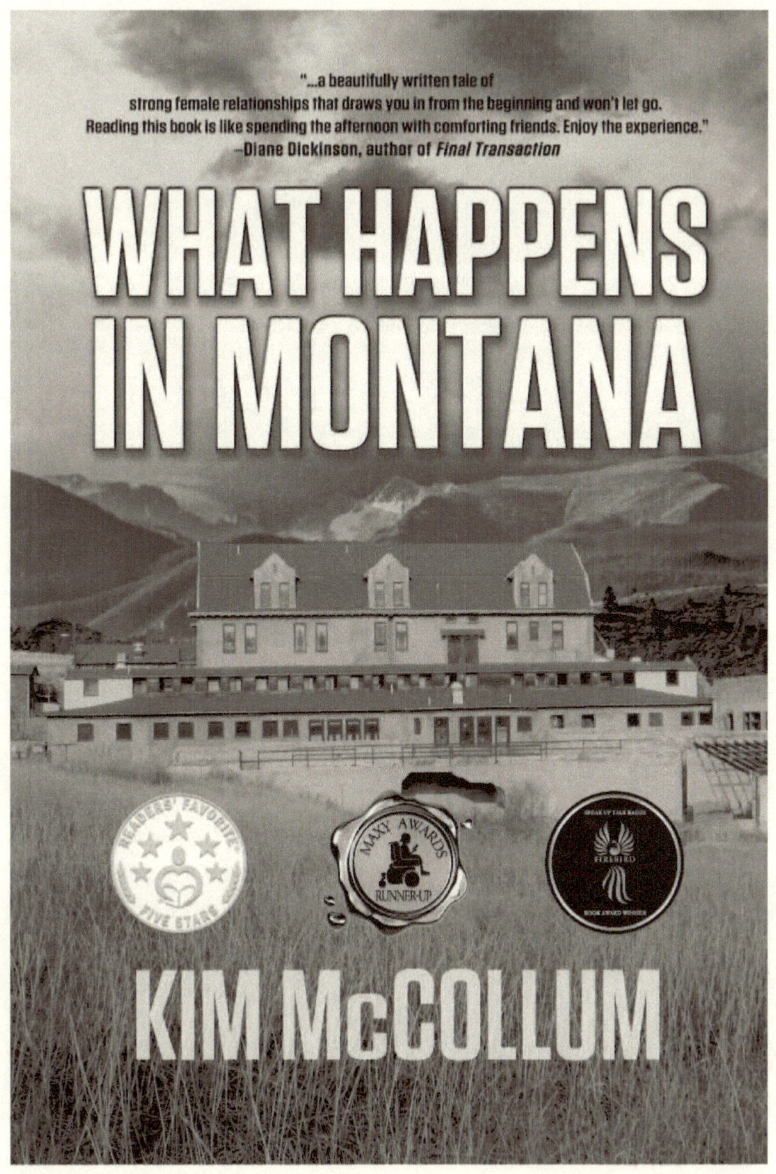

NOTE FROM KIM MCCOLLUM

Word-of-mouth is crucial for any author to succeed. If you enjoyed *Harriet Hates Lemonade*, please leave a review online—anywhere you are able. Even if it's just a sentence or two. It would make all the difference and would be very much appreciated.

Thanks!
Kim McCollum

We hope you enjoyed reading this title from:

www.blackrosewriting.com

Subscribe to our mailing list – *The Rosevine* – and receive **FREE** books, daily deals, and stay current with news about
upcoming releases and our hottest authors.
Scan the QR code below to sign up.

Already a subscriber? Please accept a sincere thank you for being a fan of Black Rose Writing authors.

View other Black Rose Writing titles at
www.blackrosewriting.com/books and use promo code
PRINT to receive a **20% discount** when purchasing.

www.ingramcontent.com/pod-product-compliance
Lightning Source LLC
Chambersburg PA
CBHW061518210726
48287CB00006B/1730